Dear Reader,

Everyone always asks a writer where she gets her ideas. Well, the idea for this book wasn't hard to come by!

My husband and I lived through a kitchen remodel this year—and I just knew that it would make a great background for a Kings of California novel.

So, meet Rafe King. He's one of three brothers who own King Construction. He's lost a bet and for the first time in years, he has to actually work at a job site. But to keep from intimidating his own employees, Rafe goes undercover as Rafe Cole.

Now, meet Katie Charles, the Cookie Queen. Katie's having her kitchen redone. She's not a big fan of the Kings, though, because one of those King cousins broke her heart. Right off the bat, she tells Rafe she has no use for the King men.

And that's a challenge Rafe simply can't ignore.

I hope you have as much fun reading this story as I did writing it. And only a couple of the kitchen "incidents" are torn from real life!

Please, visit my website at www.maureenchild.com. I love hearing from you.

Happy reading,

Maureen

KING'S MILLION-DOLLAR SECRET

BY
MAUREEN CHILD

Published in Great Britain 2012
by Mills & Boon, an imprint of Harlequin (UK) Limited,
Eton House, 18-24 Paradise Road, Richmond, Surrey TW9 1SR

© Maureen Child 2011

ISBN: 978 0 263 89163 8
ebook ISBN: 978 1 408 97182 6

951-0512

Harlequin (UK) policy is to use papers that are natural, renewable and recyclable products and made from wood grown in sustainable forests. The logging and manufacturing processes conform to the legal environmental regulations of the country of origin.

Printed and bound in Spain
by Blackprint CPI, Barcelona

Maureen Child is a California native who loves to travel. Every chance they get, she and her husband are taking off on another research trip. The author of more than sixty books, Maureen loves a happy ending and still swears that she has the best job in the world. She lives in Southern California with her husband, two children and a golden retriever with delusions of grandeur. Visit Maureen's website at www.maureenchild.com.

To Rory, Scott and Joaquin at Building and Construction Contractors, the heroes who rebuilt my kitchen, put up with my constant questions and made a palace out of a pup tent!
Thanks, you guys.

One

Rafe King liked a friendly wager as much as the next guy.

He just didn't like to lose.

When he lost though, he paid up. Which was why he was standing in a driveway, sipping a cup of coffee, waiting for the rest of the work crew to show up. As one of the owners of King Construction, it had been a few years since Rafe had actually done any on-site work. Usually, he was the details man, getting parts ordered, supplies delivered. He stayed on top of the million and one jobs the company had going at any one time and trusted the contractors to get the work done right.

Now though, thanks to one bet gone bad, he'd be working on this job himself for the next few weeks.

A silver pickup truck towing a small, enclosed trailer pulled in behind him and Rafe slanted his gaze at the driver. Joe Hanna. Contractor. Friend. And the man who'd instigated the bet Rafe had lost.

Joe climbed out of his truck, barely managing to hide a smile. "Hardly knew you without the suit you're usually wearing."

"Funny." Most of his life, Rafe hadn't done the suit thing. Actually, he was more comfortable dressed as he was now, in faded jeans, black work boots and a black T-shirt with King Construction stamped across the back. "You're late."

"No, I'm not. You're early." Joe sipped at his own coffee and handed over a bag. "Want a doughnut?"

"Sure." Rafe dug in, came up with a jelly-filled and polished it off in a few huge bites. "Where's everyone else?"

"We don't start work until eight a.m. They've still got a half hour."

"If they were here now, they could start setting up, so they could start working at eight." Rafe turned his gaze to the California bungalow that would be the center of his world for the next several weeks. It sat on a tree-lined street in Long Beach, behind a wide, neatly tended lawn. At least fifty years old, it looked settled, he supposed. As if the town had grown up around it.

"What's the job here, anyway?"

"A kitchen redo," Joe said, leaning against Rafe's truck to study the house. "New floor, new counter. Lots of plumbing to bring the old place up to code. New drains, pipes, replastering and painting."

"Cabinets?" Rafe asked, his mind fixing on the job at hand.

"Nope. The ones in there are solid white pine. So we're not replacing. Just stripping, sanding and varnish-ing."

He nodded, then straightened up and turned his gaze on Joe. "So do the guys working this job know who I am?"

Joe grinned. "Not a clue. Just like we talked about, your real identity will be a secret. For the length of the job here, your name is Rafe Cole. You're a new hire."

Better all the way around, he thought, if the guys working with him didn't know that *he* was their employer. If they knew the truth, they'd be antsy and wouldn't get the work done. Besides, this was an opportunity for Rafe to see exactly what his employees thought of the business and working for King Construction. Like that television show where employers went undercover at their own companies, he just might find out a few things.

Still, he shook his head. "Remind me again why I'm not firing you?"

"Because you lost the bet fair and square and you don't welsh on your bets," Joe said. "And, I warned you that my Sherry's car was going to win the race."

"True." Rafe smiled and remembered the scene at the King Construction family picnic a month ago. The children of employees spent months building cars that would then race on a track made especially for the event. In the spirit of competition, Rafe had bet against Joe's daughter's bright pink car. Sherry had left everyone else standing at the gate. That would teach him to bet against a female.

"Good thing you let your brothers do all the talking at the picnic," Joe was saying. "Otherwise, these guys would recognize you."

That's just the way Rafe liked it, he thought. He left the publicity and the more public areas of the business to two of his brothers, Sean and Lucas. Between the three of them, they had built King Construction into the biggest construction firm on the West Coast. Sean handled the corporate side of things, Lucas managed the customer base and crews, and Rafe was the go-to guy for supplies, parts and anything else needed on a site.

"Lucky me," he muttered, then looked up at the rumble of another truck pulling up to the front of the house. Right behind him, a smaller truck parked and the two men got out and walked toward them.

Joe stepped up. "Steve, Arturo, this is Rafe Cole. He'll be working the job with you guys."

Steve was tall, about fifty, with a wide grin, wearing a T-shirt proclaiming a local rock band. Arturo was older, shorter and wearing a shirt stained with various colors of paint. Well, Rafe thought, he knew which one of them was the painter.

"We ready?" Steve asked.

"As we'll ever be." Joe turned and pointed to the side of the house. "There's an RV access gate there. Want to put the trailer in her back yard? Easier to get to and it'll keep thieves out."

"Right."

Joe positioned his truck and trailer through the gate and in minutes, they were busy. Rafe jumped in. It had been a few years since he'd spent time on a site, but that didn't mean he'd forgotten anything. His father, Ben King, hadn't been much of a dad, but he had run the construction arm of the King family dynasty and made sure that every one of his sons—all eight of them—spent time on job sites every summer. He figured it was a good way to remind them that being a King didn't mean you had an easy ride.

They'd all grumbled about it at the time, but Rafe had

come to think that was the one good thing their father had done for any of them.

"We did the walk-through last week," Joe was saying and Rafe listened up. "The customer's got everything cleaned out, so Steve and Arturo can start the demo right away. Rafe, you're going to hook up a temporary cooking station for Ms. Charles on her enclosed patio."

Rafe just looked at him. "Temporary cooking? She can't eat out during a kitchen rehab like everyone else?"

"She could," a female voice answered from the house behind them. "But she needs to be able to bake while you're fixing her kitchen."

Rafe slowly turned to face the woman behind that voice and felt a hard punch of something hot slam into him. She was tall, which he liked—nothing worse than having to hunch over to kiss a woman—she had curly, shoulder-length red hair and bright green eyes. She was smiling and the curve of her mouth was downright delectable.

And none of that information made him happy. He didn't need a woman. Didn't want a woman and if he did, he sure as hell wouldn't be going for one who had "white picket fences" practically stamped on her forehead.

Rafe just wasn't the home-and-hearth kind of guy.

Still, that didn't mean he couldn't enjoy the view.

"Morning, Ms. Charles," Joe said. "Got your crew here. Arturo and Steve you met the other day during the walk-through. And this is Rafe."

"Nice to meet you," she said. Her green eyes locked with his and for one long, humming second there seemed to be a hell of a lot of heat in the air. "But call me Katie, please. We're going to be spending a lot of time together, after all."

"Right. So, what's this temporary cooking station about?" Rafe asked.

"I bake cookies," she told him. "That's my business and I have to be able to fill orders while the kitchen is being redone. Joe assured me it wouldn't be a problem."

"It won't be," Joe said. "Of course, you won't be able to cook during the day. We'll have the gas turned off while we work on the pipes. But we'll set it up for you at the end of every day. Rafe'll fix you up and you'll be cooking by tonight."

"Great. Well, I'll let you get to it."

She slipped inside again and Rafe took that second to admire the view of her from the rear. She had a great behind, hugged by worn denim that defined every curve and tempted a man to see what exactly was underneath those jeans. He took a long, deep breath, hoping the crisp morning air would dissipate some of the heat pumping through him. It didn't, so he was left with a too-tight body and a long day staring him in the face. So he told himself to ignore the woman. He was only here long enough to pay off a bet. Then he'd be gone.

"Okay," Joe was saying, "you guys move Katie's stove where she wants it, then Rafe can get her set up while the demolition's going on."

Nothing Rafe would like better than to set her up—for some one-on-one time. Instead though, he followed Steve and Arturo around to the back of the house.

The noise was incredible.

After an hour, Katie's head was pounding in time with the sledge hammers being swung in her grandmother's kitchen.

It was weird, having strangers in the house. Even

weirder paying them to destroy the kitchen she'd pretty much grown up in. But it would all be worth it, she knew. She just hoped she could live through the construction.

Not to mention crabby carpenters.

Desperate to get a little distance between herself and the constant battering of noise, she walked to the enclosed patio. Snugged between the garage and the house, the room was long and narrow. There were a few chairs, a picnic table that Katie had already covered with a vinyl tablecloth and stacks of cookie sheets waiting to be filled. Her mixing bowls were on a nearby counter and her temporary pantry was a card table. This was going to be a challenge for sure. But there was the added plus of having a gorgeous man stretched out behind the stove grumbling under his breath.

"How's it going?" she asked.

The man jerked up, slammed his head into the corner of the stove and muttered an oath that Katie was glad she hadn't been able to hear. Flashing her a dark look out of beautiful blue eyes, he said, "It's going as well as hooking up an ancient stove to a gas pipe can go."

"It's old, but it's reliable," Katie told him. "Of course, I've got a new one on order."

"Can't say as I blame you," Rafe answered, dipping back behind the stove again. "This thing's gotta be thirty years old."

"At least," she said, dropping into a nearby chair. "My grandmother bought it new before I was born and I'm twenty-seven."

He glanced up at her and shook his head.

Her breath caught in her chest. Really, he was not what she had expected. Someone as gorgeous as he was should have been on the cover of *GQ*, not working a construction site. But he seemed to know what he was doing and she had to admit that just looking at him gave her the kind of rush she hadn't felt in way too long.

And that kind of thinking was just dangerous, so she steered the conversation to something light.

"Just because something's old doesn't mean it's useless." She grinned. "That stove might be temperamental, but I know all of its tricks. It cooks a little hot, but I've learned to work around it."

"And yet," he pointed out with a half smile, "you've got a new stove coming."

She shrugged and her smile faded a little into something that felt like regret. "New kitchen, new stove. But I think I'll miss this one's occasional hiccups. Makes baking more interesting."

"Right." He looked as if he didn't believe her and couldn't have cared less. "You're really going to be cooking out here?"

The sounds of cheerful demolition rang out around them and Katie heard the two guys in the kitchen laughing about something. She wondered for a second or two what could possibly be funny about tearing out a fifty-year-old kitchen, then told herself it was probably better if she didn't know.

Instead, she glanced around at the patio/makeshift kitchen setup. Windows ringed the room, terra-cotta-colored tiles made up the floor and there was a small wetbar area in the corner that Katie would be using as a cleanup area. She sighed a little, already missing the farmhouse-style kitchen that was, at the moment, being taken down to its skeleton.

But when it was finished, she'd have the kitchen of her dreams. She smiled to herself, enjoying the mental images.

"Something funny?"

"What?" She looked at the man still sprawled on the tile floor. "No. Just thinking about how the kitchen will be when you guys are done."

"Not worried about the mess and the work?"

"Nope," she said and pushed out of the chair. She walked toward him, leaned on the stove top and looked over the back at him. "Oh, don't get me wrong. I'm not looking forward to it and the thought of baking out here is a little high on the ye gods scale. Still, the mess can't be avoided," she said. "As for the work that will be done, I did my research. Checked into all the different construction companies and got three estimates."

"So, why'd you choose King Construction?" he asked, dragging what looked like a silver snake from the back of the stove to a pipe jutting out from the garage wall.

"It wasn't easy," she murmured, remembering things she would just as soon put behind her permanently.

"Why's that?" He sounded almost offended. "King Construction has a great reputation."

Katie smiled and said, "It's nice that you're so protective of the company you work for."

"Yeah, well. The Kings have been good to me." He scowled a bit and refocused on the task at hand. "So if you don't like King Construction, what're we doing here?"

Sighing a little, Katie told herself she really had to be more discreet. She hadn't meant to say anything at all about the King family. After all, Rafe and the other guys worked for them. But now that she had, she wasn't going to try to lie or squirm her way out of it, either. "I'm sure the construction company is excellent. All of the referrals I checked out were more than pleased with the work done."

"But…?" He patted the wall, stood up and looked at her, waiting for her to finish.

Katie straightened up as he did and noticed that though she was five foot nine, he had at least four inches on her. He also had the palest blue eyes she had ever seen, fringed by thick eyelashes that most women would kill for. His black eyebrows looked as though they were always drawn into a frown. His mouth was full and tempting and his jaws were covered with just the slightest hint of black stubble. His shoulders were broad, his waist narrow and those jeans of his really did look amazingly good on him. A fresh tingle of interest swept through her almost before she realized it.

It was nice to feel something for an ordinary, everyday, hard-working guy. She'd had enough of rich men with more money than sense or manners.

He was still waiting, so she gave him a bright smile and said, "Let's just say it's a personal matter between me and one member of the King family."

If anything, the perpetual scowl on his face deepened. "What do you mean?"

"It's not important." She shook her head and laughed. "Honestly, I'm sorry I said anything. I only meant that it was hard for me to hire King Construction, knowing what I do about the King family men."

"Really." He folded his arms over his chest and asked, "What exactly do you think you know about the Kings?"

His gaze was narrowed and fixed on her. She felt the power of that glare right down to her bones and even Katie was surprised at the tingle of something tempting washing through her. Suddenly nervous, she glanced over the back of the stove to look at the pipes as if she knew what she was seeing. Still, it gave her a second to gather her thoughts. When she felt steady again, she said, "You mean beside the fact that they're too rich and too snobby?"

"Snobby?"

"Yes." Katie huffed out a breath and said, "Look I know you work for them and I don't want to make you uncomfortable. I only know that I never want anything to do with any of them again."

"Sounds ominous."

She laughed at the idea. Katie doubted very much that Cordell King had given her a second thought since he'd abruptly disappeared from her life six months ago. No, the Kings steamrolled their way through the world, expecting everyone else to get out of their way. Well, from now on, she was going to oblige them.

"Oh, I don't think any of the Kings of California are staying up nights wondering why Katie Charles hates their guts."

"You might be surprised," he said, dusting his hands off as he looked at her. She shifted a little under that direct stare. "You know, I'm a curious kind of guy. And I'm not going to be happy until I know why you hate the Kings."

"Curiosity isn't always a good thing," she said. "Sometimes you find out things you'd rather not know."

"Better to be informed anyway, don't you think?"

"Not always," Katie said, remembering how badly she'd felt when Cordell broke things off with her. She'd just had to ask him *why* and the answer had only made her feel worse.

Rafe smiled at her then and she noted how his features softened and even his eyes lost that cool, dispassionate gleam. Her heartbeat jittered unsteadily in her chest as her body reacted to the man's pure male appeal. Then, as if he knew exactly what she was thinking, that smile of his widened and he actually *winked* at her.

But a moment later, he was all business again.

"Your temporary gas line is hooked up. But remember, we're shutting the gas off during the day. We'll let you know when it's safe to use the stove."

"Okay. Thanks." She took a single step backward and Rafe walked past her, his arm brushing against hers as he did. Heat flashed through her unexpectedly and Katie took in a deep breath. Unfortunately, that meant she also got a good long whiff of his cologne. Something foresty and cool and almost as intriguing as the man himself. "And Rafe?"

"Yeah?"

"Please don't repeat any of what I said about the King family. I mean, I probably shouldn't have brought it up and I don't want to make anyone uncomfortable while you're working here."

He nodded. "Won't say a word. But like I said, one of these days, I'm going to hear the rest of your story."

Katie shook her head and said, "I don't think so. The Kings are part of my past and that's where I want to leave them."

By the end of the first day, Katie was asking herself why she had ever decided to remodel. Having strangers in and out of her house all day was weird, having *noisy* strangers only made it worse.

Now though, they were gone and she was left alone in the shell of what had been her grandmother's kitchen. Standing in the center of the room, she did a slow circle, her gaze moving over everything.

The floor had been torn up, right down to the black

subfloor that was older than Katie. The walls were half torn down and the cabinet doors had been removed and stacked neatly in the back yard. She caught a glimpse of naked pipes and groaned in sympathy with the old house.

"Regrets?"

She jumped and whirled around. Her heart jolted into a gallop even as she blew out a relieved breath. "Rafe. I thought you left with the others."

He grinned as if he knew that he'd startled her. Then, leaning one shoulder on the doorjamb, he folded his arms across his chest. "I stayed to make sure your gas hookup in the back room was working."

"And is it?"

"All set."

"Thanks. I appreciate it."

He shrugged and straightened up languidly as if he had all the time in the world. "It's my job."

"I know, but I appreciate it anyway."

"You're welcome." His gaze moved over the room as hers had a moment before. "So, what do you think?"

"Honestly?" She cringed a little. "It's horrifying."

He laughed. "Just remember. Destruction first. Then creation."

"I'll try to remember." She walked closer to where the sink had been. Now, of course, it was just a ripped-out wall with those naked pipes staring at her in accusation. "Hard to believe the room can come back from this."

"I've seen worse."

"I don't know whether to be relieved or appalled at that statement," she admitted.

"Go with relieved," he assured her. He walked closer, stuffing his hands into the back pockets of his jeans. "Some of the jobs I've seen took *months* to finish."

"So you've done a lot of this work?"

"My share," he said with a shrug. "Though this is the first job site I've worked on in three or four years."

The house was quiet…blessedly so, after a full day of hammers crashing into walls and wood. The decimated kitchen echoed with their voices, and outside, the afternoon was fading into twilight. There was a feeling of intimacy between them that maybe only strangers thrown together could experience.

She looked at him, taking her time to enjoy the view, and wondered. About him. About who he was, what he liked—and a part of her wondered why she wondered.

Then again, it had been a long time since she'd been interested in a man. Having your heart bruised was enough to make a woman just a little nervous about getting back into the dating pool again.

But it couldn't hurt to *look,* could it?

"So if you weren't doing construction, what were you doing instead?"

He glanced at her, long enough for her to see a mental shutter slam down across his eyes. Then he shifted his gaze away and ran one hand across the skeleton of a cabinet. "Different things. Still, good to get back and work with my hands again." Then he winked. "Even if it *is* for the Kings."

He'd shut her out deliberately. Closing the door on talking about his past. He was watching her as if he expected her to dig a little deeper. But how could she? She had already told him that she felt curiosity was overrated. And if she asked about his past, didn't that give him the right to ask about hers? Katie didn't exactly want to chat about how she'd been wined, dined and then unceremoniously dumped by Cordell King either, did she?

Still, she couldn't help being curious about Rafe Cole and just what he might be hiding.

"So," he said after a long moment of silence stretched out between them. "Guess I'd better get going and let you get busy baking cookies."

"Right." She started forward at the same time he did and they bumped into each other.

Instantly, heat blossomed between them. Their bodies close together, there was one incredible, sizzling moment in which neither of them spoke because they simply didn't have to.

Something was there. Heat. Passion.

Katie looked up into Rafe's eyes and knew he was feeling exactly what she was. And judging by his expression, he wasn't much happier about it.

She hadn't been looking for a romantic connection, but it seemed that she had stumbled on one anyway.

He lifted one hand to touch her face and stopped himself just short of his fingertips tracing along her jaw. Smiling softly, he said, "This could get…interesting."

Understatement of the century.

Two

"Meeting's over," Lucas King muttered. "Why are we still here?"

"Because I've got a question for you," Rafe answered and looked up at his brothers. Well, two of them, anyway. Sean and Lucas, his partners in King Construction. Just looking at the three of them together, anyone would know they were brothers. They all had the King coloring, black hair and blue eyes. Yet their features were different enough to point to the fact that they each had different mothers.

But the man who had been their father had linked them not just by blood, but by fostering that brotherly connection in their childhoods. All of Ben King's sons had spent time together every summer, and the differences among them melted away in the shared knowledge that their father hadn't bothered to marry *any* of their mothers.

Lucas, the oldest of the three of them, was checking his watch and firing another impatient look at Rafe. Sean, typically, was so busy studying the screen of his cell phone while he tapped out messages to God knew who, he hadn't noticed that Lucas had spoken.

The brothers held weekly meetings to discuss business, to catch up with whatever was going on in the family and simply to keep up with each other's lives. Those meetings shifted among each of their houses. Tonight, they were gathered at Lucas's oceanfront home in Long Beach.

It was huge, old and filled with what Lucas liked to call character. Of course, everyone else called it outdated and inconvenient. Rafe preferred his own place, a penthouse suite in a hotel in Huntington Beach. Sleek, modern and efficient, it had none of the quirks that Lucas seemed so fond of in his own house. And he appreciated having room service at his beck and call as well as maid service every day. As for Sean, he was living in a remodeled water tower in Sunset Beach that had an elevator at beach level just to get you to the front door.

They had wildly different tastes, yet each of them had opted for a home with a view of the sea.

For a moment, Rafe stared out at the ribbons of color on the sunset-stained ocean and took a deep breath of the cold, clear air. There were a few hardy surfers astride their boards, looking for one last wave before calling it a day, and a couple was walking a tiny dog along Pacific Coast Highway.

"What do we know about Katie Charles?" he asked, taking a swig from his beer.

"Katie who?" Sean asked.

"Charles," Lucas said, irritation for their younger brother coloring his tone. "Don't you listen?"

"To who?" Sean kept his gaze fixed on his cell phone. The man was forever emailing and texting clients and women. It was nearly impossible to get Sean to pay attention to anything that didn't pop up on an LED screen.

"Me," Rafe told him, reaching out to snatch the phone away.

"Hey!" Sean leaned out and reclaimed his phone. "I'm setting up a meeting for later."

"How about instead you pay attention to *this* one?" Rafe countered.

"Fine. I'm listening. Give me my phone."

Rafe tossed it over, then turned his gaze to Lucas. "So?" Rafe asked. "You know anything about Katie Charles?"

"Name sounds familiar. Who is she?"

"Customer," Rafe said, picking up his beer and leaning back in the Adirondack chair. "We're redoing her kitchen."

"Good for us." Sean looked at him. "So what's bugging you about her?"

Good question. Rafe shouldn't have cared what Katie Charles thought of the King family. What did it really matter in the grand scheme of things? Still, ever since leaving Katie's house earlier, he hadn't been able to stop thinking about her. And it wasn't just the flash of heat he felt when he was around her that was bugging her. She was pretty, smart, and successful, and she hated the Kings. What was up with that?

"Katie Charles," Lucas was muttering to himself. "Katie Charles. Kitchen. Cookies." He grinned and said, "That's it. Katie's Kookies. She's building a real name for herself. She's sort of a cottage industry at the moment, but people are talking about her."

"What people?" Rafe asked, frowning. "I've never heard of her before."

Sean snorted. "Why would you? You're practically a hermit. To hear about anything you'd have to actually talk to someone. You know, someone who isn't *us*."

"I'm not a hermit."

"God knows I hate to admit Sean's right. About anything. But he's got a point," Lucas said, stretching his long legs out in front of him. "You keep yourself shut up in that penthouse of yours most of the time. Hell, I'm willing to bet the only people you've actually talked to since last week's meeting are the room service operator and the crew you worked with today."

Rafe scowled at Lucas, but only because he didn't have an argument for the truth. He didn't have time to date every model in the known universe like Sean. And he had no interest in the corporate world of movers and shakers like Lucas. What the hell else was he supposed to do with his time?

"Oh, yeah," Sean said with a grin. "I forgot about that bet you made. How's it going, being back on a job site?"

"Not bad," Rafe admitted. Actually, he'd enjoyed himself more than he had expected. Being on a site with hardworking guys who didn't know he was their boss had been...fun. And there was the added plus of being around a woman who made his body tight and his brain fuzz out. Until, of course, Katie had confessed that she hated the King family.

"So," Sean asked, "if you had such a good time, why do you look like you want to bite through a box of nails?"

"You do look more annoyed than usual," Lucas said with a shrug. "What's up? And what's it got to do with Katie Charles?"

"Neither of you knows her?"

Sean and Lucas looked at each other and shrugged. "Nope."

"Somebody does."

"Somebody knows everybody," Lucas pointed out.

"Yeah, but the somebody who knows Katie is a King."

Sean snorted. "Doesn't narrow the field down by much."

"True." Hell, there were so many King cousins in California, they could probably start their own county.

"What's the deal?" Lucas picked up his beer, leaned back in his chair and waited. "Why's she bothering you?"

"Because," Rafe told him, standing up to walk to the balcony railing, "she hates the Kings."

"Hates us?" Sean laughed. "Impossible. Women *love* King men."

"That's completely true," Lucas said with a self-satisfied smile.

"Usually, maybe," Rafe said, his gaze sweeping across the froth of waves on the darkening ocean. Although his ex-wife would probably argue that point. "But this woman doesn't. Hell she barely could say the word *King* without shuddering."

"So why'd she hire us if she hates us so much?"

He turned to look at Sean. "Our company's reputation, she says. But she's not happy about it."

"And you think somebody in the family turned her against all Kings?" Lucas asked.

"What else could it be?" Rafe looked at him and shrugged.

"The real question here is," Sean said quietly, "why do you care?"

"That is a good question." Lucas looked at Rafe and waited.

Too good, Rafe thought. Hell, he didn't know why he cared, either. God knew, he didn't want to. He'd been down this road before and he'd already learned that not only didn't he know how to love, but according to his ex-wife, he was actually *incapable* of it.

So why bother with romancing a woman when you knew going in it was doomed to fail? No, he kept his relationships easy. Uncomplicated. A few hours of recreational sex and no strings attached.

Better for everyone when the rules were clear.

Yet, there was Katie.

She stirred him up in a way he'd never known before, though damned if he'd admit that to anyone else. Hard enough to get himself to acknowledge it.

"Yeah, it is a good question," Rafe muttered. "Too bad I don't have an answer."

Katie was getting used to the noise, the dust, the confusion and the presence of strangers in her house. One week and she could barely remember what quiet was like. Or privacy. Or being able to move around her kitchen to the sounds of late-night radio.

Now, her kitchen was an empty shell of a room. She glanced out one of the wide windows into the backyard and sighed. There was a small trailer parked on her grass, its doors wide open, revealing tools and equipment enough to build four kitchens.

Pickup trucks belonging to Steve, Arturo and Rafe

were also parked on her lawn and the piles of her discarded kitchen were getting bigger. Broken linoleum, old pipes, her *sink*—a beautiful, cast iron relic—lay tilted atop one of the mountains of trash and just for a second, Katie felt a twinge of panic.

This had all seemed like such a good idea at the time. Now though, she had to wonder if she'd been crazy. What if the new kitchen wasn't as good as the old? What if her new stove didn't cook as reliably? Where would she ever find another sink so wide and deep? What if her business went belly up and she'd spent her savings on a kitchen she wouldn't be able to afford?

"Oh, God…"

"Too late for panic now," a deep voice assured her from the doorway.

She turned around to look at Rafe and caught the knowing gleam in his eyes. She forced a smile. "Not full-blown panic yet. Just a little…okay," she admitted finally, "panic."

He laughed and she had a moment to think how devastating he really was before the smile on his face faded. He walked into the room and looked out at the view she'd been staring at. "It looks bad now, but it's going to be great when it's finished."

"Easy for you to say."

"Yeah, it is. This isn't my first rodeo, you know. I've done a lot of remodels and the owners always have that wild-eyed look you have right now." He lifted one shoulder in a shrug. "But they're always happy when it's over."

"Because it's over or because they love what you did to their houses?"

"A little of both, maybe," he acknowledged. "Just

wanted to let you know we found a leak in a hot-water pipe."

"A *leak?*" Katie instantly had mental images of a rising flood beneath the house.

"Relax," he said. "It's just an old, slow leak. The joint on the pipes is bad. We're going to replace it, we just need to show it to you first and get you to sign off on the work, since it's extra to the contract."

She blew out a relieved breath. "Right. Okay then. Lead the way."

Katie followed Rafe out of the patio, across the yard and through the back door to the kitchen. She couldn't even reach her favorite room in the old house by walking down the hallway. It was crowded with her refrigerator, tables holding all of her pantry items and towers of pots and pans.

The sun was blazing down out of a clear blue sky and she was grateful for California weather. If she'd had to do this remodeling job in a place renowned for rain, it would have been far worse.

Rafe held the door open for her and she walked inside to a room she barely recognized. The old subfloor was black and littered with dust. The skeletons of the cabinets stood out like picked over bones on the walls. The pipes looked forlorn somehow, as if they were embarrassed to be seen.

Steve, the plumber, was crawling up out of a hole in the floor. Katie just managed to hide a shudder. You couldn't pay her enough to crawl under the house where spiders and God knew what other kind of bug lived. When he was clear, Steve turned to flash her a smile. "If you come over here, I can show you the leak."

"Great. Leaks." She picked her way across the floor, stepping over scattered tools and bits of old wood. She stopped alongside the long, narrow opening in the floor and squatted beside Steve. He held a flashlight pointed beneath the floorboards and said, "There it is. Probably been dripping like that for years. Hasn't done any damage, so that's good. But we should put in a new copper joint."

Katie nodded solemnly as if she understood exactly what he was talking about. But the truth was, she didn't see a leak. All she noticed was a damp spot on the earth beneath the floor that probably shouldn't be there. If she actually admitted she couldn't see the leak, they might insist she go down there to see it up close and personal. So Steve's word would be good enough for her. "Okay then. Do what you have to."

"Excellent." Steve turned and said, "Hey, Rafe, why don't you show her the new sink you brought in this morning."

"My new sink's here? Already?" Now this she was interested in. As far as pipes went, all she cared about was that they carried water whichever way they were designed to carry it without leaks, thanks very much. She didn't need to understand how they did it. Hard to get thrilled over copper piping.

"I was at one of our suppliers and saw a sink I thought you'd like, so I picked it up. We'll just store it in the trailer until it's time to install." Rafe led her out of the kitchen, down the back steps and across the lawn.

Arturo had the cabinet doors spread across makeshift sawhorse work tables and was busily scraping off the old finish before sanding them. Everything was happening. Only a week and already she was seeing progress. Maybe they'd get it all done in two weeks, Katie thought, then smiled wryly to herself. And maybe she'd sprout wings and fly.

"Here it is." Rafe stopped at the trailer, reached in and drew out a huge sink, one side much deeper and bigger than the other.

"Isn't that heavy?" she asked, remembering the loud *clunk* her old cast-iron sink had made when tossed to the top of the junk pile.

"Nope. It's acrylic." He held it in one hand to prove his point. "Tougher and won't chip or rust."

She smoothed her fingers over the edge and sighed a little. It was perfect. Looking up at him, she said, "Thank you. It's great."

"Glad you like it." He tucked it back into the trailer and draped a protective work blanket over it.

"I thought the contractor was supposed to pick up the supplies for the job," she said.

He turned back to look at her and shoved both hands into the pockets of his jeans. "Joe asked me to pick up a few things at the home store. I saw the sink and..."

"How'd you know I'd like it?"

"Took a shot," he admitted.

"It was a good one."

His blue eyes were shining and a cool wind tossed his black hair across his forehead. He was tall, broad-shouldered and looked *great* in those faded jeans, she thought, not for the first time. In fact, she had dreamed about him the night before. In her dream they were back in her kitchen, alone, as they had been yesterday. But in her fantasy, Rafe had kissed her until her toes curled and she had awakened so taut with desire and tension she hadn't been able to go back to sleep.

Even her unconscious mind was working against her.

"So, Rafe Cole," she asked, "how long have you been in construction?"

She thought his features tightened briefly, but the expression was gone so quickly, she couldn't be sure. Now why would that simple question get such a reaction?

"My dad started me out in the business when I was a kid," he said, staring off at the house, keeping his gaze deliberately away from hers. "I liked it and just sort of stuck with it."

"I get that," she said, trying to put him at ease again, to regain the easiness they'd shared only a moment ago. "My grandmother started me out baking when I was a little girl, and, well, here I am."

He nodded and glanced at her. "How long have you lived here?"

"I grew up here," she said. "My dad died before I was born, and my mom and I moved in here with Nana." Her gaze tracked across the familiar lines of the old bungalow. The windows were wide, the roof was shake and the paint was peeling in spots. But the house was home. It meant security. Comfort. "I moved out for college, then mom died and a year ago, I inherited the house from Nana."

"Oh," he said softly. "I'm sorry."

It took her a second; then Katie laughed and told him, "No, she didn't die. She just moved. Nana and her sister Grace decided to share an apartment at the Senior Living Center. They figure there are lots of lonely men over there looking for love!"

He laughed at that and once again, Katie felt a rush of something hot and delicious spread through her. The man should smile more often, she thought and wondered why he didn't. The other guys working here were forever laughing and joking around. But not Rafe.

He was more quiet. More mysterious.

Just…*more*.

Rafe sat opposite his brother Sean at a local diner and waited for his burger. As for Sean, he was typing out a message or thirty on his cell phone. Okay, as far as Rafe was concerned. Gave him more time to think about Katie Charles.

The woman was haunting him.

He couldn't remember being so fixated on a single woman—not even Leslie, before he married her, had so completely captivated him. While that should have worried him, instead he was intrigued. What was it about Katie that was getting to him?

She was beautiful, sure. But lots of women were. He wanted her, but he had *wanted* lots of women. There was something else about her that was reaching out to him on so many different levels, he couldn't even name them all.

"Hey," Sean said with a laugh. "Where'd you go?"

"What?" Rafe swiveled on the bench seat and looked at his younger brother.

"I've been talking to you for five minutes and you haven't heard a word. So I was wondering just what exactly had you thinking so hard."

Rafe scowled a little, irritated to have been caught daydreaming. Jeez. Thoughts of Katie were taking up way too much of his time. "Not surprising I was thinking of something else, since you were so busy texting."

"Nice try," Sean said, still grinning. "Distract me with insults so I won't ask if you're still thinking about the cookie woman."

Rafe shot him a glare. "Her name's Katie."

"Yeah, I know."

"Anyone ever tell you how irritating you are?"

"Besides you, you mean?" Sean asked, giving their waitress a bright smile as she delivered their dinners. "You bet. All the time."

Rafe had to smile. Sean was absolutely the most laid-back King ever born. Most of them were type A's, ruthlessly pushing through life, demanding and getting their own way. Not Sean. He had a way of slipping up on whatever he wanted until it just naturally fell into his hands.

He was damn hard to annoy and almost never lost his temper. In the world of the King family, he was an original.

Once the waitress was gone, the brothers dove into their meals. This hamburger joint on Ocean Avenue had been a popular spot since the forties. Rafe and Sean were on the outside patio, where they could watch traffic and pedestrians in a never-ending stream of motion. Kids, dogs, parents with digital cameras poking out of their pockets fought for space on the crowded sidewalk. Summer in a beach town brought out the tourists.

"So," Sean said, reaching for his beer, "let's hear it."

"Hear what?"

"About the cookie lady," Sean countered, both of his eyebrows wiggling.

Rafe sighed. Should have expected that his brother would be curious. After all, Rafe hadn't talked about a woman since Leslie walked out. He remembered his ex-wife looking at him sadly and telling him that she felt "sorry" for him because he had no idea how to love someone. That he never should have married her and sentenced her to a cold, empty life.

Then he thought about Katie and it was like a

cool, soft breeze wafted through his mind. "She's… different."

"This gets better and better." Sean leaned back in his booth and waited.

Frowning, Rafe took a sip of his beer. When he spoke, it was a warning not only to his brother, but to himself. "Don't make more of this than there is. I just find her interesting."

"Interesting." Sean nodded. "Right. Like a bug collection?"

"What?"

Laughing, his brother said, "Come off it, Rafe. There's something there and you're looking. And about time too, I want to say. Leslie was a long time ago, man."

"Not that long," Rafe countered. Although, as he thought about it, he realized that he and Leslie had been divorced for more than five years. His ex-wife was now remarried to Rafe's former best friend, with a set of toddler twins and a newborn, last he heard.

"Long enough for her to move on. Why haven't you?"

Rafe shot Sean a glare that should have fried his ass on the spot. Typically enough though, Sean wasn't bothered. "Who says I haven't?"

"Me. Lucas. Tanner. Mac. Grady…" Sean stopped, paused and asked, "Do I have to name *all* of our brothers or do you get the point?"

"I get it, but you're wrong." Rafe took a bite of his truly excellent burger and after chewing, added, "I'm not carrying a torch for Leslie. It's over. Done. She's a mother, for God's sake." And if he was to be honest, he hadn't really missed her when she left. So what did that say about him?

"Yet, you're still living in a hotel suite making do with the occasional date with a beautiful airhead."

"I like living in a hotel and they're not all airheads."

"Good argument."

"Look," Rafe said, reaching for his beer. "Katie's a nice woman, but she's off limits."

"Why's that?"

"Because she's got white picket fence written all over her," Rafe explained. "She's the settle-down-and-get-married type and I've already proven I'm not."

Sean shook his head and sighed. "For a smart guy, you're not real bright, are you?"

"Thanks for the support."

"You want support?" Sean asked, digging into his burger. "Then stop being an idiot."

"Shut up. I tried the happily-ever-after thing and it blew up in my face. Not going to do it again."

"Did you ever consider that maybe the reason it didn't work was because you married the wrong woman?"

Rafe didn't even bother answering that jibe. What would have been the point?

Monday morning, the guys were still fighting with the pipes and Katie was ready for a week in Tahiti. She'd hardly slept all weekend. Though the peace and quiet were great, she'd been so busy filling cookie orders she hadn't had time to appreciate it.

Now she sipped at a cup of coffee and winced every time the whine of a drill shrieked into the air.

"The noise is worst the first week," someone from nearby said.

She turned to look at Joe Hanna, the contractor. "You're just saying that so I won't run away."

He grinned. "Once the new pipes and drains are

installed, the rest will be easier for you to live with. I promise."

He had no sooner made that vow when a shout came from the kitchen. "Arturo! Shut off the water! Off! Off!"

"Crap." Joe hustled across the yard just behind Rafe while Arturo sprinted for the water shutoff valve out front. Katie was hot on Joe's heels and stepped into the kitchen in time to see Steve crouched over a pipe with water spraying out of it like a fountain in Vegas.

Katie backed out of their way while the men grabbed towels. Then Arturo got the water off and the three men in the kitchen were left standing around as what looked like the incoming tide rolled across the floor and under the house.

"That fitting wasn't on there right, damn it," Steve muttered and dropped through the hole in the floor.

"Should have checked it out with the water on low," Joe pointed out and got a glare from Rafe in response.

"What happened?" Katie asked and both men turned to look at her.

"Nothing huge," Joe assured her. "Just got to tighten things up. Looks worse than it is."

Katie hoped so, because it looked like a lake was in her kitchen and she couldn't think that was a good thing.

Joe slapped one hand on Rafe's shoulder and said, "I should have checked his work personally before we tested it. Rafe's been out of the game for a while, so he may be rusty. But he's got potential."

Katie saw the flicker of annoyance cross Rafe's features and she shared it.

"Isn't Steve the plumber?" she asked pointedly.

"Yeah," Joe said, "but Rafe did the joint work on that pipe."

"It was fine," Rafe said. "That shouldn't have happened."

"Sure, sure," Joe told him, then looked at Katie. "My fault. Like I said, I should have kept a closer eye on the new guy's work."

Rafe was biting his tongue, no doubt worried about defending himself and maybe losing his job. Then she realized that he could be fired anyway, if Joe decided that his work was too sloppy. So before she could stop herself, she stepped in to defend him. "Rafe does excellent work. He set up my temporary kitchen, allowing me to keep my business going. He's stayed late everyday cleaning up and making sure I'm inconvenienced as little as possible. I'm sure that whatever happened with that pipe was unavoidable."

"Yeah," a voice came rumbling up from under the house. "Found the problem. The first joint worked itself loose, so the water had to go somewhere. My bad. I'll get it fixed and we'll be back in business."

Katie gave Joe a look that said quite clearly, *See? You blamed the wrong man.* She smiled at Rafe and left them to clean up the mess and get back to work.

"What was that all about?" Joe wondered.

Steve poked his head up from under the floorboards and smiled widely. "Sounds to me like the boss lady has a thing for Rafe. Lucky bastard."

"Shut up, Steve," Rafe said, but his gaze was locked on the empty doorway where Katie had been standing only a moment before.

Joe was riding him because he could and Rafe would take it because it was all part of the bet he'd lost. Good-natured teasing was all part of working a job. But Katie's defense of him had surprised him. Hell, he couldn't even remember the last time someone had stood up for him—not counting his half-brothers and cousins.

Katie Charles was like no one he'd ever met before. She didn't want anything from him. Wasn't trying to get on his good side. But then, that was because she thought his name was Rafe Cole.

It would be an entirely different story if she knew he was a King.

Three

Rafe was late getting to the job site.

Despite the bet he was in the process of paying off, he had his regular job to do, too. And dealing with a supplier who wasn't coming through for them was one of the tasks he enjoyed most.

"Look Mike," he said, tightening his grip on the phone. "You said we'd have the doors and windows on site at the medical complex by noon yesterday."

"Is it my fault if things got hung up on the East Coast?"

"Probably not," Rafe conceded, "but it's your fault if you don't get this straightened out in the next—" he checked his watch "—five hours."

"That's impossible," the older man on the other end of the line argued.

"All depends on how determined you are, now doesn't it?" Rafe wasn't going to listen to the man's excuses.

This was the second time Mike Prentice had failed to come through for King Construction. It would be the last.

Rafe didn't put up with failure. Mistakes happened to everyone, he knew that. But if a man couldn't keep track of his own business, then he was too disorganized to count on. The Kings required the people they worked with to have the same diligence they showed. "You have the materials at the job site by end of day today."

"Or…?" Mike asked.

A slow smile curved his mouth. Mike couldn't see it, but he must have heard it when Rafe answered, "You really don't want to know, do you?"

"Things happen, Rafe," the man continued to try to defend himself. "I can't stay on top of every supplier I have, you know."

"Don't see why not," Rafe countered. "I do."

"Right. Well, I'm betting that every once in a while someone stiffs the Kings, too."

"Yeah, they do." He glanced around his office at King Construction, already moving on from this particular problem. "But it doesn't happen often and it never repeats itself. This isn't the first time we've had this conversation, Mike. I took your explanation last time, but this is your second chance. I guarantee you, we'll never have this discussion again. If you can't get the supplies to us in five hours, King Construction will find a new supplier for this job."

"Now just wait a minute, let's not be hasty."

"You get *one* second chance with King Construction, Mike," Rafe told him flatly. "And this was it. Now, you have the materials there, as we agreed, or I'll put the word out to every construction outfit in the state that you can't be trusted. How many jobs you think you'll get then?"

A long moment of tense silence passed while the other man did some fast thinking. Rafe knew what was going through the guy's mind. He'd already ruined his rep with the Kings, but he still had hundreds of other construction outfits to do business with. Unless he messed this up further.

"It'll be there," the man said, but he didn't sound happy about it. "You're a hard man, Rafe."

"You should've remembered that, Mike."

Rafe hung up then, leaned back in his desk chair and spun it around until he could look out the window at the ocean scene stretching out in front of him. The King Construction building sat directly on Pacific Coast Highway and each of the brothers had an office with a view. One of the perks of being an owner.

Another perk was reaming guys who failed them.

Standing up, Rafe leaned one hand on the window, feeling the cool of the glass seep into his skin. Was he a hard man? He supposed so.

His ex-wife sure as hell thought so.

Just another reason for him to keep his distance from Katie Charles.

A woman like that didn't need a hard man in her life.

"Now, isn't this a nice view?"

Katie rolled her eyes and laughed at her grandmother. "You're impossible."

Emily O'Hara grinned, fluffed her stylishly trimmed silver hair and then winked at her granddaughter. "Honey, if you don't like looking at handsome men, they might as well bury you."

They were standing at the edge of the yard, watching the action. The men worked together seamlessly, each of them concentrating on a certain area, then helping each other out when needed. Naturally, Nana had noticed Rafe right away, but Katie could hardly blame her. The man was really worth watching.

Katie's gaze went directly to Rafe, on the opposite side of the yard. Since that morning when she'd stood up for him to Joe, Rafe had been avoiding her. She couldn't quite figure out why, either. Maybe it was a guy thing, embarrassing to have a woman defend his honor? She smiled to herself at the thought.

"Well, well. I can see now that you're doing plenty of noticing." She draped one arm around Katie's shoulders. "He's quite the hunk, isn't he?"

"Hunk?" Katie repeated with a laugh.

"You betcha. The question is, what're you going to do about it?"

"What can I do?" Katie watched Rafe as he grinned at something Arturo said and she felt a delicious flutter in the pit of her stomach.

"Honestly," Nana said with a shake of her head, "youth really is wasted on the wrong people. Katie, if you want him, go for it."

"He's not a cookie I can grab and wrap up."

"Who said anything about wrapping him up?" Nana laughed and advised, "I was thinking more that you should *unwrap* him. Just grab him and take a bite. Life's too short, honey. You've got to enjoy it while you can."

"Unbelievably enough," Katie said, "I'm not as freewheeling as my grandmother."

"Well, you could be." Nana shook her head and said, "I loved your grandfather, honey, but he's been gone a long time and I'm still alive and kicking. And, so are *you*. You've been burying yourself in your work for so long, it's a wonder you can step outside without squinting into the sun like a mole."

"I'm not that bad!"

"Didn't used to be," her grandmother allowed. "Until that Cordell twisted you all up."

Katie frowned at the reminder.

"There's a whole wide world full of people out there and half of them are men," Nana told her. "You can't let one bad guy ruin your opinion on an entire gender."

Is that what she was doing? Katie wondered. She didn't think so. Sure, Cordell King had hurt her, but she wasn't hiding. She was working. Building her business. Just because she hadn't been on a date in...good night. She hadn't been on an actual date with an actual man since Cordell and that was more than six months ago now.

How had that happened?

She used to be fun.

She used to call her friends and go out.

She used to have a life.

"Oooh, here comes the cute one," her grandmother whispered.

Katie came out of her thoughts and watched Rafe approaching them. He wasn't cute, she thought. He was dark and dangerous and so sexy just watching him walk made her toes curl. Golden retrievers were cute.

Rafe was...tempting.

"What'd you say his name was?"

"Rafe. Rafe Cole."

"Hmm..."

Katie looked at her grandmother, but the woman's expression was carefully blank. Which usually meant there was something going on in Nana's mind that she didn't want anyone else to know about. But before Katie could wriggle the information out of her, Rafe was standing in front of them. She made the introductions, then Rafe spoke up.

"I just wanted to tell you that we'll be shutting down early tonight. Joe's got a meeting and he wants Arturo and Steve there."

"Not you?" she asked.

He shook his head. "No reason for me to be there. I'm just a worker bee. Anyway," he said, with a smile for her grandmother, "it was nice to meet you."

"Good to meet you too, Rafe," Nana said with a smile.

When he walked away, Katie's gaze was locked on him. His long legs, the easy, confident strides he took, the way the sunlight glinted on his black hair. And yes, she admitted silently, she liked the view of his butt in those faded jeans, too.

Finally though, she turned her gaze to her grandmother. The thoughtful expression on her Nana's face had her asking, "Okay, what's going on? What're you thinking?"

"Me? Only wondering if he has a grandfather as good looking as he is."

"You're hiding something," Katie said, narrowing her eyes.

"Me?" Emily slapped one hand to her chest and widened her eyes in innocence. "I'm an open book, sweetie. What you see is what you get."

"Nana…"

She checked her wristwatch and said, "Oh, I have to fly. Grace and I have a double date tonight with a couple of frisky widowers. I'm meeting Grace for manicures in half an hour."

Katie laughed and gave her a hug. "You're amazing."

"So are you, when you give yourself a chance." Emily slid a look at Rafe again. "Why not invite that boy to dinner? Live a little, Katie. You like him, don't you?"

"Yeah," Katie said, shifting her gaze back to Rafe. "I do. I mean, I've only known him a week, but I've spent so much time with him, it feels like longer. He's a nice guy, Nana. A regular guy. Nothing like Cordell King and believe me, that's a good thing. I've had it with the idle rich."

"Not all rich guys are idle," Emily pointed out. "Or, jerks for that matter."

"Maybe," Katie said, but she wasn't convinced. Granted, she hadn't had a lot of experience with rich men. Cordell had been the one and only billionaire she'd ever known. But if he was an example of their breed, then he was more than enough to last her a lifetime. "From now on though, I'm only interested in regular, hardworking guys."

"You have your mother's hard head, God bless her." Nana blew out a breath and said, "Fine. This Rafe seems nice enough and he's surely easy on the eyes."

"That he is," Katie agreed, letting her gaze slide back to the man whose image had been filling her dreams lately.

"But you never really know a man until you've hit the sack with him."

"Nana!" Katie groaned and shook her head. "What kind of role model are you, anyway?"

"The good kind." Emily laughed, clearly delighted at being able to shock her granddaughter so easily. "I'm just saying, it might be interesting to take him out for a test drive, that's all."

Katie loved her grandmother, but she was in no way the free spirit Emily O'Hara was. But then Nana hadn't always been this outspoken and full of adventure. Right after Katie's mother died, Nana had seemed to realize just how short life really was and she'd thrown herself into the mix with abandon.

And while Katie admired that adventurous style and certainly understood, she just couldn't bring herself to behave the same way. Nana had had the great love of her life and now she was looking for fun.

Katie was still looking for love.

Still, the fact was, Nana was probably right about Rafe. Katie was more drawn to him than she had been to anyone, up to and including Cordell King. So maybe it was time she took a chance. Pushed herself out of the cocoon she'd wrapped herself in.

"Not interested in a test drive." Okay, that's a lie, she amended silently when that little buzz of interest popped in her veins again. "Not yet, anyway," she said aloud. "But dinner would be good. I do like him and he's so different from Cordell King."

"Uh-huh."

"What?"

"Nothing. Not a darn thing." Emily pulled her in for a hard, tight hug and said, "I'm off for some fun. I suggest you do the same. Gotta run."

Alone again, Katie silently studied Rafe Cole as he stood in the sunlight laughing with Arturo.

Fun sounded like a good idea.

"The guys are gone," Rafe said.

He had stayed deliberately, after the crew left for the

night, just to get a few minutes alone with her. Hadn't asked himself why, because he wasn't sure he'd like the answer. But he'd fallen into the habit of being the last man to leave and he actually looked forward to the times when it was just him and Katie at the house.

The neighborhood was quiet, but for the muffled, heartbeat-like sound of a basketball thumping in someone's driveway. A dog barked from close by and the ocean wind felt cool after a long day in the sun.

Katie had her curly red hair pulled back in a ponytail and her green eyes were shining in the afternoon light. A soft smile curved her mouth and Rafe felt a punch of need slam into him. He knew it would be a mistake to get her into bed. After all, not only was she so not his type, but she hated the King family. If they had sex and she found out he'd lied about who he was, it could only get ugly.

But damned if logic had anything to do with what he was feeling at the moment.

"How'd it go today?" She stepped out of the house and started for the garage. Rafe walked with her.

"We got the drywall up over the pipes and the plumbing's finished."

"Really?" She stopped and grinned. "No more naked pipes!"

The smile on her face made her eyes shine brighter and Rafe felt a tug of something hot and wicked. The woman could turn him hard without even trying. He couldn't even remember a time when he'd been this attracted, this quickly to anyone. Not even Leslie, the ex-wife from hell, had had this effect on him.

After a moment or two, he cleared his throat and said, "Yeah. It should move pretty quickly now, as long as all of your supplies come in on time."

She held up both hands, fingers crossed, and said, "Here's hoping. I really miss having a kitchen."

"Maybe, but from the smells coming from your temporary setup, it's not slowing you down any."

Laughing, she opened the garage door and stepped into the gloom. Rafe stayed with her, not ready to leave yet. He took a quick look around the garage. It was tidy, like the rest of her house. Storage shelves on one wall, washer and drier on another. There was an older model, red SUV parked dead center and a few lawn and garden tools stacked along the last wall.

"Baking the cookies is easy enough thanks to you setting up the stove for me," she said, with a nod of her head. "But oh, I miss my counter when it comes time to decorate and wrap. I've got tables set up all over the patio now, but…"

"You want your life back," he finished for her.

"*Yes*," she agreed with a sigh. "Funny, but you go along every day and you hardly notice your routine—" She paused and smiled. "You'll notice I said routine, not *rut*."

"I noticed," he said with a grin.

She stopped beside the shelves and bent down to pull a bag of charcoal free. He bent down at the same time and suddenly, their mouths were just a kiss apart. Time staggered to a standstill. His gaze dropped to her lips and everything inside him clenched when her tongue slipped out to slide along her bottom lip.

Rafe wanted a taste of her. More than he did his next breath. But her eyes told him she wasn't ready for that and if there was one thing Rafe King knew, it was how to be patient. So he straightened up and grabbed the bag.

"Let me get that for you."

She stepped back with a soft *thanks*, then continued with what she'd been saying. "Then you get ripped out of that routine and all you can think about is getting it back. That doesn't make any sense at all, does it?"

"Sure it does," he said, idly noting how the sunlight drifting in through the small garage windows shone on her hair like fire. His body was tight and his breath was strangling in his lungs. But he didn't let her know that.

"Nobody likes having their place invaded and their life turned upside down."

"What about you?" she asked. "Do you have a routine you don't want upset?"

He gave her a quick grin and set the bag of charcoal at his feet. "Men don't have routines," he corrected. "We have schedules."

"Ah." She leaned against the front fender of the van. "And your 'schedule'?"

"Same as everyone else's I guess," he said after a long minute, when he took the time to remind himself to be vague. He couldn't exactly tell her about time spent with his brothers, or at King Construction. "Work, home. Play."

"I know what you do for work. What's your idea of playtime?"

"Well now," he mused thoughtfully, meeting her gaze and allowing her to see exactly what she was doing to him, "that's an interesting question."

She sucked in a breath of air and straightened up and away from her car. He liked seeing her nervous. That told him she was feeling the same kind of attraction he was. Good to know. But he'd let her catch her breath before he pushed any harder. He wasn't used to dealing with a woman like Katie.

The women he generally spent time with were, like Rafe, only interested in a few hours of pleasure. There were no hidden agendas, no emotional traps and no expectations. Katie was different. She was new territory for him and damned if he wasn't enjoying himself.

"So?" he asked, picking up the bag of charcoal, "Barbecuing?"

She looked grateful for the reprieve. "Yes. Hamburgers sounded good to me and they're just not the same if they're not barbecued."

"Agreed," Rafe said, turning for the door. "Want me to set it up for you?"

"Only if you'll stay for dinner."

He stopped, half turned and looked at her. A slow smile curved his mouth. If he was here for dinner, he'd be damn sure staying for dessert, too. "That'd be great. But if it's all the same to you, I'll go home and shower and change first."

"Sure, that's fine."

She looked nervous again, chewing at her bottom lip. His gaze locked on that action and his insides tightened even further. Oh, yeah. He'd make it a cold shower, too.

"Okay," he said, "give me an hour? I'll get the barbecue going when I get back. I'm good at starting fires."

"That," she said, "I absolutely believe."

Four

"It doesn't mean a thing," Katie told herself while she quickly mixed up a batch of pasta salad to go with the burgers. "It's just dinner. A barbecue. Friendly. Non-threatening. Not sexual in any way…"

Oh, even *she* didn't believe that. She'd felt the tension mounting between them when they both went to reach for the bag of charcoal. For a second, she had been sure he was going to kiss her and she still wasn't sure if she'd been relieved or disappointed that he hadn't. And, she had seen his eyes when he promised to start her fire for her. He probably knew that he'd already started it.

Cooking helped center her. It always had. As a girl, she'd helped Nana out in the kitchen and slowly learned her way around a recipe. Then, she started creating her own. And she had learned early that no matter what else was happening in her life, the kitchen was her comfort zone.

She chopped celery, then mushrooms, carrots and broccoli, and added them to the cold pasta, giving it all a good stir together with the homemade pesto. When she was finished, she stored the bowl in her fridge and started on dessert.

She had to keep busy. If she stopped long enough to think about what she was doing, she'd talk herself out of it.

That brought her up short.

"Out of *what* exactly, Katie?" she demanded. "He's coming for dinner. Nobody said anything about sex."

Oh, boy.

The problem was, she really wanted Rafe Cole. She'd been around him almost nonstop for the last week and every day, he'd gotten to her just a little bit more. He was friendly and helpful and, boy, he looked darn good in his jeans. Those blue eyes of his were starring nightly in her dreams and her fingers itched to slide through his thick, black hair.

Yep, she was in bad shape and no doubt asking for trouble by instigating this dinner. But maybe it was time she had a little trouble in her life. She'd always been the good girl. Always done the "right" thing. The *safe* thing.

Heck, she'd dated Cordell King for three months and hadn't slept with him. She'd wanted to take it slow because she'd been so sure that he was the one.

It had seemed, at the time, as if fate had thrown them together. After all, it wasn't as if she stumbled across billionaires all the time in her everyday life. He had ordered an extra-large cookie bouquet to be delivered to his assistant, who was taking off for maternity leave. Katie's delivery girl hadn't been able to take the runs that day, so Katie had done the job herself.

Cordell had slipped out of his office to watch as his assistant cooed and cried over the beautifully frosted cookies that Katie presented to her. And after that, he'd walked Katie to her car and asked her to dinner. After that night, they'd been together as often as each of their schedules had allowed.

Looking back, Katie could see that she had been flattered by Cordell's attention. That the thought of a rich, successful man being interested in her had fed the flames of what she had believed was the start of something amazing. He was so handsome. So attentive. So damned sexy. Her heart had taken a leap before her mind could catch up.

Shaking her head, she realized that she had felt at the time as if she were living in a fairy tale. Where the handsome prince swooped into her poor but proud cottage and carried her off to her castle.

"Silly," she whispered, thinking back to her own actions. Thank God she hadn't slept with him. That would have only fed the humiliation when she looked back on a time where she had been involved in what she thought was something special.

As it turned out, of course, the only thing special they shared was that they were both in love with Cordell.

Grumbling under her breath, Katie let the old, hurtful memories fade away as she focused instead on the evening to come. She spooned fresh whipped cream into old-fashioned sundae glasses. Then she layered chocolate-chip cookie bits with more whipped cream and when they were finished, they too went into the fridge. She would drizzle raspberry syrup over the top of the frothy dessert just before she served it.

When the meal was done, she glanced around the temporary kitchen, checked her watch and realized that

Rafe would be arriving any minute. So she raced to the bathroom and checked her hair and makeup. Stupid, but she felt like a teenager waiting for her first date to arrive.

Nerves bubbled in the pit of her stomach and a kind of excitement she hadn't felt before hummed through her bloodstream. Staring at the woman in the mirror, she gave herself a little pep talk.

"You're going to have fun, Katie Charles. For once in your life, you're not going to think ahead to tomorrow. You're going to enjoy tonight for whatever it turns out to be." She nodded abruptly and pretended she didn't see the flash of nervousness staring back at her from her own eyes. "He's a nice guy. You're both single. So relax, already."

Easier said than done, she knew.

But there was nothing wrong with a little fun.

Right?

"You find out anything from the family?" Rafe asked his brother as he steered his truck down Katie's street.

"Not a damn thing," Sean assured him, his voice crackling with static over the cell phone. "I talked to Tanner, but since he and Ivy got married, he's pretty much useless for picking up stray news. All he talks about is their latest ultrasound picture." Sean sighed in disgust. "Seriously, you'd think they were the only people in the universe to get pregnant."

Rafe let that one go. He was glad for their brother Tanner. Ivy was a nice woman and against all odds, she was turning Tanner into a halfway decent Christmas-tree farmer.

"Then," Sean said, "I called cousin Jesse. But the only thing he knows about Katie Charles is that he favors her macadamia-nut-white-chocolate-chip cookies. His wife Bella says the peanut-butter ones are best, but their boy Joshua likes the chocolate fudge."

Rafe rubbed a spot between his eyes and took a breath. "And I care what kind of cookies they like, because…"

"Because that's the only information they had and now I want a damn cookie," Sean grumbled.

Rafe scowled as he pulled up outside Katie's house. He parked and slanted a glance at the setting sun reflecting off the gleaming front windows. "Somebody in the family knows her and I want to find out who."

"What do you care?" Sean snorted a laugh. "I mean, seriously dude, you've known her for what, a week? What's it to you if she hates the Kings?"

"I don't like it."

"You'd think you'd be used to it," Sean said. "There are plenty of people out there who feel the same."

"Not *women*."

"Good point." Sean sighed and said, "So, this is part of why you find her so interesting, huh?"

"Maybe." He didn't even know. But Katie Charles was hitting him in places he hadn't known existed. And she kept doing it. One look out of those green eyes of hers and his mind filled with all sorts of damn near irresistible images.

And it was lowering to admit that if she knew he was a King, she'd slam her front door in his face and he'd never see her again.

"Fine. I'll go back to the drawing board. Hey, I'll call Garrett," Sean suggested. "He loves a mystery, so if he doesn't have the answer he'll find it."

Sean was right. Their cousin, Garrett King, ran a security company and liked nothing better than delving for secrets. If anyone could find out who was behind Katie's feelings about the Kings, it would be Garrett.

"All right, good. Thanks."

"You busy? I'm taking the jet to Vegas tonight. Why don't you come with me? We'll hit a show, then wipe out the craps tables."

Rafe smiled. Ordinarily, he'd have appreciated the invitation. But tonight, he had something better to do. "Thanks, but I've got plans."

"With the King hater?"

"Her name is Katie, but yeah," Rafe said tightly.

"She doesn't know who you are, does she?"

"No." Irritation hummed inside him again. He'd never before had to disguise himself to be with a woman. Hell, if anything, the King name had women clamoring to get near him.

"Great. Well, pick me up some cookies before she finds out you're lying to her and you ruin what's left of our rep with her."

Rafe hung up a second or two later, his brother's words ringing in his ears. He dismissed them though, because there was no way Katie would find out Rafe's last name until he was good and ready for her to know. And that wouldn't be until he'd romanced her, seduced her and shown her just how likeable he really was.

Then he'd tell her he was a King. And she'd see how wrong she was. About all of them.

But for now, he was enjoying himself with a woman who didn't want anything from him beyond barbecuing some burgers.

He got out of the truck and headed for the house. But before he reached the porch, Katie rushed out the door and skidded to a stop when she saw him. Her curly red hair was loose around her shoulders and her long legs looked tan and gorgeous in a pair of white shorts. Her dark green T-shirt made her eyes shine as she spotted him. "Rafe, I'm so glad you're back! Follow me!"

She sprinted down her front steps and past him, headed toward her neighbor's house. She rounded a white picket fence with bright splashes of flowers climbing across it and headed up the driveway. Rafe stayed right on her heels, his mind already racing to possible disasters. Someone dying. Someone bleeding. He reached into his pocket and gripped his phone ready to dial nine-one-one.

Adrenaline pulsed through him as they rushed up the drive to the front porch of a small, Tudor-style cottage with a sloping roof and leaded windows.

"What's wrong?" he shouted.

"Nicole needs help!"

The front door of the house swung open as they approached and a harried woman with short, blond hair and a toddler on her hip sighed in relief.

"Thank God you're here, it's all over everywhere."

Katie made to run inside, but Rafe pulled her back and went in first. He didn't know what the hell was going on around here, but damned if he was going to let Katie run into the heart of whatever trouble it was.

She was right behind him though. He took a moment to glance around, while looking for whatever disaster had happened. He registered the toy cars strewn across the floor and the wooden train set. Then he heard the trouble and his heartbeat returned to normal. No one was dying but it sounded like there was an indoor fountain on full blast.

The woman was talking to Katie, but Rafe was only half listening.

"I can't turn the water off—it's like the valve is frozen

in place or something and there's water everywhere and Connor was crying.…"

"It's okay, Nicole," Katie said. "We'll get it shut off and help you clean it up."

He ignored the women and headed for the kitchen, following the loud sound of splashing. Not the way Rafe had planned on this first date with Katie going, but he could adapt. Water was shooting out from under the kitchen sink through the open cupboard doors. Already there was a small flood in the room and a kitchen rug was drifting out on the tide.

Cursing under his breath, Rafe sloshed his way through the kitchen. He crouched down in front of the sink, reached through the cascading cold water and blindly found the shutoff valve. Water poured over him in a never-ending jet. He blinked it out of his eyes, muttered an oath and grabbed hold of the damn valve. Hell, he thought, no wonder Nicole hadn't been able to turn it. It took everything he had to budge the damn thing and it didn't go easy, fighting him every inch of the way. By increments, he slowly shut down the torrent until all that was left was the mess on the floor and a steady drip under the sink.

The sudden silence was almost overpowering. Until the little boy in his mother's arms started laughing.

"Boat!" he cried, pointing to a cell phone as it floated past them.

"Fabulous," Nicole murmured and bent down to scoop it up. "Well, I needed an upgrade anyway."

"Oh, honey, I'm so sorry," Katie said, dropping one arm around her friend's shoulders. She looked at Rafe, soaking wet, and winced. "Rafe Cole, this is Nicole Baxter. Nicole, Rafe."

The woman gave him a tired smile. "I suspect I'm happier to meet you than you are me at the moment."

"No problem. I like an adventure every now and then." He pushed his hair back from his face with both hands, then swept water off his palms. Wet and cold, he caught the glimmer of regret and amusement in Katie's eyes and smiled in spite of everything. "I've got it shut off, but your pipe joint's shot. It has to be fixed."

"Of course it does," Nicole said with a sigh. She hitched her son a little higher on her hip and added, "Thanks. Really, for shutting off Old Faithful. I never would have been able to do it."

"Your husband should be able to replace it without a problem," he told her.

"My *ex*-husband's in Hawaii with his secretary," she said wryly and only then did Rafe see Katie shaking her head at him in a silent signal to shut up.

"Haven't seen him since before Connor was born," Nicole added, kissing the little guy's cheek. "But we do fine, don't we, sweet boy?"

Perfect, Rafe thought. He'd made the woman feel even worse now by reminding her of her creep of an ex. A bubble of irritation frothed inside him. What kind of man walked away from his child? Rafe didn't get it. Sure, he knew that marriages didn't always work out. But what man would walk away from his own baby? Shouldn't he try to hold his family together?

While his brain raced, a quiet, rational voice in the back of his mind warned him that he was putting his own issues out there and it was time to draw them back. His old man hadn't been even close to a normal father, but at least Ben King was always there when his kids needed him. Which was more than Rafe could say for Nicole's ex.

Still, looking at Katie's friend, holding her son so closely, reminded him of his own upbringing. Oh, his mother hadn't stuck around or anything. She'd handed him off to an elderly aunt before he was a year old and only showed up for a visit when her money was running out. Ben King hadn't married her, but he'd supported her until Rafe was eighteen.

Once he was grown, his mom had started coming to Rafe for the cash she required to live the kind of life she preferred. He didn't mind paying. It kept her out of his hair.

Now though, watching Nicole and her son brought home to him again how hard the aunt who'd raised him had had it. Oh, she'd had money for plumbing repairs, but she'd been all alone raising a boy. Just as Nicole was. And Nicole didn't have the luxury of calling a King for help.

Lucky for her, there was already a King in the neighborhood.

He looked at Katie and saw the worry for her friend shining in her eyes and he heard himself say, "Why don't you two get the back door open and sweep out as much of this water as you can?"

"Good idea," Katie agreed. "Come on, Nicole, I'll help you get this straightened up."

"You don't have to do that," the blond said. "We'll be fine. Really."

"Sure you will, I can see that," Rafe told her with a shrug, not wanting to wound her pride. "But while you two get the water out of here, I'm going to run up to the hardware store. I'll get a new joint in there and have you up and running again."

Katie *beamed* at him.

And he felt as if someone had just pinned a medal to his chest.

Their gazes locked, and the rest of the world fell away for one long, sizzling moment. Every heartbeat felt measured. Every breath a struggle.

Rafe was caught by the emotion on her face. The pride in *him*. The gratitude and the admiration. He had never known another moment like it. It was amazing, he thought, to have someone look at him as if he'd hung the moon.

And all he wanted to do was walk across the floor, take her into his arms and sweep her into a dip for a kiss that would send them both over the edge of hunger. Need was a gnawing ache inside him. He'd never experienced *that* before, either, he thought. Desire, sure. Want, absolutely.

But *need?*

Never.

"I can't ask you to do that," Nicole said, shattering the moment.

Rafe took a breath to steady himself and shook his head, clearing his thoughts, getting a grip on the emotions suddenly churning through him. As he regained control, he mentally thanked Nicole for shattering whatever it was that had so briefly hummed between he and Katie.

Looking at the blonde, he said, "You didn't ask. I offered. And don't worry about it. Besides," he added with a grin for the toddler, "with this little guy around, you're going to need water, right?"

Katie was still smiling at him as if he were some kind of comic-book hero. And she was still stirring him up inside, so he gave her a smile, then tugged his keys out of his jeans pocket. Best all around if he left now. "I'll be back in a few minutes and we'll get you set up."

"Thanks." Nicole whispered the word. "Really."

Katie gave her a brief hug, then stepped up to Rafe and slid her hand into his. "I'll walk you to the door while Nicole gets the broom and mop."

His fingers curled around hers and he felt the heat of her skin zing through his system like a raging wildfire. At the front door, Katie looked back over her shoulder to make sure Nicole was out of earshot, then said softly, "Thank you for offering to help her like that, Rafe. Nicole couldn't afford a plumber. You're really doing something amazing for her."

"It's not a problem."

"For *you*," she said with another smile. "But for a single mom, it's a catastrophe. Or it would have been. Without you. You're my hero."

Her simple words hit him with a crash. Always before, when people needed help, he wrote a check. Made a donation. It was safe, distant and still managed to salve the urge he had to help those who needed it. He hadn't realized until just now how differently helping felt when it was up close and personal.

"I've never been anybody's hero before."

She looked up at him and he knew he could lose himself in the deep, summer green of her eyes. Her delectable mouth curved at the edges. "You are now."

He reached up and cupped the back of her neck with his palm. "Keep that thought and hold on to it for later, okay?"

"I can do that," she said and went up on her toes to brush a soft kiss across his mouth. Then she stepped away and said, "Hurry back."

His lips were tingling, his breath was still strangling

in his lungs and Rafe was suddenly so damn hard he didn't think he'd be able to walk to his truck without limping.

Some hero.

Nicole and Connor joined them for the barbecue.

Katie told herself she was just being nice—Nicole was still upset and they were all tired out from cleaning up the mess in her kitchen. But the truth was, that moment with Rafe at the front door of Nicole's house had shaken Katie enough that she had wanted someone else around during dinner. Not exactly a chaperone, just someone to keep Katie from jumping Rafe the moment they were alone.

Because that's exactly what she wanted to do. He had been wonderful. Honestly, she thought back to her time with Cordell King and no matter how she tried to imagine it, she couldn't see that man diving under a kitchen sink to fix something as a favor. He was too much a suit-and-tie man. Too focused on the bottom line of his company and not so interested in the "real world."

Rafe though, was different, she thought, watching him gently toss a soft foam ball to Connor. The little boy waved both arms trying to catch it and Rafe laughed with him when he missed. The man was just…

"Amazing," Nicole said, unknowingly finishing Katie's mental sentence.

"What?"

"Him." Nicole smiled at Katie, then shifted her gaze to where her son was playing with Rafe. "That guy is one in a million, Katie."

"I was just thinking the same thing."

"Yeah?" Nicole pushed her paper plate aside, leaned

both arms on the weathered picnic table and asked, "If you think so, why'd you have Connor and I come over and horn in on your date?"

"You're not horning in," Katie argued. In the year she and her son had lived next door, Nicole had become Katie's best friend. They'd commiserated on the rotten tendencies of the men they'd had in their lives and they'd bonded over working from home. Katie had her cookie company and Nicole did the billing for several local companies.

"You're my friend, Nicole, and you're always invited over. You know that."

"'Course I know that." Nicole reached out and covered Katie's hand with her own. "You've been great to us since we moved in here. But Katie, this is the first guy I've seen you date in like forever. Don't you want some alone time?"

Katie stared at Rafe as he scooped Connor up and ran across the yard, the little boy chortling happily. "I do and I don't. Seriously, Nicole, I'm not sure what I want."

"Well I can tell you if he looked at *me*, the way he looks at *you*, I wouldn't have any trouble deciding what I wanted."

"It's complicated."

"I know. Cordell." Giving her hand a squeeze, Nicole sat back and shook her head. "He messed you up bad. But Rafe isn't Cordell."

"You're telling me," Katie said on a sigh.

"Do you really want to risk losing a great guy because you're still mad at a rotten one?"

"Have you been talking to Nana?"

Nicole laughed. "No. I haven't. But if she agrees with

me, then we're both right and you should trust us on this. Give it a shot, Katie. What've you got to lose?"

Another chunk of her heart, she thought but didn't say. But then again, if she never risked her heart, she'd never use it, would she? She'd die an old lady, filled with regrets, still holding on to her withered pride like a trophy with some of the shiny worn off.

Her gaze locked on Rafe again as he lifted the little boy high enough for tiny hands to swat at the glossy leaves of an orange tree. Her still-wary heart turned over in her chest as she watched the expression on Rafe's face. He was enjoying himself. He was relaxed, at ease with her friends, in her tiny backyard. Cordell, in the same situation, would have—never mind, he never would have been in this situation. He had preferred five-star restaurants to picnics and three-piece suits to jeans.

Cordell had swept Katie off her feet because she had never been with anyone like him. Now she knew she should have kept it that way.

But Rafe…he was different from Cordell. He was the kind of guy Katie should have met first.

And if she had, she asked herself, would she have been so hesitant to take a chance on him? No, she wouldn't have.

"Ooh, I can see by the look in your eyes you've decided to take a chance," Nicole said. "Want me to take Connor home so you can get going on that?"

Katie shook her head. "Not until after dessert," she said. "Then we'll see what happens."

She stood up and headed for the enclosed patio and her refrigerator. Behind her, she heard Connor's giggles and Rafe's deep laughter.

Her skin tingled and everything in her awoke to anticipation.

Five

"If that dessert was a sample of your cookies," Rafe said much later, "then I can understand why people are so crazy about them."

"Thank you. I can give you some to take home if you like," Katie said.

Rafe tipped his head to one side and studied her. Nicole and her son had gone home and now it was just he and Katie in the backyard. The summer night was cool, the sky overhead swimming with stars. Moonlight drifted down and did battle with the candle flames flickering in the soft breeze.

"Anxious to get rid of me?" he asked quietly.

"No," she said. "That's not what I meant. I just—oh, for heaven's sake. You'd think I'd never been on a date before." She caught herself and amended, "Not that this is a date or anything…"

Rafe grinned, enjoying that touch of nervousness. "It's not?"

"Is it?"

His smile firmly in place he admitted, "Well, I don't usually do plumbing on a date, but everything else seems about right."

Now she returned his smile and seemed to relax a little. The wind lifted her hair like a lover's caress. "It was fun, wasn't it?"

"Yeah, and it's not over yet."

"Really."

Not a question, he told himself. More of a challenge. Well, he was willing to accept it. "Really."

He stood up, walked to her side of the picnic table and pulled her to her feet. "What're you doing?"

"I want to dance with you," he said simply, drawing her closer.

Even as she went with him, she was saying, "There's no music."

"Sure there is," he told her, wrapping his arm around her waist and capturing her right hand in his left. "You're just not listening hard enough."

She shook her head at him.

"Close your eyes," he said and she did. He looked down at her, so trusting, so beautiful, and his breath caught in his chest. Her hand was warm and smooth in his, her scent—a mixture of vanilla and cinnamon—filling him. He smiled, thinking that she smelled as edible as her cookies.

"Now listen," he urged quietly, his voice hardly more than a whisper of sound.

"To what?" she answered just as quietly.

"Everything."

He swayed with her in his arms and rested his chin

on top of her head. Her body felt perfect aligned along his and he went hard and ready almost instantly. If she noticed, she didn't let him know.

As they moved in the starlight, sounds of the summer night began to encroach. Crickets singing, the distant sigh of the ocean, the wind in the trees. It was as if nature herself were providing a perfect symphony just for the two of them.

She smiled, tipped her head back, and keeping her eyes closed, moved with him as if they'd been dancing together forever. "I hear it now," she whispered. "It's perfect."

"Yeah," he said, coming to a stop, staring down at her. "It is."

Her eyes opened and she met his gaze. "Rafe?"

His hand tightened on hers and he held her closer, pulling her in firmly enough against him that she couldn't miss feeling exactly what she was doing to him. "I want you, Katie. More than I've ever wanted anything."

A tiny sigh slipped from her mouth as she confessed, "I feel exactly the same way."

He gave her a grin and slowly lowered his mouth to hers. "Good to hear."

He kissed her and the instant their mouths met, Rafe felt a punch of desire so hot, so unbelievably strong that it nearly knocked him over. In response, his arms tightened around her, all thoughts of dancing disappearing from his mind. He wanted to move with her, but dancing had nothing to do with the plans quickly forming in his mind. He needed her, more than he would have thought possible. And he wanted her even more.

His hands swept up and down her spine, defining

every curve, every valley she possessed. She moved against him, her body restless, her soft moans telling him everything he needed to know. He slipped one hand beneath the hem of her T-shirt and swept up, to caress the side of her breast. Even the lacy material of her bra couldn't keep him from enjoying the heat of her. The perfectly shaped wonder of her. His hands itched to feel her skin.

Hunger roared through him and he deepened their kiss, his tongue sweeping into her mouth, claiming everything she had and silently demanding more. She gave it to him, surrendering herself to the passion rising between them. Her tongue tangled with his, her breath sighing against his cheek as she met him stroke for stroke. Her hands clutched his shoulders, holding on tightly as she moaned in appreciation.

That soft sound was enough to push Rafe dangerously close to the edge. He tore his mouth from hers, looked down at her through eyes glazed with heat and need and said grimly, "If we don't stop right now, I'm going to throw you down onto this picnic table and give your neighbors a show."

A choked laugh shot from her throat. She didn't release her hold on him though, as if she didn't quite trust herself to be able to stand on her own two feet.

"The picnic table's not nearly as comfortable as my bed," she said, just a little breathlessly.

"Is that an invitation?"

"Sounded like one to me."

"All I need to know," Rafe muttered and swept her up into his arms.

"You don't have to carry me!"

"Faster this way," he told her, nearly sprinting across the yard toward the house.

"That works too," she said, snuggling close to him, stroking the flat of her hand across his chest.

He hissed in a breath, hit the patio door and stepped inside. "Where to?"

"Down the hall, turn left at the end."

He was already moving. His body was hard and aching. He could hardly draw a breath without fanning the flames licking at his insides. His heart pounding, Rafe entered her room and strode straight to the bed. Absently, he noticed the window seat on the front wall, colorful rugs scattered across a gleaming wood floor and a squat bookcase stuffed with paperbacks.

But his gaze was locked on the wide bed covered in an old-fashioned quilt. He stopped alongside the four-poster, tossed the covers back to reveal smooth white sheets and dropped Katie onto the mattress.

She bounced, then smiled up at him. It was all the encouragement he needed. Tearing off his clothes, he watched her as she did the same. In seconds, they were both naked and he was leaning over her. Rafe had been thinking about this moment for days. Dreaming about it every damn night.

She was haunting him, this woman who so hated the King family. She had somehow reached him in a way no other woman had and though that admission bothered him, it wasn't enough to keep him from enjoying what she was offering.

Reaching up to him, she plunged her fingers through his hair and drew his mouth down to hers. Their mouths melded and her taste was as intoxicating as ever. Her kiss sizzled inside him, making the ache in his body almost overpowering. Everything in him urged him to hurry. To take. To ease the need clamoring within him.

But the urge to savor was just as strong. His tongue

entwined with hers, he slid one hand down the length of her body, relishing the glide of her skin beneath his palm. So soft, so curvy. So just right.

Reluctantly, he broke their kiss, shifted position slightly and took one of her hard, pink nipples into his mouth. She gasped and arched against him as he suckled her, using his teeth and tongue to lovingly torture her. He felt every breath she took, heard every sigh and wanted more. Rafe inhaled her scent and lost himself in the glory of her.

She held his head to her breast as if afraid he might stop. But Rafe was just getting started. He moved to give the same attention to her other breast, feeling her heartbeat quicken, as anticipation rolled through her. He smiled against her skin, then lifted his head and looked up into her passion glazed eyes. "I've wanted this since the first moment I saw you."

"Me, too," she admitted, licking her bottom lip in an action that caused everything inside him to clench.

His fingers and thumb continued to tug and pull at her nipple, making her squirm and her breath catch in her throat. When he touched her, he saw exactly what she was feeling on her face. He loved watching her expression shift and change as she gave herself over to him and Rafe knew there was something more here than want.

Something dangerous.

Yet he couldn't have pulled away and left if it had meant his life.

That thought stark in his mind, he leaned over her again, stared down into her green eyes and asked, "What are you doing to me?"

She laughed a little and cupped his cheek in her palm. "At the moment, it's *you* doing something to *me*."

Staring into her eyes, he felt that kick of something he didn't quite recognize and after a long second or two, he let it go. Now was not the time to be thinking.

"So it is," he agreed, dipping his head for one brief, hard kiss. He felt it again. That something *more* between them. That extra jolt he'd never known before. A part of Rafe worried that he might be getting in deeper here than he had planned. But there was no way out now. No other answer but to have her. To feel her body welcoming his. To delve into her heat and take them both where they had been heading from the first.

He'd worry about consequences later. Wonder if this had been a good idea another time. For right now, there was nowhere he'd rather be.

Sliding one hand down the length of her body, he stroked her core with the tips of his fingers until she lifted her hips into his touch. Her gaze never left his. He watched passion flare and sparkle in her eyes and pushed her higher, faster. Her breath came in quick gasps. Her body trembled in his arms and he felt her pleasure as if it were his own.

Rafe couldn't get enough of looking at her face. Every emotion so openly displayed. Nothing hidden. Nothing held back. He'd never been with a woman so honestly enthusiastic. Always before, the women in his life had been controlled. As if playing the role they thought he wanted from them.

Even his ex-wife Leslie had held something back from him, as if she couldn't quite trust him enough to confide her deepest feelings and reactions. But there was no artifice with Katie.

She threw herself into the moment and in so doing, drew him with her.

"Come for me," he whispered, dipping his head

to taste her mouth. He caught her breath as it passed between her parted lips. She tasted as sweet as the cookies she was known for. "Let go, Katie. Fly."

She choked off a half laugh and held on to him, one arm draped around his shoulder. Her hips rocked into his hand and when he dipped his fingers in and out of her heat, she groaned and arched high off the bed. "Rafe…"

"Shatter, Katie. Let me watch you shatter."

Her gaze locked on his, she expelled a breath, took another and did as he asked. Her body shook as she cried out his name, her gaze never leaving his. She allowed him to see exactly what he was doing to her. What he was making her feel. And his own passion exploded in response. She bit down hard on her bottom lip and rode the wave of completion he gave her and all Rafe could think was, it wasn't enough. He had to see her face etched in pleasure again and again.

The last of her tremors had barely faded away when he pushed off the bed, grabbed his jeans off the floor and dug into the pocket.

"What're you…" She stopped and smiled when she saw him pull out a foil-wrapped condom. Stretching her arms back over her head, she sighed and said, "Pretty sure of yourself tonight then, weren't you? You came prepared."

He ripped open the foil, sheathed himself and turned back to her. "Not sure of myself. Just hopeful."

He leaned over her and Katie's arms encircled his neck. "I think, Rafe Cole, that you're *always* sure of yourself and tonight was no different."

Couldn't really argue with that, he thought. But the truth was, he had just wanted to be prepared. Unlike his father, Rafe didn't run around the world leaving illegitimate children in his wake. In fact, he had no intention of ever having children and he for damn sure wouldn't create a life because he was too lazy or too selfish to wear a condom.

None of which Katie needed to know.

Bending his head to claim another hard, fast kiss, Rafe looked into her eyes and said, "I'm not so sure of myself around you, Katie. And that's the truth."

She smiled, a slow curve of her mouth, then reached up to stroke her fingertips along his jawline. "I like hearing that."

Wryly, he said, "Thought you would. Women love to know when they've got a man dazed and confused."

"Are you dazed?" she asked, moving against him.

"With any luck," he told her, "I'm about to be."

He parted her thighs and settled himself between them. He looked his fill of her then, stroking her center with long, leisurely caresses until she was writhing with the tension.

"Yeah," he whispered, more to himself than to her, "dazed, all right."

Outside, the night was cool and quiet. In this room, the only sound was their ragged breathing and the thundering beat of their hearts. All that existed was this moment. This near-electric current of passion was flooding back and forth between them and Rafe knew he couldn't wait one more second to claim her.

For more than a week, he'd watched her, laughed with her. He'd spent more time with Katie Charles in the last week than he had with his ex-wife in the last year of their marriage. And he'd enjoyed it more, as well. She was smart and funny and talented and so damn sexy; one look from her green eyes was almost enough to floor him.

She parted her thighs wider in acceptance and sighed as he touched her. Rafe felt the slam of that soft sound ricochet inside him and ignored it. He didn't want his heart to be involved in this, so it wouldn't be. He wouldn't allow any more connection than the physical between them. And that would be enough, he assured himself.

He just had to have her, and then everything would go back to normal.

Lifting her hips to give himself better access, he slowly pushed himself into her heat. Into the very heart of her. And as her body wrapped itself around his, he hissed in a breath and fought for control.

Instinctively, she moved with him, lifting her legs high enough to wrap them around his waist and pull him in deeper, tighter, harder. He looked down at her and she opened her arms to him. Leaning over, he kissed her as he rocked his body against hers. Retreating and then advancing, he felt the magical slide of her warmth and knew it had never been better for him.

For the first time in his adult life, he wished to hell he wasn't wearing a damn condom. He wanted to feel *all* of her, without that layer separating them. But that would have been nuts, so he pushed that thought aside and moved on her again.

She lifted up from the bed and kissed him, framing his face in her hands, running her tongue along his bottom lip until she pushed him so near the edge there was no restraining himself any longer. He'd wanted to draw this out. Wanted to make it last, because he'd been dreaming of this moment for days now. But there was no more waiting. No slow and seductive.

There was only need and the desperate ache for completion.

Pushing her back onto the bed, he levered himself over her and took her hard and fast.

"Yes," she whispered, moving with him, matching his rhythm eagerly. His body pistoned into hers. Her hunger fueled his and together they reached for what they both needed.

He felt her climax hit her and as she rode out the convulsing waves of pleasure, he erupted, called her name and joined her in time to slide into oblivion, locked together.

"My hero," Katie said when she was sure her voice would work.

"Happy to oblige," he murmured, his face tucked into the curve of her neck.

She smiled to herself and stared up at the pale blue ceiling overhead. The soft sigh of his breath against her skin, the heavy weight of his body pressing onto hers and the throbbing center of her where they were still joined all came together to create perfection.

Running her hands up and down his back, she listened to the sound of his ragged breathing and felt the pounding beat of his heart. It had been so long since she'd been with someone, that maybe she was making too much of this.

But there was a tiny voice inside her, whispering to Katie that this had been *special*. That she had just shared something with Rafe that went far beyond sex.

Her heartbeat jittered unsteadily as that thought settled into her mind. Hadn't she thought what she had with Cordell was special, too? But this was different, her thoughts argued. This was so much more than she had ever felt for Cordell. Rafe touched more than her heart. He'd somehow wormed his way into her soul.

But she was rushing things and she knew it. She wasn't going to be foolishly romantic about a purely physical pleasure. Not again. She wasn't in love, for heaven's sake. Katie was a rational, logical woman and she knew that falling in love just didn't happen in a week's time.

But she could at least admit that Rafe Cole was in her heart. She cared for him or she never would have slept with him. And watching him tonight with Nicole and Connor had only heightened her feelings for him. How could she *not* be touched by a man who was so gentle with a two-year-old? So nice to a single mom who had needed help?

Rafe was the kind of man she used to dream of finding. He was hardworking and honest and kind and so very, very sexy.

"You're thinking," he murmured.

"Yep," she said.

He lifted his head and quirked a smile at her. "Why is it that good sex energizes a woman and makes a man unconscious?"

"I'd tell you," she said solemnly, "but then I'd have to kill you."

He laughed and she felt the jolt of that movement ripple throughout her body. They were still locked together. Every move Rafe made awakened already sensitized flesh and set it sizzling.

"Hmm," he whispered, as if knowing exactly what she was thinking, feeling. He moved in her again, slowly at first, eliciting another sigh from Katie. "Seems we're not finished yet."

"Not nearly," she agreed, moving with him, sliding into the pace he set as if they had been together hundreds of times and knew each other's moves instinctively. It was, Katie thought, as if they had been meant to be together. As if their bodies had been forged specifically to link into place, two halves, one whole. She couldn't help feeling that this was all as it was supposed to be. That this night had been fated in some way. That she'd been given this chance with Rafe in order to make up for the wounded heart she'd lived through months before. And it was working.

In seconds, the fire between them was burning again. Flames licked at her center and spread throughout her body. He touched her and there was magic. He became a part of her body and a corner of her heart never wanted it to end.

She looked up into those deep blue eyes of his and thought how glad she was that she'd taken this chance with him. That she had opened herself up to possibilities. To the magic that could happen between the right people.

And then her thoughts splintered as he pushed her beyond desire into passion that demanded her focus. She felt the quickening within, the first tingle of anticipation that something amazing was about to happen. Katie reached for it eagerly, hungrily, wanting to feel it all again.

He kissed her and she opened her mouth to him, welcoming his invasion. The taste of him filled her and she felt his breath on her face. His body rocked into hers over and over again and she lifted her legs higher around his waist, holding him to her, offering herself up to his pleasure.

To *their* pleasure.

And when the first, shattering jolts hit her system, she

tore her mouth free of his, whispered his name and clung to him desperately. Moments later, while she shivered and trembled in his arms, he allowed himself to follow her and she held him tightly as his body exploded into hers.

Six

"That's it," he whispered. "Unconscious for real now."

"I feel great," she admitted with a happy sigh.

He looked down into her eyes and shook his head. "You're amazing."

"Why am I amazing?" she asked, reaching up to smooth his thick black hair off his forehead.

Studying her for a moment or two, he finally said, "Most women right now would be either regretting what just happened—"

"Not me," she said.

"—or they'd be silently planning how to make this a little more permanent."

Katie frowned and shook her head. "Also not me."

"I'm getting that," he said and rolled to one side of her, pulling her with him though, so that she rested her head on his shoulder.

Snuggling close, Katie listened to the steady beat of

his heart and the quiet, every-night noises of her old house. Wind rattled her windows and the familiar creaks and groans of the house settling sounded like whispers from friends.

She felt wonderful. Better than she had in too long to remember. But, she had heard what Rafe had to say and she knew he was probably right. A lot of women right now would be plotting how to keep him in their beds. In their lives. And, she had to admit, at least silently, that it would have been easy for her to fall into that category.

But she wasn't going to fool herself or tell herself comforting lies. She knew this one night wasn't the beginning of a "relationship." If not for remodeling her kitchen, she never would have met Rafe Cole. This wasn't your ordinary dating situation, she thought firmly. He hadn't made her any promises and she hadn't asked for any.

She rose up and braced her folded arms on his chest. Her hair was in her eyes, so she shook it back and looked at him squarely. Might as well have this conversation now, she told herself and gave him a sad smile.

"Uh-oh," he murmured. "That's not a this-was-great-let's-do-it-again smile, is it?"

"No," she told him and moved one hand to smooth his hair back from his forehead. If her fingers lingered a little longer than necessary, who was to know? "This was lovely, Rafe. Really. But—"

He frowned at her, did a quick roll and had her under him in the blink of an eye. Now he was looming over her and his blue gaze was fixed and sharp. "But *what?*"

She sighed. "I just don't think we should do this again, that's all."

"You're *dumping* me?"

"Well, we're not really a couple, so it's not really dumping you, but, yes. I guess so."

"I don't believe this." He sounded astonished and Katie admitted silently that he probably wasn't used to women turning him away. Any man who looked like he did had to have women clinging to him like cat hair. She chuckled a little at her pitiful analogy and his frown deepened.

"This is funny, too?"

"No, sorry." She stroked her hand up and down his arm, tracing the line of his well-defined muscles and barely restraining another sigh of appreciation. "No, this isn't funny. I just had a weird thought and—"

He snorted. "Perfect. So not only are you dumping me, but you can't even focus on the task?"

"Why are you getting angry?"

"Why the hell wouldn't I be?"

Katie felt a small spurt of irritation shoot through her. "Just a second ago, you were proud of me for not making more of this than there was."

"Yeah, but—"

"And now you're mad for the same reason?"

He blew out a breath and stared at her for a long second. "This isn't the usual response I get from women, so pardon the hell out of me if I'm a little surprised."

"Surprised, sure. But mad? Why?" Her minor irritation faded and she gave him a patient smile. "You feel the same way, you know you do. I just said it first. I would think you'd be glad for my reaction."

"Yeah, well, I'm not," he muttered, pulling away. He leaned back against the headboard and threw one arm behind his head. Giving her a look that probably should have worried her, he said, "So exactly what was tonight about, Katie?"

"Us," she said and scooted to sit beside him. Absently, she tugged the sheet up to cover her breasts. "We both wanted this, Rafe. And I thought, why shouldn't we have it?"

"And that's it?"

"Yes." Well, not completely of course, she thought. She did care for him and if she spent too much more time with him, she could come to care a lot more. Which would be a huge mistake. Yes, Rafe was a great guy, but she didn't trust herself anymore to know the good guys from the creeps.

Cordell King had seemed like a sweetie at first, too. Then he'd had a diamond bracelet overnighted to her along with a note saying they "were just too different to make a longer relationship work." Translation, she'd always known was really, *I'm rich, you're poor, goodbye.*

So, she'd been wrong about Cordell. And confidence in her character-reading skills was low. Nope. Better she bury herself in work for a year or two and then she'd get back out there. Oh, she was glad she'd had this night with Rafe. But she wasn't going to build a future out of it. Still, she knew now that she could get back into the world and one day she'd look for a man like Rafe, she told herself. Someone strong and kind and honest.

"I don't believe you," he said grimly. "Something else is going on here and I want to know what it is."

"Excuse me?"

"You heard me, Katie. You *like* me. I know you do. So why're you cutting me loose before the sheets are even cold?"

"That doesn't matter."

He grabbed her, pulled her across his lap and held her tightly to him. "Yeah. It does. To me."

Being this close to him really wasn't a good idea when she was trying to be logical and rational, Katie thought. She fought down the impulse to slide her palms across his broad, muscular chest and said, "You're taking this all wrong, Rafe."

"What did you expect? That I'd just get dressed, say thanks for the roll in the hay and then leave?"

"Well…*yes*." Of course that's what she had expected. What man wouldn't enjoy free, no-strings-attached sex?

"Sorry to disappoint," he muttered, then tipped her chin up so that their gazes locked. "I want to know the real reason behind this."

"Rafe…"

"It's him, isn't it? The mysterious member of the King family."

Katie scowled at him, pulled free and scooted off his lap all at once. "If it is, that's my business."

"You just made it my business too, Katie. I'm getting the heave-ho because of this guy. The least you can do is tell me why."

"Because I trusted him, okay?" She blurted it out before she could stop herself and once the words started coming, there was no stopping them. "I thought I was in love with him. I thought he loved *me*. He was sweet and thoughtful and funny."

"And rich," Rafe muttered darkly. "Don't forget rich."

"Okay, yes, he was," she said. "But that's not why I fell in love with him. In fact, it's why it didn't work out in the end."

"What?"

Shaking her head, she pushed out of bed, walked to the connected bathroom and stepped inside. There she grabbed her bathrobe and pulled it on. When it was tied securely around her waist, she felt a little less vulnerable. Though the look in his eyes told her he wouldn't be leaving until he knew all of it. So she would be vulnerable anyway, she told herself. At least emotionally.

"Fine," she said at last. "You want the sad truth? He dropped me because we were too 'different.' Because I wasn't good enough. According to him our worlds were too far apart. Bottom line? Rich guy didn't want poor girl. Big surprise. There, happy now? Feel better getting *all* of my little humiliations up front?"

He simply stared at her. "Not good enough? Who the hell is he to say that about anybody?"

Unexpectedly, Katie smiled, despite the rawness of her feelings at the moment. His outrage on her behalf took a little of the sting out of her memories.

"He's a King," she said with a shrug she didn't quite feel. "Masters of the known universe. Just ask anyone. Heck, ask the guys you work with. They've probably got stories and complaints about the great King family."

He scowled at her. "Actually, the guys *like* working for King Construction. Haven't heard a word against them."

"Probably out of fear of losing their jobs," she muttered. On the other hand, maybe working for the King family was entirely different from trying to date one of them.

Frowning, he asked, "Who is he? Which King, I mean? Tell me who he is and I'll go punch him in the nose for you."

A surprised laugh shot from her throat and Katie was grateful for it. "Still my hero?"

"If you need one."

Tempting, she thought. He wasn't running for the hills. Maybe he was actually interested in her for more than a fleeting encounter. All she really had to do to find out was trust herself. Trust Rafe. She'd like to, Katie realized. But apparently she just wasn't ready.

Shaking her head, she said, "No, but thanks. I think I have to be my own hero first."

"So *you* want to punch him in the nose?"

She laughed louder. "Oh, I did, about six months ago. But I'm over it. I'm over *him*."

"No," he said, "you're not."

"Excuse me?"

He got out of bed and pulled on his jeans. "If you were over him, we wouldn't be having this conversation. We'd still be in bed, doing what we're obviously so good at."

Her amusement died in a flash. "This isn't about him. This is about me. It's about us."

He snorted and tugged on his boots. Then he grabbed his shirt off the floor, shrugged into it and stalked across the floor toward her. He stopped dead within arm's reach and then grabbed her, tugging her tightly to him. "You just told me there is no *us,* Katie, so get your stories straight."

"Let me go."

He did, but frustration simmered in the air around him. Shoving one hand through his hair, he grumbled, "What do you care what a King had to say anyway? Didn't that prove to you the man was an ass?"

"Don't you get it? I thought he was Prince Charming. Turned out he was a frog. But I never saw it." She threw both hands high and let them fall to her sides again. "How can I even trust my own judgment if I was that far off to begin with?"

"You're letting him win, Katie," he told her, bending over her, until their noses were practically brushing against each other. "By doubting yourself, you're giving that guy power he doesn't deserve."

"Maybe," she admitted. "But I'm not ready to make another mistake yet."

"What makes you so sure I'm a mistake?"

"I'm not sure," she told him quietly. "That's the problem."

He eased back a little, laid his hands on her shoulders and slowly drew them up until he held her face between his palms. His gaze was locked on her and Katie could have sworn his eyes were blue enough to drown in.

"You'll miss me."

"I know."

"I'm not going away," he said. "You'll see me every day."

"I know that, too."

Bending down, he kissed her, gently at first and then as the moments ticked past, the kiss deepened until Katie felt as though the ends of her hair were on fire. Finally though, Rafe pulled back to look at her again.

"Tonight isn't the end, Katie. It's just the beginning."

Before she could argue with him, he turned and walked out of the room.

When he got home, he placed a call.

"Sean?" he said when his brother answered. "Did you get hold of Garrett?"

"No can do," Sean said. "He's in Ireland and he's not answering his phone."

"*Ireland?*" Rafe repeated. "What's he doing over there?"

"Exactly the question I asked his twin. Griffin says Jefferson had some problems with a thief in his European company and Garrett went to investigate it."

Great timing, Rafe thought in disgust. Jefferson King, one of their many cousins, lived with his Irish wife on a sheep farm in County Mayo. Hard to believe that Jefferson, Mr. Hollywood Mogul, was happy out in the boonies, but he was. And if Jeff had a problem, then there was no telling when Garrett might come back home. To the Kings, *Family comes first* was the unofficial motto. So Garrett wouldn't leave Ireland until he'd turned the country upside down to find the answers Jeff wanted.

"Well, that's great," Rafe grumbled, stalking through the sleek, modern hotel suite he called home. The place was empty, of course, but tonight, it felt…desolate. Rafe had always preferred life in a hotel. It was easy. Uncomplicated. But tonight, it also felt…sterile.

His mind kept returning to Katie's older house with its overstuffed furniture and creaky floors. There was a sense of continuity in that bungalow, as if the walls and floors themselves held the echoes of generations of laughter and tears.

His gaze swept the interior of his own home and for the first time in years, he found it lacking. Irritated with himself, he opened the sliding glass door to his terrace and stepped outside. The cold wind slapped at him and the roar of the ocean growled unceasingly. Streetlamps below threw yellowed circles of light onto the sidewalks and out on the beach. He spotted the dancing flames of campfires blazing in the fire rings.

"So," he asked, "we still don't have any idea which one of the family is the one who messed with Katie."

"Nope," Sean said. "Not a clue. And except for the married ones, it could be anyone."

"This I know already." Rafe shoved one hand through his hair and squinted into the cold sea breeze. His body was still humming from his time with Katie, and his mind was racing, trying to figure out how it had all gone to hell so damn fast.

He didn't have an answer.

"I can ask around," Sean offered.

"Never mind," Rafe told him. "I'll do the asking myself."

"Fine," Sean said, then asked, "Hey, did you get me some cookies?"

Rafe hung up, stuffed his phone into his pocket, then leaned both hands on the wrought-iron railing in front of him. He leaned into the wind, watched the black waves moving and shifting in the moonlight and promised himself that he would find out who had hurt Katie.

A few days later, Rafe was still simmering. He was getting nowhere fast with talking to his cousins. Amazing how many Kings took off during the summer. What the hell had happened to the family's work ethic? But it wasn't just the frustration of trying to find out which of his cousins he should pummel that was making him insane.

It was Katie herself. Until her, the only woman who'd ever turned her back on him was Leslie. And at least she had *married* him first.

"Everything okay here?"

Rafe buried his irritation, turned the electric sander off and faced Joe, the man pretending to be his boss. "Fine," Rafe said shortly and moved the finished cabinet door to one side before grabbing up the next one in line.

Sanding was hot, tedious work, so his mind had plenty of room to wander. Unfortunately, it continued to wander toward Katie.

The woman was making him insane and that had never happened before. Always in his life, Rafe was in charge. He did what he wanted when he wanted and didn't much care about looking out for whoever might be in his way. Since Leslie, women were expendable in his world. Temporary. They came in, spent a few good hours with him; then they were gone, not even leaving behind a residual echo of their presence.

"Until now," he muttered, removing the safety goggles and paper mask he wore to avoid inhaling all the sawdust flying around so thickly in the air.

Joe glanced over his shoulder to make sure no one was close enough to overhear them. "Look, I don't know what's going on, but I just came from talking to Katie and she's wound so tight she's giving off sparks."

"Really?" Rafe hid a smile. Good to know he wasn't the only one. She had managed to avoid talking to him the last few days, so he hadn't known exactly how she was feeling until just this moment. It had about killed him to be here, so near to her every damn day, and not speak to her. Touch her. But he'd kept his distance because damned if he'd be the one to bend. He wanted her. She knew it. Let her come to him. She was, after all, the one who pushed him away to begin with. "She say anything?"

"She didn't have to," Joe told him. "The whole time I was talking to her about her new floor tiles, she kept looking out here at *you*."

Also good to know, Rafe thought and hid a satisfied smile.

"What's going on?"

Rafe slanted a hard look at Joe. He'd known the man for years. Trusted him. Considered him a friend, even. But that didn't mean that he was interested in Joe's opinion on this particular subject. "That's none of your business, is it?"

The older man scrubbed one hand across the top of his balding head. "No, I guess it's not. But I work for King Construction. I've got a good reputation with the company and with our clients."

"You do," Rafe said, keeping his voice down. "What's your point?"

"I've known you a long time, Rafe, and I'm going to say that my business or not, I think you need to tell that girl who you really are."

He snorted. "Not likely."

Hell, she'd kicked him loose thinking he was Rafe *Cole*. If she knew he was actually a King, who knew what she'd do?

Joe huffed out an impatient breath. "She's a nice woman and I don't like the idea of lying to her. I'm sorry I suggested this bet in the first place."

Rafe saw how uncomfortable Joe was and he was sorry for that. But he wasn't telling Katie the truth. Not yet. Not until he'd made her see how much she wanted him. How much she liked him. Then he'd tell her that she was wrong about the King family and him specifically. And she'd have to admit that she had made a mistake.

"Look, Joe," he said, "I'm sorry you're in the middle of this, but we're already too deep in the game to stop. There's no changing the rules at this late date."

"A game? Is that what this is?" Joe's eyes narrowed and Rafe had the distinct impression that his contractor was about to defend Katie's honor.

Well, there was no need.

"I don't mean Katie is a game to me, so relax."

The man's pitbull expression eased a bit and Rafe kept talking.

"Don't get all twisted up over this, Joe." Rafe slapped one hand on the man's shoulder. "We made the bet and I'm honoring it. As for telling Katie the truth, I'll do that when the time's right."

"And when's that?"

"Not now, for damn sure." Rafe narrowed his own eyes in warning. "And don't you tell her, either."

Grumbling under his breath, Joe worked his jaw furiously as if there were a hundred hot words in his mouth that he was fighting to keep inside. Finally though, he grudgingly agreed. "Fine. I won't say anything. But I think you're making a mistake here, Rafe. One that you're gonna regret real soon."

"Maybe," he said and shifted his gaze back to the enclosed patio where Katie was working in her temporary kitchen. Even from a distance, she was beautiful, he thought. But it wasn't just her beauty calling to him. It was the shine of something tender in her eyes. The knowledge that she had wanted him, desired him, without knowing who he was. She didn't want anything from him and that was so rare in Rafe's world that he couldn't let her go.

But his heart wasn't involved here and it wouldn't be, either. He had tried love. Tried marriage and failed miserably at both. Kings didn't fail. It was the one rule his father had drummed into all of them from the time they were kids.

Well, his divorce from Leslie was going to be the *only* time Rafe King failed at anything. He wouldn't risk another mistake. Wouldn't give Fate another shot at kicking his ass.

"Whether or not I regret anything," Rafe told Joe quietly, "is not your business. You just do your job and leave Katie Charles to me."

"Fine. You're the boss," Joe said after a long minute of silence. "But King or not, you're making a mistake."

Joe walked off to the kitchen where Steve and Arturo were jokingly arguing about the plastering job. Inside her temporary kitchen, Katie was busy working on another batch of her cookies and the delicious aromas wafting from the oven wrapped themselves around him. Rafe stood alone in the sunlight while his mind raced with possibilities.

Maybe Joe had a point. But being with Katie, keeping his identity a secret, didn't feel like a mistake to Rafe. So he was going to stick with his original plan. Once a decision had been made, Rafe never liked to deviate. That was second-guessing himself and if he started doing that, where would it end? No.

Better he take the fall for his own decisions than have to pay for unsolicited advice gone wrong.

Seven

Emily O'Hara was waiting for Rafe outside Katie's house late that afternoon. Again, he was the last man to leave and he had lingered even later than usual, half hoping Katie would get back from the store before he left. He wanted to talk to her. Hell, he admitted silently, that wasn't all he wanted.

Since Katie wasn't home, he was surprised to find her grandmother leaning against his truck when he walked out front to leave. She wore a hot-pink oversize shirt over a white tank top and white pants. Huge red-framed sunglasses shielded her eyes, but when she heard him approach, she pushed them up to the top of her head.

Idly filing her nails, she looked up at him as he got closer and gave him a tight smile that should have warned him something was up. But, he reminded himself, if there was one thing Rafe knew, it was women. Granted, he didn't have much experience with older females, but how hard could it be to pour on some charm and win her over?

Besides, Katie's grandmother had seemed nice enough when he first met her. What could possibly go wrong?

"Mrs. O'Hara," he said, giving her a guileless smile designed to put her at her ease, "Katie's not home."

"Oh, I know that Rafe. It's Tuesday. My girl always goes grocery shopping on Tuesdays. I've tried to shake up her world a little, but she does love a schedule." She straightened up, tucked her emery board into the oversize purse hanging from her shoulder and cocked her head to look at him. "Wait, maybe I shouldn't call you Rafe at all. Maybe you'd prefer it if I call you Mr. King?"

Rafe flinched and a sinking sensation opened up in the pit of his stomach. This he hadn't expected at all. She knew who he was. Had she told Katie? No, he thought. If she had, he'd have heard about it by now. Hell, Katie would have come at him with both barrels blazing. So the question was, why hadn't her grandmother given him up?

"Rafe'll do," he told her and stuffed his hands into his pockets. "How long have you known who I am?"

She chuckled. "Since the moment my Katie introduced you as Rafe Cole." Shaking her head, she ran one finger along the hood of the truck, looked at the dirt she'd picked up, then clucked her tongue and rubbed her fingers together to get rid of it.

"See, Katie's a good girl, but she's single-minded. At the moment, she's so focused on her business that she doesn't see anything else. Sadly, her pop culture knowledge is lacking, too. If she'd read the celebrity magazines more often, as I do..." She paused to give him another one of those cool, measuring stares. "Then she would have recognized you, too. Though I will say, you look different in jeans than you do in a tux at some fancy party."

Inwardly, he groaned. Stupid. He hadn't even thought of that. He'd been in one of those weekly tabloidesque magazines only last month. Photographers at the Save the Shore benefit had gotten shots of him squiring an actress to the affair. Not that he and Selena were a couple or anything. After one date, he'd known that a man could only talk hairdos and tanning tips for so long.

Sliding his hands from his pockets, he folded his arms over his chest in a classic defense posture. Emily might appear to be a sweet older lady, but the glint in her eye told him that he'd better walk soft and careful. But Rafe was used to sometimes-hostile negotiations with suppliers, so he was as prepared for this confrontation as he could be. Bracing his feet wide apart, he waited for whatever was coming next.

"So, not going to deny it at least," she said.

"What would be the point?"

"There is that."

Curious now, Rafe asked, "Why haven't you told Katie?"

"Interesting question," Emily acknowledged with a small smile. "I've asked that of myself a time or two in the last couple of weeks. But the truth is, I wanted to wait and see what you were up to first."

"And?"

"Still waiting." She wagged her finger at him as if he were a ten-year-old boy. She took a step or two away from the truck, walking from sunlight into shade. Her sandals clicked on the concrete driveway. When she turned to look at him again she asked, "So instead of keeping me in suspense, why don't you do us both a favor and tell me what's going on? Why are you pretending to be someone you're not?"

For one moment, Rafe caught himself wondering what it might have been like to have a woman like this one in his life. He had the distinct impression she would be a lioness when protecting Katie. He couldn't blame her for that, Rafe thought, even as he shrugged. He didn't want to be disrespectful, but damned if he'd explain himself to Katie's grandmother, either.

"Long story short," he offered, "I lost a bet so I'm working this job. Easier to work it as a nobody than one of the bosses."

"That explains why you haven't told your crew," she said thoughtfully. "It doesn't explain lying to Katie."

"No, it doesn't."

She blew out an impatient breath and prompted, "And? So?"

One look in the woman's eyes, so much like her granddaughter's, told Rafe that she wasn't going to give up until she had what she'd come here for. He didn't like being put on the spot. Didn't appreciate having to justify his actions. But, if there was one thing Rafe respected, it was loyalty and he could see that feeling ran deep in this woman.

So, though he wouldn't explain himself thoroughly, he was willing to give her the bare bones. "I like her. She hates the Kings. So I'm not about to tell her I'm one of them."

"Ever?" Emily asked, clearly dumbfounded.

"I'll have to tell her eventually," he acknowledged, "but in my own time and my own way."

"And when is that, exactly?"

Looking into her eyes, Rafe wondered why he had considered this woman to be just a nice older lady. Katie's nana had steel in her spine. He wasn't used to this. Rafe couldn't even remember the last time anyone had questioned him about anything. He was a King. He didn't do explanations or apologies. And he didn't, for damn sure, wither under a disapproving stare from a suburban grandmother.

Yet, that was just what he was doing.

"When I've convinced her that not *all* Kings are bastards," he admitted. "When she likes me enough, I'll tell her everything, prove to her she was wrong about us and then I'll get out of her life."

Emily blinked at him, then shook her head as if she hadn't heard him right. "That's your plan?"

"Something wrong with it?"

"Let me count the ways," she muttered, with yet another shake of her head.

He didn't care what she thought of his plan, he was sticking with it. But as he stood there, another idea occurred to him and he wondered why he hadn't thought of it before. Could have saved himself, and his brother Sean, a lot of trouble. Taking a step or two closer to Emily, he said, "You know which of the Kings treated her badly, right?"

She frowned so harshly, Rafe was instantly glad it wasn't *him* this formidable woman was mad at. "I do."

"Tell me," he said shortly. "Tell me who he is. I'm trying to find out, but it's taking me too long."

"Why do you care?"

"Because—" Rafe's mouth snapped shut. He took a breath and said, "I want to know who hurt her so I can hurt him back."

"One of your own family?"

He heard the surprise in her voice and a part of him shared it. The Kings always stuck together. It was practically a vow they all took at birth. It was the King cousins against the world and God help anyone who tried to undermine them. The occasional brawls and fistfights notwithstanding, none of the Kings had ever turned on another.

"Yeah," he said, realizing that cousin or not, Rafe really wanted to hit the guy responsible for Katie's defensiveness. No matter who the King cousin—or brother—was, Rafe was going to make him sorry for hurting Katie.

"Again," Emily said quietly, "I have to ask, why do you care?"

He scrubbed one hand across the back of his neck and gritted his teeth in frustration. Rafe wasn't sure himself why he cared so damn much, he only knew he did. The only possible explanation was that he didn't like the idea of a woman like Katie hating the Kings. She was…nice. Frowning at that moronic thought, he grumbled aloud, "You ask a hell of a lot of questions."

"I do indeed. So how about an answer?" she countered. "An honest one."

Rafe met her gaze and wondered if Katie would be as amazing a woman as her grandmother when she was Emily's age. He had to figure that she would. As the Kings were always saying, *it's in the blood.* And a part of him wanted to be around to see Katie as a scary-smart old woman. He dismissed that thought quickly enough though, as he knew all too well that commitment and permanence weren't in him.

Choosing his words carefully, Rafe said, "Honestly, I don't know why I care so much. I only know I do. I don't like knowing it was one of my family who caused her pain. And I don't like knowing she hates the Kings because of that one jerk—whoever he is. So give me a name and I'll take care of it and get out of Katie's life all that much sooner."

She gave him a slow, wide smile and shook her head firmly enough to have her short, silver hair lifting in the breeze. "You know what? I don't think I will."

"Why not?"

"Because, I'd rather watch you play out your plan," she admitted. "My Katie can take care of herself, you know. That guy hurt her, but he didn't break her. You know why? Because she only *thought* she was in love. You might want to remember that, Rafe."

Confusion rose up inside him, but he swallowed it back. "Fine, I'll remember."

"Good. Now, I've got a hot date, so I've got to get a move on," she announced and turned around to leave, only to whirl back to face him again. Pointing at him, she said, "Just one more thing."

"What's that?"

Her eyes narrowed and her voice dropped a couple of notches. There wasn't even the glimmer of a smile on her face. "If you break her heart, I'll hunt you down like a sick dog and make you sorry you ever set foot in Katie's house. Sound fair?"

Rafe nodded, admiration for the older woman filling him again. Family loyalty he understood completely. And he found himself again envying Katie for having someone in her life who loved her so much.

He'd never known that himself. Oh, he had his brothers and cousins, sure. His mother, though, hadn't loved him; she'd only used him as a bargaining chip, to squeeze Ben King for money. The elderly aunt who'd raised him hadn't—she'd only done her duty, as she often told him. Rafe was pretty sure his father had loved him, as much as Ben King was able. Rafe wasn't feeling sorry for himself. Things were as they were. And he'd done fine on his own.

But he had to wonder how it might have been to be raised with the kind of love he saw now, glittering in Emily O'Hara's eyes.

"I hear you."

"Good." She set her sunglasses in place, flashed him a quick smile and said, "As long as we understand each other, we'll be fine."

Then she waved one hand and hurried to a bright yellow VW bug parked at curbside. She hopped in, fired it up and was gone an instant later.

Scowling to himself, Rafe looked back at Katie's house, quiet in the afternoon light. The crew was gone, *she* was gone and the old bungalow looked as empty as he felt.

Talking to Emily had shaken him. Hearing his own plan put into words had made him realize that maybe it was as dumb as Katie's grandmother clearly thought it was. The lie he'd spun and invested so much in suddenly felt like a weight around his neck. He had to wonder if he wasn't doing the wrong thing in keeping it going.

He'd started this as a way to win her affection and respect without her knowing who he really was. But if he pulled it off, what did he really gain? She wasn't caring for the real him if she didn't *know* the real man. The sad truth was, Katie now cared about a lie. A fabrication. He'd done this to himself and couldn't see a way out without risking everything he didn't want to lose.

Rafe didn't like admitting it even to himself, but he suddenly felt more alone than he ever had in his life. And he wasn't sure what the hell to do about it.

* * *

Katie had deliveries to make bright and early the next morning. Any other day, she would have enjoyed being the one to drop off a surprise gift of cookies. She always got a charge out of seeing people's reactions to the elegantly frosted and wrapped creations. Since she'd become busier, she didn't normally have time to make deliveries herself anymore.

Usually, she had a teenager from down the street deliver her cookie orders. It helped her out and Donna made more money than she would babysitting. A win-win situation all the way around.

But Donna was on vacation with her family, so despite being so tired she could barely stand up, Katie had no choice but to load up her car with the week's orders. Specially made boxes lined her trunk and she carefully stored away the cookie bouquets and cookie towers and cookie cakes that she'd spent the last two days making. Each of them were frosted, some personalized and a swell of pride filled her as she looked at them.

She'd built this business out of nothing and she had big plans for it, too.

"And that," she told herself firmly, "is just one more reason to stay away from Rafe."

He was too male. Too overwhelming to every sense she possessed. She couldn't afford to be distracted from her goals, not even by a man who had the ability to sweep her off her feet with a single glance. And, if she hadn't already surrendered to her own hormones, he wouldn't be taking up so much of her thoughts. So she deliberately stopped thinking about Rafe—though it wasn't easy.

For now, she would devote herself to her burgeoning business. She wanted to make an even bigger name for herself. Move Katie's Kookies into a shop down on Pacific Coast Highway. Have several ovens, hire more help, expand her client list and maybe even go into online orders. She had big plans. And nothing was going to stop her from making them come true.

The scents of vanilla, cinnamon and chocolate filled her car and made Katie smile in spite of the fact that she was running on about three hours sleep. But she couldn't blame her sleeplessness entirely on the fact that she'd been baking half the night. Because when she finally did get to bed, she'd slept fitfully, tortured by dreams of Rafe. Of the night they'd had together.

And there he was again, front and center in her brain. Seeing him every day wasn't helping her avoid thoughts of him. Especially since her own body seemed determined to remind her, every chance it got, of just what she'd experienced in his arms.

"Need some help?"

Katie jolted and slapped one hand to her chest as she turned around to look at the very man she had just been thinking about. "You scared me."

"Sorry." He grinned. "I called out to you, but you didn't hear me, I guess."

No, she hadn't. She'd been too busy remembering his hands on her skin. The taste of his mouth. The slow slide of his body invading hers. Oh, boy. She blew out a breath, forced a smile and said, "I'm just preoccupied."

"I can see that," he said, glancing into the back of the SUV. "You've been busy."

"I really have," she admitted, and turned to pick up the last box, holding a dozen pink frosted cookies shaped like baby rattles.

"Let me get that," he said and reached for it before she could stop him.

Truthfully, even though it was a little uncomfortable being around him at the moment, Katie was glad he was there. She'd spent the last few days avoiding being alone with him, allowing herself only a glimpse of him now and then. Having him close enough now that she could feel his body heat was a sort of tempting torture. He looked great in his worn blue jeans and blue T-shirt with King Construction stenciled across the back. And he smelled even better, with the scent of soap from his morning shower still clinging to his skin. She wanted to go to him. To kiss him.

She caught that thought and strangled it. She was so tired, she was nearly staggering. Way too tired to trust her instincts around a man she already knew she wanted. Katie gave herself a quick, silent talking-to. Besides, she still had a full morning of deliveries.

"Thanks."

He set the box in the trunk, then shot her a look. "Are you okay?"

"Yes. Just tired."

He frowned and shifted his gaze to the mass of cookies. "You're delivering all of these yourself?"

She yawned and nodded. "Sorry. Yes. My usual delivery girl is camping in Yosemite with her family so…"

"You can hardly keep your eyes open," he accused.

As if to prove him wrong, Katie opened her eyes as wide as possible and pretended not to notice that they felt like marbles rolling in sand. "I'm fine. Really. I'll have these done in an hour or two and then I'll come home and take a nap."

From inside the kitchen, a saw buzzed into life.

"Well, maybe I'll take a nap," she said with a wry smile.

He didn't return the smile. Instead, he glowered at her, crossed his arms over his chest and said flatly, "You're not driving anywhere."

She blinked at him. "Excuse me?"

Shaking his head, Rafe said, "Katie, you're practically asleep on your feet. You try to drive and you'll end up killing someone. Or yourself."

"You're overreacting," she said and closed the trunk lid. "I can take care of myself."

"Sure you can," he agreed amiably. "When you're awake."

"I'm not your responsibility, Rafe," she argued, fighting the urge to yawn again. See? Just another reason why they wouldn't have worked out as a couple. He was too bossy and she was too stubborn.

God, she was tired. Another yawn sneaked up on her before she could stifle it and she saw his eyes narrow dangerously. Perfect. She had just given him more ammunition for his argument. To head him off before he could say anything, she spoke up quickly. "Look, I appreciate the concern, really. But I'm fine and we both have work to do. Why don't we just get on with what we were doing and let this go?"

"I don't think so." Rafe grabbed the keys from the trunk lock and held them out of reach. "I'm not kidding about this. No way am I letting you drive."

"Letting me?" she repeated incredulously as she stared up into his implacable expression. "You don't have a vote in it, Rafe. This is my car. My business, and I say I'm fine to drive."

"You're wrong." He looked over his shoulder at the house. "Wait here."

He might as well have patted her on the head and ordered her to *stay*. As if she were a golden retriever or something. And of course she would wait there. What choice did she have? Katie wondered in irritation. He'd taken her keys.

Anger churned inside her and mixed with the fatigue clawing at her. Probably not a good combination. Okay. Fine. Yes, she really *was* exhausted. But she wasn't a danger to people on the road for heaven's sake. She wasn't a complete idiot. She wouldn't drive if she didn't think she could.

The longer he was gone, the more irritated she became. She paced—in the garage, muttering to herself, rubbing her gritty eyes. One night with the man and he became territorial. Probably a good idea she'd decided to keep her distance. Imagine what he'd be like if they were actually in a relationship.

Then that thought settled in. Instead of making her angrier, it gave Katie a soft, warm glow. Who was she kidding? She'd love for someone to be that worried about her. Oh, not that she was some mindless woman to take orders from anyone. But the idea that a man would care enough to worry about her safety sort of dulled the edges of her anger. Of course, she thought wryly, that could be the exhaustion talking.

So when he finally came back, her tone hadn't softened by much as she said, "Give me my keys."

"Not a chance." He took her arm in a firm, no-nonsense grip, steered her to the passenger side of her car, opened the door and said simply, "Get in."

Stubbornly, Katie pulled free of his hold and took a determined step back. Standing her ground, she lifted her chin in defiance and met him stare for stare. "This isn't funny, Rafe."

His blue eyes narrowed on her. "Damn right it isn't. You're too self-sufficient for your own good."

"What's that supposed to mean?"

"It means that you're so focused on doing everything on your own you don't know enough to ask for help when you need it." He scowled at her as if expecting her to quail before his impeccable logic.

She didn't.

"I don't need help, and if I did, I wouldn't come to you."

He took a quick, sharp breath. "Why the hell not?"

"Because, we're not together and you're supposed to be working on my kitchen."

"We could be together if you weren't so damn hard-headed," he pointed out. "And as for working on your kitchen, I can do that when we get back."

"*We* aren't going anywhere," she argued and felt another yawn sneaking up on her. She twisted her mouth together and clamped her lips shut rather than giving into it.

"Nice try, but I saw that yawn anyway," he pointed out.

"Doesn't mean a thing," she told him.

"Damn it, Katie," Rafe said, his voice quiet, his gaze locked on hers, "Even if you don't want *my* help, you could at least admit that you're too damn tired to think straight, let alone drive."

He was leaning on the open passenger door, just an arm's reach away from her. His blue eyes were locked on her and his dark blue, steely stare told Katie he wouldn't be giving up easily.

So she tried another tactic.

"Rafe," she assured him in a calm, rational tone that completely belied the irritation still spiking inside her, "I'm completely fine. Really."

Then she yawned again.

"Uh-huh," he said, "I'm convinced. Get in. I'm driving."

"*You?*" She looked from him to the kitchen, where the crew was busy doing heaven knew what to her house and asked, "You can't just walk away from your job."

"I told the guys to let Joe know I was helping you out and that I'd be back in a couple of hours."

"You can't do that." Wouldn't he be fired? She couldn't let him lose his job over this.

"Yeah," he said, "I can. Consider us a full-service construction company. Whatever the boss—that's *you*—needs, we provide."

Katie hadn't gone to him, he'd come to her. And there was the slightest chance that he was right and she was too tired to drive all over town. But at the same time, that didn't make it okay for him to ride in and take over.

She thought about it, her mind racing, arguing with itself. Yes, he was being a jerk, but he was also being nice, in a roundabout, tyrannical sort of way. He was glaring at her, but he was worried about her. He was supposed to be working on her kitchen, but instead he was willing to drive her around town making cookie deliveries.

And she would be alone with him in the car for an hour or more. That appealed to her on so many levels it was scary. But could she really be with him and *not* with him at the same time?

Oh, she was so tired, even *she* didn't understand her any more.

"I can practically hear you arguing with yourself," he said after a long moment.

"It's easier than arguing with you," she told him.

"True. And before we start in again, you should know that I don't quit. I don't give in. Never surrender."

She tipped her head to one side and looked up at him. "I don't quit, either."

He shrugged. "Hence the trouble between us."

"Hence?" she repeated, smiling in spite of the situation.

Rafe blew out a breath. "Are you getting in, or do I pick you up and *put* you in?" he asked.

Katie sent him a hard glare. "All right, fine," she confessed. "I *might* be a little too tired to drive."

He smiled and Katie's toes curled in her comfortable flats. Oh, boy. For all of her fine notions about keeping her distance, about not letting herself fall for a guy, she was certainly doing a lot of stumbling around him.

"Now that we're on the same page, so to speak," Rafe said, "will you please get in the car?"

Her mouth twitched into a smile at the way he'd changed his command to a request. She nodded, climbing up into the passenger seat. "Thank you."

"You're welcome." He closed her door, walked around to the driver's side and slid her key into the ignition. Then he looked at her and said, "So, how does it feel to be going on our second date?"

Her eyebrows winged up when she turned her gaze on him. "Delivering cookies is a date?"

"If we say it is, yeah." He fired up the engine and looked at her again. "So? Is it?"

Katie stared at him and remembered that night. Then she remembered the last few days, being so close to him and so far away all at the same time. She remembered every haunting dream she'd had and how she would wake up, aching for his touch.

Was she being an idiot by shutting out the first nice,

normal guy she'd met in way too long? Okay, yes, he was a little bossy, but she could handle that. Would it really be so bad to take a chance? To spend some time with Rafe? To see if what she already felt for him might grow? After all, she could concentrate on her business *and* have a life, couldn't she? Isn't that what Nana and Nicole both had been trying to tell her?

Memories of Cordell rose up in her mind, but Katie fought them down with determination.

Watching Rafe, she finally said, "It's not a date unless you spring for a cup of coffee at least."

He grinned at her, clearly victorious. "One latte, coming up."

Eight

An hour and a half later, Katie looked a little more alert and Rafe was enjoying himself immensely. "No wonder you like doing this," he said, sliding into the driver's seat after making the last of the deliveries. "People are excited to see you when you bring them cookies."

She grinned. "How did the pink baby-rattle cookies go over?"

He laughed and held up a five-dollar bill. "I got a tip!"

He looked so pleased with himself, Katie had to laugh, too. "Congratulations, you're a delivery person."

"She cried, too," he said, handing Katie the five. Shaking his head, he remembered the expression on the woman's face when she opened the door and saw him standing there, holding the basket of pink frosted cookies. "The woman? The new mom? She took one look at those cookies her friend ordered from you and burst into tears. She was laughing and crying and for a minute." Then he added, "it was terrifying."

Katie reached out and patted his arm. "Not what you're used to as a carpenter?"

"No," he said simply, looking into her green eyes. She was so pleased with him, having so much fun, he couldn't help but suddenly feel like a first-class rat for lying to her.

He thought back to his conversation with Katie's grandmother and realized that she had been right. Ever since talking to Emily, he'd been rethinking this whole keep-the-lie-going thing. His lies hadn't seemed like such a big deal when he had started out on this job. But now, every day with Katie made him feel that much more like a jerk. He should have told her the truth before now.

Sure, he'd told Emily that he was sticking to his plan, but she'd made him start to doubt the wisdom in that. But he couldn't think of a good way out of this mess. Because, he realized with startling clarity, the moment he told Katie about his lies, what his real name was, it would all be over between them.

Odd that he hadn't considered that possibility before. But then, he hadn't thought that he would *want* to keep seeing her once this job was finished. Now though, he knew he didn't want her disappearing from his life at the end of this job. He wanted to keep seeing her. And the chances of that happening looked slim.

He imagined blurting out the truth right there and then. Telling her that he wasn't the man she thought he was. And in his mind's eye, he saw her features tighten with betrayal, saw the shine in her green eyes dim and then flash with fury, and he told himself that it didn't matter if he was starting to get uncomfortable with his lies.

She wasn't ready to learn the truth.

He wanted her to care for him before he told her who he was. And then? a voice in his mind whispered. But he didn't have an answer to that yet. All Rafe knew was that he wanted to be with her *now*. And he didn't want the King name ruining that.

So he was stuck with his lies, his plan, whether he wanted to be or not.

"How are you feeling?" he asked, suddenly changing the subject.

"A little more awake, thanks. The latte helped."

"Not enough," he decided. Her green eyes were shadowed and her face was too pale to suit him. The fact that he was worried about her bothered him, but there didn't seem to be anything he could do about that. "You still look tired."

"Well, don't I feel pretty?" she asked wryly.

"You're beautiful." Two words, softly spoken, and they seemed to echo in the air around them. He hadn't meant to blurt that out. It had been a knee-jerk reaction.

"Rafe—"

"Don't," he said quietly, before she could start in on her speech about how nothing had changed and she still wasn't interested in being with him. He could *feel* her reaction to his closeness. Her skin was warm and though her eyes were tired, he still noticed the gleam of desire in their depths.

Leaning in closer to her, Rafe reached out, touched her cheek with his fingertips and tipped her face up for his kiss. "Just, let me…"

She sighed and moved into him, meeting him halfway, taking what he offered, and Rafe was relieved. He didn't know if he could have taken her turning from him or pulling away. He'd been thinking about doing just this for the last few days. Thinking about *her*. The first touch of her mouth to his eased everything inside him, yet rekindled a fire that had been nothing more than glowing embers since their one night together.

His body tightened, his heartbeat thundered in his chest and Rafe had to fight every instinct he possessed to keep from grabbing her and yanking her close to him. He wanted his hands on her again. Wanted her under him, over him. Wanted her body surrendering to his.

He groaned then, knowing he couldn't have everything he wanted right now. And the longer he kissed her, the less willing he would be to stop. So he pulled back while he still could and drew a long, shaky breath.

Resting his forehead against hers, he waited for control to slide back into his body, but it was a long time coming. Especially when he could feel her short, sharp breaths against his face. Well, he thought wryly, so much for her claims of not wanting to be with him again.

Several long moments passed before he gave her a smile, looked into her eyes and said, "There. Told you we weren't done with each other."

Katie shook her head, one corner of her mouth tipping into a reluctant half smile. "You really think now is the right time for I-told-you-sos?"

"What better time?"

"You're impossible."

"I like that." He skimmed his fingers through her hair until his hand was at the back of her neck, kneading her skin with a sure, gentle touch.

"You would," she told him, sighing at his touch.

"Are we going to argue again?" he asked. "Because I warn you, I'm getting to the point where I really enjoy our 'disagreements.'"

"Maybe later." She cupped his cheek in the palm of her hand.

"At least you admit there will be a 'later.'"

"Yes," she said with a slow nod, never tearing her gaze from his. "There will be."

"Tonight." Rafe caught her hand in his. "I want to see you tonight."

"Okay," she said. "Another barbecue?"

"Oh, I think this time we'll let someone else cook. I'll pick you up at seven," he said, easing back behind the wheel.

"To go where?"

"That's a surprise." He shot her a quick grin as a plan formed in his mind while he steered the car into traffic. "All you have to do is dress up. Oh, and take a nap. I want you wide awake tonight."

"That sounds intriguing."

"Count on it."

His mind was already racing with plans and he smiled to himself as it all began to come together.

That feeling lasted until he went home to change.

The minute he walked into his hotel suite, he knew someone was there. Didn't take a genius, after all. There was a designer purse on his couch and a pair of black heels under the glass-topped coffee table.

Rafe's brain raced frantically. Had he already set up a date for tonight? He didn't think so. Hell, he hadn't seen anyone since Selena the Self Involved Actress. So who...?

"Rafe? Is that you?"

The familiar, feminine voice sent a twist of old pain mixed with regret slashing through his middle, but he fought it down and managed to give his ex-wife a half smile when she came in off the balcony.

"Leslie. What are you doing here?"

The cool, elegant brunette flashed him a brief, wry smile. "Well, good to see you too, Rafe."

Irritated at being called to the carpet on his manners when she was the one who'd shown up unannounced and let herself into *his* home, Rafe just stared at her. Waiting.

It didn't take long. Leslie never had been the patient type. "I know I should have called before just showing up here."

"That would've been good," he said.

She stood with the balcony and the bank of windows at her back. Rafe was absolutely sure she knew that the sunlight streaming in through those windows was highlighting her to a beautiful advantage. Leslie always had known how to show herself off in the best way. She was lovely, self-assured and the only woman in the world who had ever told him that he wasn't good enough.

That memory colored his tone when he spoke. "How did you get in here?"

"Oh," she said, giving him a palms-up shrug, "Declan's still the concierge here. He let me up so I could wait for you in private."

Silently, Rafe told himself that he'd be having a little chat with Declan real soon. For the moment though… "I repeat. What are you doing here?"

Leslie frowned slightly, not enough to mar her brow or anything, but he got the message. She had never had any trouble letting Rafe know that he'd disappointed her in some way. Looking back now, he couldn't even remember *why* they had gotten married in the first place.

"You always were a straightforward man," she murmured.

"As I recall, that's one of the things you didn't care for."

Her mouth flattened into a straight line briefly; then, as if she'd willed it to happen, it curved again slightly. "Look at us. It's been years since we divorced and we're still treating each other like the enemy."

He shifted a little at that, since it was true and there really was no point in it. Leslie wasn't a part of his life anymore, so why go on a forced march down memory lane?

"True. So tell me. Why are you here?"

"Honestly?" She shook her head in wonder and admitted, "I can't believe I'm here, either. But I didn't have anywhere else to turn."

She took a small breath, covered her mouth with her fingertips and let tears well in her eyes. Something inside Rafe tightened as he remembered all the times Leslie had been able to turn on the tears. During an argument, to avoid an argument or just to make the point that he was a selfish bastard—out came the tears. When they were dating, he'd felt almost heroic when he could make those tears stop. Because she looked so damn fragile when she cried. Today though, he was no longer moved. Besides, she had a different husband now. Why wasn't she home turning *him* inside out?

"Oh, Rafe," she whispered brokenly, allowing the sunlight to backlight her to perfection. "I hated coming here, truly, but I had no choice."

"Just tell me what's going on."

"It's John," she said and Rafe felt an instant stab of

worry. After all, before he became Leslie's husband, John Peters had been Rafe's best friend.

"Is he all right?"

"Physically, yes," she said with a little shake of her head. "But Rafe, he's lost his job and I don't know what to do."

For one very brief second, Rafe felt a twinge of sympathy for his old friend. He and John had met in college and until Leslie had come between them, they'd been the best of friends. Truthfully, Rafe had missed John's friendship more than he had missed being with Leslie.

A sad statement on a dead marriage.

"What's that got to do with me?" He winced at the tone in his own voice and knew that he'd sounded crueler than he'd intended when her head came up and her eyes narrowed.

"You don't have to be mean."

He sighed and glanced at his watch. He wanted to take a shower, get dressed and pick up Katie. Leslie was his past and his present was looking a lot more promising. So rather than prolonging this conversation, he got to the point. "Leslie, you're my *ex*-wife married to my *ex*-friend. Just how much sympathy do you expect?"

"I knew you wouldn't understand."

"You're right," he agreed, heading for the wet bar along the wall. He suddenly wanted a beer. "I don't."

She walked over to join him and asked for a glass of wine. Once he'd poured it and handed it to her, Leslie took a sip and said, "I need money."

Rafe almost smiled, even as he felt a brand-new sheen of ice coat his heart. He should have known. When it came right down to it, what people wanted from the

Kings was money. Never failed. "Does John know you're here?"

"Of course not. He'd be humiliated."

That much Rafe believed. The man Rafe remembered would have been horrified to know that Leslie was here asking for help. He leaned one arm on the bar top. "Just out of curiosity, say I give you the cash you need, how do you explain that to John?"

"I'll find a way," she said, lifting her chin slightly to prove her point. "I can be pretty persuasive."

"I remember." He remembered a lot, Rafe thought. Leslie had always been able to find a way to get whatever it was she wanted. That much, it seemed, hadn't changed. As he looked at his ex-wife now, he mentally compared her to Katie Charles. Katie with her soft hair and faded jeans. With the laugh that seemed to bubble up from her soul. With green eyes that flashed from humor to fury and back again in a heartbeat.

Leslie was coolly elegant.

Katie was heat and passion and—he shut his brain off before it went on an even wilder tangent.

"Rafe, I wouldn't have come to you if I'd had anywhere else to turn," she said, and for the first time, her voice held an edge of regret.

"Yeah, I know that, too." Rafe thought about Katie again and wondered what she would do if she was in Leslie's position. He didn't like to think about Katie being in trouble. Didn't want to acknowledge that it bothered him more than a little to know that she wouldn't turn to him.

Then he thought about how hard Katie worked at building her business. How she scrambled for a living. How she worked and fought for a future doing something she loved. She would do whatever she had to do to take care of herself. And he realized that Leslie was only doing the same thing now. She never would have come to him for help if she hadn't been desperate. Hell, he could read that much in her tear-sheened blue eyes. Because of Katie, Rafe felt a surge of sympathy for Leslie he might not have experienced just a few weeks ago. What was that about?

However it had ended between them, Rafe knew he couldn't ignore Leslie's request for help. Maybe he was finally letting the past go—along with the regrets and the stinging sense of failure memories of his marriage inevitably dredged up.

"Call my assistant Janice tomorrow," he told her. "She'll give you however much you need."

She let out a relieved breath and gave him a grateful smile. "Thanks. To tell the truth, I didn't really think you'd help."

"But you asked anyway."

"Had to," she said, her gaze steady and honest. "I can't stand seeing John worried and upset."

Rafe studied her. "You really love him."

"I really do," she said simply.

That should at least sting, he thought, but it didn't. Not anymore. And, if he was honest with himself, Rafe could admit that when Leslie had walked out, it had been his pride, more than his heart, that had been affected. What did that say about him? Was Leslie right when she told him that he simply wasn't capable of love?

"Les, when we were married," he asked quietly, studying the label on his beer bottle as if looking for the right words, "did you feel that way about me? Would you have protected me if I needed it?"

"You didn't need me, Rafe," she said softly. "You never really did."

"I loved you."

She smiled and shook her head. "No, you didn't."

Irritation spiked. "I guess I know what I felt."

"Don't be so insulted," she said, giving him a patient smile. "I know you cared, but you didn't *love* me, Rafe. I finally got tired of trying to get through to you."

He straightened up, set his beer down and stuffed both hands into his jeans pockets. "I seem to recall you telling me I was incapable of love."

She blinked at him, stunned. "No, I didn't."

"Yeah, you did," he argued.

"For heaven's sake, Rafe," she countered, "why would I say that?"

"Funny, I asked myself that a few times."

"Honestly, Rafe, this is one of the reasons we didn't work out," she told him with a shake of her head. "You never *listened* to me. I never said you were *incapable* of love. I said you were incapable of loving *me*."

He shifted his gaze from Leslie to the view beyond his windows. The sun was sliding into the ocean, dazzling the waves in a brilliant crimson light. A cool breeze danced in through the open balcony doors and he turned his face into it. "Either way, you were right."

"No," Leslie said. "I wasn't."

She reached out and laid one hand on his arm. "Rafe, don't you get it? You didn't love me and that hurt. So I wanted to hurt you back."

She hadn't hurt him, he realized now. She had just driven home the point he'd learned long before her. That love was something you had to be taught when you were growing up. And that was one course Rafe had never gotten.

Leslie tipped her head to one side and looked up at him. "Who is she?"

"What?" He stiffened, instantly retreating into privacy mode, shuttering his eyes, closing down his expression. He took a long, metaphorical step back and distanced himself as much as possible from the curiosity in Leslie's eyes.

"Wow," she murmured, staring at him as if he'd just performed a magic trick, "you still do that so easily."

"Do what?"

"Lock yourself away the instant anybody gets close. Used to make me crazy," she admitted. "It was as if you were on a constant red alert—just waiting for a sneak attack on your heart so you could defend against it."

He resented the description, but Rafe really couldn't deny it, either.

Shaking her head again, she said, "Don't do it, Rafe. I mean, with her, whoever she is, don't do this. Let her in. Risk it."

"Yeah, because my track record is so good."

"You don't need a track record to love someone," she told him. "All it takes is the *right* someone."

"Like John?" he asked.

"For me, yes. Exactly like John." She let her hand fall from his arm and added, "You know, John misses your friendship. You didn't have to cut him loose because of what happened between us, Rafe."

Yes, he did. Because he couldn't look at his friend without knowing that somehow, John had been able to do something Rafe had failed at. He'd made Leslie happy when Rafe couldn't. Kings didn't like losing, probably because they weren't very good at it. Thankfully, the Kings didn't have to deal with that situation often, since they rarely accepted failure.

But in these last few minutes with Leslie, Rafe could admit that whatever he had once felt at losing her was now gone. She was married, happy and a mother. Leslie had moved on, just as his brothers had said. Maybe it was time he did the same thing. Should he really allow one failure to dictate the rest of his life?

"I've missed John, too," he admitted finally. And since that statement didn't leave a bitter taste in his mouth, he heard himself ask, "How are the kids?"

Her face brightened instantly and her smile went wide and heartfelt. "They're terrific. Want to see some pictures?"

"Sure." It only took her a moment to get her purse and pull out her wallet. Then she was flipping through pictures of two beautiful kids, each of them with her hair and John's eyes. He looked at those shining faces and felt the slightest ping of envy at the proof of his ex-wife's current life.

"Nice-looking kids."

"They're great," Leslie said. "And John's a wonderful father."

"I'm glad for you," he told her and surprisingly enough, he meant it. Odd, Rafe thought. Before, when he'd thought about Leslie, there had always been a thread of sadness sliding through him. His failure. His mistake. Now, he felt nothing like that. Instead, his thoughts were filled with images of Katie Charles. Her smile. Her laugh. The feel of her skin beneath his hands.

Leslie was the past.

Was Katie the future?

"Are you okay?"

"What?"

Leslie studied him. "You looked worried there for a second."

Worried? Him? Rafe frowned slightly. He didn't

worry. He acted. "No. Not worried. Everything's fine."
He paused and then surprised himself by adding, "I'm
glad you stopped by today, Leslie."

"Yeah?" She grinned. "Now there's something you
wouldn't have said even a year ago."

"True," he admitted ruefully. "But I can say it now."

"She must really be something, your mystery woman."

"You know," he said thoughtfully, as the last of his
baggage from his failed marriage fell away, "she really
is."

"Then don't blow it, Rafe," Leslie told him. "For your
own sake, let her in."

He already had, he realized now. Hadn't meant to.
Hadn't even been aware of it. But somehow Katie had
gotten past his defenses and now he had to figure out
what that meant for him. For them.

"I should be going," Leslie said. She picked up her
bag and walked over to slip into her heels. "Thank you
again for doing this, Rafe, and I will pay you back."

"I know. Just…call Janice tomorrow."

"I will. Oh, and don't be mad at Declan for letting
me into your place. I won't do it again."

He nodded, watching her prepare to return to her
own life and world.

"There's one more thing," she said softly. "I'm sorry
about how we ended."

He snapped her a look and noted that her smile was
genuine and the tears were gone. For the first time, Rafe
could look at her and see beyond his own failures and
disappointments. He realized that there weren't hard
feelings anymore. He didn't need to continue to avoid
Leslie or even John. The past was done. It didn't matter
to him now and with that realization came a sort of

peace. So when another thought popped into his mind, he went with it.

"We could always use another legal shark at King Construction," he offered. "Tell John to call me."

Her smile was quick and bright. "He'd love to talk to you again, Rafe. Even without a job offer."

"Yeah," he admitted. "Me, too."

When Leslie left a moment later, Rafe took a second or two to enjoy the unusual sensation he felt. For years, he'd been holding on to the failure of his marriage like a damn battle flag. Internally, he'd waved it any time a woman even remotely seemed to be getting too close. That stamp of failure was enough to ensure he'd never try marriage again. Never allow someone to matter too much. As a King, he didn't fail.

But now, he was beginning to realize that maybe his marriage to Leslie hadn't had a chance from the beginning. He'd never had a shot at making it work because he had married Leslie for all the wrong reasons.

They had both been too young to know what they wanted. Too stupid to see that getting married wasn't the natural end result of dating for a year. He had blindly pushed forward even though a part of him had known going in that it wasn't right.

The problem was, he didn't feel like that about Katie. Being with her felt absolutely right. But would it still feel that way when she knew the truth?

Nine

After a long nap, Katie felt energized and a little nervous about her upcoming date. So she took moral support along when she went shopping.

"Seriously?" Nicole asked, shaking her head and grimacing. "You're not fifty years old, Katie."

Katie looked down at the dress she had tried on and frowned to herself. It was a lovely beige silk with a high neck, long sleeves and a full skirt that swirled around her knees when she did a quick turn in front of the mirror. "It's pretty."

"It's dowdy," Nicole argued and handed Connor a bottle of juice.

The little boy kicked his heels against the stroller bottom and cried out, "Pretty!"

"Connor likes it," Katie argued.

"He won't when he's thirty." Nicole shook her head again, leaned over to a nearby rack and plucked a dress free. "Try this one. It's your size."

"It's black."

"And…?"

Katie blew out a breath and said, "Fine. Be right back."

They were in a tiny boutique on Second Street. She might have had better luck in a mall, but this was closer and Katie preferred supporting the small businesses around her. After all, she was determined to be one of them someday soon and besides, the big mega stores already had a huge customer base.

She took off the beige and hung it up carefully, giving it one last wistful glance. "Are you sure?" she called out from the dressing room. "The beige one looks so elegant."

"Try the black," Nicole ordered from just outside the door. "Trust me on this."

Sighing, Katie did, dragging the black dress over her head and positioning it just right. When she closed the side zipper, she looked into the mirror and instantly thought about buying a sweater.

"I can't wear this," she complained, still staring at her reflection as if seeing a stranger. "This is so not me."

"Let's see it."

Katie opened the door a scant inch, barely giving Nicole a peek. But her friend wasn't satisfied with that and pushed the door open completely. Her eyes went wide and a slow grin curved her mouth. "Wow."

Uncomfortable, Katie looked back into the mirror. Miles of skin were exposed. She'd never worn anything like this before. And what did that say about her sad, quiet little life?

Two thin black straps snaked over her bare shoulders and the bodice was cut low enough to give an excellent view of the tops of her breasts. The material was slick and clingy and molded to every inch of her body, defining curves even she hadn't been aware of. The hem of the dress hit mid-thigh—another inch or two higher and it would've been illegal.

As it was, it was only embarrassing.

"You look amazing," Nicole said, staring into the mirror to catch her eye.

"I can't wear this."

"Why not?"

"It's just not me," Katie said, fighting the urge to tug the bodice up a little higher.

"That's exactly why you should wear it," Nicole told her, scooping Connor out of the stroller to prop him on her hip. Swinging her blond hair back behind her shoulder, she met Katie's gaze in the mirror and said, "Cordell shot your confidence out from under you."

"True." But she was the one who had allowed it to happen. Katie ran one hand over the front of the dress, smoothing the fabric. She studied her own reflection while her friend continued talking.

"If you keep hiding away, you're letting *him* decide your life for you. Don't you get it?"

Katie's gaze shifted to Nicole's in the mirror. "Yes, but—"

"No buts." Nicole shook her head firmly and ran the palm of her hand across the top of her son's head. "Trust me, I know what it's like to have your self-assurance shaken. Let's pause to remember that my husband walked out on me when I was pregnant."

"Nicole…"

"Not a bid for sympathy," she said firmly. "I'm so over him. My point is, you should be over Cordell, too."

"I am really," Katie told her and realized that she had been "over" Cordell for some time. She'd been nursing her own hurt feelings for too long, but that had stopped when she met Rafe.

Just one of his kisses was enough to sear anyone else from her mind. Her heart. Her breath caught and twisted in her lungs until she was almost light-headed as she thought about the gleam that would appear in Rafe's eyes when he saw her in this dress.

"Then what're you waiting for?" Nicole came up behind her. In the glass, the two women stood side by side, with a toddler boy grinning between them. "If you're really over that creep, then wear this dress tonight. Knock Rafe's socks off."

Katie sent her own reflection a thoughtful smile. Slowly, she straightened up, threw her shoulders back and let the initial embarrassment she'd felt slide away. She did look good. She really liked Rafe and hiding away from what she was feeling wouldn't change that any.

"Atta girl," Nicole whispered as if she could hear what Katie was thinking.

Katie's mind raced. Cordell King hadn't even been a part of her life for very long. Truthfully, she thought now, she had probably built what they'd so briefly shared into something it had never been. Meeting him had been so far out of her orbit that she had taken it as some sort of sign—that he was the one. She had been willingly blinded by the fairy tale, Katie told herself hollowly. Rich, handsome man sweeps poor but honest shopkeeper off her feet and whisks her off to his palatial estate.

She gave her reflection a rueful smile.

When her fantasy ended, she'd crawled back into her narrow routine and pulled it in after her, essentially cutting herself off from everything just so that she couldn't make a foolish mistake again. And who was *that* decision hurting? she demanded silently.

Cordell had gone on his merry way, leaving a diamond token in his wake, no doubt never once thinking about Katie. While she, on the other hand, had not only buried herself in work, but continued to hold off on another relationship just because she'd made one bad judgment call.

Straightening up slowly, she looked her reflection in the eye and asked, *Are you going to be alone for the rest of your life, Katie?*

God no. She didn't want that. She had never wanted that. Ever since she was a little girl, she'd dreamed about having a family of her own. She had heard all the stories from her grandmother and her mother, talking about the great loves of their lives and how they wouldn't have traded a minute of it—even to spare themselves the pain of losing those special men.

What, she wondered, would she look back on one day? A great cookie recipe?

"So just when exactly did I become such a coward?" she whispered.

"What?"

She shifted her gaze to Nicole's reflection and asked, "Why didn't I see this before? Why am I hiding away? I didn't do anything wrong. I just picked a lemon in the garden of love."

Nicole laughed and the baby's giggle echoed her. "Nice way of putting it, but yeah."

Every passing moment filled Katie with more strength. More confidence. Right there in the tiny dressing room, she had the epiphany of all epiphanies. She had closed herself off to life to punish herself for being wrong. It didn't even make sense. Was pain so great that you couldn't risk being happy on the off chance you might get hurt again?

It was as if she could feel her old self clawing her way to the surface, brushing past the hesitant, meek Katie and tamping her down, she hoped, never to rise again.

"Who doesn't pick the wrong guy occasionally?" she demanded.

"Preaching to the choir, girl," Nicole said ruefully.

"That's right!" Katie swung around and draped one arm around Nicole's shoulders. "*Your* guy was a jerk, too!"

Laughing, Nicole said, "Do you have to sound so excited by that?"

Katie shook her head and said, "Sorry, but I'm having a moment here. The problem's not me. It never was me. So I picked the wrong guy? So what? Doesn't mean I'll pick the wrong one again, does it?"

"Nope."

Swinging back around to face her reflection, Katie dismissed the dowdy beige dress from her mind and instead admired the sexy black one she wore. She turned and checked herself out from every angle and finally gave a sharp nod. "You were right, Nicole. This dress *is* perfect. It's going to knock Rafe's socks off."

"Hopefully," Nicole added with a sly grin, "it'll knock off a lot more than his socks."

Katie felt a flush of heat rush through her just thinking about the possibilities. Then she tugged at the zipper and said, "As soon as I'm dressed again, we're headed for the shoe department. I need some sky-high heels, too."

"Now you're talking," Nicole said and took her son out of the dressing room.

Katie thought about what Rafe's reaction to her might be and she smiled to herself. She was through pretending she didn't care about him. Finished trying to protect herself at the cost of her own happiness. Tonight was going to be a turning point for her and Rafe. She was opening herself up to the possibilities.

Katie gave her reflection one last, approving glance. Nana would be so proud.

The restaurant sat high on the cliffs at Dana Point.

There was patio dining and then there were the booths inside, safely tucked behind a glass wall, protecting diners from the cool wind. He'd left their choice of table up to Katie and was pleased when she'd opted for the patio. From here, they could not only see the ocean, but hear the pulse of it as the water met the cliffs.

With the stars overhead and the waves crashing into the rocks below, it was probably one of the most romantic places on the coast. Rafe hadn't been there in years—but he had known it was the perfect spot for the romantic evening he wanted to have with Katie.

Looking at her now, across the table from him, with the ocean breeze ruffling her dark red hair into a tumble of curls, his breath caught in his chest. Her green eyes shone in the soft candlelight burning from behind the safety of hurricane lamps in the center of their table. Her smile was infectious as she admired her surroundings, and the urge to reach out and touch her was damn near overpowering.

He'd never forget his first sight of her when she opened her door to him. That black dress clung to her body in all the right ways. Her creamy skin was displayed to perfection and the heels she wore made her already great legs look amazing.

Everything in him went hard and tight. His heartbeat was crashing in his chest and his mind filled with sensual images of just how he hoped this evening would end.

"This place is gorgeous," she said, shifting her gaze

back to him before turning her head to take in the restaurant behind them and the people sitting behind the glass wall. "I can't believe anyone would choose to be inside instead of out here."

"Me either," he said and reached for his glass of wine. He took a sip, admired the taste of it and silently toasted his cousin Travis, who owned and operated King Vineyards. The bottle of King Cabernet was perfect. As it should be. "But most women prefer to be inside where their hair doesn't get messed up by the wind."

She turned to grin at him, flipping her hair back over her shoulder. "Not me. I love the feel of the wind."

"It looks good on you," he said softly.

Katie took a sip of her wine and smiled. "The wine's good, too, even if it *is* from the King winery."

Frowning a bit, Rafe told himself he should have ordered a different wine, if only to keep her mind off the King family and her resentments toward them. Clearly, tonight would not be the night when he'd make a full confession. He would soon, though. He just had to find the right words. The right way to explain to her who he was and why he'd lied to her.

Just as he was about to change the subject, he thought better of it and decided to plunge in and try to subtly alter her opinion of the Kings.

"They can't all be bad," he said diffidently.

"Maybe not," she allowed and he felt a small stirring of hope that was dashed a moment later. "But people that rich are so removed from everyday life they tend to look at the world differently than we do."

One of his eyebrows lifted. "You know many rich people, do you?"

She smiled. "No. Just the one. But he left an impression."

"Obviously," Rafe murmured, still wishing he knew which member of his family had hurt her so badly.

Reaching across the table, Katie covered Rafe's hand with her own and his fingers trapped hers instantly, holding on to her when she would have pulled back. She tipped her head to one side and said, "The difference between you and a rich guy is that you brought me here because you thought I'd love it. He would have brought me here to impress me. That's a big difference, Rafe."

He shifted a bit in his chair, uncomfortable with her explanation. The truth was, he'd brought her here because he *had* wanted to impress her—but he'd also known that she would love this place. So that was sort of a compromise, wasn't it?

Still holding on to her hand, he stroked the pad of his thumb across her fingers and said quietly, "What if the rich guy really did bring you here because he thought you'd like it?"

She smiled and briefly gave his hand a squeeze. "It still wouldn't have been as special as you bringing me here, because I know that for a working guy, this place is so expensive, you wouldn't come here normally."

The frown he felt earlier came back as he studied her. "You know something? You're a snob, Katie Charles."

"What?" She tugged her hand free and sat up straight in her chair. "No, I'm not."

"Sure you are," he countered, suddenly feeling more relaxed. If he could make her see that she was being prejudiced, maybe she'd take the truth, when he finally told it, a little better. "On the strength of meeting one rich creep, you've decided that all rich guys aren't worth your time. So you're a reverse snob. As far as you're concerned, only poor guys need apply."

"That sounds terrible," she said, reaching for her wine. She took a sip and set the glass down again.

"But it's accurate." Rafe grinned, and took her hand in his again, despite her efforts to wriggle free.

"Nice to know what you really think of me."

"What I think is, you're a beautiful, smart, ambitious woman with one huge blind spot."

She laughed in spite of herself. "That's a heck of a description."

"This guy who treated you so badly," Rafe said, ignoring her last comment. "What was it about him that attracted you in the first place?"

Her mouth twisted a little and she took a breath, then blew it out in a huff. "Fine. I admit it. He was…" She lifted one shoulder in a half shrug. "…exciting. Different. He was rich and handsome and—"

"Hmm," Rafe teased in a thoughtful tone. She'd said exactly what he'd hoped she would say. Made it much easier to score a point here. "So the first thing you noticed about him was that he was rich?"

"Not the first," she argued quickly, then after a second or two she admitted, "but it was in the top two."

"Uh-huh."

"Fine. I see what you're saying." She shook her wind-tousled hair back from her face. "Very clever. So the poor rich man was taken advantage of by a woman who was intrigued."

"Nope, not what I'm saying at all," he told her, keeping her hand firmly in his despite the fact that she kept trying to slip free. "All I'm saying is that you liked that he was rich until it turned on you. So basically, the problem here is that he was a jerk, not that he was a *rich* jerk."

Whatever she might have said in response went

unspoken because their server chose that moment to arrive with their salads. Rafe and Katie stared into each others' eyes as the woman deftly slid icy plates in front of them and asked, "Is there anything else you need right now?"

"No, thanks." Rafe dismissed her with a smile, then turned his gaze back on Katie, who was watching him through narrowed eyes.

"Think you're pretty clever, don't you?" she asked.

"Actually, *yeah*."

She laughed and the sound of it was like music to him.

"Okay, I see your point," she acknowledged, picking up her fork. "And maybe you're a little bit right."

"Only a little?" he asked.

"Yes," she said. "I didn't like him *because* he was rich, but I do admit that was part of the attraction. Mainly since I couldn't understand why he was interested in me."

"I can."

Rafe understood completely what any man would see in Katie. What he couldn't understand was how a member of his family could be so stupid as to walk away from her. To hurt her and toss her aside. That he would never figure out. But if his anonymous relative hadn't walked away from Katie, Rafe wouldn't be with her now. So maybe he owed the bastard a thank-you—after he punched him in the face.

She smiled. "Thanks for that. And I'll think about what you said. Maybe you're right. Maybe it's not rich guys I should be mad at, but the jerks of the world."

He lifted his glass in a silent toast to her, even while thinking that if she was going to condemn the "jerks," wouldn't he technically be one of that crowd? The burden of lies fell on top of him and Rafe couldn't shrug it off anymore. He wasn't looking forward to telling her the truth, but he couldn't see a way around it.

"Deal." He reluctantly released her hand so that she could eat her salad, but he found he missed the warmth of her touch. He watched her in the flickering candlelight and though the restaurant patio was crowded with other diners, it felt to him as though he and Katie were all alone.

He didn't need dinner. Didn't need the wine. All he really needed—*wanted*—was this woman sitting across from him. She was unlike anyone he'd ever known. She didn't want anything from him. Didn't demand his attention—though she had it anyway. In another week or so, her kitchen redo would be complete and he wouldn't have a handy excuse for seeing her every day. That thought settled like a black cloud over his heart and it was just another reminder that he didn't want to let her go.

He wasn't sure if that meant they had a future or not, but what it did mean was he wanted her for more than a few stolen moments.

This had never been about a future with Katie, he reminded himself. This had started out as a way to reclaim the King family reputation. But there was more to it than that now. He had planned to simply woo her, win her and then move on. Go back to his life and leave Katie to hers.

But since that plan wasn't as appealing as it had been before, he clearly needed a new plan.

He only wished he knew what that was.

Ten

Two hours later, dinner was over and instead of taking her home, Rafe helped Katie down to the beach.

"These heels are *not* made for walking in the sand," she said with a laugh. She stopped and pulled off first one shoe then the other and looked up at him with a grin. "There. That's better."

High above them, diners still filled the restaurant patio. But here on the moonlit beach, they were alone in the shadows, as if they were the only two people on the coast. And Rafe couldn't take his eyes off her. She was the most captivating woman he'd ever known. She thought nothing of kicking off her heels to take a walk on the beach with him. She didn't worry about her hair and she didn't whine about being cold. She was… amazing and he felt a hard, solid punch of something he couldn't identify somewhere around his heart.

She laid one hand on his chest. "Rafe? You okay?"

"Yeah," he told her, "I'm fine."

But he wasn't at all sure. Leading her along the beach, Rafe held her hand and made sure she didn't get wet as the tide rushed in, leaving a foaming layer of lace on the sand. The coast was dark, but the ocean shone with moonlight glittering on its surface.

"Tonight was perfect," she said and leaned her head on his shoulder. "But you didn't have to take me to such an expensive restaurant."

He dropped her hand and laid one arm around her shoulders. "You didn't like it?"

"I loved it," she admitted. "I just don't want you to think you have to spend a lot of money to impress me."

There was a first, he told himself wryly. He couldn't remember anyone ever telling him not to spend money on them. Hell, his own mother only came around when her bank account was empty. And even thinking that made him feel like a child demanding something he couldn't have. Ridiculous. He didn't *need* anybody. He was better alone. At least he always had been. Now, he wasn't so sure. His mind was racing with thoughts that contradicted each other. Back away, one side of him said. Have a few great nights with Katie, then tell her the truth and leave her behind. But there was another voice in his mind now, too. And it was saying something completely different. That maybe Katie was what had been missing from his life. That maybe, if he could find a way to dig himself out of the hole he found himself in, he might actually find *love*.

That thought was both intriguing and terrifying to a man with so little experience with love.

She threaded her arm through his and snuggled closer and his heartbeat quickened even as his brain raced. Damn, what was going on with him? All his body wanted to do was slow down, enjoy her. Hold her. But his mind wouldn't let him relax into the moment. It kept insisting that Katie was different. Special. That she deserved honesty, damn it. That he was risking something potentially wonderful by lying to her.

"What're you thinking about?" she asked, coming to a stop so she could tip her head back to look up at him.

"You," he said.

She reached up and smoothed his hair back from his forehead and the touch of her fingers sent heat jolting through him.

"They don't look like happy thoughts. Should I be worried?"

"No," he said quickly. He threaded his fingers through her hair and she turned her face into his palm. "Did I tell you how beautiful you are?"

"Yeah, I think you mentioned it a time or two."

"Well, since I don't like repeating myself, why don't I show you instead?"

He kissed her thoroughly, completely, parting her lips with his tongue and sweeping into the warmth he'd found only with her. She welcomed him, leaning into his embrace, matching his desire with her own. He held her tightly to him, drawing her as close as possible and still it wasn't enough.

Here on this lonely stretch of beach, with the moonlight spilling down on them, Rafe could only think of her. Nothing else mattered. Only the next kiss and the next. Touching her, being with her. His brain was finally silenced by his body's overwhelming need.

He swept one hand along her side, feeling the curves of her through the silky coolness of her dress. He cupped her breast and she arched into him, a soft moan issuing from her throat. His thumb stroked the peak of her rigid nipple and even through the fabric separating him from her, he could feel her heat reaching for him.

Not enough, he thought wildly. Not nearly enough. He needed to feel her skin. Flesh to flesh. Heat to heat. He shifted her in his arms and while his mouth tantalized hers, his hand swept to the hem of her dress and inched it up, higher and higher. His palm moved over her thigh, sliding toward her core, and she parted her legs for him.

That first touch inflamed him, though the silk of her panties kept him from delving as deeply as he wanted— needed—to. He stroked her center and she shivered, that soft moan erupting over and over again as he brushed his fingertips over her most sensitive flesh.

The sea wind caressed them, the moonlight coated them in a silvery light and all Rafe was aware of was the woman in his arms. The woman he wanted above all things. He pushed the edge of her panties to one side, stroked that one tender spot at the heart of her and felt her tremble in his arms, quaking and shivering. Again and again, he touched her, pushing her higher, faster. He dipped his fingers deep, stroking her, inside and out. Her legs parted farther as she plastered herself against him. Rafe's tongue twisted with hers, he took her breath, each labored gasp, as she twisted and writhed against him, hungry for the climax shuddering just out of reach.

He reveled in her response. Loved knowing that she was as hungry for him as he was for her. He continued to push her, using his hand, his fingers, to urge her toward completion, needing to feel her surrender.

Then it was there, a release crashing down over her with enough force to leave them both shaken.

Her hands clutched at his shoulders, and her hips rocked into his hand, riding him as he took her quickly, inexorably into a shower of stars.

When it was done, when she hung limp in his arms, he tore his mouth from hers. It nearly killed him to stop, but he gathered his strength and rested his forehead against hers, each of them struggling for breath that wouldn't come. After several long seconds, he smoothed her skirt back down and whispered, "Let's go back to your place."

"Yes," she said, her voice husky with satisfaction and growing need. "Let's go now."

He grinned at her, swept her up into his arms and carried her back across the beach to the cement stairs leading up to Pacific Coast Highway.

Laughing, she said, "Rafe, I can walk, you know."

He brushed a quick kiss across her mouth. "Yeah, but I really liked carrying you before. Thought it was worth repeating."

At the head of the stairs, he took a left and made for the restaurant. He was suddenly grateful he hadn't used valet parking. They wouldn't have to stand around and wait for the car to be brought up. Instead, he'd make a dash to the lot and swing back around to pick her up.

Kissing her again, he dropped her to her feet, cupped her face in his palms and said, "Wait here. I'll get the car."

"I can come with you."

"Faster if I run for it and those heels aren't made for running."

"True," she said, glancing down at the sexy black heels she'd stepped into again the moment they were off the beach. "Hurry up."

"Back in a flash," he promised and raced off into the parking lot.

Katie watched him go, her gaze locked on him until he was swallowed up by the crowd of cars and the hazy light thrown from the yellow fog lamps. Her heart was pounding and every inch of her body was tingling, throbbing still from the effects of the orgasm still rattling through her.

The ocean wind was cold now, but it couldn't even touch the heat flooding her body. She smiled to herself, thinking that the splurge on the dress and shoes had been totally worth it. Having him touch her, take her, on the beach beneath the moon had been an experience she would never forget. The man was far too sexy for his own good and his touch was magic.

The whole night had been perfect and was, she told herself with another smile, about to get even better.

She was going to be happy, damn it. She wasn't going to deprive herself of the chance to be with Rafe because of old fears and trust issues. She wouldn't pass up a shot at happiness because of past mistakes. Besides, she had been thinking about what Rafe had said earlier all night.

He had a point. Part of what had attracted her to Cordell had been the fact that he was rich. So what did that say about her? She couldn't really blame his actions on the fact that he had money any more than she could blame her response on the fact that she *wasn't* wealthy.

They were just people.

And people made mistakes, right? The important thing was to learn from them and try not to make the *same* mistakes over and over again.

She remembered the feel of Rafe's arms coming

around her. The slow, intimate caresses. The heat of desire and the warmth of love rushing between them and her breath caught in her chest. She hadn't realized it until just this moment, and now that she had, she couldn't imagine how it had escaped her for this long.

Katie was in love.

Real love. She knew the difference this time and she wrapped herself up in the amazing sensations as they spiraled through her. What she'd thought she felt for Cordell before wasn't even a glimmer of what she felt for Rafe now. He was everything she had hoped to find. He was the man she had been waiting for all of her life.

How had it happened so quickly?

But even as she wondered that, she smiled to herself, remembering that Nana had always said "Love doesn't go by the clock." One moment was all it took when it was real. One amazing moment when the world suddenly became clear and your heart knew exactly what it wanted and needed.

She sighed a little and held her newfound knowledge close. Tonight was a night she would remember forever.

"Katie?" A deep voice called her name. "Katie Charles? Is that you?"

A small thread of something unpleasant unwound throughout her system as Katie turned slowly toward that too-familiar voice. She saw him instantly, but then he was hard to miss. Tall, gorgeous, black hair long enough to lay on his collar and sharp blue eyes fixed on her.

Cordell King.

She stood her ground and lifted her chin as he walked to her. She shouldn't have been surprised to see him.

She knew he lived in Laguna Beach and this restaurant, being the most expensive one in miles, would surely be a draw to him. But what did amaze her was the fact that she felt *nothing* for him. There were no leftover feelings trapped inside her. Not even anger, though as he smiled at her as if they were long lost friends, she could feel a spark of irritation flash into life.

"It's great to see you," Cordell said as he got close enough. He swept her into a brief hug whether she wanted to go or not, then released her. "You look amazing."

"Thanks," she said, even more grateful now that she'd bought the fabulous black dress. Imagine if she'd run into him wearing that beige one.

He glanced around, then asked, "Are you here alone? Can I buy you a drink?"

"No, you can't," she said, amazed that he had even asked. "I'm sure the woman you're with wouldn't appreciate the company."

"No date," he said. "I'm here meeting a couple of my brothers."

"Well, I'm here with someone else. He's just gone to get the car."

"Oh." He shrugged and gave her that slow, easy smile that had first tugged at her. "Well, not surprising you've got a date. You look great."

"You said that already."

"Yeah, I know," he told her. That smile came back, but when she didn't respond, he continued. "Look, Katie. I'm actually glad we ran into each other. I've been doing a lot of thinking about you lately."

Now that was surprising. "Is that right?"

"Yeah," he said, stepping in a little closer. "I was

going to call you, but doing this in person is even better."

"Why's that?" she asked sharply, folding her arms over her chest. "You didn't think breaking up with me was important enough to do in person. You overnighted me a diamond bracelet along with that charming note that said something along the lines of 'Our worlds are just too different.' Remember?"

He had the good grace to wince at the reminder, but it wasn't enough to shut him down completely. *Oh, no, not a King,* she thought.

"Okay, I could've handled that better," he acknowledged. "But I did send you diamonds."

And she'd sold them to help pay for the kitchen remodel, Katie told herself.

"I never asked for diamonds," she pointed out.

"No, but—" He stopped, took a breath and said, "Look, we're getting off the subject."

"Which is?" The toe of her shoe tapped against the cement, making a staccato sound that played counterpoint to the conversation.

"I'd like to give our relationship another chance," he said. "I mean, we had a great time for a while—"

"Until you dumped me, you mean?" she interrupted, that spark of irritation flashing into quite the little blaze.

"Yeah, well." He shrugged as if that were water under the bridge. "That was then, this is now. And, babe, looking at you now makes me think we could work things out if we tried."

"Babe?" she repeated, taking one step toward him. "Don't you call me 'babe.'"

"Hey." He lifted both hands in the air as if he were

surrendering, but that meant nothing. "Relax, I just thought—"

"You just thought that I'd what? Leap into your arms at the *gracious* offer of being able to go out with you again?"

He smiled and that simply infuriated her. Cordell King had bruised her heart so badly, she'd completely lost sight of who and what she was. He'd shattered her confidence and made her question her own ability to judge a person's character.

"All I'm saying is—" he started.

But Katie cut him off with a single wave of her hand. She was through. She didn't want to hear his lame excuses. He'd hurt her and now he behaved as though it had never happened. Well, maybe most of the Kings were able to skate through life without ever once having to face up to what they'd done, but Cordell was going to get a piece of her mind. At last.

"Don't bother. I'm not interested in what you have to say. Do you really think I would go out with you again after how you treated me? Seriously? Does that sweet smile and charm really work for you?"

"Usually," he admitted, taking a long step back as if finally understanding that she wasn't thrilled to see him. He took a quick look around as if to assure himself that they were alone.

They were. But it wouldn't have mattered to Katie either way.

"Amazing," she said, "that there are so many women out there allowing themselves to be dazzled by good looks and empty promises."

"Now just a minute," he countered in his own defense. "I didn't make you any promises."

"Oh, no," she acknowledged. "Just the unspoken

promise of one human being to treat another with a bit of respect."

"It was a good time, okay? That's all. As for tonight, I saw you and thought—"

"I know exactly what you thought, Cordell, and I can tell you it's never going to happen."

He shook his head, blew out a breath and said, "Okay, I can see that this was a mistake, so—"

The sound of a rumbling engine came to her and Katie glanced at the parking lot. Rafe was driving his truck around to the front to pick her up and as he approached, she pointed at him.

"You see that truck? Driving it is a better man than you'll ever be, Cordell. He's a carpenter. He's not rich, but he's got more class than you could hope to have. He's honest and kind and sweet and—"

"Okay!" Cordell took another step away from her and his features clearly said that he wished he were anywhere but there. "I get the picture."

"Good." She set her hands at her hips and took a deep, calming breath of the cool, fresh air. Katie felt better than she had in months. Being given the chance to face Cordell and tell him exactly what she thought of him had been…liberating.

She was still watching him with a gleam of triumph in her eyes when she heard the truck stop and the driver's side door open and slam shut.

"Cordell?" Rafe shouted as he came closer.

Katie slowly swiveled her head to stare at him. How did he know Cordell?

"Rafe?" Cordell said his name on a laugh. *"You're* the poor but honest carpenter? The paragon of virtue Katie just slapped me upside the head with? *You?"*

Rafe didn't say another word. He bunched his fist

and threw a punch to Cordell's jaw that had the man sprawled out on the cement before he could take his next breath. Then Rafe stood over him, glaring in fury. "You son of a bitch."

"You *know* each other?" Katie asked, her voice hitching higher on every word.

Rubbing his jaw, Cordell scrambled to his feet, his glare burning into Rafe as if he could set fire to him with only the power of his will. "You could say that. Rafe's my cousin."

Katie staggered back a step or two, her gaze locked on the man turning to face her now. "Rafe *King?*"

"I can explain," he said.

She noticed he wasn't denying it.

"So much for the poor but proud carpenter, huh?" Cordell muttered, his gaze snapping from his cousin to the woman staring at both of them as if they'd just crawled out from under the same rock. "Katie, I admit it. I treated you badly and I'm sorry for it. But at least I never lied to you, which is more than I can say for my cousin."

"Shut up, Cordell."

"You want to try another shot at me, Rafe?" he offered. "Go for it."

"Both of you stop it," Katie demanded, suddenly feeling like a bone being tugged between two snarling dogs.

Fury tangled with hurt and mixed into a knot of emotions in the pit of her stomach. She was so shaken she could hardly stand, but still, she had to look at Rafe. She read regret in his eyes, though that didn't do a thing toward assuaging what she was going through.

Tears stung her eyes, but she refused to let them fall. Damned if she'd give her tears to the Kings. Again. No, instead, she went with the fury, letting her anger pulse inside her until she could hardly breathe for the fire churning inside her.

"Was this a game?" she demanded, ignoring Cordell, giving her attention only to the man she had thought she knew so well. "Did you have a good time? Are you going to run off to your country club now with lots of fun stories about how you wormed your way into the cookie queen's bed?"

"You slept with her?" Cordell said.

Rafe sent him a death glare, then focused on Katie. "It wasn't a game. Damn it, Katie, you're...*important* to me."

"Oh, sure," she said, sarcasm dripping from her tone, "I can sense that. Lies are always an indicator of a real depth of feeling."

"I was going to tell you the truth."

"What stopped you?" she asked tightly. "Could it be shame?"

"Katie, if you'll just listen for a second..." He took a step closer and she skipped back in reaction.

"Stay away from me," she muttered, shaking her head as if she could wipe away the memory of these last few minutes. "I can't believe this is happening."

"Katie let me explain," Rafe said.

"This should be good," Cordell murmured.

"Don't you have somewhere to go?" Rafe challenged.

"I'm not going anywhere," his cousin said.

"Then I will," Katie told both of them. She couldn't stand here listening to either one of them.

"Not before you hear me out," Rafe said, grabbing her arm to hold her still when she would have sailed past him.

Katie pulled free, ignoring the instinct to stay within the grip of his warmth. "Fine. Talk."

He shot another look at his cousin, then focused on her as if she were the only person in the world. "I made a bet with Joe. The contractor."

"A *bet?* You bet on me?" Oh, she thought grimly, this just got better and better. Now it wasn't just Rafe lying to her, but Joe, too. And probably Steve and Arturo, as well. They must have had some fun lunchtime conversations talking about how stupid she was. "I can't believe you did that."

"No," he snapped, then ran one hand through his hair. "It wasn't about you. I lost a bet and had to work a job site. Your job site. Then I met you and found out you hated all the Kings because of what this moron did to you—"

"Hey!"

"—so I didn't tell you who I was. I wanted you to get to know me. To like me. Then I was going to tell you the truth, I swear it."

"*That* was your plan?" Cordell asked. "And you call me a moron."

"Be quiet, Cordell." Katie shook her head in disbelief and gave her full attention to Rafe again. His eyes were flashing with emotion, but she couldn't read them and wouldn't have bothered if she could. She was beyond caring what he was feeling. Her own emotions were too wild. Too tangled and twisted to be able to make sense of them. All she knew was that she was hurting and, once again, a *King* was at the center of her pain. "You were going to show me that I was wrong about your family by *lying* to me?"

He scrubbed one hand across his jaw and muttered

something she didn't quite catch. Then he said, "Katie, let me take you home so we can talk this out."

Cordell snorted a short laugh.

Neither of them so much as glanced at him.

"I'm not going anywhere with you, Rafe," she said quietly. Looking up into his beautiful blue eyes for the last time, she silently said goodbye to her hopes, her dreams and the love she had so recently discovered. How could she love a man she didn't even know? And that knowledge made the pain in her heart much more fierce. "Just leave me alone."

She started walking and only paused when he called out, "You need a ride home."

"I'll call a cab," she said without even looking at him.

Katie couldn't bear it for another minute. Couldn't look at him one more time, knowing that he'd lied to her every day they were together. None of it had been real. None of it had meant a thing.

She had fallen in love with a stranger.

And now she was alone again.

As the restaurant valet called for a taxi, she realized that she had been right earlier.

Tonight *was* a night she would always remember.

"So," Cordell asked, "you want to get a drink?"

"Sure," Rafe grumbled, "why not?"

The two cousins headed for the restaurant bar and Rafe didn't miss the fact that Katie's gaze locked on them both as they walked past her. He could almost feel the fury radiating off her and damned if he could blame her for it.

Amazing, he thought, just how fast a perfect night

could go to hell. As they stepped into the restaurant, Cordell shivered.

"Did you feel those icicles she was shooting at us?"

"Felt more like knives to me," Rafe said and led the way into the wood-paneled bar. A dozen or more people were scattered around the glass-walled room at tiny round tables boasting flickering candlelight. Rafe ignored everyone else and headed directly for the bartender. He took a seat, ordered two beers, then turned to look at his cousin as Cordell took the stool beside him. "This wasn't how I saw tonight ending up."

"Guess not," Cordell said amiably. "So how long have you been seeing Katie?"

"A few weeks." Rafe picked up his beer and took a long swallow.

"A few weeks? Hell, I dated her for three months and never got past her front door."

Rafe smiled to himself. That was good to hear. If Cordell had said something about sleeping with Katie, then Rafe would have had to kill him and there would have been hell to pay from the rest of the family.

As it was, he was fighting down an urge to hit Cordell again just for the heck of it. But what would be the point? Katie had made it all too clear that it wasn't just Cordell she was angry at anymore. Seemed there was plenty of outraged fury to spread over the whole King family.

And he'd brought it all on himself.

Rafe rubbed the back of his neck and gritted his teeth against the urge to howl in frustration. Ironic that just when he'd decided to come clean and confess all, he'd lost everything before he had the chance. He should have told her sooner, he knew. But he hadn't wanted to risk what they had.

Now, it no longer mattered because what they had was gone.

His cousin nudged him with an elbow. "So why'd you lie to Katie?"

"Why were you a jerk to her?"

Cordell shrugged. "According to most of the women I go out with, that's what I'm best at."

"That's just great," Rafe said, nodding grimly.

"You're avoiding the question," his cousin said. "Why'd you lie to Katie?"

"You heard me explain it to her," Rafe said, studying his own sorry reflection in the mirror across from him.

"Yeah," Cordell agreed. "But I'm thinking it was more than that."

Listening to his cousin was making Rafe bunch his fists again. He didn't want to be here with Cordell. He wanted to be with Katie. Wanted to make her understand...*what?* What could he possibly say now that wouldn't paint him as the same kind of ass as Cordell?

She had lumped all the Kings into one bad basket and as it turned out, he told himself, she was right.

"What're you talking about, Cordell?"

"Only that you really liked her. And once you found out she hated all Kings—"

"Thanks to you," Rafe added.

Cordell shrugged and nodded. "Thanks to me, then you decided that you didn't want to blow it by telling her the truth."

"Wrong. I had a plan. I was going to tell her."

"Sure you were," his cousin said on a snort of laughter.

"If there's something funny about this," Rafe muttered, "I wish you'd share it. Because I just don't see it."

"I know." Cordell took a long pull of his beer and looked into the mirror, meeting Rafe's gaze with a smile. "And that's the funniest part. Man, if your brothers could see you now."

"You want to step outside and finish that fight?"

"Nope," Cordell said, "and hitting me won't change a thing for you anyway."

"Meaning?"

"Meaning, you're in love with her." Cordell laughed, took another drink of his beer and shook his head. "Another King bites the dust."

"You're wrong." Rafe looked into the mirror, met his own gaze and assured himself that Cordell couldn't have been more wildly off base. He wasn't in love. Had no wish to be in love.

Which was a good thing, he decided grimly. Since the only woman who might have changed his mind about that now wanted nothing to do with him.

Eleven

Katie spent the next few days buried in work.

There was simply nothing better for taking your mind off your problems then diving into baking. She devoted herself to building cookie cakes, decorating birthday cookies and churning out dozens of her clients' favorites.

The scents of cinnamon, vanilla and chocolate surrounded her, giving her a sense of peace that actually went nowhere toward calming her. Inside, her heart was torn and her mind was still buzzing with indignation and hurt. In her dreams, she saw Rafe's face, over and over again, as he looked at her and said, "I can explain." She saw Cordell laughing, Rafe furious and herself, shattered.

He'd said she was "important" to him. As what? A means to winning a bet? As a personal challenge to change her mind about the Kings? And if she was so important to him, why hadn't he tried to talk to her since that night? Why had he been able to let her go so easily?

God, she wasn't making sense. She didn't want him back, did she? So why should she care that he wasn't calling? Wasn't coming over?

Again and again, she relived that night and each time the images danced through her brain, the pain she felt ratcheted up another notch. Her own fault, she knew. She had trusted. Big mistake. She had known going in that she should keep her distance from Rafe. Instead though, she'd followed her heart again, choosing to forget that that particular part of her anatomy was fairly unreliable.

"How many times are you going to go over this anyway, Katie?" she murmured. Shaking her head grimly, she boxed up a dozen chocolate-chip cookies and tied the pink and white striped container with a cotton-candy-colored ribbon.

No matter what else was happening in her life, at least her business was surviving. Thriving, even. The stacks of boxes waiting to be delivered gave her a sense of accomplishment and pride. And that was exactly what she needed at the moment.

This temporary kitchen was her solace. Here she could remember who and what she was. Remind herself that she was building a future for herself. And if that future didn't involve Rafe Cole—she frowned and mentally corrected, Rafe *King*—she would find a way to deal with it.

While the latest batch of cream-cheese cookies baked, Katie wandered to the windows and looked out at the backyard. It was slowly returning to what it had once been. The piles of discarded flooring and plasterboard were gone. Blue tarps covering the grass had been folded and stored away in the crew's trailer, with only squares of dried grass to mark where they had been. The crew was nearing the end of the job and Katie's heart ached at the thought. Her last connection to Rafe was quickly dissolving.

Despite her determination to be strong and self-sufficient, a small, whiny part of her wanted to see Rafe again. Didn't seem to care that he had lied to her. Repeatedly. There was still a dull pain wrapped around her heart and she knew instinctively that it wouldn't stop hurting any time soon.

She hadn't seen Rafe since that night at the restaurant. Apparently his "bet" with Joe had ended the moment she discovered the truth. Rafe had simply walked away without a backward glance, as far as she knew, and it didn't look as though he'd be back. Really, it was as if he had never been here at all, she thought, watching Steve and Arturo carry in the last of the newly refinished cabinet doors.

Katie had walked through her kitchen only that morning in the pre-dawn silence. The pleasure she would have taken in the remodel was muted by the absence of the man who was taking up far too many of her thoughts.

The kitchen was exactly as she had pictured it. The tile floors and granite countertops were in place. All that was left was the finishing work. A few more doors, installing the new drawer pulls and light fixtures, and then her house would be hers again. The crew would leave and she would be alone, with no more contact with King Construction.

Or Rafe.

That twinge of pain twisted in her chest again and

she wondered if it would always be a part of her. She sighed and so didn't hear a thing when Joe entered the patio kitchen.

"Katie?"

She whirled around, startled, to face the man who had been a part of what she now thought of as the Great Lie. He looked uncomfortable, as he had since discovering that she now knew the truth.

Her voice was cool, but polite. "Hello, Joe."

She actually saw him flinch. Though Rafe hadn't been around, she knew that he had been in contact with Joe to tell him that the jig, so to speak, was up.

He shifted position as if he were nervous. "Just wanted to let you know your new stove will be delivered and installed tomorrow morning."

"That's good, thanks."

"The inspector's signed off on everything so we'll move the refrigerator back into the kitchen this afternoon."

"All right." It was almost over, she thought. She wouldn't spend another day cooking in her temporary kitchen. The batch of cookies in the oven now would be the last she baked in her old stove.

"And," he continued, "the guys will be here to help the installers. Then they'll do the last of the finishing jobs and we'll be out of your hair by tomorrow afternoon."

"Okay."

Katie tucked her hands into the pockets of her jeans and as she stood there watching Joe in his misery, she almost felt sorry for him. None of this was his fault. The morning after that scene at the restaurant Joe had explained what had happened and all about the bet Rafe had lost to him.

He'd apologized for going along with Rafe's lies,

but Katie knew he also hadn't had much choice in the matter, either. As an employee, he could hardly argue with the boss. With that thought in mind, she managed to give the man a small smile.

"I have to admit, I'm looking forward to getting my life back," she said. She wouldn't confess to missing Rafe. Not to Joe. Not to anyone.

"Yeah," he muttered, voice still gloomy. "I'll bet."

She noticed he was crumpling an invoice in one tight fist and asked, "Is that the last one?"

He looked down at the paper as if surprised to see it. Then he smoothed it out before holding it out to her. "Your last payment includes the little extras you asked for along the way that were off contract."

Katie nodded and walked over to take it. She didn't even glance at the total. "I'll have a check for you tomorrow."

"That'll be fine." He turned to leave, then stopped and looked at her again. "I'm really sorry, Katie. About everything."

She flushed and now it was her turn to be uncomfortable. Blast Rafe King for putting her in this position. "It wasn't your doing."

"It was, in a way," he insisted, apparently unwilling to let it go that easily. "You know, Rafe's actually a good guy."

"Of course you'd say that," she told him with a sad smile. "You work for him."

"I do," Joe argued, animation coming into his face at last as he tried to defend his employer. "And that's why I'm in a position to know just what kind of man he is. You can tell a lot about a person in the way they treat the people around them. Rafe's not an easy man, but he's a fair one."

"To whom?" Only moments ago, she'd been feeling sympathetic toward Joe since Rafe had put him in such an awkward position. But now, outrage began to bristle inside her. "Was it fair to lie to me? To force you to go along with the lie?"

Joe scowled and scrubbed one hand over his jaw. "No, it wasn't. But he was paying off his bet to me, so I think we should cut him some slack. Not all employers would have had the spine to honor the debt like that."

"Honor?" A burst of laughter shot from Katie's throat.

"Yeah," he said flatly. "Honor. I don't know what happened between you two and I don't want to know. But I can tell you that Rafe's not a man who goes out of his way to treat people badly."

"Just a happy accident, then?" she sniped and instantly regretted it when Joe winced. Honestly, why was she taking her anger and hurt out on him? He hadn't done anything to her beyond supporting Rafe's lies. It was Rafe who had set everything in motion. Rafe who had slept with her and *still* lied to her. Rafe who had let her believe that something amazing was coming to life between them, all the time knowing that it was a sham.

Katie struggled for control and found it. Forcing a smile she didn't feel, she said, "Joe, why don't we just call this a draw and agree not to talk about Rafe King?"

A moment or two passed when it looked as though he might argue with her. But at last, Joe nodded in surrender. "That's fine, then. I'll just let you get back to work and go see if I can help the boys finish up any faster."

She watched him go, then took a deep breath and tried to push Rafe from her mind. Again.

Naturally, it didn't work.

It had been almost a week since he'd last seen Katie Charles.

Rafe felt like a caged man. He was trapped in his own memories of her no matter what he did to try to shake them loose. Her image haunted his dreams, and awake, he couldn't seem to keep thoughts of her at bay. Didn't matter where he was or what he did, Katie was never more than a thought away.

Hell, he'd even considered calling one of the women he knew, to dive back into his life. Get back in the normal swing of things. But damned if he'd been able to make himself do it. No, he had a charity event he had to go to in a few days, but until then, he wasn't going out.

Didn't have the patience to put up with any of the women he knew and wasn't interested in finding someone new.

He just wanted to be alone. But not by himself. Which didn't make sense even to him.

He had tried holing up in his suite at the hotel, locking himself away with only his racing brain to keep him company. But the hotel rooms felt sterile, impersonal, and the echoing emptiness had pounded on him until he thought he might lose what was left of his mind.

So here he sat, trying to focus on inventory and supply sheets while images of Katie taunted him. To make matters worse, there was Sean. The problem with coming into King Construction offices, Rafe told himself, was that he couldn't really avoid his brothers.

"What is your problem?" Sean asked.

"I'm fine," Rafe insisted, keeping his head down, his gaze on the paperwork scattered across his desk. "Just get off my back, all right?"

Sean laughed. "Trust me when I say, I'd love to. But you're making everyone around here nuts. When Janice was doing some phone work for me, she *begged* me to get you out of the office."

That's great, he thought. Always before, Rafe had kept his personal and business lives separate. Now though, it seemed his lousy attitude was bleeding into the office. Hell, maybe he should take some time off. But if he did that, his mind would have far too much time to think about Katie. So whether his assistant was happy about it or not, he wasn't going anywhere.

Rafe scowled and looked up to watch his brother stroll around the perimeter of his office. When Sean stopped at a shelf and plucked a signed baseball off its pedestal, Rafe grumbled, "Put that down." When he complied, Rafe demanded, "Why is *my* assistant doing work for you anyway? Don't you have your own? What happened to Kelly?"

Sighing, Sean walked over and perched on the edge of Rafe's desk. "She eloped last weekend."

"That's the third assistant you've lost this year, isn't it?"

"Yeah. I've got to stop hiring the pretty ones," Sean mused. "Inevitably, they run off and get married and leave me swinging in the wind."

"Well, call the temp agency and get someone in here. Just leave Janice alone."

"Funny," Sean said, his eyes narrowing as he watched Rafe thoughtfully, "she'd rather work for me these days."

Disgusted, Rafe muttered, "Yeah, well, she doesn't."

"Better she work for me than quit. And until you lighten up, nobody wants anything to do with you. So why don't you just tell me what's going on?"

"Work," Rafe said flatly, his gaze giving nothing away as he glared at his brother. "You should try it."

"Just so you know? The whole 'King Glare' thing doesn't work on me. I can do it too, remember?"

Rafe tossed his pen to the desktop and, giving into the irritation flooding his system, jumped out of his chair as if he couldn't bear to sit still any longer. Turning his back on his brother, he stared out the window at the spread of sunlit ocean before him. There were a few sailboats out on the water today and in the distance, fishermen lined the pier. Gray clouds gathered on the horizon and the wind whipped the waves into choppy whitecaps.

"So," Sean asked again, "what's going on?"

He glanced back over his shoulder. He knew his younger brother wouldn't go away until he got some answers. And a part of Rafe wanted to say it all out loud anyway, so he blurted, "Found out which King hurt Katie."

"Yeah? Who?"

"Cordell."

"Should have thought of him," Sean mused with a nod. "He goes through women faster than Jesse used to."

At mention of their now-married cousin, Rafe almost smiled. As a former professional surfer, Jesse King's reputation with the ladies had been staggering. Of course, that was before he married Bella and became a father.

"How'd you find out who it was?"

Rafe muttered an oath and looked at Sean. "Ran into Cordell when I took Katie to dinner."

"Ouch." Sean nodded thoughtfully, clearly understanding the situation.

"Yeah. That about covers it." Pushing one hand through his hair, Rafe looked back at the ocean and said, "It all happened pretty fast. I punched him. Then he told Katie who I was. Then she left."

"And you let her go."

Swiveling his head around, he glared at Sean again. "What was I supposed to do? Hold her captive?"

"Or talk to her?"

"She was through talking," Rafe assured him, remembering the look in her eyes as she faced him down. He'd seen the pain glittering brightly in tears she hadn't let fall. He'd heard the betrayal in her voice and felt the sharp sting of his own lies catching up with him.

"So that's it?" Sean asked.

"That's it." Deliberately, Rafe turned his back on the view, ignored his brother and took a seat behind his desk again. Picking up his pen, he stared blindly at the supply sheets.

"Can't believe you're going to let her get away."

"I didn't *let* her do anything," Rafe muttered, still not looking up at Sean. "Katie makes her own decisions. And now she has more reason than ever to hate the Kings. Most especially, *me*."

Blowing out a breath, Sean stood up but didn't leave. "And you're okay with that?"

"Of course I am," Rafe lied and mentally congratulated himself on just how good he was getting at it. "I always intended to walk away from her, Sean. It just happened a little faster than I'd planned."

God, that was a lie, too.

"Right." Sean slapped one hand down on top of the papers, forcing Rafe to look up at him.

"Butt out, Sean," he ground out.

"Hell no," his brother said, frustration simmering in the air between them. "You're not usually a stupid guy, Rafe. But this time, you're being an idiot."

No, he wasn't. Katie didn't want to see him and he couldn't blame her. Besides, it was better this way. If she was mad at him, she wouldn't stay hurt for long. She'd get over it. So would he. He was no good at love and he knew it. Better he hurt her now than destroy her later.

"Thanks for the input." Rafe peeled Sean's hand off the papers. "Now go away."

"If you don't go after her," Sean said quietly, "you'll regret it."

Rafe already regretted it. Enough that his soul felt as if it was withering and his heart could barely summon the energy to beat.

"I've had regrets before," he finally said. "Let's remember Leslie."

"Uh-huh. Speaking of your ex…I hear you hired her husband."

Rafe sighed. Yes, he had hired John. And he was forced to admit that he might not have if he hadn't met Katie. Being with her had allowed him to face his own past. And the talk with Leslie had been eye-opening enough that he'd been able to reach out to an old friend. Maybe he and John would actually be close again someday.

If they were, that too would be laid at Katie's feet. Her optimism and rosy outlook on life had affected him more than he would have thought possible. Rafe shifted in his chair. He didn't want to talk about any of this. Hell, he didn't want to talk at all.

"So the question is," Sean continued, oblivious to the fact that Rafe wanted him gone, "why is it you can make peace with John and Leslie, but you won't go see the woman you're crazy about?"

Several silent, tense seconds passed before Rafe finally asked, "Are you going to leave? Or do I have to?"

"I'll go," Sean said amiably. "But that won't solve your problem for you."

"Yeah?" Rafe countered. "What will?"

Sean laughed at him and shook his head as he opened the door. "You already know the answer to that, Rafe. You just don't want to admit it."

Twelve

"It's really gorgeous, honey," Emily O'Hara said as she walked through the completely remodeled kitchen. "I love the floor and the counters are just beautiful."

Katie should have been cooing over her finished kitchen too, but somehow she couldn't muster up the enthusiasm for it. Heck, in the two days since the crew left, she hadn't even made a single batch of cookies in her shiny new stove.

Her gaze swept the remodeled room, trying to see it as Nana was, from the slate gray tiles to the pearlized blue granite counters to the dark blue walls and she felt... nothing. It was all perfect and it meant...nothing.

"All right, sweetie," her grandmother said, coming up to give her a brief, comforting hug. "You've got the kitchen of your dreams, but you're standing there looking as if you just found out cookies had been banned. Tell me what's wrong."

The tears that Katie had been holding at bay for days crested again and before she could stop them, one or two trailed down her cheeks. Her heart ached and it felt as though there were a boulder sitting on her chest. She could hardly draw a breath without wheezing. "Oh, Nana, *everything's* wrong."

"Honey…" The older woman sighed and steered Katie across the room. An ancient, round pedestal table and captain chairs sat before the wide window where sunlight splashed and curtains danced in a soft wind. Emily pushed her granddaughter into one of the chairs, then sat down beside her. "Talk to me."

Where to start? Katie wondered. With the fact that she was in love with a man she didn't really know? That she'd allowed herself to get bamboozled by the King family? *Again?* Or should she just admit that she wasn't getting over it this time? That she would *never* get over it? That she couldn't sleep, she couldn't eat, she didn't even want to bake anymore. And that was saying something. She just couldn't bring herself to care about anything but the gaping hole in her own heart.

"It's Rafe," she said, slumping back into her chair. "He lied to me."

"I know."

"What?" Katie blinked at her grandmother and waited for an explanation. But the older woman just sat there in the sunlight, smiling benevolently. "How? What? How?"

Emily reached over, patted Katie's hand, then sighed and leaned back in her chair. "I know his real name is Rafe King, if that's what you're talking about."

"Well, yeah, it is."

"Do you want tea? We should have some tea."

"I don't want tea," Katie said, stopping her grandmother before the woman could get up. "I want some answers. You know about Rafe? For how long?"

She waved one hand dismissively. "Oh, I knew the minute you introduced us."

"How?" Katie just stared at her in rapt confusion. "Do you have some kind of inner lie radar that I didn't get?"

"No, and I don't think I'd want it, either. Sometimes lies can be a good thing," Emily said, her gaze locked on Katie.

"Lying is *not* a good thing. You're the one who taught me that, remember?"

Again, Emily waved a hand, effectively wiping away that little nugget of so-called wisdom. "That was different. You were ten. Now you're an adult and surely you've learned that sometimes a small, harmless lie is far better than a hurtful truth."

"This lie wasn't harmless," Katie argued, remembering the sting of betrayal when she'd discovered Rafe's game. "And you still haven't told me how you knew who he was."

"If you read popular magazines once in a while, you would have known him too," Nana said with a huff. "There's always one King or another's picture in there. I recognized Rafe from a picture taken at a movie premiere."

"A premiere." Katie shook her head and felt her heart drop through the floor. He was used to dating actresses and going to fabulous parties. Oh, he must have gotten such a laugh from the spur-of-the-moment barbecue in her backyard.

Annoyance flickered into anger and soon that hot little bubble of fury was frothing into real rage. "I can't believe it. He must have thought I was an idiot for not recognizing him." She paused for a glare at her grandmother. "And why didn't you *tell* me?"

"Because," Emily said. "You needed your life shaken up a little. Besides, he's a cutie-patootie and you can't hang *all* of the Kings for what one of them did."

"*Two* of them now," Katie reminded her.

"All right, yes, Rafe's not looking too good at the moment," Emily admitted. "But did you give him a chance to explain?"

"Oh, he explained. I was a bet gone wrong."

"Katie…"

She shook her head and held up both hands. "No, Nana, there's no excuse for what he did. He lied to me and that's it."

"I lied to you too, sweetie," her grandmother pointed out in a small voice.

Sighing, Katie said, "Yeah, but you didn't do it to hurt me."

"No, I didn't. And maybe that wasn't Rafe's intention, either."

"We'll never know, will we?" Katie muttered, as anger seeped away into the wide black hole she seemed to be carrying around inside her these days.

"You could find out if you'd stop hiding away in your house and go see him." Emily frowned and looked at her steadily. "Are you really going to become a hermit while he's out having a good time?"

That caught her attention quickly enough. Rafe was having a good time? Where? And a moment later the more important question—*with who?*—leaped into mind.

"What do you mean?" Katie asked, voice tight.

Her nana sighed again and reached for the morning paper, still folded and unopened on the kitchen table.

"Honestly, Katie, if you paid a little more attention to current events…"

"What does that have to do with anything?"

Silently, Emily discarded the news section and went straight to Lifestyles. Thumbing through it, she finally found what she was looking for and folded it back. Then she laid it down in front of Katie and stabbed a grainy black-and-white picture with her manicured nail. "It means, you can find out a lot by keeping up with gossip. Like for example…there."

Katie looked at the picture and felt the tightening in her chest ratchet up until she couldn't get any air in her lungs. She was light-headed. That had to be the reason her vision was narrowing until all she could see was the picture in the paper. The picture of an unsmiling Rafe in a tuxedo at a charity fundraiser, with a blond sporting boobs twice the size of Katie's clinging to his arm.

"When was—" She broke off as she read the caption under the photo. "Two nights ago."

"*He's* not curled up in the fetal position like someone else I could mention," Emily murmured.

"That rat. That *creep*." Katie slowly rose from her chair, clutching the paper in her fists. Her gaze still locked on the picture, all she could see was Rafe's face, glaring at the camera as if he were wishing the photographer into the darkest bowels of Hell.

"Atta girl," her grandmother whispered.

"He told me I was *important* to him," Katie said, fury coloring her voice until it quivered and shook with the force of it. "He must have been lying *again*. If I was so damn important, how is he out with this bimbo?"

"To be fair, we're not sure she's a bimbo," Nana said.

Katie glared at her. "Whose side are you on?"

"Right."

"Does he think I'm stupid?" Katie asked, not waiting for an answer. "Did he really believe I wouldn't find out that less than a week after—after—that he'd be dating the rich and pointless again? Does he think I don't read the paper?"

"Well," Emily pointed out easily, "you don't."

"I will from now on," Katie promised, giving the paper a hard shake.

"So, what're you going to do about this?"

Katie finally lifted her gaze and looked into her grandmother's eyes. With cold, hard determination she said simply, "I'm going to go dethrone a King."

Rafe couldn't settle.

He felt uncomfortable in his own skin.

Which left him nowhere to run.

Not that he would. Kings didn't run. Kings didn't hide.

But then if that were true, why wasn't he over at Katie's house right now, demanding she listen to him? Grumbling, he stood up, walked to the window of his office and stared out at the view without even seeing it. The ocean could have dried up for all the notice he gave it. There might as well have been empty sand dunes stretching out into eternity out there. He didn't care. It didn't matter. Nothing did.

He'd tried going back to his life, but it was a damned empty one. Hell, he couldn't even go into his hotel suite anymore. The silence was too much to take. So instead, he stayed here. At the office. He'd been sleeping on the damn couch, if you could call it sleep.

Every time he closed his eyes, he saw Katie, as she had been that last night. Quivering in his arms. Kissing him breathless. Then finally, staring at him out of hurt-filled eyes. And if he had been able to figure out how to do it, he'd have punched his own face in days ago.

The intercom buzzed and he walked to stab a finger at the button. "Damn it, Janice, I told you I didn't want to be disturbed."

"Yes, but there's—" she said, then added, "Wait! You can't go in!" just before his office door crashed open.

Katie stood in the doorway, her green eyes flashing at him dangerously. Her hair was a wild tumble of curls around her shoulders. She wore a black skirt, a red button-down shirt that was opened enough that he could see where her silver necklace dipped into the valley of her breasts. And she was wearing those black high heels she'd been wearing their last night together.

Altogether, she looked like a woman dressed for seduction. But with the fury in her eyes, any man she was aimed at might not survive. Rafe was willing to take his chances. And if she did end up putting him down, he couldn't think of a better way to go.

"Sorry," Janice was saying as she brushed past Katie with a frown. "She got past me and—"

"It's okay, Janice. Close the door on your way out."

"Yes sir," she said and, though curiosity was stamped on her face, she did what he asked and left he and Katie alone.

"It's good to see you," he said, knowing that for the understatement of the century.

"It won't be in a minute," Katie promised and stalked toward him like an avenging angel on a mission. She dipped one hand into the black purse hanging off her shoulder and came back up with a folded newspaper.

Once she had it, she threw it at him. He caught it instinctively and gave it a quick glance. Ah. Now he knew what was behind the fresh fury driving her. And weirdly, it gave him a shot of hope that she wasn't lost to him completely since that picture had definitely pissed her off.

"Did you think I wouldn't see it?" she said, her voice little more than a snarl. "Or was it just that you didn't care if I saw it? Game over, bet won, moving on? Was that it?"

"It wasn't a game, Katie," he said and his tone was as tight as the tension coiled inside him. "I told you that. Or I tried to."

"And I should believe you," she said, dropping her purse onto the closest chair and stabbing one finger at the newspaper he tossed to his desk. "Because clearly you missed me so much you had to rush out and drown your sorrows in that blonde double D."

He grinned at her, even knowing that would only feed the flames of her wrath. Rafe couldn't help himself. Hell, he could hardly believe she was standing here. Even gloriously furious, she was the only woman who could make his heart lift out of the darkness he carried inside him. The only woman who made him want to smile. Who made him want to promise her any damn thing she wanted as long as she never left him again.

He thought briefly about what Cordell had said at the restaurant the other night. *Another King bites the dust.* He'd argued the point then, out of sheer stubbornness and a refusal to see the truth for what it was.

But now that Katie was standing here in front of him, bubbling with a fury that had her green eyes flashing like fireworks, he knew he couldn't deny the facts any longer. Not even to himself. More importantly, he didn't want to.

He was in love for the first time in his life.

And damned if he'd lose her.

"Don't you dare laugh at me," she warned.

"Not laughing." Reaching out, he grabbed hold of her shoulders and only tightened his grip when she tried to twist free. "Katie, that blonde is an actress. Under contract to my cousin Jefferson's film company. I had to go to the charity thing anyway and he asked me to escort her to get her some media."

She wasn't mollified. "And I should believe that *why?*"

"Because she was boring and vapid and I had a terrible time because she wasn't you. And…because I won't lie to you again, Katie."

Some of the fight went out of her. The rigidity in her shoulders faded enough that he risked easing his grip on her. She didn't step away from him when she had the opportunity and Rafe silently considered that a good sign.

"I miss you," he said before he could gauge his words and try to predict her reaction.

Her delectable mouth flattened into a grim line. "I'm still furious with you."

"I get that." But she was *here* and he was taking that as a good sign. She looked up at him with those gorgeous green eyes and Rafe knew that he had only this one shot. This one chance to redeem himself. To somehow salvage the most important relationship he'd ever known.

So the words came slowly, but they came.

Words he had never thought to say to anyone.

"I wasn't ready for you," he started and read the confusion in her eyes. "The bet with Joe? It shouldn't have been a big deal. But then I met you and found out you hated the Kings and I knew if I told you the truth, you'd never look at me again."

She frowned, and bit into her bottom lip as if trying to keep herself from talking so that she could hear him out completely.

"I told myself that I wanted to change your mind about the King family," he said and watched a flash of something in her eyes come and go. "But it wasn't only that. Like I said, I knew you'd never look at me again if you knew. And I *wanted* you to look at me, Katie," he said, shifting one hand to cup her cheek. "I wanted a lot more than that, too."

"You got more, Rafe," she said, her voice so quiet he had to strain to hear her. "You got more than I ever gave anyone before. I *loved* you. So when I found out you had lied to me, it hurt far deeper than anything Cordell made me feel."

"I know," he told her, mentally holding fast to the word *loved*. If she had loved him then, she had to love him still. It couldn't burn out that fast, no matter how angry she was. "I know."

He pulled her close and kissed her once, twice. It was soft and hard, passionate and tender. That one kiss carried his heart and he nearly sighed in relief when she leaned into him to return that kiss, however hesitantly she did it.

Pulling back, he let his gaze move over her features, as if burning this moment, her expression, into his brain. Finally though, he drew away and said, "I told you I wasn't ready for you and that's the honest truth. But I don't know how I could have been prepared for what you would do to me."

"Rafe…"

He shook his head and laid his fingertips over her

mouth. "No, let me say it. You grew up with your grandmother, your mom. You knew you were loved and you knew how to respond to it. I didn't. My dad was a lousy role model and I hardly knew my mother. When I got married, it was for all the wrong reasons and when she left, my ex let me know that it was *my* failings, my inability to love, that ruined everything—"

Katie's eyes shone brightly as she reached up to smooth her palm across his jaw. "She was wrong."

"No," he said, "she wasn't. Because until I met you, I didn't know how to love."

"Oh, Rafe…"

His heart felt light for the first time in days. His soul was warm again because she was near. Rafe knew that this one woman was the center of his world. If he couldn't convince her to take a chance on him—to love him in spite of all the reasons she shouldn't—then he'd never have anything worth a damn.

"Look, I'm a bad bet," Rafe told her, determined to be completely honest with her even if it cost him what he wanted most. "I know that. But I love you, Katie. In my whole life, I've never loved anything else."

Tears glittered in her eyes and his stomach hitched. Happy tears? Or goodbye?

She took a breath, let it slide from her lungs and admitted, "I want to believe you."

Rafe smiled and pulled her in close to him, where she could feel the hammering of his heart in his chest. Where she would feel the strength of his love wrapping itself around her.

"Take a chance on me, Katie," he whispered, dipping his head to kiss the curve of her neck. He inhaled the scent of her and smiled as cinnamon and vanilla surrounded him. "I swear you'll never regret it."

"Rafe?"

He pulled back to look into her eyes and before she could speak again he said, "Marry me, Katie. Marry me and let me live with you in that great old house. Let me make you happy. I know I can. I'll prove to you that I can be what you need."

"Yes, I'll marry you." Finally, a slow smile curved her mouth and she reached up with both hands to cup his face between her palms. "Don't you know that you're *already* everything that I need?"

"Thank God," he whispered and kissed her again, a promise of more to come.

"After all, you did build me a nearly perfect kitchen."

"Nearly?" he asked with a grin.

"Well, I've suddenly decided that since I'm marrying a carpenter, he should be able to build me a pantry."

"Anything you want, Katie," he promised with a grin. "But I warn you, as soon as he finds out we're getting married, my brother Sean's going to want cookies."

"For family?" she said, *"Anything."*

Rafe dropped his head and rested his forehead against Katie's, feeling his world, his life slide into place again. The woman he loved was in the circle of his arms, and the future was suddenly looking bright. He was right where he wanted to be. Where he was supposed to be.

With Katie Charles, the cookie queen.

Epilogue

Katie grinned as she looked out the kitchen window at her crowded backyard. "I never dreamed there were so many Kings in California."

Julie King, married to Travis, laughed as she pulled a bowl of pasta salad from the fridge. "And this isn't all of them by any means."

"Wait until your wedding," Maggie King, wife of Justice warned her. "They'll *all* be there for that."

"Yep," Jericho's wife Daisy agreed. "They never miss a wedding. Jeff and Maura will even come in from Ireland for that."

"It's a little intimidating," Katie admitted, unwrapping a platter of cookies designed especially for their engagement party. There were dozens of golden crowns, frosted in yellow or white, with Katie and Rafe inscribed on them.

She glanced down at the emerald engagement ring

glittering on her finger and almost hugged herself just to make sure she was awake and not dreaming all of this. But remembering the night before, when Rafe had made love to her for hours and then held her as she slept was enough to convince her that yes. Her life really was perfect.

It had been a month since she'd stormed her way into his office and he laid siege to her heart with the truth. And in that time, she hadn't once regretted taking a chance on Rafe. He'd shown her in countless little ways just how important she was to him. He'd built her that specially designed pantry just as he'd promised. He sent her flowers, made her dinner and when she was tired, he gave her a fabulous foot rub that inevitably led to long, lovely hours in bed.

"Uh-oh," Daisy said with a laugh. "I know that smile."

"What?" Katie grinned, embarrassed to be caught daydreaming.

"It's the same one I get when I remember how I ended up with a gorgeous baby girl." Standing up, Daisy smiled. "And speaking of Delilah, think I'll just go and make sure Jericho's not teaching her how to do something dangerous. The man's got a thing about his daughter being the first female Navy SEAL."

"I know how she feels," Ivy King said, rubbing a rounded belly. "Tanner already plans on our poor baby being the next computer genius of the universe. But no pressure."

As Daisy left and the other King wives laughed and chatted about their kids and their husbands, Katie took a minute to enjoy where she was. Her nana had been right all along of course. Which Emily had continued to remind her of over the last month. Love was worth taking a chance on. Because Katie had risked it, she was about to marry the man she loved, become a part of a huge family and, one day, start her own.

Babies. They would come soon. Rafe had already talked about how he wanted to add to the next generation of the King family.

"It's funny," Katie said softly to the women who were already her friends as well as almost-relatives. "Just a few months ago, I hated the Kings."

"Yeah," Jackson's wife Casey said as she unwrapped a sheath of plastic cups, "we all heard about Cordell. If it helps, everyone knows he's a dog."

Maggie chimed in with, "Justice offered to beat him up, as soon as Cordell arrived today, but apparently Rafe already took care of it."

"Yeah, he did," Katie assured them. "But as much as I hate to admit it, without Cordell being a jerk, I might never have fallen in love with Rafe."

"So, it was worth it then?" Jesse's wife Bella asked.

"More than," Katie assured them. Then she glanced out the window to see her neighbor Nicole walking into the yard with her son in tow. "A friend of mine just showed up. I'll be back to finish up the potato salad!"

"No, you won't," Julie told her. "This is *your* engagement party. Go out and enjoy it. We'll take care of the setup."

Smiling, Katie left her beautiful kitchen and walked into the yard. Her grandmother and aunt were in heaven, playing with all of the King kids. The men were gathered around the brick barbecue Rafe had finished building only last week, arguing over the best way to grill steaks. She caught a glimpse of Rafe in the middle of them all and couldn't help smiling. She had been so wrong. The rich weren't snobby. At least, the Kings weren't. They were just people.

"This is some party," Nicole said as she walked up and gave Katie a hug.

"It is. And I'm so glad you came."

"Wouldn't have missed it. As your future matron of honor, it's my duty to sit here and have a beer and eat steak." Nicole picked Connor up and placed him on her hip. "And your ring bearer wants a cookie."

Katie laughed, delighted, and leaned in to kiss Connor. "My special ring bearer can have as many cookies as I can sneak him!"

When two strong, familiar arms snaked around her middle from behind, Katie leaned back into Rafe's chest with a sigh of satisfaction.

"Hi, Nicole," he said, planting a quick kiss on Katie's head. "Glad you could make it."

"Are you kidding? Wouldn't be anywhere else," she told him. Then with a wry smile at the two of them, she added, "I'll just take Connor in to grab a cookie. We'll see you later."

Rafe turned her to face him and Katie flung her arms around his neck. He kissed her hard and long and deep and when her head was buzzing and her balance had completely dissolved, he lifted his head and looked down at her. "Have I told you today how much I love you?"

"You have," she said, "but I never get tired of hearing it."

"Good. I plan to say it often. Just so you never forget it."

"Not a chance," she promised.

He rested his forehead against hers. "So, after meeting the thundering herd of Kings, you still want to marry me next month?"

His tone was joking, but she knew that a part of him

was still worried that something might happen to tear them apart. He might not believe that he was capable of love, but Katie knew differently. Rafe King had more love to give than most men, simply because he'd never known it before. And she knew that once his heart was given, it was forever.

"You're not getting away from me now, Rafe," she said softly. "We're getting married and I am going to love you forever."

His eyes flashed, his mouth curved, and he pulled her in hard against him for a hug that left her breathless. But who needed to breathe when you were surrounded by love?

When he finally let her go, he draped one arm around her shoulders and, together, they walked into the circle of family.

* * * * *

He needed more time with her.

His mind filled with a vision of Alexa chasing his kids around, all wet from the tub. Warm memories pulled him in with a reminder of the family life he should be having right now and wasn't because of his workload. Having Alexa here felt so right.

It was right.

And so he wasn't sending her home in the morning. He not only needed her help with the children, he wanted her to stay for personal reasons. The explosive chemistry they'd just discovered didn't come around often. Hell, he couldn't remember when he'd ever burned to have a particular woman this much. So much the craving filled his mind as well as his body.

The extension of their trip presented the perfect opportunity to follow that attraction to its ultimate destination.

Landing her directly into his bed.

Dear Reader,

As an avid reader myself, I adore connected stories! When I'm intrigued by a secondary character in a novel, I'm ecstatic when that character gets his or her own happily-ever-after. It's especially a thrill when readers write to me, asking about a potential book for one of my characters.

In this case, readers have been asking for Seth Jansen's story since his extended family first appeared in one of my novels, *Explosive Alliance*, and then again in my early Desire novels *Baby, I'm Yours* and *Under the Millionaire's Influence*. This book—*Billionaire's Jet Set Babies*—can be read as a stand-alone. However, if you would like to find those earlier reads about Seth and his family, they have all been reissued in ebook form.

Thanks again to all of you who sent shout-outs for Seth Jansen's story. I had a blast penning the long-awaited happily-ever-after for this jet-setting hero!

Cheers,

Catherine Mann

www.CatherineMann.com

BILLIONAIRE'S JET-SET BABIES

BY
CATHERINE MANN

Published in Great Britain 2012
by Mills & Boon, an imprint of Harlequin (UK) Limited,
Eton House, 18-24 Paradise Road, Richmond, Surrey TW9 1SR

© Catherine Mann 2011

ISBN: 978 0 263 89163 8
ebook ISBN: 978 1 408 97183 3

951-0512

Harlequin (UK) policy is to use papers that are natural, renewable and recyclable products and made from wood grown in sustainable forests. The logging and manufacturing processes conform to the legal environmental regulations of the country of origin.

Printed and bound in Spain
by Blackprint CPI, Barcelona

USA TODAY bestselling author **Catherine Mann** is living out her own fairy-tale ending on a sunny Florida beach with her Prince Charming husband and their four children. With more than thirty-five books in print in more than twenty countries, she has also celebrated wins for both a RITA® Award and a Booksellers' Best Award. Catherine enjoys chatting with readers online—thanks to the wonders of the wireless internet, which allows her to network with her laptop by the water! To learn more about her work, visit her website, www.catherinemann. com, or reach her by snail mail at PO Box 6065, Navarre, FL 32566, USA.

To Amelia Richard: a treasured reader, reviewer and friend. Thank you for all you've done to help spread the word about my stories. You're awesome!

One

Alexa Randall had accumulated an eclectic boxful of lost and found items since opening her own cleaning company for charter jets. There were the standard smart phones, portfolios, tablets, even a Patek Philippe watch. She'd returned each to its owner.

Then there were the stray panties and men's boxers, even the occasional sex toys from Mile High Club members. All of those items, she'd picked up with latex gloves and tossed in the trash.

But today marked a first find ever in the history of A-1 Aircraft Cleaning Services. Never before had she found a baby left on board—actually, *two* babies.

Her bucket of supplies dropped to the industrial blue carpet with a heavy thud that startled the sleeping pair. Yep, two infants, apparently twins with similar blond curly hair and cherub cheeks. About one year old, perhaps? A boy and a girl, it seemed, gauging from their pink and blue smocked outfits and gender-matched car seats.

Tasked to clean the jet alone, Alexa had no one to share her shock with. She flipped on another table lamp in the main compartment of the sleek private jet, the lighting in the hangar sketchy at best even at three in the afternoon.

Both kids were strapped into car seats resting on the leather sofa along the side of the plane, which was Seth Jansen's personal aircraft. As in *the* Seth Jansen of Jansen Jets. The self-made billionaire who'd raked in a fortune inventing some must-have security device for airports to help combat possible terrorist attacks on planes during takeoffs and landings. She admired the man's entrepreneurial spirit.

Landing his account would be her company's big break. She needed this first cleaning of his aircraft to go off without a hitch.

Tiny fists waved for a second, slowing, lowering, until both babies began to settle back to sleep. Another huffy sigh shuddered through the girl before her breaths evened out. Her little arm landed on a piece of paper safety-pinned to the girl's hem.

Narrowing her eyes, Alexa leaned forward and read:

Seth,
You always say you want more time with the twins, so here's your chance. Sorry for the short notice, but a friend surprised me with a two-week spa retreat. Enjoy your "daddy time" with Olivia and Owen!
XOXO,
Pippa

Pippa?

Alexa straightened again, horrified. Really? Really!

Pippa Jansen, as in the *ex*-Mrs. Jansen, had dumped off her infants on their father's jet. Unreal. Alexa stuffed her fists into the pockets of her navy chinos, standard uniform for A-1 cleaning staff along with a blue polo shirt bearing the company's logo.

And who signed a note to their obviously estranged baby daddy with kisses and hugs? Alexa sank down into a fat chair across from the pint-size passengers. Bigger question of the day, who left babies unattended on an airplane?

A crappy parent, that's who.

The rich and spoiled rotten, who played by their own rules, a sad reality she knew only too well from growing up in that world. People had told her how lucky she was as a kid—lucky to have a dedicated nanny that she spent more time with than she did with either of her parents.

The best thing that had ever happened to her? Her father bankrupted the family's sportswear chain— once worth billions, now worth zip. That left Alexa the recipient of a trust fund from Grandma containing a couple of thousand dollars.

She'd used the money to buy a partnership in a cleaning service about to go under because the aging owner could no longer carry the workload on her own. Bethany—her new partner—had been grateful for Alexa's energy and the second chance for A-1 Aircraft Cleaning Services to stay afloat. Using Alexa's contacts from her family's world of luxury and extravagance she had revitalized the struggling business. Alexa's ex-husband, Travis, had been appalled by her new occupation and offered to help out financially so she wouldn't have to work.

She would rather scrub toilets.

And the toilet on this particular Gulfstream III jet was very important to her. She had to land the Jansen Jet contract and hopefully this one-time stint would impress him enough to cinch the deal. Her business needed this account to survive, especially in today's tough economy. If she failed, she could lose everything and A-1 might well face Chapter 11 bankruptcy. She'd hardly believed her luck when she'd been asked by another cleaning company to subcontract out on one of the Jansen Jets—this jet.

Now that she'd found these two babies, she was screwed. She swept particles of sand from the seat into her hand, eyed the fingerprints on the windows, could almost feel the grit rising from the carpet fiber. But she couldn't just clean up, restock the Evian water and pretend these kids weren't here. She needed to contact airport security, which was going to land Jansen's ex-wife in hot water, possibly him as well. That would piss off Jansen. And the jet still wouldn't be serviced. And then he would never consider her for the contract.

Frustration and a hefty dose of anger stung stronger than a bucket full of ammonia. Scratch cleaning detail for now, scratch cinching this deal that would finally take her company out of the red. She had to locate the twins' father ASAP.

Alexa unclipped the cell phone from her waist and thumbed her directory to find the number for Jansen Jets, which she happened to have since she'd been trying to get through to the guy for a month. She'd never made it further than his secretary, who'd agreed to pass along Alexa's business prospectus.

She eyed the sleeping babies. Maybe some good could come from this mess after all.

Today, she would finally have the chance to talk to the boss, just not how she'd planned and not in a way that would put him in a receptive mood…

The phone stopped ringing as someone picked up.

"Jansen Jets, please hold." As quickly as the thick female Southern drawl answered, the line clicked and Muzak filled the air waves with soulless contemporary tunes.

A squawk from one of the car seats drew her attention. She looked up fast to see Olivia wriggling in her seat, kicking free a Winnie the Pooh blanket. The little girl spit out her Piglet pacifier and whimpered, getting louder until her brother scrunched up his face, blinking awake and none too happy. His Eeyore pacifier dangled from a clip attached to his blue sailor outfit.

Two pairs of periwinkle-blue eyes stared at her, button noses crinkled. Owen's eyes filled with tears. Olivia's bottom lip thrust outward again.

Tucking the Muzak-humming phone under her chin, Alexa hefted the iconic Burberry plaid diaper bag off the floor.

"Hey there, little ones," she said in what she hoped was a conciliatory tone. She'd spent so little time around babies she could only hope she pegged it right. "I know, I know, sweetie, I'm a stranger, but I'm all you've got right now."

And how crummy was that? She stifled another spurt of anger at the faceless Pippa who'd dropped her children off like luggage. When had the spa-hopping mama expected their father to locate them?

"I'm assuming you're Olivia." Alexa tickled the bare foot of the girl wearing a pink smocked dress.

Olivia giggled, and Alexa pulled the pink lace bootie from the baby's mouth. Olivia thrust out her bottom lip—until Alexa unhooked a teething ring from the diaper bag and passed it over to the chubby-cheeked girl.

"And you must be Owen." She tweaked his blue tennis shoe—still on his foot as opposed to his sister who was ditching her other booty across the aisle with the arm of a major league pitcher. "Any idea where your daddy is? Or how much longer he'll be?"

She'd been told by security she had about a half hour to service the inside of the jet in order to be out before Mr. Jansen arrived. As much as she would have liked to meet him, it was considered poor form for the cleaning staff to still be on hand. She'd expected her work and a business card left on the silver drink tray to speak for itself.

So much for her well laid plans.

She scooped up a baby blanket from the floor, folded it neatly and placed it on the couch. She smoothed back Owen's sweaty curls. Going quiet, he stared back at her just as the on hold Muzak cued up "Sweet Caroline"— the fourth song so far. Apparently she'd been relegated to call waiting purgatory.

How long until the kids got hungry? She peeked into the diaper bag for supplies. Maybe she would luck out and find more contact info along the way. Sippy cups of juice, powdered formula, jars of food and diapers, diapers, diapers…

The clank of feet on the stairway outside yanked her upright. She dropped the diaper bag and spun around fast, just as a man filled the open hatch. A tall and broad-shouldered man.

He stood with the sun backlighting him, casting his face in mysterious shadows.

Alexa stepped in front of the babies instinctively, protectively. "Good afternoon. What can I do for you?"

Silently he stepped deeper into the craft until overhead lights splashed over his face and she recognized him from her internet searches. Seth Jansen, founder and CEO of Jansen Jets.

Relief made her knees wobbly. She'd been saved from a tough decision by Jansen's early arrival. And, wow, did the guy ever know how to make an entrance.

From press shots she'd seen he was good-looking, with a kind of matured Abercrombie & Fitch beach hunk appeal. But no amount of Google Images could capture the impact of this tremendously attractive self-made billionaire in person.

Six foot three or four, he filled the charter jet with raw muscled *man*. He wasn't some pale pencil pusher. He was more the size of a keen-eyed lumberjack, in a suit. An expensive, tailored suit.

The previously spacious cabin now felt tight. Intimate.

His sandy-colored hair—thick without being shaggy—sported sun-kissed streaks of lighter blond, the kind that came naturally from being outside rather than sitting in a salon chair. His tan and toned body gave further testimony to that. No raccoon rings around the eyes from tanning bed glasses. The scent of crisp air clung to him, so different from the boardroom aftershaves of her father and her ex. She scrunched her nose at even the memory of cloying cologne and cigars.

Even his eyes spoke of the outdoors. They were the same vibrant green she'd once seen in the waters off the Caribbean coast of St. Maarten, the sort of sparkling green that made you want to dive right into their cool depths. She turned shivery all over just thinking about taking a swim in those pristine waters.

She seriously needed to lighten up on the cleaning supply fumes. How unprofessional to stand here and gawk like a sex-starved divorcée—which she was.

"Good afternoon, Mr. Jansen. I'm Alexa Randall with A-1 Aircraft Cleaning Services."

He shrugged out of his suit jacket, gray pinstripe and almost certainly an Ermenegildo Zegna, a brand known for its no-nonsense look. Expensive. Not surprising.

His open shirt collar, with his burgundy tie loosened did surprise her, however. Overall, she got the impression of an Olympic swimmer confined in an Italian suit.

"Right." He checked his watch—the only non-*GQ* item on him. He wore what appeared to be a top-of-the-line diver's timepiece. "I'm early, I know, but I need to leave right away so if you could speed this up, I would appreciate it."

Jansen charged by, not even hesitating as he passed the two tykes. *His* tykes.

She cleared her throat. "You have a welcoming crew waiting for you."

"I'm sure you're mistaken." He stowed his briefcase, his words clipped. "I'm flying solo today."

She held up Pippa's letter. "It appears, Mr. Jansen, your flight plans have changed."

Seth Jansen stopped dead in his tracks. He looked back over his shoulder at Alexa Randall, the owner of a new, small company that had been trying to get his attention for at least a month. Yeah, he knew who the drop-dead gorgeous blonde was. But he didn't have time to listen to her make a pitch he already knew would be rejected.

While he appreciated persistence as a business professional himself, he did not like gimmicks. "Let's move along to the point, please."

He had less than twenty minutes to get his Gulfstream III into the air and on its way from Charleston, South Carolina, to St. Augustine, Florida. He had a business meeting he'd been working his ass off to land for six months—dinner with the head of security for the Medinas, a deposed royal family that lived in exile in the United States.

Big-time account.

Once in a lifetime opportunity.

And the freedom to devote more of his energies to the philanthropic branch of this company. Freedom. It had a different meaning these days than when he'd flown crop dusters to make his rent back, in North Dakota.

"This—" she waved a piece of floral paper in front of him "—is the point."

As she passed over the slip of paper, she stepped aside and revealed—holy crap—his kids. He looked down at the letter fast.

Two lines into the note, his temple throbbed. What the hell was Pippa thinking, leaving the twins this way?

How long had they been in here? And why had she left him a damn note, for Pete's sake?

He pulled out his cell phone to call his ex. Her voice mail picked up immediately. She was avoiding him, no doubt.

A text from Pippa popped up in his in-box. He opened the message and it simply read, Want 2 make sure you know. Twins r waiting for you at plane. Sorry 4 short notice. XOXO.

"What the h—?" He stopped himself short before he cursed in front of his toddlers who were just beginning to form words. He tucked his phone away and faced Alexa Randall. "I'm sorry my ex added babysitter duties to your job today. Of course I'll pay you extra. Did you happen to notice which way Pippa headed out?"

Because he had some choice words for her when he found her.

"Your ex-wife wasn't here when I arrived." Alexa held up her own cell phone, her thumb swiping away a print. "I tried to contact your office, but your assistant wouldn't let me get a word out before shifting me over to Muzak. It's looped twice while I waited. Much longer and I would have had to call security, which would have brought in child services—"

He held up a hand, sick to his gut already. "Thanks. I get the picture. I owe you for cleaning up after my ex-wife's recklessness as well."

His blood pressure spiked higher until he saw red. Pippa had left the children unattended in an airplane at his privately owned airport? What had his security people been thinking, letting Pippa just wander around the aircraft that way? These were supposed to be the days of increased precautions and safety measures, and yet they must have assumed because she was his ex-wife that garnered her a free pass around the facility. Not so.

Heads were going to roll hard and fast over this. No one put the safety of his children at risk.

No one.

He crumpled the note in his fist and pitched it aside. Forcing his face to smooth so he wouldn't scare the babies, he unstrapped the buckle on his daughter's car seat.

"Hey there, princess." He held Olivia up high and thought about how she'd squealed with delight over the baby swing on the sprawling oak in his backyard. "Did you have fruit for lunch?"

She grinned, and he saw a new front tooth had come in on top. She smelled like peaches and baby shampoo and there weren't enough hours in the day to take in all the changes happening too quickly.

He loved his kids more than anything, had since the second he'd seen their fists waving in an ultrasound. He'd been damn lucky Pippa let him be there when they were born, considering she'd already started divorce proceedings at that point. He hated not being with them every day, hated missing even one milestone. But the timing for this visit couldn't be worse.

Seth tucked Olivia against his chest and reached to ruffle his son's hair. "Hey, buddy. Missed you this week."

Owen stuck out his tongue and offered up his best raspberry.

The petite blonde dressed in trim, pressed chinos popped a pacifier into Owen's mouth then knelt to pick up the crumpled note and pitch it into her cleaning bucket. "I assume today isn't your scheduled visitation."

She would be right on that. Although why the disdain in her voice? Nobody—single parent or not—would appreciate having their kids dumped off in their workplace. Not to mention he was mad as hell at Pippa for just dropping them off unannounced.

What if someone else had boarded this plane?

Thank God, this woman—Alexa—had been the one to find them. He knew who she was, but Pippa hadn't known jack when she'd unloaded his children.

Of all the reckless, irresponsible…

Deep breath. He unbuckled Owen as well and scooped him up, too, with an ease he'd learned from walking the floors with them when they were infants. Just as he'd needed calm then, he forced it through his veins now.

Getting pissed off wouldn't accomplish anything. He had to figure out what to do with his children when he was scheduled to fly out for a meeting with multimillion dollar possibilities.

When he'd first moved to South Carolina, he'd been a dumb ass, led by glitz. That's how he'd ended up married to his ex. He'd grown up with more spartan, farm values that he'd somehow lost in his quest for beaches and billions.

Now, he itched inside his high-priced starched shirt and longed for the solitude of those flights. But he had long ago learned if he wanted to do business with certain people, he had to dress the part and endure the stuffy business meetings. And he very much wanted to do business with the Medina family based out of Florida. He glanced at his watch and flinched. Damn it. He needed to be in the air already, on his way to St. Augustine. At the moment, he didn't have time for a sandwich, much less to find a qualified babysitter.

He would just have to make time. "Could you hold Owen for a second while I make some calls?"

"Sure, no problem." Alexa stopped straightening his jacket on the hanger and extended her arms.

As he passed his son over, Seth's hand grazed her breast. Her very soft, tempting breast. Just that fast touch pumped pure lust through his overworked body. It was more than just "nice, a female" kind of notice. His body was going on alert, saying "I will make it my mission in life to undress you."

She gasped lightly, not in outrage but more like someone who'd been zapped with some static. For him, it was more like a jolt from a light socket.

Olivia rested her head on his shoulder with a sleepy sigh, bringing him back to reality. He was a father with responsibilities.

Still, he was a man. Why hadn't he noticed the power of the pull to this woman when he'd walked onto the plane? Had he grown so accustomed to wealth that he'd stopped noticing "the help"? That notion didn't sit well with him at all.

But it also didn't keep him from looking at Alexa more closely.

Her pale blond hair was pulled back in a simple silver clasp. Navy chino pants and a light blue shirt— the company uniform—matched her eyes. It also fit her loosely, but not so much that it hid her curves.

Before the kids, before Pippa, he would have asked Alexa for her number, made plans to take her out on a riverboat dinner cruise where he would kiss her senseless under a starry sky. But these days he didn't have time for dating. He worked and when he wasn't on the job he saw his kids.

With a stab of regret, his gaze raked back over her T-shirt with the A-1 Aircraft Cleaning logo. He'd seen that same emblem in the cover letter she'd sent with her prospectus.

He also recalled why he hadn't gotten any further than the cover letter and the fledgling business's flyer—where he'd seen her headshot.

Following his eyes, she looked down at her shirt and met his gaze dead-on. "Yes, I have a proposal on your desk." Alexa cocked one eyebrow. "I assume that's why you were looking at my shirt?"

"Of course, why else?" he answered dryly. "You should have received an answer from my secretary."

"I did, and when you're not in a hurry—" she smoothed back her already immaculate hair "—I would appreciate the opportunity to explore your reasons for rejecting my initial bid."

"I'll save us both some time. I'm not interested in the lowest bidder or taking a risk on such a small company."

Her sky-blue eyes narrowed perceptively. "You didn't read my proposal all the way through, did you?"

"I read until my gut told me to stop." He didn't have time to waste on page after page of something he already knew wasn't going to work.

"And you're saying that your gut spoke up quickly."

"Afraid so," he said shortly, hoping to end an awkward situation with his best boardroom bite. A suspicion niggled. "Why is it you're here cleaning today instead of someone from my regular company?"

"They subcontracted A-1 when they overbooked.

Obviously I wasn't going to turn down the opportunity to impress you." She stood tall and undaunted in spite of his rejection.

Spunky and hot. Dangerous combo.

He fished his phone from his suit coat again. "I really do need to start making some calls."

"Don't let me keep you." She dipped her hand into the diaper bag and pulled out two rice cakes. She passed one to Owen and the other to Olivia. All the while Owen tugged at her hair, watching the way the white-blond strands glittered in the light. "That should keep them quiet while you talk."

Interesting that Alexa never once winced, even when Owen's fingers tangled and tugged. Not that he could blame his son in the least.

Seth thumbed the numbers on his phone and started with placing a call to his ex-wife—that again went straight to voice mail. Damn it. He then moved on to dialing family members.

Five frustrating conversations later, he'd come up empty on all counts. Either his kids were hellions and no one wanted to watch them, or he was having a serious run of bad luck.

Although their excuses were rock solid. His cousin Paige was on lockdown since her two daughters had strep throat. His cousin Vic had announced his wife was in labor with child number three—which meant *her* sisters were watching her other two kids, in addition to their own. But damn it, he'd needed to take off five minutes ago.

Brooding, he watched Alexa jostle Owen on her shapely hip. She was obviously a natural with kids. She wasn't easily intimidated, important when dealing with his strong-willed offspring. She'd protected the kids when she found them alone on the plane. He'd seen proof of her determination and work ethic. An idea formed in his head, and as much as he questioned the wisdom of it, the notion still took root.

In spite of what he'd told her, he had read more of her proposal than the cover letter, enough to know something about her. He was interested in her entrepreneurial spirit—she'd done a solid job revitalizing a company that had virtually been on financial life support. Still, his gut told him he couldn't afford to take a risk on this part of his business, especially not now. Now that he was expanding, he needed to hire a larger, more established cleaning chain, even if it cost him extra.

But he needed a nanny and she'd passed the high-level background check needed to work in an airport. Her life had been investigated more thoroughly than anyone he would get from a babysitting service. Not to mention a babysitting service would send over a total stranger that his kids might hate. At least he'd met this woman, had access to her life story. Most importantly, he saw her natural rapport with the twins. He would be nearby in the hotel at all times—even during meetings—if she had questions about their routine.

She was actually a godsend.

Decision made, he forged ahead. "While I don't think your company's the right one to service Jansen Jets, *I* have a proposal for *you*."

"I'm not sure I understand?"

"You fly with me and the kids to St. Augustine, be Owen and Olivia's nanny for the next twenty-four hours and I'll let you verbally pitch your agency's proposal to me again, in detail." The more he spelled it out, the better the idea sounded. "I'll give you a few pointers about why my gut spoke up so quickly in case you want to make adjustments for future proposals to other companies. I'll even pass along your name to possible contacts, damn good contacts. And of course you'll be paid, a week's worth of wages for one day's work."

Was he taking advantage here? He didn't think so. He was offering her a business "in" she wouldn't have otherwise. If her verbal proposal held together, he would mention her business to some of his connections. And yes, give her those tips to help cinch a deal elsewhere. She would land jobs, just not his.

She eyed him suspiciously. "Twenty-four hours of Mary Poppins duty in exchange for a critique and some new contacts?"

"That should be long enough for me to make alternative arrangements." There'd been a time when twenty-four hours with a woman would be more than enough time to seduce her as well. His eyes roved over Alexa's curves once more, regretting that he wouldn't be able to brush up on those skills during this trip.

"And you trust me, a stranger, with your children?" Disdain dripped from her voice.

"Do you think this is the right time to call me a crummy father?" Though he had to appreciate her protective instincts when it came to his children.

"You could just ring up a nanny service."

"Already thought of that. They wouldn't get here in time and my kids might not like the person they send. Olivia and Owen have taken to you." Unable to resist, he tapped the logo just above her breast. Lightly. Briefly. His finger damn near shot out a flame like a Bic lighter. "And I do know who you are. I read enough of your proposal to learn you've passed your security check for airport work."

"Well, tomorrow is usually my day off..." She dusted the logo on her shirt, as if his touch lingered. "You'll really listen to my pitch and give me tips, mention my company to others?"

"Scout's honor." He smiled for the first time all day, seeing victory in sight.

"I want you to know I'm not giving up on persuading you to sign me up for Jansen Jets as well."

"Fair enough. You're welcome to try."

She eyed both the children then looked back to him. He knew when he'd presented an irresistible proposition. Now he just needed to wait for her to see this was a win-win situation.

Although he needed for her to realize that quickly. "I have about two minutes left here," he pressed. "If your answer's no, get to it so I can make use of the rest of my time to secure alternative arrangements." Although God only knew what those might be.

"Okay." She nodded in agreement although her furrowed brow broadcast a hefty dose of reservation. "You have yourself a deal. I'll call my partner to let her know so she can cover—"

"Great," he interrupted. "But do it while you buckle up the kids and yourself. We're out of here." He settled Olivia back into her car seat with a quick kiss on her forehead.

Alexa looked up quickly from fastening Owen into his safety seat. "Where's the pilot?"

He stared into her pale blue eyes and imagined them shifting colors as he made her as hot for him as he was for her. God, it would be damn tough to have this jaw-dropping female working beside him for the next twenty-four hours. But his children were his top priority.

So he simply smiled—and, yes, took a hefty dose of pleasure in seeing her pupils widen with awareness. "The pilot? That would be me."

Two

Her stomach dropped and she prayed the Gulfstream III wouldn't do the same in Seth Jansen's hands.

Turning off her cell after deleting four missed calls
from her mother and leaving a message for her partner,
Bethany, Alexa double-checked the safety belts for both
children and buckled her own. Watching Seth slide into
the pilot's seat, she reminded herself he owned a charter
jet company so of course it made sense he could pilot
a plane himself. She'd flown on private aircraft during
her entire childhood, trusting plenty of aviators she'd
never even met to get her safely from point A to point B.
So why was she so nervous with this guy at the helm?

Because he'd thrown her off balance.

Boarding the plane earlier, she'd had such optimism,
a solid approach in place and control of her world. In the

span of less than ten minutes, Seth Jansen had seized control of not just the plane, but her carefully made plan.

The kind of bargain he'd proposed was so unexpected, outrageous even. But too good an opportunity to pass up. She needed to take a deep breath, relax and focus on learning everything she could about him, to give her an edge in negotiations.

Even knowing he must have his pilot's license, she wouldn't have expected someone as wealthy as him willing to fly himself. She'd thought he would have someone else "chauffeuring" while he banged back a few drinks or took a nap. Like her dad would have done during their annual family vacation, a one-week trip that was supposed to make up for all the time they never spent together during the year.

Not that she saw much of either of her parents even then. While on vacation, the nanny had taken her to amusement parks or sightseeing or to the slopes while her father attended to "emergency" business and her mother went to the spa.

Simmering over old memories, Alexa polished the metal seatbelt buckle absently with the hem of her shirt as she watched Seth Jansen complete his preflight routine.

The door to the cockpit had been left open. Seth adjusted the mic on the headset, his mouth moving, although she couldn't hear him as the engines hummed to life. Smooth as silk, the plane left the hangar, past a row of parked smaller aircraft until he taxied to the end of the runway and stopped.

Nerves pattered up from her stomach to the roots of her hair. The jet engines roared louder, louder still, and yet she could swear she heard Seth's deep voice calmly blending with the aerial symphony.

Words drifted back…

"Charleston tower… Gulfstream alpha, two, one, prepared… Roger… Ready for takeoff…"

The luxury craft eased forward again, Seth's hands steady on the yoke and power. Confidence radiated from his every move, so much so she found herself relaxing into the butter-soft leather sofa. Her hands fell to rest on the handle of each car seat, claiming her charges. Her babies, for the next twenty-four hours.

Her heart squeezed with old regrets. Her marriage to Travis had been an unquestionable failure. While part of her was relieved there hadn't been children hurt by their breakup, another part of her grieved for the babies that might have been.

The nose of the plane lifted as the aircraft swooped upward. Olivia and Owen squirmed in their seats. Alexa reached for the diaper bag, panic stirring. Did they want a bottle? A toy? And if they needed a diaper change there wasn't a thing she could do about that for a while. Just when the panic started to squeeze her chest, the noise of the engines and the pacifiers she'd used to help their ears soothed them back into their unfinished nap.

The diaper bag slid from her grip, thudding on the floor. Relaxing, she stared across the aisle out the window as they left Charleston behind. She also left behind an empty apartment and a silent phone since her married friends had dropped away after her divorce.

Church steeples and spires dotted the ocean-locked landscape. So many, the historic town had earned nicknames of the Holy City and the City by the Sea. After their financial meltdown, her parents had relocated to a condo in Boca Raton to start over—away from the gossip.

How ironic that her parents' initial reservations about Travis had been so very far off base. They'd begged him to sign a prenuptial agreement. She'd told them to take their prenup and go to hell. Travis had insisted he didn't care and signed the papers anyway. She thought she'd found her dream man, finally someone who would love her for herself.

Not that the contract had mattered in the end since her father had blown through the whole fortune anyway. By the time they'd broken up, her ex hadn't wanted anything to do with her, her messy family dysfunction, or what he called her germaphobic ways.

The way Travis had simply fallen out of love with her had kicked the hell out of her self-esteem there for a while. She couldn't even blame the breakup on another woman. No way in hell was she going to let a man have control of her heart or her life ever again.

All the more reason she had to make a go of her cleaning business and establish her independence. She had no other marketable skills, apart from a host of bills and a life to rebuild in her beloved hometown.

So here she was, on a plane bound for St. Augustine with a stranger and two heart-tuggingly adorable babies. The coastline looked miniscule now outside the window as they reached their cruising altitude.

"Hey, Alexa?"

Seth's voice pulled her attention away from the view. He stood in the archway between the cockpit and the seating area.

Her stomach jolted again. "Shouldn't you be flying the plane?"

"It's on autopilot for the moment. Since the kids are sleeping, I want you to come up front. The flight isn't long, but it will give us the chance to talk through some specifics about your time with the twins."

She saw the flinty edge of calculation in his jewel-toned eyes. He may have offered her a deal back at the airport, but now he intended to interview her further before he turned over his children to her. A flicker of admiration lit through the disdain she had felt for him earlier.

Giving each baby another quick check and finding them snoozing away, binkies half in, half out of their slack mouths, she unbuckled, reassured she could safely leave them for a few minutes. She walked the short distance to Seth and stopped in the archway, waiting for him to move back to the pilot's seat.

Still, he stood immobile and aloof, other than those glinting green eyes that swept over her face. The crisp scent of him rode the recycled air to tempt her nose, swirling deeper inside her with each breath. Her breasts tingled with awareness, her body overcome with the urge to lean into him, press the aching fullness of her chest against the hard wall of manly muscles.

She shivered. He smiled arrogantly as if completely cognizant of just how much he affected her on a physical level. Seth stepped back brusquely, returning to the pilot's spot on the left and waving her into the copilot's seat on the right.

Strapping in, she stared at the gauges around her, the yoke moving automatically in front of her. Seth tapped buttons along the control panel and resumed flying the plane. Still, the steering in front of her mirrored his movements until she felt connected to him in some mystical manner.

She resented the way he sent her hormones into overdrive with just the sound of his husky voice or the intensity of his sharp gaze. She was here to do a job, damn it, not bring a man into her already too complicated life.

Twisting her fingers together in her lap, she forced her thoughts back to their jobs. "What's so important about this particular meeting that it can't be rescheduled?"

"I have small mouths to feed. Responsibilities." He stayed steadily busy as he talked, his eyes roving the gauges, his hands adjusting the yoke. "Surely you understand that, and if not, then I don't even need to read your proposal." He winked.

"Thank you for the Business 101 lecture, Mr. Jansen." She brushed specks of dust from a gauge. "I was really just trying to make conversation, but if you're more comfortable hanging out here alone, I'll be glad to return to the back."

"Sorry... And call me Seth," he said with what sounded like genuine contrition. "Long day. Too many surprises."

She glanced back at the sleeping babies, suddenly realizing they had miniature versions of his strong chin. "I can see that. What do you do to relax?"

"Fly."

He stared out at the expanse of blue sky and puffy clouds, and she couldn't miss the buzz radiating from him. Jansen Jets wasn't just a company to him. He'd turned his hobby, his true love, into a financial success. Not many could accomplish such a feat. Maybe she could learn something about business from him after all.

"You were looking forward to this time in the air, weren't you? What should have been your relaxing hour for the day has become a stressor."

"I've gotta ask…" He looked over at her quickly, brow furrowed. "Is the psychoanalysis included in the cleanup fee?"

She winced as his words hit a little too close to a truth of her own. Travis used to complain about that same trait. Well, she did have plenty of practice in what a shrink would say after all the time she'd spent in analysis as a teenager. The whole point had been to internalize those healthier ways of thinking. She'd needed the help, no question, but she'd also needed her parents. When they hadn't heard her, she'd started crying out for their attention in other ways, ways that had almost cost her life.

Her thoughts were definitely getting too deep and dark, and therefore too distracting. Something about this man and his children made her visit places in her mind she normally kept closed off. "Like I said, just making small talk. I thought you wanted me to come up here for conversation, to dig a little deeper into the background of your new, temporary nanny. If you don't want to chat, simply say so."

"You're right. I do. And the first thing I've learned is that you don't back down, which is a very good thing. It takes a strong person to stand up to the twins when they're in a bad mood." He shuddered melodramatically, his complaint totally undercut by the pride in his voice. Mr. Button-Up Businessman loosened up a little when he spoke of his kids. "What made you trade in your white gloves at tea for white glove cleaning?"

So he knew a little about her privileged upbringing as well. "You did more than just read my cover letter."

"I recognized your name—or rather your return to your maiden name. Your father was once a client of a competing company. Your husband chartered one of my planes."

"My ex-husband," she snapped.

He nodded, his fingers whitening as his grip tightened on the yoke. "So, back to my original question. What made you reach for the vacuum cleaner?"

"Comes with the business."

"Why choose this particular line of work?"

Because she didn't have a super cool hobby like he did? She'd suffered a rude awakening after her divorce was finalized a year ago, and she realized she had no money and no marketable skills.

Her one negligible talent? Being a neat-freak with a need to control her environment. Pair that with insights into the lifestyles of the rich and spoiled and she'd fashioned a career. But that answer sounded too half-baked and not particularly professional.

"Because I understand the needs of the customer, beyond just a clean space, I know the unique services that make the job stand out." True enough, and since he seemed to be listening, she continued, "Keeping records of allergies, favored scents, personal preferences for the drink bar can make the difference between a successful flight and a disaster. Flying in a charter jet isn't simply an air taxi service. It's a luxury experience and should be treated as such."

"You understand the world since you lived in it."

Lived. Past tense. "I want to be successful on my own merits rather than mooch off the family coffers."

Or at least she liked to think she would have felt that way if there had been any lucre left in the Randall portfolio.

"Why work in this particular realm, the aircraft world?" He gestured around the jet with a broad hand.

Her eyes snagged on the sprinkling of fair hair along his forearm. Tanned skin contrasted with the white cuffs of his rolled up sleeves and wow did her fingertips ever itch to touch him. To see if his bronzed-god flesh still carried the warmth of the sun.

It had been so long since she'd felt these urges. Her divorce had left her emotionally gutted. She'd tried dating a couple of times, but the chemistry hadn't been there. Her new business venture consumed her. Or rather, it had until right now, when it mattered most.

"I'm missing your point." No surprise since she was staring at his arm like an idiot.

"You're a…what…history major?"

"Art history, and being that close means you read my bio. You do know a lot more about me than you let on at first."

"Of course I do or I never would have asked you to watch my children. They're far more precious to me than any plane." His eyes went hard, leaving no room for doubt. Any mistakes with his son and daughter would not be tolerated. Then he looked back at the sky, mellow Seth returning. "Why not manage a gallery if you need to fill your hours?"

Because she would be lucky if working in a gallery would cover rent on an apartment or a lease on an economy car, much less food and economic stability. Because she wanted to prove she didn't need a man to be successful. And most importantly, *because* she didn't ever again want the freaked out feeling of being less than six hundred dollars away from bankruptcy.

Okay, sort of melodramatic since she'd still owned jewelry she could hock. But still scary as hell when she'd sold off her house and car only to find it barely covered the existing loans.

"I do not expect anyone to support me, and given the current economy, jobs in the arts aren't exactly filling up the want ad sections. Bethany has experience in the business, while I bring new contacts to the table. We're a good team. Besides, I really do enjoy this work, strange as that may seem. While A-1 has employees who handle cleaning most of the time, I pitch in if someone's out sick or we get the call for a special job. I enjoy the break from office work."

"Okay, I believe you. So you used to like art history, and now you enjoy feeding people's Evian habits and their need for clean armrests."

The deepening sarcasm in his voice had her spine starching with irritation. "Are you making fun of me for the hell of it or is there a purpose behind this line of questioning?"

"I always have a purpose," he said as smoothly as he flew the plane. "Will your whim of the week pass, once you realize people take these services for granted and your work is not appreciated? What happens to my aircraft then? I'll be stuck wading through that stack of proposals all over again."

He really saw her as a flighty, spoiled individual and that stung. It wasn't particularly fair, either. "Do you keep flying even when people don't appreciate a smooth or on-time flight, when they only gripe about the late or bumpy rides?"

"I'm not following your point here. I like to fly. Are you saying you like to clean?"

"I like to restore order," she answered simply, truthfully.

The shrinks she'd seen as a teen had helped her rechannel the need for perfection her mother had drilled into Alexa from birth. She'd stopped starving herself, eased off searching the art world for flawless beauty and now took comfort from order, from peace.

"Ah—" a smile spread over his face "—you like control. Now that I understand."

"Who doesn't like control?" And how many therapy sessions had she spent on *that* topic?

He looked over at her with an emerald-eyed sexy stare. The air crackled as if a lightning bolt had zipped between them. "Would you like to take over flying the plane?"

"Are you kidding?" She slid her hands under her thighs even though she couldn't deny to herself just how tempting the offer sounded.

Who wouldn't want to take a stab at soaring through the air, just her and the wide-open blue rolling out in front of the plane? It would be like driving a car alone for the first time. Pushing an exotic Arabian racehorse to gallop. Happier memories from another lifetime called to her.

"Just take the yoke."

God, how she wanted to, but there was something in his voice that gave her pause. She couldn't quite figure out his game. She wasn't in the position to risk her livelihood or her newfound independence on some guy's whims.

"Your children are on board." She knew she sounded prim, but then hey, she was a nanny for the day.

"If it appears you're about to send us into a nosedive, I'll take over."

"Maybe another time." She leaped up from the seat, not about to get sucked into a false sense of control that wouldn't last. "I think I hear Olivia."

His low chuckle followed her all the way back to both peacefully sleeping children.

Alexa could hear his husky laugh echoing in her ears two hours later as they settled into their luxurious hotel room in St. Augustine, Florida.

She had seen the best of the best lodgings and the Casa Monica—one of the oldest hotels in the United States—was gorgeous by any standards, designed to resemble a castle. The city of St. Augustine itself was rich with history and ornate Spanish architecture, the Casa Monica being a jewel. The hotel had been built in the 1800s, named for St. Monica, the mother of St. Augustine, the city's namesake.

And here she was with Seth and his babies. She could use a little motherly advice from a patron saint's mom right now.

She also needed to find some time to touch base with Bethany at work. Even though she was sure Bethany could manage—it had been her company at one time—she really did need to speak with her partner and give Bethany her contact information.

Seth had checked them into one of the penthouse suites, with a walk-out to a turret with views of the city. The suite had two bedrooms connected by a sitting area. The mammoth bath with a circular tub called to her muscles, which ached from working all day then lugging one of the baby carriers around. Then her thoughts went to images of sharing the tub with a man…not just any man…

She turned back to the room, decorated in blue velvet upholstery and heavy brocade curtains. Seth had claimed the spare bedroom, leaving her the larger master with two cribs inside. She trailed her fingers over the handle to Olivia's car seat on the floor beside the mission style sofa in the sitting room. Olivia's brother rested in his car seat next to hers.

"Your twins sleep well. They're making this job too easy, you know."

"Pippa doesn't believe in bedtimes. They usually nap hard their first day with me." Seth strode into the spare bedroom. "Expect mayhem soon enough when they wake up recharged. Owen's a charmer, so much so it's easy to miss the mischief he's plotting. He's always looking for the best way to stack furniture and climb his way out. You can see where he's already had stitches through his left eyebrow. As for Olivia, well, keep a close eye on her hands. She loves to collect small things to shove up her nose, in her ears, in her mouth…"

Affection swelled from each word as he detailed his children's personalities. The man definitely loosened up when around his kids or when he was talking about them. He seemed to know his offspring well. Not what she would have expected from a distant dad. Intrigued, she moved closer.

Through the open door, she could see him drape his suit coat on the foot of the bed. He loosened his tie further and unbuttoned his collar, then worked the buttons free down his shirt.

Alexa backed toward her own room. "Um, what are you doing?"

Seth slipped his still-knotted tie over his head and untucked the shirt. "Owen kicked his shoes against me when I picked him up after we landed." He pointed to smudges down the left side. "I need to change fast before my meeting."

His all-important meeting. Right. Seth had told her he was having dinner with a bigwig contact downstairs and she could order whatever she wanted from room service. He would be back in two to three hours. If she could get the kids settled in the tub, she could sit on the side and make some work calls while watching them. Check voice mail and email on her iPhone, deal with the standard million missed calls from her mom before moving on to deal with work. Her staff wasn't large, just four other employees, including Bethany. Her partner was slowing down, but could hold down the fort. In the event an emergency arose, Bethany would make sure things didn't reach a boiling point. So she was in the free and clear to spend the night here. With the kids.

And Seth.

She thumbed a smudge from the base of the brass lamp. "Can't have shoe prints all over you at the big meeting. That's for sure."

"Could you look in the hang-up bag and get me another shirt?"

"Right, okay." She spun away before he undressed further. She charged over to the black suitcase resting on top of a mahogany luggage rack.

Alexa tugged the zipper around and...oh my. The scent of him wafted up from his clothes, which should be impossible since they were clean clothes. But no question about it, the suitcase had captured the essence of him and it was intoxicating.

Her fingers moved along the hangers until she found a plain white shirt mixed in with a surprising amount of colorful others. Mr. Buttoned-up Businessman had a wild side. An unwelcome tingle played along her skin and in her imagination. She slapped the case closed.

Shirt in hand, she turned back to Seth who was now wearing only his pants and a T-shirt. His shoulders stretched the fabric to the limit. Her fingers curled into the shirt in her hands, her fingertips registering Sea Island Cotton, high-end, breathable, known for keeping the wearer's body cool throughout the day.

Maybe she could use some Sea Island Cotton herself because she was heating up.

Alexa thrust the shirt toward him. "Will this do?"

"Great, thanks." His knuckles brushed hers as she passed over his clothes as if they were intimately sharing a space.

And more.

Awareness chased up her wrist, her arm, higher still as the intimacy of the moment engulfed her. She was in a gorgeous hotel room, with a hot man and his beautiful children, helping him get dressed. The scene was too wonderful. Too close to what she'd once dreamed of having with her ex.

She jerked back fast. "Any last minute things to tell me about the kids when I order up supper?"

"Owen is allergic to strawberries, but Olivia loves them and if she can get her hands on them, she tries to share them with her brother. So watch that—hotels do the strawberry garnish thing on meals."

"Anything else?" She tried to pull her eyes away

from the nimble glide of his fingers up the buttons on his shirt.

"If you have an emergency, you can contact me at this number." He grabbed a hotel pen and jotted a string of numbers on the back of a business card. "That's my private cell line I use only for the kids."

"Got it." She tucked it in the corner of the gold gilded mirror. She could handle a couple of babies for a few hours.

Right?

"Don't lose it. And don't let Owen find it or he will eat it." He unbuckled his belt.

Her jaw dropped.

He tucked in his shirttails—and caught her staring. Her face heating, she turned away. Again.

Looking out the window seemed like a safe idea even though she'd been to St. Augustine about a dozen times. She could see Flagler College across the way, a place she'd once considered attending. Except her parents refused to pay if she left Charleston. Students at the Flagler castlelike fortress must feel as if they were attending Hogwarts. In fact, the whole city had a removed-from-reality feel, a step out of time. Much like this entire trip.

A Cinderella carriage pulled by a horse creaked slowly by as a Mercedes convertible whipped around and past it.

As Charleston had the French Huguenot influence, buildings here sported a Spanish Renaissance flair, and if Seth didn't get dressed soon, she would run out of things to look at. He was too much of a threat to her world for her to risk a tempting peek.

Her body hummed with awareness even when she

didn't see him. What a hell of a time for her hormones to stoke to life again.

"You can turn around now." Seth's voice stroked along her ragged nerves.

She chewed her lip, spinning back to face him, a man too handsome for his own good—or hers. "I've taken care of babies before."

Not often, but for friends in hopes she could prepare herself for the day it was her turn. A day that had never come around.

"Twins are different." He tugged the tie back over his head.

If he was so worried, he should cancel his meeting. She wanted to snap at him, but knew her irritability for what it was. Her perfect plan for the day had gone way off course, complicated even more by how damn attracted she was to the man she wanted to woo for a contract, not as a bed partner.

Memories of rustling sheets and sweat-slicked bodies smoked through her mind. She'd had a healthy sex life with her ex, so much so that she hadn't considered something could be wrong until everything fell apart. She definitely couldn't trust her body to judge the situation.

"Seth," she said his first name so easily she almost gasped, but forced herself to continue, "the twins and I will manage. We'll eat applesauce and fries and chicken nuggets then skyrocket your pay-per-view bill with cartoon movies until our brains are mush. I'll watch Olivia with small objects, and Owen's charm won't distract me from his climbing or strawberry snitching. They'll be fine. Go to your meeting."

He actually hesitated before grabbing his jacket from

the edge of the bed. "I'll be downstairs in the bar if you need me."

Oh, her body needed him all right. Too much for her own good. She was better off using her brains.

Seth stepped from the elevator into the lobby full of arches that led to the bar and restaurant. He scanned the chairs and sofas of rich dark woods with red-striped fabrics. Looking further, he searched past the heavy beams and thick curtains pulled back at each archway.

Thank God, somehow he'd managed to make it here ahead of his dinner partner. He strode past an iron fountain with Moorish tiles toward the bar where he was supposed to meet Javier Cortez, a cousin to royalty.

Literally. Cortez was related to the Medina family, a European monarchy that had ended in a violent coup. The Medinas and relatives had relocated to the United States, living in anonymity until a media scoop exposed their royal roots last year.

Cortez had served as head of security to one of the princes prior to the newsbreak and now oversaw safety measures for the entire family. Landing the Medinas as clients would be a huge coup.

Seth hitched up onto a stool at the bar, waving to the bartender for a seltzer water. Nothing stronger tonight.

Jansen Jets was still a small company, relatively speaking, but thanks to an in, he'd landed this meeting. One of those "Human Web" six degrees of separation moments—his cousin's wife's sister married into the Landis family, and a Landis brother married the illegitimate Medina princess.

Okay, that was more like ten degrees of separation. Thankfully, enough to bring him to this meeting. From this point on he had to rest on his own merits. Much like he'd told Alexa. *Alexa...*

Damn it all, did every thought have to circle back around to her?

Sure he'd noticed her on a physical level when he'd first stepped on the plane, and he'd managed the attraction well enough until he'd caught her eyes sliding over his body as he'd undone his pants. The ensuing heat wave sure hadn't been a welcome condition right before a meeting.

But he needed her help, so he would damn well wrestle the attraction into submission. His kids were his number one priority. He'd tried calling his ex multiple times since landing in St. Augustine, but only got her voice mail. Life had been a hell of a lot less complicated when he was flying those routes solo in North Dakota.

There didn't seem to be a damn thing more he could do about his mess of a personal life. Hopefully he could at least make headway in the business world.

Starting now.

The elevator dinged, doors swished open and Javier Cortez stepped out. Predictably the bar patrons buzzed. The newness of having royalty around hadn't worn off for people. The forty-year-old royal cousin strode out confidently, his Castilian heritage fitting right into the hotel's decor.

The guy's regal lineage didn't matter to Seth. He just appreciated the guy's hard-nosed efficiency. This deal would be sewn up quickly, one way or another.

"Sorry I'm late." Cortez thrust out his hand. "Javier Cortez."

"Seth Jansen." He stood to shake Javier's hand and then resettled onto a barstool beside the other guy.

The bartender placed an amber drink in front of Javier before he even placed an order. "I appreciate your flying down to meet with me here." He rattled the ice and looked around with assessing eyes. "My wife loves this place."

"I can see why. Lots of historic appeal."

It was also a good locale to conduct business, near the Medinas' private island off the coast of Florida. Although Seth hadn't been invited into that inner sanctum yet. Security measures were tight. No one knew the exact location and few had seen the island fortress. The Medinas owned a couple of private jets, but were looking to increase their transport options to and from the island as their family expanded with marriages and new children.

Cortez tasted his drink and set it on the cocktail napkin. "Since my wife and I are still technically finishing up our honeymoon, I promised her a longer stay, the chance to shop, laze around by the pool, soak up some Florida sun before we head back to Boston."

What the hell was he supposed to say to that? "Congratulations."

"Thanks, thanks. I hear you have your kids and their sitter with you."

Of course he'd heard, even though Seth had only been in town for about an hour. The guy was a security whiz and obviously didn't walk into a meeting unprepared. "I like to work in time with them whenever I can, so I brought the kids and Mary Poppins along."

"Excellent. Then you won't mind if we postpone the rest of this discussion."

Crap. Just what he didn't need.

The stay here extended. Less taken care of tonight, more tomorrow and even the next day. "Of course."

Cortez stood, taking his drink with him as he started back toward the elevator. Seth abandoned his seltzer water.

They stepped into the elevator together, and Cortez swiped his card for the penthouse level. "My wife and I would enjoy having you and your kids meet us for breakfast in the morning, your sitter, too. Around nine? Great," he said without waiting for an answer. "See you there."

Holy hell. Breakfast in a restaurant with a one-year-old was tough enough. But with two of them?

He stepped out onto the top floor, Javier going right as he went left.

The closer he came to the suite's door, the louder the muffled sounds grew. Squealing babies. Damn. Was one of them hurt? He double-timed toward his room, whipped the key card through just as the door opened.

Alexa carried a baby on each hip—two freshly bathed and wet naked babies. Her cheeks were flushed, her smile wide. "I just caught them. Holy cow, they've got some speed for toddlers."

He snagged a towel from the arm of the sofa and held it open. "Pass me one."

She handed Owen over and Seth saw…

Her shirt was soaking wet, clinging to every perfect curve. Who would have thought Mary Poppins could rock the hell out of a wet T-shirt contest?

Three

Alexa plucked at her wet company shirt, conscious of the way it clung to her breasts. She didn't need the heat in Seth's eyes. She didn't need the answering fire it stirred in her. They both had different goals for what remained of their twenty-four-hour deal. They were best served focusing on the children and work.

Turning away, she hitched Olivia up on her hip and snagged the other towel from where she'd dropped it on the sofa to chase the racing duo around the suite. "You're back early from your dinner meeting."

"You need some clothes." The sound of his confident footsteps sounded softly behind her on plush carpet.

"Dry ones, for sure." She glanced through to the bathroom. Towels were draped on the floor around the circular tub, soaking up all the splashes. "I let the babies use the Jacuzzi like a kiddie pool. A few plastic cups and they were happy to play. Supper should be arriving soon. I thought you were room service when I heard you at the door."

"They'll need cleaning up again after supper." He tugged out two diapers and two T-shirts from the diaper bag.

"Then I'll just order more towels." She plucked the tiny pink T-shirt from his hand and busied herself with dressing Olivia to keep from noticing how at ease he was handling his squirming son.

"Fair enough." He pressed the diaper tapes in place, his large masculine hands surprisingly nimble.

"Did your meeting go well?" She wrestled a tiny waving arm through the sleeve.

"We didn't get through more than half a drink. He had to postpone until the morning." A quick tug later, he had Owen's powder-blue shirt in place. He hoisted his son in the air and buzzed his belly before setting him on his feet. "I'll just call room service and add my order to the rest."

He wasn't going back to work? They would be spending the rest of the evening here. Together with the children, of course. And after the toddlers drifted off? He'd mentioned Pippa kept them up late. With luck the pint-size chaperones would burn the midnight oil.

"Too bad your dinner companion couldn't have told you about the delay before you left Charleston. You would have had time to make other arrangements for the children." And she would have been at home in her lonely apartment eating ice cream while thinking about encountering Seth on his plane. Because without question, he was a memorable man.

"I'm glad to have the time with them. I assume you can arrange to stay longer?"

"I'll call my partner back as soon as the kids are asleep. She and I will make it work."

"Excellent. Now we just need to arrange extra clothes and toiletries for you." He reached for the room phone as Olivia and Owen chased each other in circles around their father. "When I order my supper I'll also have the concierge pick up something for you to change int—"

"Really, no need." She held up a hand, an unsettling tingle tripping up her spine at the thought of wearing things purchased by him. "I'll wear the hotel robe tonight and we can have the hotel wash my clothes. The kids and I will kill time tomorrow browsing around downtown, shopping while you finish your meeting. You do have a double stroller, don't you?"

"Already arranged. But you are going to need a change of clothing sooner than that." The furrows in his brow warned her a second before he said, "My business prospect wants to have breakfast with the kids and there's not a chance in hell I can carry that off on my own. It's my fault you're here without a change of clothes."

A business breakfast? With two toddlers? Whose genius idea was that? But she held her silence and conceded to the need for something appropriate to wear.

She stifled a twinge of nerves at discussing her clothing size. She was past those days of stepping on the scales every morning for her mom to check—what a hell of a way to spend "mother-daughter" time. And thank God, she was past the days of starving herself into a size zero.

Size zero. There'd been an irony in that, as if she could somehow fade away...

Blinking the past back, she said, "Okay then, tell them to buy smalls or eights, and my shoes are size seven."

His green eyes glimmered wickedly. "And underwear measurements?"

She poked him in the chest with one finger. "Not on your life am I answering that one." God, his chest was solid. She stepped away. "Make sure to keep a tally of how much everything costs. I insist on reimbursing you."

"Unnecessarily prideful, but as you wish," he said it so arrogantly she wanted to thump him on the back of his head.

Not a wise business move, though, touching him again. One little tap had nearly seared her fingertip and her mind. "I pay my own way now."

"At least let me loan you a T-shirt to sleep in tonight rather than that stifling hotel robe."

His clothes against her naked flesh?

Whoa.

Shaking off the goose bumps, she followed the toddling twins into the master bedroom. The rumble of his voice followed her as Seth ordered his meal, her clothing and some other toiletries...

Olivia and Owen sprinted to check out the matching portable cribs that had been set up on the far side of the king-size bed, each neatly made. Everything had been provided to accommodate a family. A real family. Except she would crawl under her own covers all alone wearing a hot guy's T-shirt.

Alexa wrapped her arms around her stomach, reminded

of the life she'd been denied with the implosion of her marriage. A life she purposefully hadn't thought about in a year since she'd craved a real family more than her next breath. Being thrust into this situation with Seth stirred longings she'd ignored for too long. Damn it, she'd taken this gamble for her company, her employees, her future.

But in doing so, she hadn't realized how deeply playing at this family game could cut into her heart.

Playing pretend family was kicking his ass.

Seth forked up the last bite of his Chilean sea bass while Alexa started her warm peach bread pudding with lavender cream. They'd opted to feed the babies first and put them to bed so the adults could actually dine in peace out on the turret balcony. Their supper had been set up by the wrought-iron table for two, complete with a lone rose in the middle of the table. Historical sconces on either side of the open doors cast a candlelit glow over the table.

Classical music drifted softly from inside. Okay, so it was actually something called "The Mozart Effect— Music for Babies," and he used it to help soothe Olivia and Owen to sleep. But it still qualified as mood-setting music for grown-ups.

And holy crap, did Alexa ever qualify as a smoking hot adult.

She'd changed into one of his T-shirts with the fluffy hotel robe over it. She looked as if she'd just rolled out of his bed. An ocean breeze lifted her whispery blond hair as late evening street noises echoed softly from the street below. Tonight had been the closest he'd come to experiencing family life with his children.

He hadn't dated much since his divorce and when he had, he'd been careful to keep that world separate from his kids. Working side by side with Alexa had more than cut the tasks in half tonight. That made him angry all over again that he'd screwed up so badly in his own marriage. He and Pippa had known it was a long shot going in, but they'd both wanted to give it a chance, for the babies. Or at least that's what he'd thought, until he'd discovered Pippa wasn't even sure if he was the biological father.

His gut twisted.

Damn it all, Olivia and Owen were *his* children. *His* name was on their birth certificate. And he refused to let anyone take them from him. Pippa vowed she wasn't going to challenge the custody agreement, but she'd lied to him before, and in such a major way, he had trouble trusting her.

He studied the woman across from him, wishing he could read her thoughts better, but she held herself in such tight control at all times. Sure, he knew he couldn't judge all females by how things had shaken down between him and Pippa. But it definitely made him wary. Fool him once, shame on her. Fool him twice. Shame on him.

Alexa Randall was here for one reason only. To use him to jump-start her business. She wasn't in St. Augustine to play house. She didn't know, much less love, his kids. She was doing a job. Everybody in this world had an agenda. As long as he kept that knowledge forefront in his mind, they would be fine.

He reached for his seltzer water. "You're good with kids."

"Thanks," she said tightly, stabbing at her pudding.

"Seriously. You'll make a good mother someday."

She shook her head and shoved away her half-eaten dessert. "I prefer to have a husband for that and my only attempt at marriage didn't end well."

The bitterness in her voice hung between them.

He tipped back his crystal glass, eyeing her over the rim. "I'm really sorry to hear that."

Sighing, she dipped her finger in the water and traced the rim of her glass until the crystal sang. "I married a guy who seemed perfect. He didn't even care about my family's money. In fact, he sided with my dad about signing a prenup to prove it." Faster and faster her finger moved, the pitch growing higher. "After always having to second-guess friendships while growing up, that felt so good—thinking he loved me for myself, unconditionally."

"That's how it's supposed to work."

"Supposed to. But then, I'm sure you understand what it's like to have to question everyone's motives."

"Not always. I grew up in a regular farming family in North Dakota. Everyone around me had working class values. I spent my spare time camping, fishing or flying."

"Most of my friends in private school wanted the perks of hanging out with me—shopping trips in New York. For my sixteenth, my mother flew me and my friends to the Bahamas." She tapped the glass once with a short fingernail. "The ones with parents who could afford the same kind of perks were every bit as spoiled as I was. No wonder I didn't have any true friends."

Having to question people's motives as an adult was tough enough. But worrying as a kid? That could mark a person long-term. He thought of his children asleep in the next room and wondered how he would keep their lives even-keeled.

"So your ex seems like a dream guy with the prenup… and…?"

"His only condition was that I not take any money from my family." Her eyes took on a faraway, jaded look that bothered him more than it should have for someone he'd just met. "My money could go into trust for our kids someday, but we would live our lives on what we made. Sounded good, honorable."

"What happened?" He lifted his glass.

"I was allergic to his sperm."

He choked on his water. "Uh, could you run that by me again?"

"You heard me. Allergic to his swimmers. We can both have kids, just not with each other." She folded her arms on the edge of the table, leaning closer. "I was sad when the doctor told me, but I figured, hey, this was our call to adopt. Apparently Travis—my ex—didn't get the same message."

"Let me get this straight." Seth placed his glass on the table carefully to keep from snapping the stemware in two with his growing anger. "Your ex-husband left you because the two of you couldn't have biological children together?"

"Bingo," she said with a tight smile that didn't come close to reaching her haunted blue eyes.

"He sounds like a shallow jerk." A jerk Seth had an urge to punch for putting such deep shadows in this woman's eyes. "I would be happy to kick his ass for you. I may be a desk jockey these days, but I've still got enough North Dakota farm boy in me to take him down."

A smile played at her lips. "No worries. I kick butts on my own these days."

"Good for you." He admired her resilience, her spunk. She'd rebuilt her life after two nearly simultaneous blows from life that would have debilitated most people.

"I try not to beat myself up about it." Sagging back in the wrought-iron patio chair, she clutched the robe closed with her fists. "I didn't have much practice in making smart choices about the people I invited into my life. So it stands to reason I would screw that one up, too."

"Well, I'm a damn good judge of character and it's obvious to me that *he* screwed up." Seth reached across the table and touched her elbow lightly where the sleeve fell back to reveal the vulnerable crook. "Not you."

Her eyes opened wider with surprise, with awareness, but she didn't pull away. "Thanks for the vote of confidence, but I know there had to be fault on both sides."

"Still, that's not always easy to see or say." His hand fell away.

"What about *your* ex?" She straightened the extra fork she hadn't needed for her dinner. In fact, she hadn't eaten much of her fire-grilled sea scallops at all and only half of her bread pudding. Maybe the cuisine here didn't suit her. "Does she make it a regular practice to run off and leave the kids?"

"Actually, no." Pippa was usually diligent when it came to their care. In fact, she usually cried buckets anytime she left them.

Alexa tapped the top of his hand with a whisper-soft touch. "Come on now. I unloaded about my sucky marriage story. What's yours?"

Normally he preferred not to talk about his failures. But the moonlight, good food—for him at least—and even better company made him want to extend the evening. If that meant spilling a few public knowledge facts about his personal life, then so be it.

"There's no great drama to share—" And yeah, he was lying, but he preferred to keep it low-key. He was used to glossing over the truth in front of his kids, who were too young to understand paternity questions. "We had a fling that resulted in a surprise pregnancy—" Pippa had just failed to mention the other fling she'd had around the same time. "So we got married for the children, gave it an honest try and figured out it wasn't going to work. We already had divorce papers in motion by the time the babies were due."

"If you don't mind my asking—" she paused until he waved her on "—why did you get married at all then?"

He'd asked himself the same question more than once, late at night when he was alone and missing the twins. "Old-fashioned, I guess. I wanted to be around my kids all the time. I wanted it to work." Wanted the babies to be his. "It just…didn't."

"You're so calm about it," she said with more of those shadows chasing around in her eyes.

Calm? He was a holy mess inside, but letting that anger, the betrayal, fly wouldn't accomplish anything. "I have the twins. Pippa and I are trying to be good parents. At least I thought we were."

Her hand covered his completely, steadily. "By all appearances you're doing a great job. They're beautiful, sweet babies."

The touch of her soft skin sent a bolt of lust straight through his veins, pumping pulsing blood south. He wrestled his thoughts back to the conversation, back to the care of his offspring. "They're hell on wheels, but I would do anything for them. Anything."

So there was no need for him to stress over the fact that Alexa turned him on so hard his teeth hurt. He'd been too long without sex, only a couple of encounters in the year since his divorce. That had to be the reason for his instantaneous, out of control reaction to this woman.

Gauging by the pure blue flame in her eyes, she was feeling it, too.

He was realizing they had a lot more than just a hefty dose of attraction in common. They were both reeling from crappy marriages and completely focused on their careers. Neither of them was looking for anything permanent that would involve more messy emotions.

So why not hook up? If he wanted to act on their attraction and she was cool with the fact that being together had no effect on his business decisions, this could be the best damn thing to happen to him in months. *She* could be the best thing to happen to him in months.

Yeah, this could work.

Simple, uncomplicated sex.

They had an empty second bedroom waiting for them. He always carried condoms these days. One surprise pregnancy was enough. They had moonlight, atmosphere. She was even already half-undressed. There was nothing stopping him from seeing if she was amenable.

Decision made, Seth pulled the rose from the vase and stroked it lightly down her nose. Her eyes blinked wide with surprise, but she didn't say a word, didn't so much as move. Hell, yeah.

Emboldened, he traced her lips with the bud before he leaned across the table and kissed her.

Four

The warm press of Seth's mouth against hers surprised Alexa into stillness—for all of three heartbeats. Then her pulse double-timed. Surprise became desire. The attraction she'd been feeling since first laying eyes on him, since he'd taken off his tie, since she'd felt the steamy glide of his gaze over her damp clothing now ramped into hyperdrive.

He stood without breaking contact, and she rose with him as they stepped around the small table into each other's arms. She gripped his shoulders, her fingers sinking into the warm cotton of the shirt she'd chosen for him earlier. Her defenses were low, without a doubt. The romantic meal, moonlit turret and alluring dinner companion had lulled her. Even the soft classical music stroked over her tensed and frazzled nerves. It had been so long since she'd relaxed, too busy charging ahead with rebuilding her life. Even opening up about her divorce had felt—if not good—at least cathartic.

It had also left her bare and defenseless.

The man might be brusque in the way he spoke sometimes, but, wow, did he ever take his time with a kiss. She slid one hand from his shoulder up to the back of his neck, her fingers toying with the coarse texture of his hair. Her body fit against his, her softness giving way to the hard planes of his chest. The sensitive pads of her fingers savored the rasp of his late day beard as she traced his strong jaw, brushed across his cheekbones and back into his thick hair.

His mouth moved over hers firmly, surely, enticing her to open for him. Her breasts pressed more firmly against him as she breathed faster and faster with arousal. The scent of aftershave mingled with the salty sea air. The taste of lime water and spices from his dinner flavored their kiss, tempting her senses all the more to throw reason away. The bold sweep of his tongue made her hunger for more of this. More of *him*.

How easy it would be to follow him into his bedroom and toss away all the stress and worries of the past years as quickly as discarded clothes. Except, too soon, morning would come and with it would come all those concerns, multiplied because of their lack of self-control.

God, this was so reckless and unwise and impulsive in a way she couldn't afford any longer. Scavenging for a shred of self-control, she pushed at his shoulders since she couldn't seem to bring herself to tear her mouth away from his.

Thank goodness he took the hint.

He pulled back, but not far, only a whisper away.

Each breath she took drew in the crisp scent of him. The starlight reflected in his green eyes staring at her with a keen perception of how very much she ached to take this kiss further.

Her chest pumped for air even though she knew full well the dizziness had nothing to do with oxygen and everything to do with Seth's appeal. Slowly he guided her back to her chair—good thing since her legs were wobbly—and he returned to his as well, his eyes still holding her captive. He lifted his crystal glass, sipping the sparkling water while watching her over the rim.

She forced a laugh that came out half strangled. "That was unexpected."

"Really?" He placed his glass on the table again. The pulse visibly throbbing in his neck offered the only sign he was as shaken as she was by what they'd just shared. "I've wanted to kiss you since I first saw you on board my plane. At that moment, I thought that attraction was mutual. Now, I *know* it is."

His cool arrogance smoked across the table.

A chilling thought iced the heat just as quickly as he'd stoked it. "Is that why you asked me to watch your children? Because you wanted a chance to hit on me?" She sat straighter in her chair and wished she wore something more businesslike than a borrowed terry-cloth robe and his shirt. "I thought we had a business arrangement. Mixing business and personal lives is never a good idea."

"Then why did you kiss me back?" He turned the glass on the tablecloth.

"Impulse."

His eyes narrowed. "So you admit you're attracted to me."

Duh. Denying the mutual draw would be pointless. "You know that I am, but it doesn't mean I've been making plans to act on the feeling. I think Brad Pitt's hot as hell, but I wouldn't jump him even if given the opportunity."

"You think I'm Brad Pitt-hot?"

Damn the return of his arrogant grin.

"I was just making a point," she snapped.

"But you think I'm hot."

"Not relevant." She flattened her hands on the table. "I'm not acting on the impulse any further tonight or ever. If that means you renege on your offer to read my proposal and refer me to others in the business, then so be it. I will not sleep my way into a deal."

She pushed to her feet.

"Whoa, hold on." Standing, he circled the table to face her, stroking her upper arm soothingly. "I didn't mean to imply anything of the sort. First, I don't believe you're the kind of person to get ahead in the world that way. And second, I have never paid for sex, and I never intend to."

She froze, his touch sending fresh skitters of awareness up her arm. The darkness and distant night sounds isolated them with too much intimacy.

Alexa eased back a step toward their suite and the soft serenade of Mozart on the breeze. "Have you looked into finding someone else to take care of your children?"

Still, he didn't move. He didn't have to. His presence called to her as he simply stood a couple of steps away, his broad shoulders backlit by the moon, starlight playing across his blond hair, giving him a Greek godlike air.

"Why would I need to do that?" he asked. "You're here for them."

"Our agreement only lasts for twenty-four hours," she reminded him, holding onto the door frame to bolster her wavering resolve.

"I thought we established the time frame had expanded because my meeting with Javier Cortez fell through tonight." He stepped closer, stopping just shy of touching her again. "You even rearranged things at your work to accommodate our business agreement."

He was right, and she'd allowed him to scramble her thoughts once more. She locked onto his last three words and pushed ahead. "Our *business* agreement."

"You're angry."

"Not…angry exactly. Just frustrated and disappointed in both of us."

His eyes flared with something indefinable. "Disappointed?"

"Oh—" she suddenly understood his expression "—not disappointed in the kiss. It was… Hell, you were here, too. There's no denying the chemistry between us."

Another arrogant grin spread across his face. "I agree one hundred percent."

"But back to the Brad Pitt principle." She stiffened her spine and her resolve. "Just because there's an attraction doesn't mean it's wise to act on it. I'm disappointed that we did something so reckless, so unprofessional. My business has to be my primary focus, just as you've said your children are your main concern."

"Having my priorities in order doesn't cancel out my attraction to you. I can separate business from pleasure." He held her with his laser hot gaze. "I'm very good at multitasking."

Anger did build inside her now alongside the frustration. "You're not hearing me! This thing between us is too much, too soon. We barely know each other and we both have high stakes riding on this trip." She jabbed him in the chest with one finger. "So, listen closely. No. More. Kissing."

She launched through the door and into the suite before he could shake her resolve again. But as she raced across the luxurious sitting area into her bedroom, his voice echoed in her ears and through her hungry senses.

"Damn shame."

She completely agreed. Sleep tonight would be difficult to come by as regrets piled on top of frustrated desire.

Staring off over the city skyline, Seth leaned back in his chair, staying on the turret balcony long after Alexa left. The heat of their kiss still sizzling through him, he finished his seltzer water, waiting for the light in her room to turn off.

He'd only met her today, and he couldn't recall wanting any woman this much. The strength of the attraction had been strong enough on its own. But now that he'd actually tasted her? He pushed the glass aside, his deeper thirst not even close to quenched.

Now he had to decide what to do about that feeling. She was right in saying that giving in to an affair wasn't wise. They both had important reasons to keep their acquaintance all business.

His life was complicated enough. He needed to keep

his life stable for his kids. No parade of women through the door, confusing them.

He eyed his smartphone on the table where it had been resting since his four attempts to contact Pippa. She still wasn't returning his messages, and his temper was starting to simmer. What if there had been something wrong with one of the kids and he needed to contact her? She should at least pick up to find out why he was trying to reach her.

His phone vibrated with an incoming call. He slammed his chair back on all four legs and scooped up his cell fast. The LED screen showed a stored name... his cousin Paige back in Charleston.

Not Pippa.

Damn it.

Even his extended family kept in better contact with him than the mother of his kids. His cousins Paige and Vic had both moved from North Dakota, each starting their families in the Charleston area. With no other family left out west, Seth had followed and started his own business.

He picked up without hesitation. "Paige? Everything okay?"

"We're fine." His cousin's voice was soft as if lowered to keep from waking her children. Classical guitar music played softly in the background. "The girls are both finally asleep. I've been worried about you all afternoon. How are you and the twins? I feel so bad that I couldn't help you out."

"No need to call and apologize. We prefer to steer clear of strep throat."

"Actually I'm calling about Vic and Claire..."

Oh. Hell. In the chaos with the twins, he'd actually

forgotten that his cousin Vic's wife had gone into labor today. "How's she doing?"

"She delivered a healthy baby boy just before midnight. Nine pounds thirteen ounces, which explains the C-section. But Mom and baby are doing great. His big sister and big brother can't wait to meet him in the morning." Two boys and a girl. A family.

Seth scratched the kink in his neck. "Send my congratulations when you see them. I'll swing by for a visit when I get back in town."

"I'll let them know." The reception crackled as it sounded like she moved her phone to the other ear. More guitar music filled the airwaves... Bach, perhaps? "Actually, I called for a different reason. Now that Claire's had the baby and Vic has picked up their kids, her sister Starr says she can watch the twins. They know her two kids. They'll have a blast. You could fly Olivia and Owen up early in the morning before your first meeting."

"That's a generous offer..."

"My girls won't be contagious in another day or two once the antibiotics kick in, so I can relieve her then. No worries."

Her plan sounded workable. And yet, he hesitated, his gaze drawn back to the suite where Alexa slept. "You're all busy with your own families, and I have a plan in place here."

"You're family," Paige insisted sincerely. "We want to help."

"I appreciate that." Except he genuinely wanted his kids near him—and he wanted to keep Alexa near him, too.

The thought of cutting his time with Alexa short—it just wasn't happening. Crazy, really, since he could contact her later, after this deal was cinched. If she was even still speaking to him once she realized he never intended to give her the Jansen Jets contract.

No. His time to get to know Alexa was now. He needed to figure out this unrelenting draw between them and work through it. She was here, and he intended to keep it that way. "Thanks, Paige, but I meant it when I said I'm set. I have help."

"Hmm…" Her voice rose with interest. "You have a new nanny?"

His family chipped in most of the time, but he didn't want to take advantage so he hired a couple of part-time nannies on occasion, all of which Paige would already know about. "Not a nanny. More of a sitter, a, uh, friend actually."

"A female friend?" she pressed, tenacious as ever.

"She's a female, yes." *Definitely* female.

"That's it?" Paige laughed. "That's all you're going to tell me, eh?"

"There's not much to tell." Yet. His eyes drifted back to the suite as he envisioned Alexa curled up asleep, wearing his shirt.

"Ah," she said smugly, "so you're still in the early stages, but not too early, right, or she wouldn't be there with your children. Because, as best as I can remember, you haven't dated much and none of those women ever got anywhere near the twins."

His cousin was too insightful. The way she homed in on the intensity of his draw to Alexa so quickly made him uncomfortable.

He shot up from his seat. "That's enough hypothesizing about my personal life for one night. I need to go."

"I'm not giving up. I'll want details when you return,"

Paige insisted, getting louder and louder by the second. "And I want to meet her. I know you guard your privacy, but I'm family and I love you."

"Love you too, cuz."

"So you'll talk to me? Let me know what's going on in your world rather than hole up the way you did after Pippa—"

"I hear a kid," he cut her short. "Gotta go. Bye." He thumbed the off button and flipped the phone in his palm, over and over.

Guilt kicked around in his gut for shutting down Paige and for taking advantage of Alexa's help. He should send Alexa back to Charleston and then impose on the sister of a cousin-in-law because his ex-wife had dumped his kids off without warning...

Hell, his life was screwed up, and he needed to start taking charge. He'd meant it when he said he could separate the personal from the professional. But he also heard Alexa when she said this was moving too fast for her. She needed more time, time they wouldn't have if she went back to Charleston while he stayed here. He suspected once she went home, she would erect mile-high walls between them, especially once she learned he'd never planned to sign her cleaning company.

He needed longer with her *now*.

His mind filled with a vision of Alexa chasing his kids around, all wet from the tub. Warm memories pulled him in with a reminder of the family life he should be having right now and wasn't because of his workload. Having Alexa here felt so right.

It *was* right.

And so, he wasn't sending her back in the morning. In fact, he had to find a way to extend their window of time together. He not only needed her help with the children, but he also wanted her to stay for more *personal* reasons. The explosive chemistry they'd just discovered didn't come around often. Hell, he couldn't remember when he'd ever burned to have a particular woman this much. So much the craving filled his mind as well as his body.

The extension of their trip presented the perfect opportunity to follow that attraction to its ultimate destination.

Landing her directly into his bed.

Sunlight streamed through the window over the array of clothes laid out on the bed. So many clothes. Far more than she needed for a day or two.

Although as Alexa looked closer, she noticed the variety. It was as if whoever had shopped for her had planned for any contingency. Tan capris with a shabby chic blouse. A simple red cocktail dress. A sexy black bathing suit that looked far from nannylike and made her wonder who'd placed the order. At least there was a crocheted cover-up. And for this morning's breakfast…

She wore a silky sundress, floral with coral-tinted tulips in a watercolor print. Strappy gold sandals wrapped up and around her ankles. She scraped her hair back with a matching scarf that trailed down her back.

There was a whole other shopping bag that a quick peek told her held more clothes, underwear, a nightgown and a fabric cosmetics bag full of toiletries. Once upon a time, she'd taken these kinds of luxuries for granted, barely noticing when they appeared in her room or at a hotel.

These days she had a firm grasp on how hard she would have to work to pay for even one of these designer items. What a difference a year could make in a person's life. Yet, here she was again, dancing on the periphery of a world that had almost swallowed her whole.

Steeling her resolve to keep her values firmly in place, she strode from the bedroom into the sitting area where Seth was strapping the twins into the new, top-of–the-line double stroller.

He looked up and smiled. The power of his vibrant green eyes and dimples reached across the room, wrapping around her, enticing her to move closer into the circle of that happiness. A dangerous move. She had to step away, for her own peace of mind. She wasn't wired to leap into intimacy with a stranger.

A stranger who became more intriguing by the second.

Surely a billionaire who knew how to work a stroller couldn't be totally disconnected from everyday reality. That insight buoyed her, and inspired her. Actively learning more about him would help her on many levels. Knowing more about him was wise for her work.

For work, damn it, not because of this insane attraction.

"Are you ready?" he asked.

"Yes, I believe I am." She could do this. She could keep her professional face in place, while discovering if Seth Jansen harbored any more surprises in that hulking hot body of his.

"Glad the clothes fit. Although for breakfast with the twins, we might be better off draping ourselves in rain ponchos."

Before she could laugh or reply, his phone rang and

he held up a hand. "Hold on, I've got to take this. Work call coming in."

He started talking into his cell and grabbed his briefcase off the sofa. Opening the door, he gestured her ahead. She wheeled the stroller forward, out into the hall and toward the elevator.

The fabric slid sensuously against her skin with each step as she pushed the stroller into the elevator while Seth spoke on his phone to his partner...Rick... briefcase in his other hand. Each glide of the silky dress against her skin reminded her how vibrantly in tune her senses were this morning, and, as much as she wanted to credit the sunshine, she knew it was last night's kiss that had awakened something inside her.

Something that made professional goals tougher to keep in focus.

Two floors down, the doors slid open to admit an older couple dressed casually in sightseeing clothes that still shouted Armani and Prada. They fit right in with the rest of the clientele here. Except the woman carried a simple canvas bag with little handprints painted on it and signed in childlike handwriting. Stenciled along the top of the bag were the words Grandma's Angels. Alexa swallowed a lump of emotion as she counted at least eleven different scrawled signatures.

The husband leaned closer to his wife, whispering, pointing and smiling nostalgically. The wife knelt to pick up a tiny tennis shoe and passed it to Alexa. "You have a beautiful family."

Before Alexa could correct her, they reached the lobby and the couple exited. She glanced sheepishly toward Seth and found him staring at her with assessing eyes as he tucked away his phone. Her mouth went dry.

She grabbed the stroller, grateful for the support as the now increasingly predictable wobbly knees syndrome set in.

Ever aware of his gaze following her, she wheeled the twins from the elevator. She needed to get her thoughts in order ASAP. She was seconds away from meeting royalty for breakfast, pretty heady stuff even given her own upbringing. Seth was certainly coming through on his promise to introduce her to prestigious connections. Knowing the Medina family could be a serious boon to her fledgling business.

Although she was confused by a person who invited twin toddlers to a business breakfast at a restaurant with silk, antiques and a ceiling hand-painted with twenty-four karat gold.

The clink of silverware echoing from the room full of patrons, she didn't have to wonder for even a second which pair of diners to approach. A dark-haired, aristocratic man stood from a table set for six, nodding in their direction. A blonde woman sat beside him, a flower tucked behind her ear.

The wheels of the stroller glided smoothly along the tile floor as they passed a waiter carrying plates of crepes on his tray. Alexa stopped by their table.

Seth shook the man's hand. "Javier, I'd like you to meet—"

The man took her hand. "Alexa Randall. A pleasure to meet you," Javier said with only a hint of an accent. He motioned to the elegant woman beside him. "This is my wife, Victoria."

"Lovely to meet you." Victoria smiled welcomingly, while tucking her fingers into the crook of her husband's arm. He covered her hand automatically with a possessive and affectionate air.

Good God, this place was chock full of couples swimming in marital bliss. First the elderly couple in the elevator. Now her dining companions for breakfast. She didn't even dare look at the couple feeding each other bits of melon at the table next to them.

The numbers of fawning couples here defied national divorce statistics. Although, now that she thought about it, she and Seth had enough breakups to even out the scales.

Leaning into the stroller, Victoria grinned at the twins and spun a rattle attached to the tray. "Would you mind if I held one of these sweethearts?"

Seth pulled back the stroller canopy. "Sure, this is Owen—" he picked up his son "—and this is Olivia."

As Victoria reached down, the little girl stretched her arms up toward Alexa instead. Alexa's heart squeezed in response. So much so, it scared her a little. These babies were quickly working their way into her affection. Victoria eased back gracefully and left Alexa to settle the baby girl into her high chair beside her brother's. The adults took their seats and placed their orders, so far, with no mishaps.

As the waitress placed each person's dish on the table, Victoria spread her linen napkin across her lap. "I told Javier he really put you on the spot insisting you bring along babies, but the twins are total dolls." She tickled Olivia's chin. "Hopefully you'll warm up to me, sweetie, so I can entertain you while Alexa eats her breakfast, too."

"I think I can manage, but thank you." She reached past her smoked salmon bagel for her goblet of juice.

How well did this woman and her husband already know Seth? What kind of information might she learn during this breakfast about Seth and his possible contacts?

While Javier detailed the must-see sights in St. Augustine, Olivia and Owen fed themselves fruit—which scared Alexa to her last frazzled nerve as she watched to be sure strawberries stayed on Olivia's tray but not Owen's.

Seth shoveled in steak and eggs, spooning oatmeal into the twins' mouths, while holding a conversation. She was in awe.

And a little intimidated.

She'd almost flooded the floor last night during their bath. If he hadn't shown up early, she wasn't sure how she would have wrestled them both into clothes. Whenever she thought she'd moved everything dangerous out of their reach...

Oh, God...

She lunged for Olivia just as Seth smoothly pulled the salt shaker from her grasp. Her pulse rate doubled at the near miss with catastrophe. So much for using this breakfast to learn more about Seth from the Cortez couple. She would be lucky to make it through the meal with her sanity intact.

Victoria rested her knife at the top of her plate of half-eaten eggs Benedict. "I hope he's treating you to some vacation fun after all these stodgy business meetings are over."

"Pardon?" Alexa struggled to keep track of the twins and the conversation in the middle of a business meeting and a dining room full of tourists.

Glasses and silverware clinked and clattered. Waiters

angled past with loaded trays as people fueled up for the day ahead.

Victoria swiped her mouth with the linen napkin. "You deserve some pampering for watching the kids solo here at the hotel during the day."

"I'm helping out with temporary nanny detail."

Leaning closer, Victoria whispered, "It's obvious he doesn't look at you like a nanny."

She couldn't exactly deny that since she was likely searing him with her own glances, too. "Honestly we don't know each other that well."

Victoria waved away her comment, her wedding rings refracting light from the chandelier. "The length of time doesn't always matter when it comes to the heart. I knew right away Javier was the one." She smiled affectionately at her new husband, who was deep in conversation with Seth. "It took us a while to find our way to each other, but if I'd listened to my heart right off, we could have been saved so many months of grief."

"It's a business arrangement," she said simply, hoping if she repeated it enough she could maintain her objectivity. "Only business."

"Of course," Victoria conceded, but her smile didn't dim. "I'm sorry. I didn't mean to be nosy. It's just that given what I understand from Javier, Seth has been a workaholic since his divorce. He hasn't had time for relationships."

"There's nothing to apologize for." Alexa knew full well she and Seth were sending out mixed signals. As much as she'd been determined to keep things professional with Seth the businessman, she found herself drawn to Seth the father. A man so tender with his children. At ease with a baby stroller. As adept at flying a spoonful of oatmeal into a child's mouth as he was at piloting a plane through the sky.

These surprise insights proved a potent attraction, especially after living with her own distant father and then the way her ex had checked out on her.

Victoria's voice pulled Alexa out of her musings.

"Honestly, my thoughts may be selfish. I was thinking ahead that if Javier and Seth settle on a contract, then I was hoping we would get to see more of each other. As much as I adore my husband, his world is narrow and he's suspicious of expanding the circle. I'm always grateful for some girl time."

"That would be lovely, thank you." Alexa understood perfectly about lonely inner circles, too much so. She felt a twinge of guilt over her thoughts about using the Cortezes for contacts.

All her life she'd been warned about gold diggers. She'd always known the chances of someone seeing through the money to love her for herself was slim. And still she'd made a royal mess. She didn't want to let the Cortez money and their Medina connections blind her to who they really were.

"I mean it. And regardless of how much time we spend visiting, let's enjoy the day…let's have fun."

Fun? She should be home, at work. She took a deep breath. This situation would help her at work. Or she hoped so.

She couldn't ignore the fact that her wish to stay right here was increasing by the second. "I appreciate how helpful you've been here at breakfast. The twins are my responsibility. We're going sightseeing with the stroller, maybe do a little shopping."

"Perfect," Victoria declared. "I'm at loose ends. I

love a good walk and shopping. And after that, we can wear them out at the pool."

Alexa did have a swimsuit and she had absolutely no reason not to take Victoria up on her generous offer. No reason other than a deep-seated fear of allowing herself to be tempted back into a world she'd been determined to leave behind. A way of life embraced by Seth and his precious children. Her eyes were drawn back to the twins.

Just as Owen wrapped his fist around one of his sister's strawberries—a food he was allergic to.

Panic gripped Alexa as she saw the baby's lightning fast intent to gobble the forbidden fruit. "No! Owen, don't eat that."

Lurching toward him, she grabbed his chubby wrist just before his hand reached his mouth. His face scrunched into utter dejection as his tiny world crumbled over the lost treat. Alexa winced a second ahead of his piercing scream. Seth leaned in to soothe the temper tantrum. Before Alexa could even form the words of warning…

Olivia flipped the bowl of oatmeal straight into Javier Cortez's lap.

Five

The cosmos must have been holding a serious grudge against him because the sight of Alexa in a bathing suit sucker-punched him clean through.

Seth stopped short by the poolside bar outside the hotel and allowed himself a moment to soak in the sunlit view, a welcome pleasure after a tense work day that had started with his kid dumping oatmeal in a prospective customer's lap. Thank goodness Javier Cortez had insisted it didn't matter.

And Alexa had acted fast by scooping up both twins and taking them away for the day.

Now, she looked anything but maternal as she rubbed sunscreen down her arms, laughing at something Victoria said. The twins slept in a playpen under the shade of a small open cabana. Only a half dozen others had stayed this late in the day—a young couple drinking wine in the hot tub and a family playing with a beach ball in the shallow end.

His attention stayed fully focused on the goddess in black Lycra.

He should be celebrating the success of his day's meeting. Javier wanted him to tour the landing strip at the king's private island off the coast of St. Augustine. Their time here was done. The king's island even came equipped with a top-notch nanny for the twins, a nanny the king kept on staff for his grandchildren's visits.

And yet, Seth was all the more determined than ever to keep Alexa with him, to win her over, to seduce her into his bed again and again until he worked this tenacious attraction out of their systems. He hadn't yet attained that goal but was determined to keep her around until he succeeded.

The black bathing suit was more modest than the strings other women wore that barely held in the essentials. Still, there was no denying her sensuality. Halter neckline, plunging deeply until the top of her belly button ring showed.

A simple gold hoop.

His hands itched to grasp her hips and slide his fingers along the edges, slipping inside to feel the satiny slickness he knew waited right there. For him.

Splashing from the deep end snapped him back to reality. Damn, he seriously needed to rein in those kinds of thoughts out here in public. Even when they were alone. He needed to be patient. He didn't want to spook her into bailing on this time they had together.

He thought back to how fast she'd retreated after their kiss. She'd been undeniably as turned on as he was and yet, she'd avoided him that morning as they'd

prepared for the day. Although he thought he sensed
a bit of softening in her stance as the day wore on. At
breakfast he'd thought he caught her eyes lingering on
him more than once. He could see the memory of their
kiss written in her eyes as she stared at him with a
mixture of confusion and attraction.

Shoving away from the bar, Seth strode alongside
the pool toward Alexa. "Good afternoon, ladies."

Jolted, she looked over at him. Her eyes widened and
he could have sworn goose bumps of awareness rose
along her arms. She yanked her crocheted cover-up off
the glass-topped table and shrugged into it almost fast
enough to hide her breasts beading with arousal. His
own body throbbed in response, his hands aching to
cradle each creamy globe in his palms.

"Seth, I didn't expect you back this early."

Out of the corner of his eyes, he saw Victoria gather
her beach bag. "Since you're done for the day, I take it
my husband's free, so if you'll both excuse me…"

The woman made a smooth—and timely—exit.

Seth sank down into her vacated lounger beside
Alexa as a teenager cannonballed into the deep end.
"Did you and the babies have a good afternoon?"

"No problems or I would have called you. I wrote
down everything the children ate and when they went
to sleep. The pool time wore them out." She toyed with
the tie on her cover up—right between her breasts.

He forced his gaze to stay on her face. "I want you
to extend your time with us for a couple more days."

Her jaw went slack with surprise before she
swallowed hard. "You want me to stay with you and
the children?"

"Precisely."

"My business is a small operation—"

"What about your partner?"

"I can't dump everything on her indefinitely and still meet our obligations."

His point exactly as for why hers wasn't the company for Jansen Jets—hers wasn't large enough and didn't have adequate backup resources. He leaned forward, elbows resting on his knees. "I thought you were cleaning my plane to meet with me."

"That certainly was my intent—and to impress you with A-1's work." She hugged her legs. "But I do clean other aircraft in addition to my obligations to office work."

"That doesn't leave much time for a private life." Late day sun beating down on his head, he shrugged out of his suit jacket and draped it over the back of the lounger. He loosened his tie. God, he hated the constraining things.

"I'm investing in my future."

"I understand completely." His eyes gravitated toward his children, still sleeping peacefully in the playpen—Olivia on her tummy with her diapered butt up in the air, Owen on his back with his arms flung wide.

"You've achieved your goals. That's admirable. I'm working on my dream now." Determination coated each word as fully as the sunscreen covered her bared skin.

He *really* didn't need to be thinking about her exposed body right now.

Already, he was on the edge of a new deal with Javier Cortez to supply charter jets for the royal Medinas. That huge boon would take his company to the next level and free him up to set up an entire volunteer, nonprofit foundation devoted to search and rescue operations. His first love, what had drawn him into flying in the first place. That love of flying had helped him develop and patent the airport security device that had made him a mint. Once he took his business to the next level, funding and overstretched government budgets wouldn't be an issue…

So damn close to achieving all his business dreams.

Yet, still he was restless. "Let's forget arguing about tomorrow and business. We can hash that out later. Right now, I'm off the clock. I want to make the most of our time left in St. Augustine tonight."

"What exactly did you have in mind?" She eyed him suspiciously.

Had he imagined her softening on the all-business stance? There was only one way to find out.

Standing, he snagged his suit coat. "We're going to spend the evening out."

"With twins? Don't you think breakfast was pushing our luck?"

He grinned, scooping up his groggy daughter. "Trust me. I can handle this."

"All right, if you're sure."

"Absolutely." He palmed his daughter's back as she wriggled in his arms and tugged at his collar. "Wait until you see what I have planned. You'll want to dress comfortably, though. And we should probably pack extra clothes for the kids in case they get dirty."

Alexa pulled up alongside him, Owen in her arms. Seth reached for the door inside—

Until her gasp stopped him short.

"Did you forget something?" he asked.

When Alexa didn't answer, he glanced and found her

staring back at him with horror. What the hell? Except as she raised a shaking hand to point, he realized she wasn't looking at him. Her attention was focused fully on Olivia.

More precisely, on Olivia's bulging left nostril.

Sitting on the edge of the hotel sofa in their suite, Alexa struggled to contain the squirming little girl in her lap while pushing back the welling panic. The whole ride up in the elevator had been crazy, with Seth attempting to check his daughter's nose and the child growing more agitated by the second.

How in the world had Olivia wedged something up her nostril? More importantly, *what* had she shoved into there?

Alexa winced at the baby's bulging left nostril. She hadn't taken her eyes off Olivia for a second during their time at the pool—except when Olivia had been sleeping. Had she woken up? Found something in the playpen? Perhaps something blew inside the pen with her?

Panic gripped her. What the hell had she been thinking, allowing herself to believe she could care for these two precious children? She willed herself to stop shaking and deal with the crisis at hand.

Seth knelt in front of her, trying to grasp his daughter's head between his palms. "I can get this out if you will just hold her still long enough for me to push my thumb down the outside of her nose."

"Believe me, I'm trying my best." Alexa's heart pumped as hard and fast as Olivia's feet as the little girl screamed, kicking her father in the stomach. Her face turned red; her skin beaded with sweat from hysteria.

Sinking back on his haunches, Seth looked around their suite. "Is there any pepper left from last night's dinner?"

"Housekeeping cleared away everything. Oh, God, I am so sorry. I don't know how this happened—"

A crash echoed through the room.

Alexa looked at Seth, her panic mirrored in his eyes. "Owen!"

They both shot to their feet just as a pitiful wail drifted from behind the velvet sofa. Holding Olivia around the waist, Alexa ran fast on Seth's heels, only to slam against his back when he stopped short.

Owen sat on the floor, blessedly unharmed, just angry. His "tower"—which consisted of a chair, a pillow and the ice bucket—now lay on its side by the television. Handprints all over the flat screen testified to his attempt to turn on the TV by himself.

Seth knelt beside his son, running his hands along the toddler's arms and legs. "Are you okay, buddy? You know you're not supposed to climb like that." His thumb brushed over his son's forehead, along the eyebrow that still carried a scar from past stitches. "Be careful."

Picking up Owen, Seth held him close for a second, a sigh of relief racking through his body so visibly Alexa almost melted into the floor with sympathy. God, this big manly guy who plowed through life and through the skies alone had the most amazing way of connecting with his kids.

What would it have been like to grow up with a father like him? A dad so very present in his children's lives?

Standing, Seth said, "I'm going to have to take Olivia to the emergency room. Swap kids with me. You can stay here with Owen."

"You still trust me?"

"Of course," he responded automatically even though his mouth had gone tight. With frustration? Fear?

Or anger?

He leaned toward her. Olivia let out a high-pitched shriek and locked her arms tighter around Alexa's neck, turning her face frantically from her father.

Seth frowned. "It's okay, kiddo. It's just me."

Patting Olivia's back, Alexa swayed soothingly from side to side. "She must think you're going to pinch her nose again."

"Well, we don't have much choice here. I need to take her in." He set down Owen and clasped his daughter.

Olivia's cries cranked up to earsplitting wails, which upset her brother who started sobbing on the floor. If Olivia kept gasping would whatever was in her nose get sucked in? And then where would it go? Into a lung? The possibilities were horrifying. This parenting thing was not for the faint of heart.

"Seth, let me hold her rather than risk her becoming even more hysterical." She cradled the little girl's head, blond curls looping around Alexa's fingers as surely as the child was sliding into Alexa's heart. "You and I can go to the emergency room and take both kids."

Plowing a hand through his hair, Seth looked around the suite again as if searching for other options. Finally he nodded and picked up his son. "That's probably for the best. We just have to get a car." He grabbed the room phone and dialed the hotel operator. "Seth Jansen here. We need transportation to the nearest E.R. waiting for us. We're headed to the elevator now."

She jammed her feet into the flip-flops she'd worn to the pool, grateful she'd at least had time to change out of her swimsuit, and followed Seth out into the hall. The elevator opened immediately—thank God—and they plunged inside the empty compartment. He jostled his restless son while she made *shhh, shhh, shhh* soothing sounds for Olivia, who was now hiccupping. But at least the little girl wasn't crying.

The floors dinged by, but not fast enough. The doors parted and the elderly couple they'd seen on their way down to breakfast stepped inside.

Dressed to the nines in jewels and evening wear, the woman wasn't carrying her canvas bag made by her grandchildren, but she still radiated a grandma air. She leaned toward Olivia and crooned, "What's the matter, sweetie? Why the tears?"

Lines of strain and worry pulled tighter at the corners of Seth's mouth. "She shoved something up her nose," he said curtly, his gaze locked in on the elevator numbers as if willing the car to move faster. "We're headed to the E.R."

As if sensing her dad's intent, Olivia pressed her face into Alexa's neck.

The grandmother looked back at her husband and winked knowingly. The older gentleman, dressed in a tuxedo, reached past Alexa so quickly she didn't have time to think.

He tugged Olivia's ear. "What's that back there behind your ear, little one?" His hand came back around with a gold cuff link in his palm. "Was that in your ear?"

Olivia peeked around to see and like lightning, the grandmother reached past and swiped her finger down Olivia's nose. A white button shot out and into the woman's hand. She held it up to Seth's shirt. A perfect match. They hadn't even noticed he was missing one from near his neck.

Surprise stamped on his handsome face, Seth stuffed the button into his pocket. "She must have pulled it off when I picked her up by the pool."

Alexa gasped in awe at how easily the couple had handled mining the button from Olivia's nose. "How did you two manage that so smoothly?"

The grandpa straightened his tuxedo bow tie. "Lots of practice. You two will get the knack before you know it."

In a swirl of diamonds and expensive perfume, the couple swept out of the elevator, leaving Alexa and Seth inside. The doors slid closed again. She sagged back against the brass rail. Relief left her weak-kneed all the way back to the penthouse floor while Seth called downstairs on his cell to cancel their ride to the E.R.

Stopping just outside their door, he tucked his phone in his pocket and slid a hand behind her neck. "Thank you."

"For what? I feel like I've let you down." The emotions and worry after the scare with Olivia had left her spinning. She could only imagine how he must feel.

"Thank you for being here. Chasing these two is more challenging than flying a plane through a thunderstorm." He scrubbed a hand over his jaw. "My family tells me I'm not too good at asking for help. But I gotta admit having an extra set of hands and eyes around made things easier just now."

His emerald-green gaze warmed her along with his words. Given her history with men, the whole trust notion was tough for her. But right now, she so desperately wanted to believe in the sincerity she saw in his eyes. She felt appreciated. Valued as a person.

Giving that much control to another person scared her spitless. "You're welcome."

She thought for a moment he was going to kiss her again. Her lips tingled at the prospect. But then he glanced at the two children and eased back. "Let's get the diaper bag so we can move forward with our night out on the town."

Blinking fast, she stood stock-still for a second, barely registering his words. They still had a whole night ahead of them? She was wrung out, as if she'd run an emotional marathon. With her defenses in the negative numbers, an evening out with Seth and his children was too tantalizing, too tempting a prospect. Hell, the man himself was too tempting. Not that she had the choice of opting out.

She just really hoped the evening sucked.

The evening hadn't sucked.

In fact, Seth had followed through with the perfect plans so far, starting off with a gourmet picnic at a park near a seventeenth century fort by the harbor. The children had toddled around, eaten their fill and gotten dirty. So precious and perfect and far more normal than she would have expected.

Then Seth had chartered a carriage ride through the historic district at sundown. Olivia and Owen had squealed with delight over the horse. And the last part of the outing hadn't ended in a half hour as she'd expected.

Once the kids' bedtime arrived, Seth had simply paid the driver to continue down the waterside road while the children slept in their laps. The *clop, clop, clop* of the Belgian draft's hooves lulled Alexa as she cuddled the sweet weight of Owen sleeping in her arms.

The night was more than Cinderella-perfect. Cinderella only had the prospect of happily ever after. For tonight, Alexa had experienced the magic of being a part of a real family during this outing with Seth and his children.

Although Cinderella's driver likely wasn't sporting ear buds for an iPod. Alexa appreciated the privacy it offered as she didn't have to worry about him eavesdropping.

Being a part of a family taking a magical moonlit carriage ride presented a tableau she'd dreamed about. The way Olivia nestled so trustingly against her father's chest. The obvious affection between him and his children during their picnic. He'd built a relationship with them, complete with familiar games and songs and love.

But even as she joined in this family game for now, she couldn't lose sight of her real role here. Or the fact that Seth Jansen was a sharp businessman, known for his drive for perfection and no-nonsense ways.

She knew he wanted her. Could he be devious enough to use his children to keep her here? She thought of earlier, by the pool, how he'd focused all that intensity on her. His eyes had stroked over her, hot and hungry.

Exciting.

There'd been a time when she couldn't show her body in a bathing suit—for fear people would find out her secret, because of her own hang-ups. She'd worked past that. She'd come to peace with herself. But as her thoughts drifted toward the possibility of intimacy with another person, she faced the reality of sharing that secret part of herself, to explain why she had such extensive stretch marks in spite of never having had a child.

Even though she'd found resolution inside, it wasn't something she enjoyed revisiting.

She rested her chin on Owen's head, Seth sitting across from her holding Olivia. "How did your business meeting go?"

"We're moving forward, closer to a deal than before. My gut tells me there's a real possibility I can land this one."

"If he hasn't ended the negotiations, that's got to be a positive sign." She settled into the professional discussion, thinking of how far she'd come from her teenage years of insecurity.

"That's my take." He nodded, then something shifted in his eyes. "It appeared you had fun with Victoria today."

More memories of his interest at the pool, of his kiss last night steamed through her as tangibly as the heat rising from the paved road. A cooling breeze rolled off the harbor and caressed her shoulders, lifting her hair the way his fingers had played through the strands.

Her hand lifted to swipe back a lock from her face. "I feel guilty calling this work when it really has been more of a vacation."

"You've had twins to watch over. That's hardly a holiday."

"I've had a lot of help from you and Victoria." The carriage driver tugged the reins at a stop sign, a towering adobe church on the corner. "Not that any of us could stop that oatmeal incident."

He chuckled softly. "Thank goodness Javier's more laid back than I would have given him credit for."

"It was gracious of him to acknowledge that the breakfast with toddlers was his idea." She shuffled Owen into a more comfortable position as the baby settled deeper into sleep. "What made you think of taking a carriage ride to help the twins wind down?"

"I spent so much time outdoors growing up." He patted his daughter's back softly. "I try to give that to my kids when I can."

"Well, this was a great idea…" The moonlight played across the water rippling in the harbor. "The night air, the gorgeous scenery, the water, it's been quite a break for me, too."

"I never get tired of the year-round good weather here." As he sat across from her, he propped a foot beside her on the seat.

"What about January through March?" She shivered melodramatically. "The cold wind off the water is biting."

His laugh rode the ocean breeze as he opened up more as the evening wore on. "You've obviously never visited North Dakota. My uncle would get icicles in his beard in the winter."

"No kidding?"

"No kidding." He scratched his chin as if caught in the memories. "My cousins and I still went outside, no matter how far the temperature dropped, but it's a lot easier here when it doesn't take a half hour to pull on so many layers of clothes."

"What did you like to do in North Dakota?" she asked, hungry for deeper peeks into this intriguing man.

"Typical stuff, snowmobiling, hiking, horseback

riding on the farm. Then I discovered flying..." He shrugged. "And here I am now."

Yet there was so much more to him than that, this man who'd come from a North Dakota farm and made billions off his interest in airplanes.

The carriage shocks squeaked as the large wheels rolled along a brick side-road. How was it she felt tipsy when she hadn't even had so much as a sip of alcohol?

He nudged the side of her leg with his foot. "What about you? What did you want to do when you were a kid?"

"Art history, remember?" she said evasively.

"Why art history?"

"An obsession with creating beauty, I guess."

And now they were dancing a little too close to uncomfortable territory from her past. She pointed to the old-fashioned sailboat anchored near the shore with the sounds of a party carrying across the water. "What's up with that?"

He hesitated for a moment as if he understood full well she was trying to redirect the conversation. "It's a pirate ship. The *Black Raven*. They do everything from kids' parties to the more adult sort." He gestured toward a couple in buccaneer and maid costumes strolling down the sidewalk. "Then there are regular bar hours. People come in costume. I thought about having a party for the kids there someday—during regular hours, of course."

"I can envision you in a Jack Sparrow-style pirate shirt so you wouldn't have to tug at your tie all the time."

"You've noticed that?"

She shrugged, staying silent.

"There are lots of things I hope to teach my kids." He pointed toward the sky. "Like showing them the Big Dipper there. Or my favorite constellation, Orion's belt. See the orange-looking star along the strand? That's Betelgeuse, a red star. There's nothing like charting the sky."

"Sounds like you have a pirate's soul. If you'd been born before airplanes…"

"Star navigation can be helpful if you're lost," he pointed out. "Betelgeuse saved my ass from getting lost more than once when the navigational instruments went on the fritz during a search."

She thought back to her research on him from when she'd put together her proposal. "You started your company doing search and rescue."

"I'm still active in that arena."

"Really?" Why hadn't she seen information about that kind of work? That could have been useful in her proposal. She wanted to kick herself for falling short. "I didn't realize that."

"SAR—search and rescue—was my first love. Still is," he said with undeniable fire.

"Then why do you do the corporate charter gig?" The image of Seth Jansen was more confusing with each new revelation. She hadn't expected so many layers, so much depth.

"Search and rescue doesn't pay well. So the bigger my business…"

"The more good you can do." And just that fast the pieces came together, the billionaire, the father, the philanthropist. And on top of everything he was hot?

God, she was in serious deep water here.

His gaze slid to hers, held and heated. In a smooth

move, he shifted off the seat across from her to sit beside her. The scent of his crisp aftershave teased her nose, while his hulking magnetism drew her. Before she could think, she swayed toward him.

They still held both sleeping children, so nothing could or would happen. But the connection between them was tangible. His eyes invited her to lean against him and his arm slid around her shoulders, tucking her closer as the carriage rolled on.

How far did she want to take this? She hadn't forgotten his request that she extend her stay, even if he hadn't brought it up again. Then there was the whole tangle of her wanting to work for him…

And there were these two beautiful children who obviously came first with him, as they should. She understood how deeply a child could be affected by their growing up years. She carried the scars of her own childhood, complete with fears about opening herself to another relationship, making herself vulnerable to a man by baring her secrets as well as her body.

The carriage jerked to a halt outside their hotel, and her time to decide what to do next came to an end.

Seth set his iPod in the hotel's docking station and cued up the twins' favorite Mozart for tots music. The babies had been too groggy for baths after the carriage ride, so he and Alexa had just tucked them into their cribs, each wearing a fresh diaper and T-shirt.

Leaving him alone with Alexa—and completely awake.

Their evening together had given him an opportunity to learn more about her, the person, rather than the businesswoman. Guilt tweaked his conscience. She had a life and a company and a tender heart. She also had some misguided notion she could persuade him to sign a contract with her cleaning service. He'd told her otherwise, but he suspected she believed she could change his mind.

He needed to clear that up now, before things went further.

While he would do anything for his kids, he had other options for their care now and he couldn't deny the truth. He was keeping her here because he wanted to sleep with her, now, away from Charleston, in a way that wouldn't tangle their lives up with each other. Because, damn it all, no matter how much he wanted her in his bed, he didn't have the time or inclination to start a full out relationship. He would not, under any circumstances put his children through the upheaval of another inevitable breakup.

He plowed his fingers through his hair. He was left with no choice. He had to come clean with Alexa. He owed it to her. If for no other reason than because of the way she'd been so patient with his children, more than just watching over them, she'd played with them.

Rolled a ball.

Kissed a minor boo-boo.

Wiped away pudding smudges from their faces.

Rested her cheek on a sleeping baby's head with such genuine affection while they rode in the carriage like an honest to God family.

A dark cloud mushroomed inside him. He pivoted toward the living room—and found her waiting in the open doorway. She still wore the tan capris and flowing blouse she'd had on for their picnic, except her feet were bare.

Her toes curled into the carpet. "Earlier tonight, you mentioned extending our stay. What was that all about?"

He should be rejoicing. He had achieved exactly what he wanted in enticing her to stay.

Yet now was his time to man-up and tell her the whole story. "There's been a change in plans. I'm not returning to Charleston in the morning."

"You're staying here?" Her forehead crinkled in confusion.

He glanced back at his kids, concerned with waking them, and guided Alexa into the living area, closing the bedroom door behind him.

"Not exactly." He steered her to the blue velvet sofa and sat beside her. "Tomorrow, Javier and I are moving negotiations to the king's island to peruse his landing strip and discuss possibilities for increasing security measures."

"That's great news for you." She smiled with genuine pleasure.

Her obvious—unselfish—happiness over his success kicked his guilt into high gear. "I need to be up-front with you."

"Okay—" her eyes went wary "—I'm listening."

"I want you to come with me to the island." He tucked a knuckle under her chin, brushed his mouth over hers. The connection deepened, crackled with need. "Not because of business or the kids. But because I want *you*. I want *this*."

He hesitated. "And before you ask, I do still intend to introduce you to the contacts just like I promised on day one. And I will listen to your business proposal and give you advice. But that's all I can offer."

Small consolation to his burning conscience right

now. He truly wished he could do more for her and for her business.

Realization dawned in her eyes, her face paling. "I'm not going to land the Jansen Jets contract, no matter what I say."

"I'm afraid not. Your company is simply not large enough. I'm sorry."

She gnawed her plump bottom lip, then braced her shoulders. "You don't have to apologize. You told me as much that first day, and I just didn't want to hear you."

"The way your service is growing shows promise, and if this had been a year from now, the answer might have been different." That made him wonder what it would have been like to meet her a year from now, when his kids were older and the sting of his divorce had lessened.

"Then I go home now."

Was that anger or regret he saw chasing across her expression? It looked enough like the latter that he wasn't going to miss the opportunity to press what little advantage he had. "Or you could go with me to the island. Just for the weekend."

Her lips pressed tightly, thinning. "You may always get weekends free, but Bethany and I trade off every other one. I've already taken two days off work in the hope of a business proposition you never intended to fulfill. I can't keep imposing on her indefinitely."

"I meant what I said. I do intend to make good on introducing you to new connections and helping you beef up your presentation. Damn it, I'm trying hard to be honest with you." He reached to loosen his tie and then realized he wasn't wearing it anymore. "I'll pay the difference you need to hire temporary help while you're away—"

Her eyes went wide with horror. "You've already paid me enough. It's not about the money."

"Take it anyway. Consider it an exchange for your help with the kids. And I do need your help."

"You want me to stay for the twins?" She crossed her arms defensively.

"It's not that simple. I can't untangle my kids from what's going on between us. So yeah, they factor into this decision." They had to factor into every decision he made. "My children like you. That counts for a lot. They've seen too much upheaval in their lives already. I try to give them as much stability as I can."

"They've only known me for a couple of days and then I'll be gone." Her fingers dug into her elbows.

She had a point there. The thought of them growing too attached…

Shaking his head, he refocused. His plan for the weekend was solid. Second-guessing himself would only derail things. He loosened her grip and held her soft hands in his. "I like how happy Owen and Olivia are with you."

"I adore them, too." Obvious affection tinged her words, along with regret. "But even if I agree to this crazy proposition of yours, I'll be leaving their lives when we all go home."

"Maybe. Maybe not." Where had that come from? Only seconds ago he'd been thinking about how he needed to have an affair now because indulging in more once they returned home wasn't an option.

Was it?

She tugged her hands from his. "I'm not ready for

any kind of relationship, and I'm still not happy about the business end of things between us."

He should be rejoicing at those words. Should be. He cradled her face in his palm. "Then consider having a fling with me."

"A fling?" She gnawed her bottom lip slowly as she repeated the word. "Fling? No attachment or expectations. Just pure indulgence in each other?"

Already her suggestive words sent a bolt of lust straight to his groin. If she could seduce him this thoroughly with just a few words, what more did she hold in store with her hands, her body?

"That's the idea," he growled softly in agreement. "We pick up where we left off last night at dinner."

So he waited for her decision, the outcome more important than it should have been for someone of such brief acquaintance. But then she smiled, not full out, just a hint of possibility.

She reached, skimming her fingers down the front of his chest lightly as if still making up her mind. The feel of her featherlight touch made his erection impossibly harder.

Her hand stopped just shy of his belt, her eyes assessing, yet still holding the briefest hint of reservation. "For how long?"

He clasped her hand and brought her wrist to his mouth. Her pulse leaped under his kiss.

"For the weekend." Or more. He wasn't sure of a hell of a lot right now. But he was certain of one thing. He wanted Alexa. "Starting now."

Six

Alexa leaned into the restrained strength of Seth's touch. He was such a giant of a man with amazing control. She'd been aching for the feel of his hands on her skin since she'd first seen him. Yes, she was angry over the doused hopes of signing a contract with his company. However, in other ways, she was relieved. The end of their business acquaintance freed her to pursue the attraction between them.

As much as she wanted to attribute the power of her desire to months of abstinence, she knew she hadn't felt anything near this compulsion for other attractive men who'd crossed her path. She wanted him, deeply, ached to have him with such a craving it was all she could do not to fling herself onto him.

Even in her spoiled princess days, she'd guarded her body closely. She'd only slept with two men before her husband and no one since. Each relationship had come after months of dating. This was so out of character for her, which emphasized the tenacious attraction all the more.

The prospect of a no-strings affair with Seth, especially now that she wasn't trying to win a contract with him, was more temptation than she could resist.

She angled her face into his hard hand, turning to press a kiss into his palm. A primitive growl of desire rumbled from him in response, stirring and stoking molten pleasure deep in her belly.

Without moving his hand from her face, he leaned to kiss her bared neck. The glide of his mouth sent delicious shivers down her spine. Her head lolled back to give him fuller access.

He swept her hair aside with a large confident hand that skimmed down to palm her waist. Nipping, kissing, his mouth traced along her throbbing pulse. His chin nudged aside one shoulder of her blouse, his late-day beard raspy and arousing against her flushed skin.

His body hummed with restraint. Straining tendons along his neck let her know just how much it cost him to go slowly. His meticulous attention to detail sent a fresh shiver of anticipation through her.

She grabbed his shirt, her fist twisting in the warm cotton as she hauled him closer, urged him on. He shot to his feet and scooped her into his arms. Her fingers linked behind his neck as she steadied herself against his chest. Part of her warned that she should stop, now; but an even more insistent part of her urged her to see this through. Then maybe she would be free of the frenetic lure of this man. She could get back to the carefully planned, safe life she'd built for herself.

Seth angled sideways through the door into the spare room. Gauzy curtains hung from rings around the wrought-iron canopy frame overhead. He lowered her gently into the poofy white spread. Stepping back, he began unbuttoning his shirt while she watched—not that he seemed the least concerned with her gaze clinging to him.

In fact, he appeared all the more aroused by her appreciation. He shrugged off the shirt and unbuckled his belt, the low lighting from the bedside lamp casting a warm glow over his bared flesh.

One long zip later… Oh, yeah, he was most definitely as turned on as she was. The rigid length of his arousal reached up his rock solid abs. Golden hair sprinkled along his defined chest. He was a sculpted god of a man, and for tonight, he was all hers…

But as she devoured him with her eyes, unease skittered up her spine at the prospect of turning the tables. While she'd conquered the eating disorder of her teenage years, her body still carried marks and signs of how close she'd come to dying.

Twisting sideways, she reached to turn off the lamp and prayed he wouldn't argue. She truly didn't want to have this discussion right now. *Click.* The room went dark then shadowy as her eyes adjusted to the moonlight streaming through the sheers on the window, the thicker brocade curtains pulled back.

She waited and thank God, Seth stayed silent. Brows pinching together, his head tilting to the side offered the only signs he'd registered her turning off the light.

Swallowing the patter of nerves, she sat up and swept her loose shirt upward and over her head. As she shook her hair free, he kicked aside his pants and leaned over her, angling her back to recline against the piled pillows. His hand fell to the top button on her capris. Up close, she could see the question in his eyes as he waited for her consent.

Arching upward, she slid her fingers into his hair and tugged his mouth toward hers. The feel of him was becoming familiar as they deepened contact, her lips parting, opening, welcoming him. Losing herself in the kiss, she barely registered his deft work pushing aside her pants and freeing the front clasp of her bra.

The cool air contrasted with the warmth of his hard muscled body. Tension built inside her, a need to take this farther, faster. She tugged at Seth's shoulders, whispering her need, her desires, but he wouldn't be rushed.

He nipped, licked, laved his way down her neck and to her breasts, drawing on her tightening nipples with the perfect mixture of tongue and tug. Her fingernails grazed down his back, tendons and muscles flexing under her stroke in response.

The glide of his hand between them sent her stomach muscles tensing. He slowed, pausing to flick her belly button ring. "This drove me insane when I saw it earlier, exposed by that sexy deep V of your bathing suit. Ever since, all I could think of was touching it. Touching you."

"Then I like the way you think," she whispered, then gasped.

His tender torment continued until her head thrashed along the deep downy pillow. She hooked her leg around his, bringing his stony thigh to rest against her aching core. Rocking against him only made her more frustrated, liquid longing pulsing through her veins and flushing her skin.

The air conditioner swirled the scents of his aftershave, her shampoo and their desire into a perfume of lust, intoxicating her with each gasping breath. He angled off her, and she moaned her frustration.

"Shh." He pressed a finger to her mouth. "Only for a second."

His hand dipped into a drawer in the bedside table. He came back with a box of condoms. Thank heaven, someone had the foresight to plan ahead. She couldn't even bring herself to condemn him for assuming this could happen…because here they were, the only place she wanted to be at the moment.

Then the thick pressure of him between her thighs scattered any other thoughts as he pushed inside her. Large and stretching and more than she'd expected. She hooked her legs around his waist, opening for him, welcoming him and the sensation of having him fully inside her.

Smoothly, he rolled to his back while their bodies stayed connected. She lay sprawled on top of him. Bowing upward, she straddled him, taking him impossibly deeper. His eyes flamed as he watched her with the same intensity she knew she'd lavished on him when he'd undressed for her. He gripped her waist, and she rolled her hips against him.

Her head flung back at the pure sensation, the perfect angle as he nudged against the circle of sensitivity hidden inside her. And again, he moved, thrusting, pumping, taking her need to a whole new level of frenzy until she raked her nails down his chest, desperate for completion. She didn't know herself, this out of control woman all but screaming for release. She'd thought she knew her body and the pleasures to be found in bed. But nothing came close to this…this fiery tingle along her every nerve.

Then they were flipping position again and he was on top of her, pumping faster, the head of his arousal tormenting that special spot inside her again and again until…

Sensation imploded, sparks of white light dotting behind her eyes. His mouth covered hers, taking her gasps and moans and, yes, even her cries of pleasure into him the way she still welcomed him into her body.

The bliss rippled through her in tingling aftershocks even as he rolled to his side, tucking her against his chest. He drew the covers over them and kissed the top of her head tenderly, stroking her back. His heart thumped hard and loud against her ear in time with her own racing pulse.

What the hell had just happened?

The best sex of her life.

And as the wash of desire cooled inside her that thought scared her more than a little. Already she wanted him again. Far too much. She needed distance to shore up her own defenses. Establishing her independence after her divorce had been damn difficult. She couldn't allow herself to turn clingy or needy again—no matter how amazing the orgasm.

Once his breathing evened out into a low snore, she eased herself from his arms, needing to think through what had just happened between them. She inched off the bed, slowly, carefully, her feet finally touching the carpet.

She tugged on her shirt and panties, the fabric gliding

across her well-loved body still oversensitized from the explosiveness of her release. She pulled open the door to the sitting area with more than a little regret.

"You're leaving?" His voice rumbled softly from the bed.

She turned toward him, keeping her head high. "Just returning to my room for the night."

Gauzy white curtains and his large lounging body gave off the air of a blond sheikh…. Good Lord, her mind was taking fanciful routes and fantasies.

"Uh-uh." He shook his head, sliding his hands behind his neck, broad chest all but calling to her to curl right back up again. "You're not ready to sleep together."

"I want to." God, did she ever want to.

"Glad to hear it. Hold on to that thought for our weekend together." He swung his feet to the floor and was beside her in a heartbeat. He kissed her just once, firmly but without moving, as if simply sealing his imprint on her.

As if she didn't already carry the feel of him in her every thought right now.

He stepped back into his room. "Sleep well, Alexa. We leave early for the island. Good night."

The door closing after him, he left her standing in the middle of the sitting room ready to burst into flames all over again.

From inside the chartered jet, Alexa felt the blazing sun flame its way up the morning sky on her way to a king's getaway. The Atlantic Ocean stretched out below, a small dot of an island waiting ahead.

Their destination.

Waking up late, she and Seth had been too rushed for

conversation. They'd dressed the kids and raced to the lobby just as the limousine arrived to pick them up along with Javier and his wife. The luxury ride to the small airport had given her the opportunity to double-check with Bethany and clear the schedule change. Bethany seemed so excited at the prospect of new contacts, she gave two thumbs-up. So there were no obstacles to Alexa's leaving. The ride had been so smooth and speedy she'd been whisked onto the jet before she'd even fully wiped the sleep from her eyes.

Breakfast had been waiting for them on the flight, although she'd been told they would land within a half hour. She had monitored the babies plucking up Cheerios, while nibbling on a *churro*—a Spanish doughnut. It had all seemed so normal, as if her insides weren't still churning from what had happened between her and Seth the night before.

And wondering what would happen when they landed on the isolated island for the weekend.

Her eyes gravitated to the open door leading to the cockpit where Seth flew the jet, Javier sitting in the copilot's seat. Their night together scrolled through her mind in lush, sensual detail. He'd touched her, aroused her, fulfilled her in ways she'd never experienced before. And while she was scared as hell of where this intense connection might lead her, she couldn't bring herself to walk away. Not yet.

Victoria touched her arm lightly. "They're both loners, but I think they're going to work well together."

"I'm sure they will." Loner? She hadn't thought of Seth quite that way, more brusque and businesslike. Except when he was around his kids, then he really opened up. Like he had when talking to her during their carriage ride.

And while making love, he'd held nothing back.

"Are you all right?" Victoria asked.

Alexa forced a smile. "Sorry to be so quiet." She searched for something to explain her preoccupation with a certain hot pilot only a few feet away. "It's just surreal that we would go to a king's home with babies in tow."

"Deposed king—and indulgent grandfather. If it makes you worry less, he's not in residence at the moment. He's visiting his doctors on the mainland, follow-ups on some surgery he had. We'll have the island all to ourselves, other than the staff and security, of course." She replenished the pile of Cheerios on Olivia's tray. The company that had stocked and cleaned the jet had done their job well. "The twins will find anything they need already there. He even keeps a sitter on staff."

"So none of the king's family is in residence at the moment? No other children?"

"None. The other family members have their own homes elsewhere. Since the family has reconciled, they're all visiting more often."

"More air travel." That explained why they were courting Jansen Jets.

"And more need for security with all these extra trips."

That also explained how Seth fit the bill all the better with his background in search and rescue, and security devices for airports. "How scary to have to worry so much about a regular family vacation."

Victoria huffed her blond bangs from her forehead.

"The press may have eased up from the initial frenzy, but they haven't backed off altogether. Even relatives have to be on guard—and stay silent at all times."

Alexa struggled not to squirm. She was used to the background checks that accompanied working at an airport. "I hear you. No speaking to the press."

"Their cousin Alys is still persona non grata after speaking to the press. She moved back to another family compound in South America. I guess you could say she's even in exile from the exiled."

"That's so sad, but understandable." Alexa had grown up in a privileged world, but these people took privileged to a whole new level.

When the silence stretched, she followed Victoria's puzzled stare and realized…Alexa closed her fist around her napkin. She'd been scrubbing a smudge on the silver tray obsessively. Her flatware was lined up precisely and she'd even brushed some powdered sugar into a tiny pile.

Smiling sheepishly, she forced her fists to unfurl and still. "When I'm nervous, I clean."

Victoria covered Alexa's hand with her own. "There's nothing to sweat, really."

Easier said than done when she'd barely survived her home life growing up. It was one thing to stand on the periphery of that privileged world, restoring order to the messes made by others. It was another thing entirely to step into the lushness of overindulgence that had once threatened to swallow her whole. But she was committed to this weekend. Literally. There was no escape.

She stared out the window at the island nestled in miles and miles of sparkling ocean. Palm trees spiked from the lush landscape. A dozen or so small outbuildings dotted a semicircle around a larger structure.

The white mansion faced the ocean in a U shape, constructed around a large courtyard with a pool. Details were spotty but she would get an up close view soon enough. Even from a distance she couldn't miss the grand scale of the sprawling estate, the unmistakable sort that housed royalty.

The plane banked as Seth lined up the craft with a thin islet alongside the larger island. A single strip of pristine concrete marked the private runway. As they neared, a ferry boat came into focus. To ride from the airport to the main island? They truly were serious about security.

She thought she'd left behind this kind of life when she'd cut ties with her parents. She'd been happy with her peripheral role, knowing what the rich needed but free of the complications of that life for herself.

Yet here she was.

Did she really want to even dip her toe in this sort of affluent world again? What choice did she have at the moment? Her gaze slid back to Seth. No choice really given how deeply she ached to be with him again.

Or maybe she had a choice after all: the option to take control on their next encounter rather than simply following his lead.

And she would make damn sure he was every bit as knocked off balance by the experience as she'd been.

The night unfolded for Seth, full of opportunities.

He'd concluded his deal with Javier and would spend tomorrow formulating plans for the future. He was ready to celebrate. With Alexa. Hopefully she would be in the same mindset.

He closed the door to the nursery where the twins would spend the night under the watchful eye of one of the resident nannies.

Just before their bedtime, he'd tried Pippa again, on the off chance she would pick up and could wish the kids good-night. She'd actually answered, sounding overly chipper, but cut the call short once he'd attempted to put Owen and Olivia on the line. Something about the whole conversation had been "off" but he couldn't put his finger on the exact problem.

Most likely because all he could think about right now was getting Alexa naked again.

He entered their quarters. More like a luxurious condominium within the mansion. He and Alexa had been given separate rooms in the second floor corner suite, but he hoped he could keep her distracted through the night until she fell asleep in his arms, exhausted by good sex.

Great sex.

Searching the peach and gray room, he didn't see signs of her other than her suitcase open on her bed. His shoes padded softly against the thick Persian rug past a sitting area with an eating space stocked more fully than most kitchens.

The quiet echoed around him, leaving him hyperaware of other sounds…a ticking grandfather clock in the hall…the crashing ocean outside… Through the double doors, the balcony was as large as some yards.

And Alexa leaned on the railing.

A breeze gusted from the ocean plastering her long

tiered sundress to her body, draping her curves in deep purple.

He stopped beside her. "Penny for them?"

She glanced at him sideways, the hem of her dress brushing his leg like phantom fingers. "No money for no work, remember? I've done nothing here to earn even a cent. The nanny takes over the kids, and I have to admit, she's good at charming them."

"You would rather they cried for you?"

"Of course not! I just…I like to feel useful. In control."

"Most women I know would be thrilled by an afternoon with a manicurist and masseuse."

"Don't get me wrong, I enjoy being pampered as much as anyone. In fact, I think you deserve a bit of relaxation yourself." She tapped a pager resting on the balcony wall. "The nanny can call if she needs us. What do you say we head down to the beach? I found the most wonderful cabana where we can talk."

Talk?

Not what he'd been fantasizing about for their evening together. But Alexa apparently had something on her mind, given the determined tilt of her chin. He took her hand in his. Her short nails were shiny with clear polish. The calluses on her fingers from cleaning had been softened and he felt the urge to make sure she never had to pick up a scrub brush ever again.

Keeping his hand linked with hers, he followed her down the winding cement steps toward the beach. She kicked off her sandals and waited for him to ditch his shoes and socks.

Hand in hand, they walked along the shore, feet sinking into the sand as they made their way toward a white cabana. With each step closer he could feel the tension ramping up in her body.

"I'd hoped today would offer you breaks, be a sort of vacation."

She glanced up, a smile flickering. "This is paradise. I've been in some impressive mansions over the years, but even I'm a floored by this place. No kidding royalty. Your business is going to a whole new level with this deal."

"That's the plan." So why did he still feel so... unsettled? He gestured inside the cabana where she'd ordered two low lounge chairs with a small table of refreshments between them.

Her eyes flickered wide for a second before she plunged inside, choosing a chair and eyeing the wine, cheese and grapes. She'd obviously planned this chance to...talk?

She wriggled her toes in the sand and plucked a grape. A wave curled up closer and she stretched her legs out until the water touched the tips of her feet. "This truly is paradise."

He dropped into the chair beside her. "Then why are you so tense?"

"Why do you want to know?"

"Why do you think?" He poured deep red wine into two crystal glasses and let his eyes speak as fully as his words.

She took one of the drinks by the stem and sipped. "Victoria called you a loner."

"Interesting." And he wasn't sure what that had to do with anything.

"You have so much family in Charleston, I hadn't thought of you that way." The wind rippled and flapped the three canvas walls of the cabana. "You do have family there, right? You called them when you found the babies, to ask for help."

"I have two cousins—Vic and Paige. I grew up with them in North Dakota when my parents died in a car accident." He reached for his wine. "Their SUV slid off the road in a storm when I was eleven." He downed half of the fine vintage as if it was water.

"I'm so sorry." She touched his wrist lightly as he replaced his drink.

"No need to feel sorry for me. I was lucky to have family willing to take me in." He hesitated. "My parents didn't have any assets when they died. My aunt and uncle never said anything about the extra mouth to feed, but I vowed I would pay them back."

"Look at you now. You've truly accomplished the amazing."

He stared out over the dark water and the darker night sky. "Too late to give anything to them… It took me a while to find my footing. Too long."

"Good God, Seth, you're all of what…"

"Thirty-eight."

"A self-made billionaire by thirty-eight." Her laugh stroked over his senses like the ocean breeze. "I wouldn't call that a slow start."

But he was still chasing dreams around the country. "I didn't set out on this path. I wanted to fly for the Air Force, even started ROTC at the University of Miami, but lost out on a medical snafu that isn't an issue anywhere but the Air Force. So I finished my degree and came home. Ran a flight school while flying my veterinarian cousin around to farms until the family all relocated to South Carolina."

He could feel her undivided attention on him. He wasn't sure why he was spilling all of this about himself, but somehow the words kept coming out. Strange as hell since she'd been on the mark in calling him a loner in spite of his large family.

"I wrestle with wanting to give my kids everything while worrying about teaching them working class values. I think about it a lot, how to help them have their own sense of accomplishment."

"The fact that you're even thinking about it says you're ahead of the game." She reached for his hand this time, linking her fingers and squeezing. "You do well by them."

He lifted her hand to kiss her wrist. "You grew up in a privileged world but came out with a strong work ethic. Any tips?"

She laughed bitterly. "My parents had shallow values, spending every penny they inherited to indulge themselves. My father bankrupted the family trust fund, or rather I should say they both did. Now, I have to work in order to eat like most of the rest of the world, which isn't a tragedy or sob story. Just a reality."

He'd known about her father's crappy management of the family's finances and sportswear line. But… "What about your marriage settlement?"

"We signed a prenup. My father's lawyers were worried Travis was a fortune hunter. I told Travis I didn't care about any contracts but he insisted." She spread her arms without letting go of his hands. "No alimony for either of us."

Frustration spiked inside him. "He doesn't care that you were left penniless? The jackass."

"Stop right there." She squeezed his hand insistently.

"I signed the prenup, too, and I don't want your sympathy."

"Okay, I hear you."

What was she thinking right now? He wished he was better at understanding the working of a woman's mind. He'd brought her to the island for seduction, and somehow, out here tonight, they'd ended up talking about things he didn't share with others. But Alexa had a way of kicking down barriers, and he'd had as much sharing as he could take for one night.

The rush of the ocean pulling at the sand under his feet seemed as if it tugged the rest of the world with it. He'd brought Alexa to this island for a reason: to seduce her so thoroughly he could work through this raw connection they felt.

Except, as he leaned in to kiss her, he was beginning to realize the chances of working her out of his system was going to be damn near impossible.

Her hand flattened to his chest. "Stop."

"What?" His voice came out a little strangled, but he held himself still. If a woman said no, that meant no.

"Last time we did this, you were the boss." She slid from her lounger and leaned over to straddle his hips. The warm core of her seared his legs even through her cotton dress and his slacks. "This time, Seth, I'm calling the shots."

Seven

Seth's brain went numb.

Did Alexa actually intend to have sex with him outside, in a seaside cabana? If so, she wouldn't get an argument from him. He was just surprised, since she'd insisted on leaving his bed the night before. He'd assumed she was more reserved given how she'd wanted to keep the light off.

Although the way she tugged at his shirttails, he couldn't mistake her intent, or her urgency.

Moonbeams bathed her in a dim amber glow. Still straddling his hips, Alexa yanked the hem free then ripped, popping the buttons, sending them flying into the sand. Surprise snapped through him just as tangibly. Apparently he'd underestimated her adventurous spirit.

Wind rolled in from the ocean across his bare chest. His body went on alert a second before her mouth flicked, licked and nipped at his nipple the way he'd lavished attention on her the night before.

He cupped her hips, his fingers digging into the cottony softness of her bunched dress. "I like the way you think, Alexa."

"Good, but you need to listen better." She clasped his wrists and pulled them away. "This is *my* turn to be in control."

"Yes, ma'am." Grinning at her, he rested his hands on the lounger's armrests, eager to see her next move.

Wriggling closer, she sketched her mouth over his, over to his ear. "You won't be sorry."

Her hands worked his belt buckle free, her cool fingers tucking inside to trace down the length of his arousal. He throbbed in response, wanted to ditch their clothes and roll her onto the sandy ground. The more she stroked and caressed, the more he ached to do the same to her. But every time he started to move, she stopped.

Once he stilled again, she nipped his ear or his shoulder, her fingers resuming the torturously perfect glide over him. His fingers gripped the rests tighter, until the blood left his hands.

Alexa swept his pants open further, shifting. As he started to move with her, she placed a finger over his lips. "Shh... I've got this."

Sliding from his lap, she knelt between his legs and took him in her mouth, slowly, fully. Moist, warm ecstasy clamped around him, caressed him. His head fell back against the chair, his eyes closing, shutting out all other sensation except the glide of her lips and tongue.

Her hands clamped on his thighs for balance. With

his every nerve tuned into the feel of her, even her fingers digging into his muscles ramped his pulse higher. Wind lifted her hair, gliding it over his wrist. The silky torment almost sent him over the edge.

The need to finish roared inside him, too much, too close. He wasn't going there without her. Time for control games to come to an end.

He clasped her under her arms and lifted her with ease, bringing her back to his lap.

"Condom," he growled through clenched teeth. "In my wallet. Leftover from the hotel."

Laughing softly, seductively, she reached behind him and tucked her fingers into his back pocket. The stroke of her hand over his ass had him gritting his teeth with restraint. Then she pitched his wallet to the ground with a wicked glint in her eyes.

What the hell?

She leaned sideways, toward the table of wine and cheese. Pitching aside a napkin, she uncovered a stack of condoms. "I came prepared."

His eyebrows rose at the pile of condoms, a dozen or so. "Ambitiously so."

"Is that a problem?" She studied him through her lashes.

God, he loved a challenge and this woman was turning out to be a surprise in more ways than one since she'd blasted into his life such a short time ago. "I look forward to living up to your expectations."

"Glad to hear it." She tore open one of the packets and sheathed him slowly.

Backlit by the crescent moon, she stood. She bunched the skirt of her dress and swept her panties down, kicking them aside. A low growl of approval rumbled inside him as he realized her intent. She straddled him again, inching the hem of her dress up enough so the hot heat of her settled against his hard-on.

Cradling his face in her hands, she raised up on her knees to kiss him. Her dress pooled around them, concealing her from view as she lowered herself onto the length of his erection. The moist clamp of her gripped him, drew him inside until words scattered like particles of sand along the beach.

The scent of the ocean clung to her skin. Unable to resist, he tasted her, trekking along her bared shoulder and finding the salty ocean flavor clung to her skin. He untied the halter neck of her dress, the fabric slithering down to reveal a lacy strapless bra. Her creamy breasts swelled just above the cups and with a quick flick of his fingers, he freed the front clasp.

Freed her.

Lust pumped through him along with anticipation. He filled his hands with the soft fullness, the shadowy beauty of her just barely visible in the moonlight.

His thumbs brushed the pebbly tips. "Someday we're going to make love on a beach with the sun shining down, or in a room with all the lamps on so I can see the bliss on your face."

"Someday..." she echoed softly.

Were those shadows in her eyes or just the play of clouds drifting past?

Her face lowered to his, blocking out the view and his thoughts as she sealed her mouth to his, demanding, giving and taking. With the lighting dim, his other senses heightened. The taste of her was every bit as intoxicating as the lingering hint of red wine on her tongue. Burying himself deep inside her, deeper still, he reveled in the purr of pleasure vibrating in her throat.

He stroked down her spine until his hands tucked under her bottom. Her soft curves in his palms, he angled her nearer, burning for more of her, more of them together. Her husky sighs and moans grew louder and closer together. Damn good thing since he was balancing on the edge himself, fulfillment right there for the taking.

Waves crashed in the distance, echoing the rush of his pulse pounding in his ears. Sand rode the air and clung to the perspiration dotting their skin, the gritty abrasion was arousing as she writhed against him. He tangled his hand into her satiny hair and gently tugged her head back. Exposing her breasts to his mouth, he took the tip of one tight bud and rolled it lightly between his teeth.

She sighed, her back arching hard and fast, her chanted "yes, yes, yes," circling him. Wrapping and pulsing around him like the moist spasms of her orgasm. Her cries of completion mingled with the roar of crashing waves.

Blasting through his own restraint.

Thrusting through her release, he triggered another in her just as he came. The force slammed through him, powerful and eclipsing everything else as he flew apart inside her into a pure flat spin nosedive into pleasure. His arms convulsed around her with the force of his completion.

He forced his fist open to release her hair even though she hadn't so much as whimpered in complaint. In fact, her head stayed back even as he relinquished her hair, the locks lifted and whipped by the wind into a tangled mass.

Gasping, she sagged on top of him, her bared breasts against his heaving chest. He didn't have a clue how long it took him to steady his breathing, but Alexa still rested in his arms. He retied the top of her sundress with hands not quite as steady as he would like. She nuzzled his neck with a soft, sated sigh.

He slid from under her, smoothing her dress over her hips, covering her with more than a little regret. With luck, though, there would be more opportunities to peel every stitch of clothing from her body.

For now, though, it was time to go inside. He refastened his pants and tucked the remaining condoms in his pocket. Not much he could do about his shirt since the buttons were scattered on the beach. He snagged the nursery pager and clipped it to his waistband before turning back to Alexa.

Scooping her in his arms, he started barefoot toward the mansion. She looped her arms around his neck, her head lolling onto his shoulder. Climbing the steps to their second floor suite, he walked through the patio filled with topiaries, ferns and flowering cacti. He'd enjoyed her power play on the beach. It had certainly paid off for both of them. But that didn't mean he was passing over control completely.

Tonight, she would sleep in his bed.

Alexa stretched in the massive sleigh bed, wrapped in the delicious decadence of Egyptian cotton sheets and the scent of making love with Seth. She stared around the unfamiliar surroundings, taking in oil paintings and heavy drapery.

She dimly remembered him carrying her from the beach to his bed. For a second, she'd considered insisting he take her to her room and leave her there. But his arms felt so good around her and she'd been so deliciously sated from their time in the cabana, she'd simply cuddled against his chest and slept.

God, had she ever slept. She couldn't remember when she'd last had eight uninterrupted hours. Could be because every muscle in her body had relaxed.

Yes, she knew she hadn't turned on the glaring lights, literally and in theory, by avoiding telling him about the issues in her past. But taking control last night had given her the confidence to invite Seth the rest of the way into her life.

Through the thick wood door, she heard voices in the other room; Seth's mingled with the babble of the twins. She smiled, looking forward to the day already. Except her suitcase and other clothes were in her bedroom, and she couldn't walk out there as is with the children nearby.

Swinging her feet to the floor, she grabbed her dress off the wing chair and pulled it on hastily. The crumpled cotton shouted that she'd spent the night with a man, but at least the twins wouldn't pick up on that. She could say "good morning" to them and then zip into her room to put on something fresh before she greeted the rest of the household.

At the door, she paused by a crystal vase of lisianthus with blooms that resembled blue roses. She plucked one out, snapped the stem and tucked the blossom behind her ear. Her hands gravitated to the flowers, straightening two of the blooms again so they were level with the rest, orderly. Perfect. She pulled open the door to the living area.

Another voice mingled in the mix.

An adult female voice.

Alexa froze in the open doorway. She scoured the room. Seth sat in a chair at the small writing desk, a twin on each knee as they faced the laptop computer in the middle of a Skype conversation.

A young woman's face filled the screen, her voice swelling from the speakers. "How are my babies? I've missed you both so very, very much."

Oh, God. It couldn't be. Not right now.

If Alexa had harbored any doubts as to the woman's identity, both babies chanted, "Ma-ma, Ma-ma, Ma-ma."

"Olivia, Owen, I'm here." Her voice echoed with obvious affection.

Pippa Jansen wasn't at all what she'd expected.

For starters, the woman didn't appear airheaded; in fact she had a simple, auburn-haired glamour. She wore a short-sleeved sweater set and pearls. From the log cabinlike walls and mountainous backdrop behind Pippa, she didn't appear to be at a plush spa or cruise ship getaway as Alexa had assumed.

Pippa didn't look to be partying or carefree. She appeared...tired and sad. "Mommy's just resting up, like taking a good nap, but I'll see you soon. We'll have yogurt and play in the sandbox. Kisses and hugs." She pressed a hand to her lips then wrapped her arms around herself. "Kisses and hugs."

Olivia and Owen blew exuberant baby kisses back. Both babies were so happy, so blissfully unaware. Alexa's heart ached for both of them. Her hands twitchy, she straightened a leather-bound volume of *Don Quixote* on a nearby end table.

Tension radiated from Seth's shoulders as he held a baby on each knee. "Pippa, while I understand your need for a break, I need some kind of reassurance that you're not going to drop off the map again once we hang up. I need to be able to reach you if there's an emergency."

"I promise." Her voice wavered. "I'll check in regularly from now on. I wouldn't have left this way if I wasn't desperate. I know I should have stayed to tell you myself, but I was scared you would say no, and I really needed a break. I watched through an airport window until you got on your plane. Please don't be angry with me."

"I'm not mad," he said, not quite managing to hide the irritation in his voice. "I just want to make sure you're all right. That you never feel desperate."

"This time away is good for me, really. I'll be back to normal when I come back to Charleston."

"You know I would like to have the children more often. When you're ready to come back, we can hire more help when they're with you, but we can't have a repeat of what happened at the airport. The twins' safety has to come first."

"You're right." She fidgeted with her pearls, her nails chewed down. "But I don't think we should talk about this now, in front of the babies."

"You're right, but we do have to discuss it. Soon."

"Absolutely." She nodded, almost frantically, pulling a last smile for the babies. "Bye-bye, be good for Daddy. Mommy loves you."

Her voice faded along with her picture as the

connection ended. Olivia squealed, patting the screen while Owen blew more kisses.

Alexa sagged against the door frame. She'd been prepared to hate Pippa for the way she'd been so reckless with her kids. And while she still wasn't ready to let the woman off the hook completely, she saw a mother running on fumes. Someone who was stressed and exhausted. She saw a mother who genuinely loved her children. Pippa had obviously reached her breaking point and had wisely taken them to their father before she snapped.

Of course sticking around to explain that to him would have been a far safer option. But life wasn't nearly as black and white as she'd once believed.

She'd seen Seth angry, frustrated, driven, affectionate, turned on… But right now, as Seth stared at the empty computer screen, she saw a broad-shouldered, good man who was deeply sad.

A man still holding conflicted feelings for his ex-wife.

Seth set each of his kids onto the floor and wished the weight on his shoulders was as easy to move.

Talking to Pippa had only made the situation more complicated just when he really could have used some simplicity in his personal life. He and Alexa had taken their relationship to a new level last night, both with the sex and sharing the bed. And he'd looked forward to cementing that relationship today—and tonight.

The call from Pippa had brought his life sharply back into focus. She was clearly at the end of her rope. While he wanted more time with his children, he didn't want to get it this way.

And this certainly wasn't how he'd envisioned kicking off his day with Alexa.

Glancing back over his shoulder at her in the doorway, he said, "You can come in now."

He'd sensed her there halfway through the conversation with his ex. Strange how he'd become so in tune with Alexa so quickly.

"I didn't mean to eavesdrop." She stepped deeper into the room, a barefoot goddess in her flowing purple dress with a flower behind her tousled hair.

Gracefully she sank down to the floor in front of the babies and a pile of blocks. He took in her effortless beauty, her ease with his kids. She was his dream woman—who'd come into his life at a nightmare time.

Right now, he couldn't help but be all the more aware of her strength, the way she met challenges head-on rather than running from her troubles. She'd rebuilt her entire life from the ground up. He admired that about her. Hell, he just flat out liked her, desired her and already dreaded the notion of watching her walk away.

"The conversation wasn't private." He shoved up from the chair and sat on the camelback sofa. "Olivia and Owen were just talking with their mother. Raising a baby is tough enough. The added pressure of twins just got to her. She's wise to take a break."

She glanced up sharply. "Even though she left them unattended on the airplane?"

"I'm aware that the way she chose to take that break left more than a little to be desired in the way of good judgment." He struggled to keep his voice level for the kids. For Alexa, too. He couldn't blame her for voicing the truth. "I'll handle it."

"Of course. It's really none of my business." She gnawed her bottom lip, stacking blocks then waiting for Olivia to knock the tower over. "Why don't I take the kids for a couple of hours? Give you some time to—"

"I've got them." He watched his son swipe his fist through the plastic blocks with a squeal of delight. "I'm sure you want a shower or a change of clothes."

In a perfect world he would have been joining her in that shower. As a matter of fact, in his screwed up, imperfect world he needed that shower with her all the more. What he would give for twenty minutes alone with her under the spray of hot water with his hands full of soap suds and naked Alexa. He swallowed hard and filed those thoughts away at the top of his "to do" list.

Although to get to everything on that list he would need more time. A lot more time.

"Really, it's no trouble." She patiently stacked the blocks again in alphabetical order while Olivia tried to wedge one, the *w*, in her mouth. "I'm getting good at balancing them on both hips. They can run out some energy on the beach while you finish up last minute busi—"

"I said I have them. They are my children," he snapped more curtly than he'd intended, but the discussion with Pippa had left him on edge. Wrestling for control was tough as hell with anger and frustration piling up inside him faster than those blocks made a Leaning Tower of Pisa.

Hurt slashed across her face before she schooled her features into an expressionless mask. "I'll change then, and take care of my own packing. How much longer until we leave the island?"

"We're flying out in an hour." Not that he intended to let that stop him from pursuing her. As much as he'd hoped to win her over during their trip, he now realized that wasn't going to be enough. He needed more—more time with her, more *of* her. While his relationship with Pippa had been a disaster, he was wiser for the experience now. He could enjoy Alexa in his life without letting himself get too entangled, too close.

Staring at his babies on the floor, he listened to the echo of tread as she walked away. Thought harder on the prospect of her walking away altogether.

Away, damn it.

He was going to lose Alexa if he didn't do something. He was fast realizing that no matter what his concerns about bringing a new woman into his children's lives, he couldn't let her leave.

"Alexa?"

Her footsteps stopped, but she didn't answer.

God, for about the hundredth time he wished they'd met a year from now when this would have been so much easier. But he couldn't change it. The time was now.

He wanted Alexa in his life.

"I'm sorry for being an—" He paused short of cursing in front of his children. "I'm sorry for being a jerk. I know you didn't sign on for this, but I hope you'll give me a chance to make it up to you."

She stayed silent so long he thought she would tell him to go to hell. He probably deserved as much for the way he was botching things with her right now. Her lengthy sigh reached him, heaping an extra dose of guilt on his shoulders.

"We'll talk later, after you have your children settled."

"Thanks, that's for the best." Problem was, with Pippa, he wasn't sure how or when things in his life would ever be *settled*. All the more reason to keep his emotions in check when dealing with either woman in his life. Starting now.

Because, their island paradise escape was over. It was time to return to the real world.

Riding on the ferry out to the king's private airstrip, Alexa gripped the railing as they neared Seth's plane on the islet runway. The twins, buckled into their safety seats, squealed in delight at the sea air in their faces as they waved goodbye to the tropical paradise.

She feared she was saying goodbye to far more than that.

Her eyes trekked to Seth, who was standing with the boat captain. Not surprising, since Seth had all but shut down emotionally around her since his conversation with his ex-wife.

Alexa twirled the stem of a sea oat in her hand, then tickled the twins' chins with it. They were cute, but it would be helpful if they spoke a few more words so they could hold up the other end of a conversation. There was no one else to talk to. Javier and his wife had opted to stay on the island for a couple of extra days. Alexa envied them. Deeply. The time here with Seth before that Skype call had been magical, and she wanted more.

As smoothly as the ferry moved along the marshy water, her mind traveled to dreams of extending her relationship with Seth. Could what they'd shared be just as powerful under the pressure of everyday life?

A daunting thought to say the least, especially when he had begun pulling away after his conversation with Pippa.

Thinking of that call, Alexa reached for her own phone. She should check for messages from Bethany. She'd turned her cell off last night and let it recharge—and, yes, probably because she didn't want interruptions. The way she'd made love with Seth on the beach…the way he'd made love to her afterward…

Heat pooled inside her, flushing her skin until she could have sworn she had an all-over sunburn.

Her phone powered up and she checked… No messages from Bethany, but the expected nine missed calls from her mother. Just as she started to thumb them away, the phone rang in her hand.

Her mom.

She winced.

Was her mother's perfectly coiffed blond hair actually a satellite dish that detected when her daughter turned on her phone?

Wind tearing at her own loose hair, she considered ignoring that call altogether as she had the others. But Olivia giggled and Alexa's heart tugged. If she felt this much for these two little ones so quickly, how much more must her mother feel for her?

Guilt nudged her to answer. "Hey, Mom. What's up?"

"Where are you, Lexi? I have been calling and calling." Laughter and the clank of dishes echoed over the phone line. Her parents had taken what little cash they had left and bought into a small retirement community chock-full of activities. How they continued to pay the bills was a mystery. "Lexi? Are you listening?

I took a break from my 'Mimosas and Mahjong' group just to call you."

God, why couldn't her mother call her Alexa instead of Lexi? "Working. In Florida."

Crap. Why hadn't she lied?

And was the island even part of Florida? Or was it the royal family's own privately owned little kingdom? She wasn't sure and didn't intend to split hairs—or reveal anything more than necessary to her mother.

"Oh, are you near Boca? Clear the rest of your day," her mother ordered. "Your dad and I will drive over to meet you."

"I really am working. I can't just put that on hold. And besides, I'm in Northern Florida. Very far away." Not far enough at the moment.

"You can't be working. I hear children in the background."

She hated outright lying. So she dodged with, "The boss has kids."

"Single boss?"

Not wading into those waters with her mother. "Why was it that you called?"

"Christmas!"

Huh? "The holidays are months away, Mom."

"I know, but we need to get these things pinned down so nothing goes wrong. You know how I like to have everything perfect for the holidays."

And that need for perfection differed from the rest of the year how, exactly? "I'll do my best to be there."

"I need to know, though, so we have an even number of males and females at the table. I would just hate to have the place setting ruined at the last minute if you cancel."

So much for her mother's burning need to see her only child. She just needed an extra warm body at the table, a body with female chromosomes. "You know what, Mom, then let's just plan on me not being there."

"Now, Lexi, don't be that way. And wipe that frown off your face. You're going to get wrinkles in your forehead early, and I can't afford collagen treatments for you."

Deep breaths. She wasn't her mother. She'd refused to let her mom have power over her life.

But control seemed harder to find today than usual after she'd lowered so many barriers with Seth last night.

Her mother had her own reasons for the way she acted, most of which came from having a control freak mother of her own. Holiday photos were always color-coordinated, perfectly posed and very strained.

But understanding the reasons didn't mean accepting the hurtful behavior. Alexa had worked hard to break the cycle, to get well and make sure that if she ever had a child of her own, the next generation would know unconditional love, rather than the smothering oppression of a parent determined to create a perfectly crafted mini-me.

Her eyes slid down to Olivia who was trying her best to stuff her sock in her mouth. God, that kid was adorable.

Alexa's hand tightened around the phone, another swell of sympathy for her mom washing over her. She could do this. She could talk to her mother while still keeping boundaries in place. "Mom, I appreciate that you want to have me there for the holidays. I will get back to you at the end of the month with a definite answer one way or the other."

"That's my good girl." Her mother paused for a second, the background chatter and cheers the only indication she was still on the line. "I love you, Alexa. Thanks for picking up."

"Sure, Mom. I love you, too."

And she did. That's what made it so tough sometimes. Because while love could be beautiful, it also stole control, giving another person the power to cause hurt.

As the ferry docked at the airstrip and Alexa dropped the phone back into her bag, her eyes didn't land on the kids this time. Her gaze went straight to Seth.

Eight

Her stomach knotted with each step down the stairway leading from the private jet. Back where she'd started in Charleston a few short, eventful days ago.

The flight hadn't given them any opportunity to discuss what they would do after landing. The kids had been fussy for most of the journey, not surprising given all the upheaval to their routine. Seth had been occupied with flying the plane through bumpy skies.

And all those pockets of turbulence hadn't helped the children's moods. Or hers for that matter. Her nerves were shot.

Alexa hitched Olivia on her hip more securely. The early morning sun glinted off the concrete parking area of the private airport that housed Jansen Jets. She saw Seth's world with new eyes now. Before she'd viewed him and his planes from a business perspective. She'd seen his hangars at the private airport and his jets, and thought about what a boon it would be to service his fleet. Now, she took in the variety of aircraft, in awe of how much he'd acquired in such a short time.

From her research on him she'd learned that about ten years ago he'd purchased the privately owned airport, which, at that time, sported two hangars. Now there were three times as many filled with anything from the standard luxury Learjets to Gulfstreams like the one she'd flown in today. In fact, one of those Lears taxied out toward the runway now.

As she looked back at the hangars, she also saw smaller Cessnas. Perhaps for flight training like he'd done back in North Dakota? Or was that a part of the search and rescue aspect he obviously felt so passionately about?

There was so much more to Seth than she'd originally thought.

An open hangar also gave her a peek of what appeared to be a vintage plane, maybe World War II era. Not exactly what she expected a buttoned-up businessman to own. But a bold, crop-dusting North Dakota farm boy who'd branched out to South Carolina, who'd built a billion-dollar corporation from the ground up? That man, she could envision taking to the skies in the historic craft.

She'd wanted to get to know more about Seth, to understand him, at first to win his contract and then to protect herself from heartache. Instead she was only more confused, more vulnerable, and unable to walk away.

Her feet hit solid ground just as she heard a squeal from the direction of the airport's main building, a one-story red brick structure with picture windows. An auburn-haired woman raced past a fuel truck toward the plane, her arms wide.

Pippa Jansen.

The beauty wore the same short-sleeve sweater set she'd had on during the Skype conversation earlier. She raced toward them, a wide smile on her face.

Olivia stretched out her hands, squealing, "Ma-ma, Ma-ma…"

Pippa gathered her daughter into her arms and spun around. "I missed you, precious girl. Did you have fun with Daddy? I have your favorite *Winnie the Pooh* video in the car."

She slowed her spin, coming face-to-face with Alexa. A flicker of curiosity chased through Pippa's hazel eyes. The Learjet engines hummed louder in the background as the plane accelerated, faster, faster, swooping smoothly upward. Owen pointed with a grin as he clapped.

Her son's glee distracted her and she turned to kiss his forehead. "Hello, my handsome boy."

His face tight with tension, Seth passed over his son. "I thought we were going to talk later today?"

"I decided to meet you here instead. After I heard the children's voices this morning, I just couldn't stay away any longer. I missed them too much, so I flew straight home. Your secretary gave me your arrival time since it related to the children." She kissed each child on top of the head, breathing deeply before looking up again, directly at Alexa. "And who might you be?"

Seth stepped up, his face guarded. "This is my friend Alexa. She took time off work to help me with the twins since I had an out of town business meeting I couldn't cancel. Your note said you were going to be gone for two weeks."

"The weekend's rest recharged me. I'm ready to be with my children again." Her pointy chin jutted with undeniable strength. "It's my custodial time."

He sighed wearily, guiding them toward the building, away from the bustle of trucks and maintenance personnel. He stopped outside a glass door at the end of the brick building. "Pippa, I don't want a fight. I just want to be sure you won't check out on them again without notice."

"My mother's in the car. I'm staying with her for a while." She adjusted the weight of both babies, resettling them. "Seth, I'm going to take you up on the offer to hire extra help when I'm with them, and I'd like to write up more visitation time into our agreement. They've been weaned for a couple of months, so the timing is right. Okay?"

He didn't look a hundred percent pleased with the outcome but nodded curtly. "All right, we'll meet tomorrow morning in my office at ten to set that in motion."

"Good, I'm so relieved to see them. My time away gave me a fresh perspective on how to pace myself better." She passed Olivia to Seth. "Could you help me carry them out to the car? You'll get to see my mom and reassure yourself." She glanced at Alexa. "You won't mind if I borrow him for a minute?"

"Of course not." It was clear Alexa wasn't invited on this little family walk.

Seth slid an arm around Alexa's shoulder. "This won't take long." He pulled out a set of keys and unlocked the glass door in front of him. "You can wait in my office space here where it's cooler."

An office here? Jansen Jets Corporate was located downtown. But then of course he would have an office here as well.

"I'll be waiting."

He dropped a kiss on her lips. Nothing lengthy or overtly sexual, but a clear branding of their relationship in front of his ex. Surprise tingled through her along with the now expected attraction.

Pippa looked at her with deepening curiosity. "Thank you for being there for my babies when Seth needed an extra set of hands."

Alexa didn't have a clue how to respond, so she opted for a noncommittal. "Owen and Olivia are precious. I'm glad I could help."

Stepping into the back entrance to Seth's office, she crossed to a corner window and watched the couple carrying their children toward a silver Mercedes sedan parked and idling. Pippa's older "twin" sat behind the wheel. Her mother, no doubt.

A sense of déjà vu swept over Alexa at the mother-daughter twin look. It could have been her with her own mom years ago. More than the outward similarity, Alexa recognized a fragility in Pippa, something she'd once felt herself, a lack of ego. Having rich parents provided a lot of luxuries, but it could also rob a person of any sense of accomplishment. Her parents bought her everything, even bought her way out of bad grades... which had been wrong.

Just as it would be wrong to write off Pippa's reckless escape from motherhood for the weekend. Yes, she was an overwhelmed mom, but she was also a parent with resources. She could hire help. There were a hundred better options than leaving her children unattended on an aircraft. Pippa's excuse about watching through a window was bogus. How could she have helped them from so far away if something had gone wrong?

Alexa's fists dug into the windowsill, helplessness sweeping over her. There was nothing she could do. These weren't her children. This wasn't her family. She had to trust Seth to handle the situation with his ex-wife.

Spinning back to the office, she studied the space Seth had created for himself. It was a mass of contradictions, just like the man himself. High-end leather furniture filled the room, a sofa, a wing recliner and office chair, along with thick mahogany shelves and a desk.

She also saw a ratty fishing hat resting on top of a stack of books. The messy desktop was filled with folders and even a couple of honest to God plastic photo cubes—not exactly what she'd expected in a billionaire's space. It was tough for her to resist the desire to order the spill of files across the credenza.

Forcing her eyes upward, she studied the walls packed with framed charts and maps, weathered paper with routes inked on them. In the middle of the wall, he'd displayed a print of buffalo on the plains tagged Land of Tatanka.

The land looked austere and lonely to her. Like the man, a man who'd been strangely aloof all day. Her fingers traced along the bottom of the frame. Even as he embraced the skies and adventure here, there was still a part of him that remembered his stark North Dakota farm boy roots.

The opening door pulled her attention off the artwork

and back to the man striding into the room. His face was hard. His arms empty and loose by his sides.

She rested her hand on his shoulder and squeezed lightly. "Are you okay?"

"I will be." He nodded curtly, stepping away.

Only a few minutes earlier he'd kissed her and now he was distant, cold. Had it been an act? She didn't think so. But if he didn't want her here, if he needed space, she could find her own way home. She started toward the door leading out of his office and into the building.

"Alexa," he called out. "Hold on. We have some unfinished business."

Business? Not what she was hoping to hear. "What would that be?"

He walked to the massive desk and pulled a file off the corner. "I made a promise when you agreed to help me. Before I spoke to Pippa this morning, I put in some calls, arranged for you and your partner to interview with four potential clients who commute into the Charleston area, both at the regional airport and here at my private airstrip." He passed her the folder. "Top of the list, Senator Matthew Landis."

She took the file from his hand, everything she could have hoped for when she'd first stepped onto his plane, cleaning bucket in hand. And now? She couldn't shake the sense he was shuffling her off, giving her walking papers. While, yes, that's what they'd agreed upon, she couldn't help worrying that he was fulfilling the deal to the letter so they could be done, here and now.

Her grip tightened on the file until the edges bent. "Thank you, that's great. I appreciate it."

"You still have to seal the deal when you meet them, but I had my assistant compile some notes I made that I

believe will help you beef up your proposal." He sat on
the edge of the desk, picked up a photo cube and tossed
it from hand to hand. "I also included some ways I think
you may be missing out on expansion opportunities."

He hadn't left money on the dresser, by God, but
somehow the transaction still felt cheap given the bigger
prize they could have had together.

"I don't know how to thank you." She clasped the
folder to her chest and wondered why this victory felt
hollow. Just a few days ago she would have turned
cartwheels over the information in that folder.

"No. Thank *you*. It was our agreement from the start,
and I keep my word." *Toss, toss,* the cube sailed from
hand to hand. "And while I am genuinely sorry I can't
pass over my fleet to A-1, I have requested that your
company be called first for any subcontracting work
from this point on."

His words carried such finality she didn't know
whether to be hurt or mad. "That's it then. Our business
is concluded."

"That was my intention." He pitched the cube side
to side, images of Owen and Olivia tumbling to rest
against a paperweight.

Okay, she was mad, damn it. They'd slept together.
He'd kissed her in plain view of his ex-wife. She
deserved better than this.

She slapped the file down on his messy desk and
yanked the cube from midair. "Is this a brush-off?"

He did a double take and took his photos back from
her. "What the hell makes you think that?"

"Your ice cold shoulder all day, for starters." She
crossed her arms over her chest.

"I'm clearing away business because from this point

on, if we see each other, it's for personal reasons only." He clasped her shoulders, skimming his touch down until she stepped into his embrace. "No more agendas. Holding nothing back."

She looked up at him. "Then you're saying you want to spend more time together?"

"Yes, that's exactly what I'm telling you. You've cleared your calendar until tomorrow, and it's not even lunchtime yet. So let's spend the day together, no kids, no agendas, no bargains." He brushed her hair back with a bold, broad palm. "I can't claim to know where this is headed, and there are a thousand reasons why this is the wrong time. But I can't just let you walk away without trying."

Being with this guy was like riding an emotional yo-yo. One minute he was intense, then moody, then happy, then sensual. And she was totally intrigued by all of him. "Okay then. Ask me out to lunch."

A sigh of relief shuddered through him, his arms twitching tighter around her waist. "Where would you like to go? Anywhere in the country for lunch. Hell, we could even go out of the States for supper if you can lay hands on your passport."

"Let's keep it stateside this time." This time? She shivered with possibility. "As for the place? You pick. You're the one with the airplanes."

With those words, reality settled over her with anticipation and more than a little apprehension. She'd committed. This wasn't about the babies or her business any longer. This was about the two of them.

She'd explored the complex layers of this man, and now she needed to be completely open to him as well.

They had one last night away from the real world to decide where to go next.

One last night for her to see how he handled knowing everything about her, even the insecure, vulnerable parts that were too much like those she'd seen in his ex-wife.

Seth parked the rental car outside the restaurant, waiting for Alexa's verdict on the place he'd chosen.

He could have taken her to Le Cirque in New York City or City Zen in D.C. He could have even gone the distance for Savoy's in Vegas. But thinking back over the things she'd shared about her past, he realized she wasn't impressed with glitz or pretension. They'd just left a king's island, for Pete's sake. Besides, she'd grown up with luxurious trappings and, if anything, seemed to disdain them now.

The North Dakota farm boy inside him applauded her.

So he'd fueled up one Cessna 185 floatplane and taken off for his favorite "hole-in-the-wall" eating establishment on the Outer Banks in North Carolina. A seaside clapboard bar, with great beer, burgers and fresh catch from the Atlantic.

A full-out smile spread across her face. "Perfect. The openness, the view... I love it."

Some of the cold weight he'd been carrying in his chest since saying goodbye to his kids eased. He sprinted around the front of the 1975 Chevy Caprice convertible—special ordered, thanks to his assistant's speedy persistence. He opened the door for Alexa. She swept out, her striped sundress swirling around her knees as she climbed the plank steps up to the patio dining area. The Seat Yourself sign hammered to a wooden column was weatherworn but legible.

He guided her to a table for two closest to the rocky shoreline as a waitress strolled over.

"Good to see you, Mr. Jansen. I'll get your Buffalo blue-water tuna bites and two house brews."

"Great, thanks, Carol Ann." Seth passed the napkin-rolled silverware across the table. Alexa fidgeted with the salt and pepper shakers until he asked, "Something wrong? Would you like to go somewhere else after all?"

She looked up quickly. "The place is great. Really. It's just… Well… I like to order my own food."

"Of course. I apologize. You're right, that was presumptuous of me." He leaned back in his chair. "Let me get Carol Ann back over and we can add whatever you would like."

"No need. Truly. It's just for future reference. And I actually do like the sound of what you chose, so it's probably silly that I said anything at all." She smiled sheepishly. "You may have noticed I have some… control issues."

"You appreciate order in your world. Plenty to admire about that." God knows, his world could stand a little more order and reason these days. The unresolved mess with Pippa still knocked around in his head. "That's a great asset in your job—"

He stopped short as the waitress brought their plates of Buffalo tuna bites, mugs of beer and glasses of water.

Alexa tore the paper off her straw and stirred her lemon wedge in her water. "Control's my way of kicking back at my childhood."

"In what way?" He passed an appetizer plate to her.

"When I was growing up there wasn't a lot I could

control without bringing down the wrath of Mom." She speared the fish onto her plate. "She may have depended on those nannies to free up her spa days and time on the slopes but her expectations were clear."

"And those were?"

"Great grades, of course, with all the right leadership positions to get into an Ivy League school. And in my 'spare time' she expected a popular, pretty daughter. Perfectly groomed, with the perfect boyfriend." She stabbed a bite and brought it to her mouth. "Standard stuff."

"Doesn't sound standard or funny to me." Out of nowhere, an image flashed through his mind of Pippa sitting in the front seat of the car with her mother, both women wearing matching sweater sets and pearls with their trim khakis.

"You're right. That kind of hypercontrol almost inevitably leads to some kind of rebellion in teens. Passive aggressive was my style in those days. The problem started off small and got worse. I controlled what I ate, when I ate, how much I ate." She chewed slowly.

A chill shot through him as he recalled her ordering the blocks for his kids. Her careful lining up of her silverware. Little things he'd written off as sweet peculiarities of a woman who liked the proverbial ducks in a row.

Now, his mind started down a dark path and he hoped to God she would take them on a detour soon. He didn't know what to say or do, so he simply covered her other hand with his and stayed quiet.

"Then I learned I could make Mom happy by joining the swim team. And what do you know? That gave me another outlet for burning calories. I felt good, a real rush of success." She tossed aside her fork. "Until one day when I peeled away my warm-up suit and I saw the looks of horror on the faces of the people around me…"

Squeezing her hand softly, he wished like hell he could have done something for her then. Wishing he could do something more now than just listen.

"I'm lucky to be alive actually. That day at swim practice, right after I saw the looks on their faces, I tried to race back to the locker room, but my body gave out… I pretty much just crumpled to the ground." She looked down at her hands fidgeting with the silverware. "My heart stopped."

He clasped her hand across the table, needing to feel the steady, strong beat of her heart throbbing in her wrist. There were no words he could offer up right now. But then he'd always been better at listening than talking anyway.

"Thank goodness the coach was good at CPR," she half joked, but her laugh quickly lost its fizz. "That's when my parents—and I—had to face up to the fact that I had a serious eating disorder."

She pulled away from him and rubbed her bare arms in spite of the noonday sun beating overhead. "I spent my senior year in a special high school—aka hospital— for recovering bulimics and anorexics." She brushed her windswept hair back with a shaky hand. "I was the latter, by the way. I weighed eighty-nine pounds when they admitted me."

This was more—worse—than he'd expected and what he'd expected had been gut-twisting enough. He thought of his own children, of Olivia, and he wanted to wrap her up in cotton while he read every parenting book out there in hopes that he could spare his kids this kind of pain. "I'm so damn sorry you had to go through that."

"Me, too. I'm healthy now, completely over it, other than some stretch marks from the seesawing weight loss and gain."

"Was that why you preferred to keep the lights off?"

"When we were making love? Yes." She nodded, rolling her eyes. "It's not so much vanity as I wasn't ready to tell you this. I fully realize those lines on my skin are a small price to pay to be alive." She reached for her beer, tasted the brew once, and again, before placing the mug on the red-checkered cloth. "My stint in the special high school cost me a real prom, sleepovers with ice cream sundaes and dates spent parking with a boyfriend. But it also screwed up Mom's Ivy League aspirations for me. So I won control of something for a while, I guess."

"What happened after you graduated?"

"Dad bought my way into a college, and I married the man of their choice." She patted her chest. "A-1 Cleaning is the first independent thing I've done on my own, for me."

Admiration for her grew, and he'd already been feeling a hefty dose where she was concerned. But she'd broken away from every support system she had in place—such as they were—to forge her own path. Turning her back on her family had to be tough, no matter how strained the relationship. He could also see she'd grown away from the world Pippa still seemed to be suffocating in.

He hadn't been expecting this kind of revelation from her today. But he knew he'd better come up with the right response, to offer the affirmation she should have gotten from those closest to her.

"What other things would you like to do? Anything… I will make it happen."

She leaned back in her chair, her eyes going whimsical. "That's a nice thought. But the things I regret? I need to accept I can't have them and be at peace with that."

"Things such as?"

"I can't go back and change my teenage years. I need to accept that and move forward."

The sadness in her voice as she talked about her lost past sucker punched him with the need to do something for her. To give her back those parts of her life her parents had stolen by trying to live out their own dreams through their kid. He couldn't change the past.

But he could give her one of those high school experiences she'd been denied.

Nine

Alexa shook her hair free as they drove along the seaside road with the convertible top down. She adored his unexpected choices, from the car to the restaurant. The red 1975 Chevy Caprice ate up the miles down the deserted shore of the Outer Banks. She'd marveled at how lucky they were to get such a classic car, but then learned Seth's assistant had taken care of the arrangements.

How easy it was to forget he was a billionaire sometimes, with all the power and perks that came with such affluence.

The afternoon sun blazed overhead, glinting on the rippling tide. Sea oats and driftwood dotted the sandy beach along with bare picket fences permanently leaning from the force of the wind. Kind of like her.

Leaning and weathered by life, but not broken, still standing.

She studied the brooding man beside her. Seth drove on, quietly focused on the two-lane road winding ahead of them. What had he thought of her revelations at lunch? He'd said all the right things, but she could see his brain was churning her words around, sifting through them. She couldn't help but feel skittish over how he would treat her now. Would he back away? Or worse yet, act differently?

Tough to tell when he'd been in such an unpredictable mood since talking with Pippa. That made Alexa wonder if she should have waited to dish out her own baggage? But she couldn't escape the sense of urgency pushing her, insisting they had only a narrow slice of time. That once they returned to Charleston permanently, this opportunity to fully know him would disappear.

She hooked her elbow on the open window, her own face staring back at her in the side mirror. "Seth? Where are we going? I thought the airport was the other way."

"It is. I wanted to make the most of the day before we leave." He pointed ahead toward a red brick lighthouse in the distance. "We're headed there, on that bluff."

The ancient beacon towered in the distance. She could envision taking the kids there for a picnic, like the one they'd shared at the fort in St. Augustine. "It's gorgeous here. I love our South Carolinian low country home, but this is special, too, different. I can't believe I've never been here before."

Her parents had always opted for more "exotic" vacations.

"I thought you would appreciate it. You seem to have

an eye for the unique, an appreciation for entertainment off the beaten path."

"I'm not sure I follow what you mean."

"Like when we had the picnic at the old fort. You saw it with an artist's eye rather than looking for an up-to-date, pristine park. Must be the art history major in you. This place and this car are certainly pieces of history. Did I read you right on that?"

"You did, very much so." The fact that he knew her this well already, had put so much thought into what she thought, made her heart swell. The twisting road led higher over the town, taking them farther away and into a more isolated area.

When she looked around her, she also realized… "You brought me here to make out, didn't you?"

"Guilty as charged."

"Because of what I said at the restaurant about missing the high school experience of parking and making out with a guy."

"Guilty again. It's private, bare, stripped away nature, which in some ways reminds me of North Dakota as a whole. There's something…freeing about leaving civilization behind." He steered the car off the paved road, onto a dirt trail leading toward the lighthouse. "It's good to leave baggage behind, and it's safe to say we both have our fair share."

Nerves took flight in her belly like the herons along the shore. "Like what I told you at lunch?"

"In part. Yes." Tires crunched along the rocky road, spitting a gritty cloud of dirt behind them. "It's clear we're both members of the Walking Wounded Divorce Club, both with hang-ups. But we have something else in common, an attraction and a mutual respect."

The way he'd analyzed them chilled her in spite of the bold shining sun overhead and the thoughtfulness of his gesture. He'd pinpointed them so well, and yet… "You make it sound so logical. So calculated. So… coldly emotionless."

Stopping the car at the base of the lighthouse, the top of the bluff, he gripped the steering wheel in white-knuckled fists. "Believe me, there's nothing cold about the way I'm feeling about you. I want you so much I'm damn near ready to explode just sitting beside you."

Breathless, she leaned against her door, the power of his voice washing over her as tangibly as the sun warming her skin.

He turned toward her, leather seat squeaking, his green eyes flinty. "Just watching you walk across the room, I imagine resting my hands on your hips to gauge the sway." His fingers glided along her shoulder. "Or when I see the wind lift your hair, I burn to test the texture between my fingers. Everything about you mesmerizes me."

Tension crackled between them like static in her hair, in his words. "Before this past weekend, I'd been celibate for over six months. Attractive women have walked into my life and not one of them has tempted me the way you do."

There was no missing the intensity of his words—or the intent in his eyes. His fingers stroked through her hair, down to the capped sleeves of her sundress, hovering, waiting. "Did anyone ever tell you what a truly stunning woman you are, how beautiful you will still be when you're eighty-five years old? Not that it matters what the hell I, or anyone else, thinks."

While she was flattered, his words also left her blushing with self-consciousness.

She resisted the urge to fidget. "Okay, I hear you. Now could you stop? I don't need you to flatter me because of what I said earlier. I'm beyond needing affirmation of my looks."

"I'm not flattering. I'm stating facts, indisputable, beyond perceptions."

She realized now that he'd brought her out to this place for a private conversation, a better place to discuss her past than a crowded restaurant. She should have realized that earlier.

"Thank you and I hear you. Skewed perceptions played a part in what I went through." Her hands fell to his chest. "But I'm over that now. It was hard as hell, but I'm healthy and very protective of that particular fact."

"Good. I'm glad to hear it, and I don't claim to be an expert on the subject. I only know that I want to tell you how beautiful, how sexy you are to me. Yet, that seems to make you uncomfortable."

The ocean breeze lifted her hair like a lover's caress, the scent so clean and fresh that the day felt like a new beginning.

"Maybe I like to speak with actions."

"I'm all about that, too." His hands brushed down the sleeves of her dress. "When I touch you, it turns me inside out to feel the curves, the silky softness, the way you're one hundred percent a woman."

He inched the bodice down farther, baring the top of her breasts.

Realization raised goose bumps along her skin as she

grasped his deeper intent for bringing her here... "Are you actually planning for us to make love, here?"

He nuzzled the crook of her neck. "Do you think you're the only one who can initiate outdoor sex?"

"That was at night."

"Hidden away where no one could see us." Where they could barely see each other.

Her thoughts cleared as if someone had turned the sun up a notch. Out here, there was no turning off the lamp or shrouding herself in darkness. Oh hell, maybe she wasn't as over the past as she'd thought. She'd controlled everything about their lovemaking before.

This place, now, out in the brightest light of all, meant giving over complete control. That sent jitters clear through her. But the thought of saying no, of turning down this chance to be with him, upset her far more.

He cupped her face in both hands. "Do you think I would ever place you at risk? I chose this place carefully because I feel certain we're completely alone."

Alone and yet so totally exposed by the unfiltered sunshine. Seth was asking for a bigger commitment from her. He was requiring her trust.

Toying with his belt, she said, "Out here, huh? In full daylight. No drawing the shades, that's for sure."

"Sunscreen?" He grinned.

She raised an eyebrow and tugged his belt open. "You expect to be naked that long? You're a big talker."

His smile faded, his touch got firmer. "So you're good with this."

"I'm good with *you*," she murmured against his lips.

"I like the sound of that." He slanted his mouth over hers.

The man knew how to kiss a woman and kiss her well. The way he devoted his all to the moment, to her, in his big bold way, made her want to take everything he offered here today. She'd shared everything about herself at lunch. Giving all here seemed the natural extension of that if she dared.

And she did.

Easing back from him, she shrugged the sleeves of her dress down, revealing herself inch by inch, much the way he'd undressed for her their first time together. In some ways, this was a first for them. A first without barriers.

Her bodice pooled around her waist. With the flick of her fingers, she opened the front clasp on her lacy bra. And waited. It was one thing to bare herself in the dark, but in the daylight, everything showed, her journey showed. Her battle with anorexia had left stretch marks. Regaining her muscle tone had taken nearly six years.

Meeting his gaze, she saw…heat…passion…and tenderness. He touched her, his large hands so deft and nimble as they played over her breasts in just the ways she enjoyed best, lingering on *her* erogenous zones, the ones he must have picked up on from their time together.

She arched into his palms, her grip clenching around his belt buckle. Her head fell to rest against the leather seat. The sun above warmed every inch of her bared flesh as fully as his caresses, his kisses.

His hands swept down to inch the hem upward until he exposed her yellow lace panties. Just above the waistband, he flicked a finger against her belly button ring.

She smiled at a memory. "That was my treat to myself the first time I wore a bikini in public."

"I'll buy you dozens, each one with a different jewel."

Laughing softly, she traced his top lip with the tip of her tongue. He growled deeply in his throat. But he only allowed her to steal control for an instant before he stroked lower, dipping a finger inside her panties, between her legs, finding her wet and ready.

Her spine went weak and he braced her with an arm around her waist, holding her. She unbuttoned his shirt, sweeping it aside and baring his brazened chest to her eyes, her touch. The rasp of his crisp blond hair tantalized her fingertips.

She inhaled the scent of leather and sea, a brand-new aphrodisiac for her. "We should move this to the backseat where we can stretch out somewhat."

"Or we can stay here and save the backseat for later."

She purred her agreement as she swung her leg over to straddle his lap. The steering wheel at her back only served to keep her closer to him. Everything about this place was removed from the real world, and she intended to make the most of it. She opened his pants and somehow a condom appeared in his hand. She didn't care where or how. She just thanked goodness he had the foresight.

His hands palmed her waist, her arms looping around his neck. He lowered her onto him, carefully, slowly filling her. Moving within her. Or was she moving over him? Either way, the sensation rippled inside her, built to a fever pitch. Every sensation heightened: the give of the butter-soft leather under her knees, the rub of his trousers against the inside of her thighs.

The openness of the convertible and the untouched

landscape called to her. The endless stretch of ocean pulled at her, like taking a skein of yarn and unraveling it infinitely. Moans swelled inside her, begging to be set free to fly into that vastness.

He thrust his hands into her hair and encouraged her in a litany detailing how damn much he wanted her, needed her, burned to make this last as long as he could because he was not finishing without her. The power of his words pulsed through her, took her pleasure higher.

Face-to-face, she realized there wasn't a battle for control. They were sharing the moment, sharing the experience. The insight exploded inside her in a shower of light and sensation as she flew apart in his arms. Her cries of completion burst from her in abandon, followed by his. Their voices twined together, echoing out over the ocean.

Panting, she sagged against his chest, perspiration bonding their bodies. Their time together here, away from the rest of the world, had been perfect. Almost too much so.

Now she had to trust in what they'd shared enough to test it out when they returned home.

Seth revved the Cessna seaplane's engines, skimming the craft along the water faster and faster until finally, smoothly...*airborne*.

A few more days on the Outer Banks would have been damn welcome to give him a chance to fortify his connection with Alexa. To experience more of the amazing sex they'd shared in the front seat of the convertible, then the backseat. Except he was out of time.

He had to meet with Pippa tomorrow and hammer

out a new visitation schedule. That always proved sticky since the ugly truth lurked behind every negotiation that he might not be the twins' biological father. If Pippa ever decided to push that, things could go all to hell. He would fight for his kids, but it tore him up inside thinking of how deep it would slice if he lost. Acid burned in his gut.

If only life could be simpler. He just wanted to enjoy his children like any parent. The way his cousin Paige enjoyed hers. The way his cousin Vic was celebrating a new baby with his wife, Claire. That reminded him of what a crappy cousin he'd been in not calling to congratulate them. Paige had texted him that Claire was staying in the hospital longer because of the C-section delivery. He needed to stop by and do the family support gig.

That also meant introducing Alexa to the rest of his family. Soon. His relatives were important to him. He wasn't sure how he was going to piece together his crazy ass life with hers, but walking away wasn't an option. He also wasn't sure how Alexa would feel about his big noisy family, especially given how strained her relationship was with her own.

If only life was as easy to level out as an airplane.

Easing back on the yoke, he scanned his airspeed, along with the rest of the control panel.

Alexa touched the window, an ocean view visible beyond. "I grew up with charter jets, but I've never flown on one of these before. And I certainly didn't have a fleet of planes at my fingertips 24/7."

"This wasn't among my more elite crafts, but, God, I love to fly her."

"I can tell by how relaxed you are here versus other

times." She trapped the toy bobble head fisherman suction-cupped to the control panel. Her finger swayed the line from the fishing pole. "I can hardly believe how much we've done since waking up. Starting in Florida, stopping in South Carolina, North Carolina by lunch. Now home again."

"I still owe you supper, although it'll be late."

"Can we eat it naked?"

"As long as I have you all to myself."

She laughed softly. "While I enjoyed our time in the convertible, I haven't turned into that much of an exhibitionist."

"Good," he growled with more possessiveness than he was used to feeling. "I don't share well."

She toyed with the sleeve of her dress, adjusting it after the haphazard way they'd thrown on their clothes as the sun started to set. "I appreciate that you didn't get weirded out by what I shared with you at the restaurant."

"I admire the way you've taken everything life threw at you and just kept right on kicking back," he answered without hesitation.

He meant every word.

"I'm determined not to let other people steal anything more from me—not my parents or my ex."

"That attitude is exactly what I'm talking about."

"I'm not so sure about the kick-ass thing." Her hand fell to her lap. "It's wacky the way a piece of cheesecake can sometimes still hold me hostage. Sounds strange, I know. I don't expect you to understand."

"Explain it to me." He needed to understand. He couldn't tolerate saying or doing something that could hurt her.

She sagged back in her seat. "Sometimes I look at it

and remember what it was like to want that cheesecake, but then I would measure out how many calories I'd eaten that day. Think how many laps I would need to swim in order to pick up that fork for one bite. Then I would imagine the disappointment on my mother's face when I stepped on the scale the next morning."

What the hell? Her mother made her weigh in every morning? No wonder Alexa had control issues.

He wrestled to keep his face impassive when he really wanted to find her parents and… He didn't know what he would do. He did know he needed to be here for Alexa now. "I wish I'd known you then."

She turned to look at him. "Me, too."

Suddenly he knew exactly where he wanted to take Alexa tonight. "Do you mind staying out late?"

"I'm all for letting this day last as long as possible."

"Good. Then I have one more stop to make on my way to take you home."

Of all the places she thought Seth might take her, Alexa wouldn't have guessed they would go to a hospital.

Once they'd landed, Seth had said he wanted to visit his cousin's new baby. Her heart had leaped to her throat at the mention of an infant. A newborn.

Her skin felt clammy as she rubbed her arms. Was she freaked out because of the baby or because of her own hospital stay? Right now, with her emotions so close to the surface, she couldn't untangle it all.

Damn it, she was being silly. It wasn't like she would even go in to see the new mom. This visit would be over soon and she could clear the antiseptic air with deep breaths outside. Seth was walking in on his own

while she hung out at the picture window looking into
a nursery packed full of bassinets. Her gaze lingered
on one in particular, front row, far left.

Baby Jansen.

She could barely see anything other than a white
swaddling blanket and a blue-and-yellow-striped cap.
But she could tell the bundle was bigger than most of
the others, nearly ten pounds of baby boy, according
to Seth. Alexa touched the window lightly, almost
imagining she could feel the satiny softness of those
chubby newborn cheeks.

A woman stepped up alongside her and Alexa inched
to the side to make room.

The blonde woman—in her late thirties—wore a
button that proclaimed Proud Aunt. "Beautiful little
boy." She tapped the glass right around Baby Jansen
territory. "Can you believe all that blond hair? Well,
under the hat there's lots of blond hair."

Alexa cocked her head to the side. "Do I know you?"

The woman grinned, and Alexa saw the family
resemblance so strongly stamped on her face she might
as well have pulled back her question.

"I'm Paige, Seth's cousin. While I was getting coffee,
I saw you walking in with him. My brother, Vic, is this
baby's daddy."

It was one thing meeting his family with Seth
there to handle the introductions, to define their still
new relationship. This was awkward to say the least.
Why, why, why hadn't she waited in his SUV outside?
"Congratulations on your new nephew."

"Thank you, we have lots to celebrate. Hope you'll
join us at the next family get-together." She cut her
brown eyes toward Alexa. "How did the trip with

Seth and the twins go? They're sweet as can be, but a handful, for sure."

Seth had told his family about her? Curiosity drowned out the rattle of food carts, the echo of televisions, even the occasional squawk of a baby.

"Nice trip. But it's always good to be home," she answered noncommittally. "The twins are back with their mother now."

Paige nodded, tucking her hair behind her ears. "Pippa's, well…" She sighed. "She's Pippa, and she's the twins' mom. And Seth's such a good daddy. He deserves to have a good woman to love him, better than…well…you know."

Sort of. Not really. And she should really cut this short and get all of her answers from Seth. "I'm not in a position to—"

Pivoting, Paige stared her down with an unmistakably protective gleam in her golden-brown eyes. "I'm just asking you to be good to my cousin, to be fair. Pippa screwed him over, literally. There are days I would really like to give her a piece of my mind, but I hold back because I love those kids regardless of whether they're my blood or not. But I don't think I could take seeing him betrayed like that again. So please, if you're not serious, walk away now."

Whoa, whoa, whoa. Alexa struggled to keep up the barrage of information packed into that diatribe. "I don't know what to say other than your family loyalty is admirable?"

"Crap. Sorry." Paige bit her bottom lip. "I should probably hush now. I'm rambling and being rude. Hormones are getting the best of me, compounded even more by the nursery and being pregnant—a whoops, but a happy whoops. And I already get so emotional with how Pippa used Seth, the way she still uses him. I'm sure you're lovely, and I look forward to seeing you again."

Paige squeezed her arm once, before rushing away in a flurry of tissues and winces, leaving Alexa stunned. She looked back into the nursery, then at the departing woman, going over what she'd said, something about whether or not the twins were related to her. And how Pippa had screwed Seth over. Literally.

What the hell? Had Pippa actually cheated on Seth? But he'd said they split before the twins were even born. Not that a pregnant woman couldn't have an affair, but it seemed less likely... Unless... Pippa had the affair while she and Seth were dating, and it only came out later?

An awful possibility smoked through her mind— perhaps the twins weren't his biological children?

She dismissed the thought as quickly as it came to her. He would have shared something like that with her.

Her perceptions of the man jumbled all together. At first, she'd assumed he was like her wealthy parents, too often looking for a way to dump off their kids on the nearest caregiver. Yet, she'd seen with her own eyes how much he loved them, how he spent every free waking moment with them.

If what she suspected was true, why hadn't he said something to her when they'd deepened their relationship? Sure they'd only known each other a short time, but she'd told him everything. He'd insisted on her being open, vulnerable even, when they'd made love by the lighthouse.

Had he been holding back something this important?

She wanted to believe she'd misunderstood Paige. Rather than wonder, she would ask Seth once the timing was right. They would laugh together over how she'd leaped to conclusions. She wanted to trust the feelings growing between her and Seth. More than anything, she wanted this to be real.

And if she was right in her suspicions that he was holding back?

Her eyes skipped to a family at the far end of the picture window. A grandma and grandpa were standing together, shoulder to shoulder, heads tilted toward each other in conversation as they held two older grandchildren up to see their new sister. The connection, the family bond, was undeniable.

She'd seen it earlier today when Seth and Pippa discussed their children. Yes, there was strife between them, but also a certain connection, even tenderness. Disconcerting, regardless. But if they still felt that way after such a betrayal…it gave Alexa pause. It spoke of unresolved feelings between them.

Steadying herself, she pressed her hand to the window. She'd ached for a real family connection growing up, yearned to create such a bond in her marriage. She knew what it felt like to stand on the outside.

And she refused to live that way ever again.

Ten

He wanted Alexa in his life, as well as in his bed.

As Seth drove Alexa home to her downtown Charleston condo after seeing his new nephew, he kept thinking about how right it felt having her sit beside him now. How right it had felt earlier taking her to the hospital with him. Having Alexa with him at such an important family moment made the evening even more special. He hoped when they got to her place, he could persuade her to just pick up some clothes and go with him to his house.

Beams of light from late night traffic streaked through the inky darkness as they crossed the Ashley River. The intimacy of just the two of them in his Infiniti SUV reminded him of making love in the classic Chevy convertible on the Outer Banks. God, was that only a few hours ago? Already, he wanted her again.

And what did she want?

He glanced out of the corner of his eye. She rested her head on the window, cool air from the vent lifting her hair. Shadows played along the dark circles under her eyes, in the furrows along her forehead. He was surprised—and concerned.

"Tell me." He skimmed a strand of hair behind her ear. "What's bothering you?"

She shook her head, keeping her face averted with only the glow of the dashboard lights to help him gauge her mood. She hugged her purse to her chest until the folder inside crackled.

"Whatever it is," he said, "I want to hear it, and don't bother saying it's nothing."

"We're both exhausted." She looked down at her hands, at least not staring out the window but still not turning to him. "It's been an emotional ride since we met, a lot crammed into a short time. I need some space to think."

Crap. She'd asked him earlier if he was giving her the brush-off and now he wondered the same thing. "You're backtracking."

"Maybe."

"Why?" he demanded, considering pulling off the six-lane highway so he could focus his full attention on her.

"Seth, I've worked hard to put my life back together again, twice. As a teenager. And again after my divorce. I'm stronger now because of both of those times. But I still intend to be very careful not to put myself in a dangerous position again."

What the hell? This wasn't the kind of conversation

they should have with him driving. He needed his focus planted firmly on her.

He eyed the fast food restaurant ahead and cut over two lanes of traffic, ignoring the honking horns. He pulled off the interstate and parked under the golden arches.

Hooking his arm on the steering wheel, he pinned her with his gaze. "Let me get this straight. You consider me *dangerous?* What have I done to make you feel threatened?"

"A relationship with you, I mean—" the trenches in her forehead dug deeper "—could be…maybe the better word is chancy." Headlights flashed past, illuminating her face with bright lights in quick, strobelike succession.

Some of the tension melted from his shoulders. His arm slid from the wheel and he took her hand in his. "Any relationship is risky. But I believe we've started something good here."

"I thought so, too, especially this afternoon. I opened up to you in ways I haven't to anyone in as long as I can remember." Her hand was cold in his. "But a relationship has to be a two-way street. Can you deny you're holding back?"

Holding back? Hell, he was giving her more than he'd imagined shelling out after the crap year he'd been through. What more did she want from him? A pint of blood? A pound of flesh?

But snapping those questions at her didn't seem wise. "I'm not sure what you mean."

"You have reservations about us as a couple." She didn't ask. She simply said it.

He couldn't deny she was right on the money.

Now he had to figure out how to work around that in a way that would still involve her packing a sleepover bag to go to his place. "Would it have been better for us to meet a year from now? Absolutely."

"Because?" she pressed.

Damn, he was tired and just wanted to take Alexa to his bed. This wasn't a conversation he wanted to have right now. He didn't much want to have it ever. "A year from now, my divorce wouldn't be as fresh— neither would yours. My kids would be older. Your business would have deeper roots. Can you deny the timing would be better for both of us?"

She shook her head slowly, the air conditioner vent catching the scent of her shampoo. "You know all the reasons why I have issues. I've been completely open with you, and I thought you'd been the same with me."

A buzz started in his brain. She couldn't be hinting at what he thought…

"Your cousin told me about Pippa, how she cheated on you. I can understand why that would make you relationship wary and it would have been helpful to know that."

The buzz in his head increased until he felt like he was being stung by hundreds of bees. Angry bees. Except the rage was his. "Paige had no business telling you that."

"Don't blame her. She thought I already kn—"

"How exactly was I supposed to work that into conversation? Hey, my ex-wife doesn't know for sure if my children are actually mine." His hands fisted. "In fact, she lied to me about that all the way to the altar. Now where would you like to go for dinner?"

Her face paled, her eyes so sympathetic her reaction slashed through all the raw places inside him.

"Seth, I am so sorry."

"I am their father in every way that matters." He slammed his fist into the dash. "I love my kids." His voice cracked.

"I realize that," she said softly, hugging her purse to her stomach.

"It doesn't matter to me whose blood or biology flows through their veins." He thumped his chest right over his heart that he'd placed in two pairs of tiny hands nearly a year ago. "They're *mine*."

"I'm sure they would agree." She paused then continued warily, "Have you taken a paternity test? They certainly look like you."

He didn't need any test to validate his love for those kids. "Back off. This isn't your business."

Her blue eyes filled with tears. "That's my whole point. We may have baggage, but I'm ready to be open about mine. You're not."

"Good God, Alexa, we've barely known each other for a week and you expect me to tell you something that could cripple my kids if they ever found out?"

"You think I would go around telling people? If so, you really don't know me at all." She held up her hands. "You know what? You're one hundred percent correct. This is a mistake. *We* are a mistake. The timing is wrong for us to have a relationship."

The thought of her backing out blindsided him. "Well, there's nothing I can do about the timing."

"My point exactly. Seth, I want to go home now, and I don't want you to follow me inside, and I don't want you to call me."

That was it? Even after their encounter on the Outer Banks, the way they'd come together so magnificently, she was slamming the door in his face? "Damn it, Alexa. Life isn't perfect. I'm not perfect, and I don't expect you to be, either. It's not about all or nothing here."

She chewed her bottom lip and he thought he might be making headway until she looked out the window again without answering.

"What do you want from me, Alexa?"

She turned slowly to him, blue eyes clouded with pain and tears. "Just what I said. I need you to respect my need for space."

Her mouth pursed shut, and she turned her head back toward the window. He waited while four cars cleared the fast food drive-through window and still she wouldn't look at him. He knew an ice-out when he saw one.

Stunned numb, he drove the rest of the way to her condo, a corner unit in a string of red brick buildings made to fit in with the rest of the historic homes. Her place. Where she belonged and he wasn't welcome.

How the hell had it gone so wrong so quickly? So he hadn't told her about Pippa cheating. He would have gotten around to it soon enough.

"Goodbye, Seth." She tore open the door and ran up the walkway into her apartment before he could make it farther than the front of the car.

Frustration chewed his gut as he settled behind the wheel again. He was doing his best here and she was cutting him off at the knees. The way she'd clutched her purse to her chest, she looked like she couldn't get out of the car fast enough. She had probably mangled the folder he'd given her.

An ugly, dark thought snaked through him. That she'd wanted her new contacts and now that she had them, she was looking for a way out. She'd used him. Just as Pippa had used him.

And just that quickly the thought dissipated. He knew Alexa was nothing like Pippa. Sure, they'd come from similar backgrounds, but Alexa had broken free of the dependent lifestyle. She was making her own way in the world. Honestly. With hard work. And she'd been up-front with him from the very start.

If anything, he was the one who'd held back.

Damn it.

She was right.

His head *thunked* against the seat. He'd been carrying so much baggage because of Pippa that he might as well have been driving one of those luggage trucks at the airport. He'd screwed up in that relationship in so many ways and felt the failure all the more acutely in the face of his cousins' marital bliss. To the point that he'd even held back from fully participating in their lives. Sure he'd moved here to be with them, but how close had he let anyone get? How many walls had he built?

None of which was fair to his cousins. And it most definitely wasn't fair to Alexa.

So where did he go from here? Talking to her now would likely only stoke her anger, or worse, stir her tears. Once she had a chance to cool down, he needed to approach her with something more than words. He needed strong actions to show Alexa how special, how irreplaceably important she was to him.

How very much he loved her.

Love.

The word filled his head and settled in with a flawless landing. Damn straight he loved her, and she deserved to know that.

And if she still said no? Then he would work harder. He believed in what they'd shared these past days, in what they'd started to build together.

He hadn't given up in his professional life. Against the odds, regardless of what people told him about waiting until he was older, more established, he'd accomplished what he set out to do.

Now it was time to set his sights on winning over Alexa.

Alexa Randall had accumulated an eclectic box full of lost and found items since opening her own cleaning company for charter jets. There were the standard smart phones, portfolios, tablets, even a Patek Philippe watch. She'd returned each to its owner.

Then there were the stray panties and men's boxers, even the occasional sex toys from Mile High Club members. All of those items, she'd picked up with latex gloves and tossed in the trash.

But the pacifier lying beside a seat reminded her too painfully of the precious twins she'd discovered nearly two weeks ago. Memories of their father pierced her heart all the more.

Her bucket of supplies dropped to the industrial blue carpet with a heavy thud. Ammonia fumes from the rag in her fist stung her eyes. Or maybe it was the tears. Heaven knew, she'd cried more than her fair share since leaving Seth's car after their awful argument a week ago. God, this hurt more than when she'd divorced.

The end of her marriage had been a relief. Losing Seth, however, cut her to the core. So much so, she couldn't escape the fact that she loved him. Truly, deeply loved him.

And he'd let her go.

She'd half expected him to follow her or do something cliché like send bunches of flowers with stock apologies. But he'd done none of that. He'd stayed quiet. Giving her the space she'd demanded? Or walking away altogether?

Her husband and parents would have shouted her down, even going so far as to bully her until she caved.

That made her question how she'd reacted that night to his news about the children. She may have grown in how she stood up for herself since the days when she'd tried to control stress through her eating habits. While she was happy for that newfound strength, perhaps she needed to grow even more to be able to return to a problem and fix it. Real strength wasn't about arguing and stomping away. It was going back to a sticky situation and battling—compromising—for a fair resolution.

And she had no one to blame but herself for condemning him because he hadn't told her all his secrets right away. How fair had that been?

Yes, he'd held back. Yet to the best of his ability, he'd lived up to everything he'd promised, everything he was able to give right now. Why was she realizing this now rather than days ago when she could have saved herself so much pain?

Most likely because she'd hidden her head in the sand the past few days, crying her eyes out and burying herself in paperwork at the office. Today was her first day actually picking up a bucket—and what a day it was with so many reminders of Seth and his kids.

She looked around the private luxury jet owned by Senator Landis, parked at the Charleston airport—not Seth's private field. But still, with that pacifier in hand from one of the Landis babies, she couldn't help but think of Owen and Olivia, and wonder how they were doing. She'd missed their sweet faces this week as well, and she liked to think they'd felt a connection to her, too, even during their short time together.

Her ultimatum had hurt more than just her. She stared into the bucket, more of those tears springing to her eyes. Blaming them on ammonia wouldn't work indefinitely.

She sank down onto the leather sofa, her mind replaying for the millionth time the harsh words they'd shared. She looked around the pristinely clean aircraft and wished her life was as easy to perfect.

Perfect?

Her mind snagged on the word, shuffling back to something Seth had said about it not being the perfect time, but life wasn't perfect. He didn't expect her to be perfect... And... What? She reached for the thought like an elusive pristine cloud until—

An increasing ruckus outside broke her train of thought. The sound of trucks and people talking in a rising excited cacophony of voices. She stood and walked toward the hatch. Bits of conversation drifted toward her.

"What's that up—?"

"—airplane?"

"P-47 Thunderbolt, I th—"

"Can you read what—?"

"—wonder who is Alexa?"

Alexa? Airplane?

A hope too scary to acknowledge prickled along her skin. She stepped into the open hatch, stopping at the top of the metal stairs. Shading her eyes, she scanned the crowd of maintenance workers and aircraft service personnel. She followed the path of their fingers pointing upward.

A World War II-era plane buzzed low over their section of the airfield, a craft that looked remarkably like the one she'd seen in Seth's hangar. Trailing behind, a banner flapped against the bright blue sky. In block red letters, it spelled out:

I Love You, Alexa Randall!

Her breath hitched in her throat as she descended the steps one at a time, rereading the message. By the time her feet hit concrete, it had fully sunk in. Seth was making a grand gesture to win her back. Her. Alexa Randall. At an imperfect time. In spite of her frustrated fears that were far from rational.

She'd thought she'd left her growing up years behind her, but she'd been hanging on to more than a need to make the world around her perfectly in order. She'd still subconsciously held onto the old, misguided mantra that *she* had to be perfect as well.

Seth had told her that didn't matter to him.

Maybe she needed to remember Seth didn't need to be perfect, either.

And she couldn't wait for him to land so she could tell him face-to-face.

The plane circled once more, message rippling for the entire airport to see. Then the craft descended, drifting downward into a smooth landing only twenty feet away from her.

The engine shut off with a rattle. The whirring rotor on the nose slowed and finally *click, click, clicked* to a stop. And there he was. *Seth.* Big, blond, bold and all *hers.*

He jumped out of the old craft, wearing khakis, hiking boots and a loose white shirt. His broad shoulders blocked out the sun and the crowd. Or maybe that was just because when he walked into her world, everything else went fuzzy around the edges.

She threw away the rag in her hand and raced toward him. A smile stretched across his face, his arms opening just as wide. She flew into his embrace, soaking up the crisp, clean scent of him.

She kissed him. Right there in front of the cheering crowd of airport personnel as he spun her around. The other voices and applause growing dimmer in her ears, she lost herself in the moment and just held tight to Seth. Even after her feet touched ground again, her head still twirled.

Moisture burned behind her eyelids, the happy kind of tears. How amazing to find her perfect love in accepting their imperfections.

He whispered in her ear. "Now maybe we can take this conversation somewhere a bit more private."

"I happen to be cleaning that plane right behind you and no one's due to show up for at least a half hour."

He scooped her into his arms—which launched another round of applause from the crowd—and he jogged up the steps, turning sideways to duck into the plane. He set her on her feet and right back into his arms.

Holding him closer, she laughed into his neck, his shirt warm against her cheek. "How did you know I was here?"

"I had an inside track on your work schedules. Senator Landis is a cousin of mine, sort of, with his wife being the foster sister of my cousin's wife… My family. There are a lot of us." He guided her to the leather sofa. "Before we talk about anything else, I need to tell you a few things."

Good or bad? She couldn't tell from the serious set of his face. "Okay, I'm listening."

"I've spent the past week working out some new custody arrangements with Pippa. The twins will be spending more time with me, and we've hired a new nanny for when they're with her." He looked down at their joined hands, his fingers twitching. "I'm not ready to run that paternity test. I don't know if I ever will be. The other guy who could be their biological father doesn't want anything to do with them. So, I want to leave things as they are for now. I just want to enjoy watching my kids grow up."

"I can understand that." She wanted that same joy in her life. The way he loved the twins made total sense to her. She'd been completely certain she would love an adopted child during her first marriage. "I'm sorry for pushing you away."

His knuckle glided gently along her cheekbone. "And I'm sorry for not being more open with you."

She cradled his face in her hands. "I can't believe the way you flew out there. You're crazy, did you know that?"

"When it comes to you, yes I am." He pressed a

lingering kiss into her palm, before pointing a thumb toward his airplane outside. "Did you get my message?"

"There wasn't any missing it." She tipped her face to his.

"I meant it, every word." His emerald eyes glinting with a gemstone radiance and strength. "I should have said them to you that night. Even before that. I was so zeroed in on my need to keep my kids' lives stable I focused on the idea of making sure they didn't have a parade of women through their lives. I almost missed the bigger message knocking around in my brain."

Her arms around his neck, she toyed with his sun-kissed hair. "And that message would be?"

"Marry me, Alexa." He pressed a hand to her lips, his fingertips callused. "I realize this is moving too fast in some ways and in other ways I haven't moved quickly enough. But if you need to wait a while, I can be patient. You're worth it."

"I know," she said confidently, realizing for maybe the first time she did deserve this man and his love. They both deserved to be happy together. "And I love you, too. The bold way that you touch me and challenge me. How tenderly you care for your children. You are everything I could want, everything I never even knew I could have."

"I love you, Alexa." He stroked her hair back from her face. "You. The beautiful way you are with my kids. The way you try to take care of everyone around you. But I also want to be here to take care of you when you demand too much of yourself. I love the perfect parts of us being together—and even the parts of us that aren't perfect but somehow fit together. Bottom line, you have to trust me when I say I love you and I want to be with you for the rest of my life."

"Starting now," she agreed.

"Starting right this second, if you're done here."

She scooped up her bucket. "As a matter of fact, I am. What did you have in mind?

"A date, an honest to God, going out to dinner together date—" he punctuated each plan with a kiss "—followed by more dates and making out and sex— lots of sex—followed by more romancing your socks off."

She sighed against his mouth, swaying closer to him. "And we get married."

"Yes, ma'am," he promised, "and then the real romancing begins."

Epilogue

A year later

She couldn't have asked for a more romantic wedding.

And it had nothing to do with pomp and circumstance. In fact she and Seth had bypassed all of that and planned a beach wedding in Charleston that focused on family. A very *large* family, all in attendance.

Her bouquet in one hand, Alexa looped her other arm around her husband's neck and lost herself in the toe-tingling beauty of their first kiss as man and wife. Her skin warmed from the late day sun and the promise of their honeymoon in the outer banks—of Greece.

The kiss still shimmering to the roots of her upswept hair, Alexa eased back down to her toes. Applause and cheers echoed with the rustle of sea oats. She scooped up Olivia and Seth hefted up Owen. Arm in arm with her husband, she turned to face the hundred guests. Waves rolled and crashed in time with the steel drums playing as they walked back down the aisle lined with lilies and palm fronds. The sun's rays glittered off the sand and water like billions of diamonds had been ordered special for the day.

The twins, now nearly two and nonstop chatter bugs, clapped along with the guests. Shortly before the wedding, Seth had quietly seen the doctor about running a paternity test. As Alexa had suspected all along, the babies were Seth's biological children. His relief had been enormous. He'd credited her love with giving him the strength to take that step.

A love they were celebrating today.

Sand swirled around her ankles, the perfume of her bouquet swelling upward—a mix of calla lilies, orchids and roses, with trailing stephanotis. The attire had been kept casual, with pink flowing sundresses for both bridesmaids. For the men, khakis with white shirts— and rose boutonnieres that had arrived in the *wrong* color. But she knew it was a sign that they were ideal for her wedding because the deep crimson rose was a lovely wink and nod to the beauty of the imperfect.

And her dress... White organza flowed straight down from the fitted bodice with diamond spaghetti straps. No heels to get caught in the sand, just bare feet, miles of pristine beach and crystal blue waters. A very familiar and dear World War II vintage aircraft flew overhead carrying a banner for the entire wedding party to see.

Congratulations, Mr. and Mrs. Seth Jansen.

Cabanas with dining tables filled the beach, complete with a large tent and jazz band for dancing later. She'd let her new caterer-cousin choose the menu and design a detailed sandcastle wedding cake fit for a princess. And ironically enough, she had an entire Medina royal family in attendance as well as the Landises, considered by some to be American political royalty.

A play area with babysitters on hand had been roped off for children with their own special menu and cupcakes with crystallized sugar seashells on top. Although already kids were playing outside the designated area carefully arranged for them. They were happily building a sandcastle town with new moms Paige and Claire overseeing them. Just the way it should be—with everyone enjoying the day.

She and Seth had wanted their wedding to celebrate family, and they'd succeeded. Even her family was in attendance. While their relationship would likely never be close, enjoying a peaceful visit with them went a long way in soothing old hurts.

She and Seth had spent the past year building their relationship, strengthening the connection they'd felt so tangibly from the start. She'd also spent the past twelve months building her business and confidence. Her favorite work? Servicing the search and rescue planes on the philanthropic side of Jansen Jets. It was not the whole company, but certainly the part most near and dear to Seth's heart.

They were both living out their dreams.

She looked from their applauding relatives to her new husband. And what do you know?

He was already staring right back at her, his eyes full of love. "Is everything turning out the way you wanted today?"

She toyed with his off-color rose boutonniere. "The day couldn't be any more perfect."

And the best part of that? She knew each of their tomorrows promised to be even better.

* * * * *

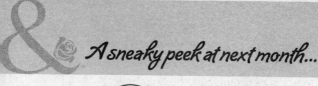

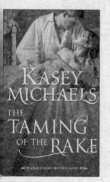

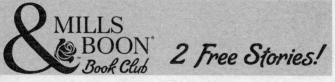

MILLS & BOON® Book Club — 2 Free Stories!

Get your free stories now at
www.millsandboon.co.uk/freebookoffer

Or fill in the form below and post it back to us

THE MILLS & BOON® BOOK CLUB™—HERE'S HOW IT WORKS: Accepting your free stories places you under no obligation to buy anything. You may keep the stories and return the despatch note marked 'Cancel'. If we do not hear from you, about a month later we'll send you 2 Desire™ 2-in-1 books priced at £5.49* each. There is no extra charge for post and packaging. You may cancel at any time, otherwise we will send you 4 stories a month which you may purchase or return to us—the choice is yours. *Terms and prices subject to change without notice. Offer valid in UK only. Applicants must be 18 or over. Offer expires 31st July 2012. **For full terms and conditions, please go to www.millsandboon.co.uk/freebookoffer**

Mrs/Miss/Ms/Mr (please circle) _____

First Name _____

Surname _____

Address _____

_____

_____ Postcode _____

E-mail _____

Send this completed page to: Mills & Boon Book Club, Free Book Offer, FREEPOST NAT 10298, Richmond, Surrey, TW9 1BR

Find out more at
www.millsandboon.co.uk/freebookoffer

Visit us Online

0112/D2XEA/REV

The World of Mills & Boon®

There's a Mills & Boon® series that's perfect for you. We publish ten series and with new titles every month, you never have to wait long for your favourite to come along.

Blaze.
Scorching hot, sexy reads

By Request
Relive the romance with the best of the best

Cherish™
Romance to melt the heart every time

Desire™
Passionate and dramatic love stories